Ever-After

Volume I

The Sleepless Cafe

Tall, dark, and handsome, the fortuneteller said.
Romagene laughed—until Dalton Traverre de Plessis entered
The Sleepless Café. Then, Romagene's barista job went from
boring to bizarre in the time it took her to make a mug of tea.
Because under the black silk shirt of the man who ordered it,
beat the heart of a vampire.

THE SLEEPLESS CAFE

Annie R McEwen

I've never believed in tall, dark, handsome strangers. It's not that I don't believe they exist, I just wouldn't ever expect to see one in my life even if a fortune teller said I would. I might believe in a chunky redhead with a good heart and a tendency toward neck boils. That's the kind of men that have crossed my path before, so I was pretty skeptical when Tamara, the house psychic at The Sleepless Café, translated the Tarot cards on the table between us.

"Yes. Um hmm, very nice. Young. But also old. An old soul in a young body."

"Are you talking about Jeffy? Because he's just a friend from high school. He's—"

"No, a friend is not what the cards are telling me. This man is more, much more. And yet..." Tamara brought a card closer to her face and squinted at it. "In some ways, much less."

Young but old? More but less? What was Tamara talking about? Was she lit? If she was, The Sleepless wasn't responsible. I've been the barista on every Saturday Psychic Night for a year, and I've never known her to drink anything stronger than herbal teas.

I have to admit, she's been right about everything else she's predicted. That's why I was sitting at the psychic's table in a back corner instead of closing the café early and going home for some shut-eye after a dead night. In February, Tamara had told me to expect improvement in my finances. The next week, Artie, the café's owner, took me off employee probation and gave me a raise. In July, Tamara said I would go somewhere beautiful, and a few days later, my first cousin Lily invited me for a week at her parents' cabin in the Ozarks.

Given Tamara's batting average of three hundred plus, I didn't have any reason to disbelieve the young/old/less/more/tall/dark/handsome man stuff. Still…I started to ask her a follow-up question, but was too slow. She swept the Tarot cards into her tote bag and stood.

"Well," she chirped, smiling brightly as she tugged down her Morticia Addams stretchy black dress. "There it is, and aren't you lucky? Twenty-five dollars, Tea Baby."

"Don't call me that, please."

"Uh, okay. It's just that everybody—"

"Yeah, I know they do." Tea Baby. Just one of the things I hate about The Sleepless. Artie started calling me that on my first night and everybody picked it up. A generous person would say I got the nickname because I'm small (five-feet, no inches) and delicately formed ("like a porcelain doll," Grandma used to say), but I knew it was just one of Artie's odious little ways to keep me from thinking I was more important than he wanted me to be.

I handed over two tens and a five, watching Tamara take the bills and slither out the door. I had the cash ready, although tips had been poor for a Saturday night. Artie wouldn't admit it, but The Sleepless was sliding slowly downhill. Two chain coffee shops and a café serving snob appeal Fair Trade teas had opened in the neighborhood the past year. The Sleepless' clientele were being relentlessly siphoned away, and I was starting to assess my options.

Past time to go, anyway. I was tired of the place, the menu (one-third classic teas, one-third herbal, one-third kratom and kava), and the clientele, who spent too much time nursing not enough drinks and leaving too few tips. More than anything, I was tired of the hours. The Sleepless opened at nine p.m. and closed at five in the morning. I was the first one in and the last one out. The one who had no life in the sun anymore, like a vampire.

No surprise, I thought as I wiped down tables and started the closing routine, that the décor at The Sleepless was something I called "fang nouveau" behind Artie's back. Because the walls were painted red and the light bulbs were tinted, the place and everyone in it looked like they'd been dipped in diluted blood. The furniture was black, Gothic, and self-consciously shabby, like a Victorian yard sale. Over the bar, a mirror-backed display case held Artie's collection of mourning jewelry and *memento mori* photographs. The photos gave me the creeps. Dead babies propped up in their cradles, a bride seated next to her dead husband of two days.

The customers—insomniacs, slumming tourists, goths, wannabe undead—loved that stuff. Loved the murky ambiance, the corpse photos, the hair jewelry, the black glass skulls the drinks were served in. But I was as tired of the décor as I was the rest of The Sleepless. It was time to move on before business got so slow Artie started laying off people. Maybe I could get a job as a budtender in a medical marijuana dispensary. Couldn't be any worse than where I was now, though I'd heard there weren't tips.

Counters cleaned, receipts totaled, the dregs of kratom emptied, furniture wiped down, my closing ritual was complete. I leaned against the bar and stared at the clock, willing the hour hand to move from four to five when I could lock the doors. The last customers had been two college students at two-thirty. They shared a single kratom (two straws) and left in twenty minutes. No tip.

The door creaked, and I groaned internally. What sort of person visits a tearoom at four in the morning?

The sort of person worth waiting for, apparently. That was the first thought I had when the man came through the doorway and stood just inside for a long moment, looking around the café while I looked at him. Tall, dark, and handsome, just like Tamara had said. I didn't believe in love at first sight, but there was such a thing as instant attraction, and this man was...

Very attractive. He was maybe six-one, six-two. His muscular body under black jeans and a snug black tricot tee was as perfectly defined as if he were wearing nothing at all, a thought that made my mouth go dry. His skin, what I could see of it, was smooth and pale as ivory, with the same subtle sheen. His face was like something on an ancient coin—broad forehead, aquiline nose, high cheekbones, the sort of jaw called "chiseled" in romance novels. He was clean-shaven, but the faint shadow of a beard and mustache gave him a sort of Corsican bandit air. His hair was somewhere between mahogany and jet black, depending on how the blood-washed light in The Sleepless played on it. It fell almost to his shoulders, one thick strand bisecting his eyebrow like a swipe of ink. His mouth...I stared at his mouth. Wide with a gently curving tilt at one side, ironic and yet promising. And his eyes...

"Hello," he said in a deep, velvety voice, like Elvis Presley. The voice made me want to vault the bar and land, kneeling, at the man's feet even though I hate Elvis, except for the voice. True, Elvis' eyes were famous, but this man's were—

"How may I serve you?" My voice, but where the hell did those words come from? Some Peter Cushing movie that infected my brain on Movie Night at the café? "I-I mean—"

Smooth as a cat, the man slid onto a barstool and looked directly, warmly, at me. Without even the second's resistance a sane woman would have to any strange man staring at her, I opened myself to his gaze. How could I not? In it was everything I ever wanted, but didn't get. The pony my parents wouldn't buy me when I was ten. The rose petal costume my sister wore for the ballet recital while I had to dress in an elf suit. Ronnie Sumner, who I was sure would ask me to my high school prom, yet asked my best friend Alison instead. The art museum jobs I couldn't snag even with two degrees, leaving me to support myself for the past year as a barista. It was all there, inches away, in those deep, dark, amber-shot eyes.

His mouth was moving. I forced myself to hear what it was saying and move my own mouth in reply.

"Oh, yes, of course, we have Earl Grey." Thank God, something to occupy my hands if not my brain.

It got easier after that. First, though, there was a little barista stuff, starting with him inviting me to have a drink, too. I literally cringed at the idea of drinking with that beautiful man in the café's kitschy skulls. Instead, I rooted around under the bar for Artie's private reserve cups. Found them. Two black cut-glass goblets, heavy and elegant. They rang when you tapped them. I washed them briskly and dried them with a fresh bar towel, agonizing the whole time. I was sure it was taking an irritating amount of time.

No worries. When I turned around with the washed/dried/filled/plated goblets, the man was still looking at me. Patiently, attentively, with his luminous, Baltic amber eyes. There was no irritation in them, just a lot of other things I couldn't quite identify, but suddenly wanted more than a vacation in Tahiti or a new car. As I put the two goblets down on the bar, his eyes never left mine, and I couldn't—*didn't want to*—look away from them even for a second. Was it my imagination or were they dilated? Admittedly, the light was poor in The Sleepless, but his pupils really were enormous and deep, twin pools of shadow I wanted to dive into, falling, falling...

"My name is Dal." Each of his words was a drop of liquid silk, faintly accented. "You must be Romagene."

I was so pathetically happy he didn't call me Tea Baby, I didn't even ask how he knew my name. My vocal chords had stopped working and I just nodded.

"Romagene," he repeated, every syllable gliding and brushing across my nipples. "Would you like to sit with me, Romagene?"

What I would've liked was to clamber over the bar into his lap, but I forced myself to walk, slowly, from behind the bar to his side. As I did, Dal turned his body on the barstool to face me. I slid onto the stool next to him. Our knees brushed. The contact couldn't have been more charged if I'd put my finger in an electrical outlet.

We sat, knee to knee, our inside elbows resting on the bar, and waited for the tea to cool. The cat that had gotten my tongue finally went somewhere else and I asked, "Is there more to your name than Dal?"

"Dalton Laurent Traverre de Plessis."

"Wow."

"Too much." He grinned, displaying even white teeth.

One more smile like that and I might take off my clothes. "It's a lot of name. It's nice, though."

"So is Romagene."

I made a face. "My great-grandma was a Gypsy. At least, that's what my grandmother had said. You know, Romany, Roma—"

"Yes." He waved, almost impatiently. "You have Gypsy blood. I can hear it."

"Hear it? You mean, it's talking or—?"

"Whispering. But very clear." He took a sip of his tea, and the cut-glass goblet chimed gently when he settled it in the saucer again. With his every gesture, something inside me chimed, too. A distant, crystal bell that vibrated as though he'd flicked it. "Then again, I have very acute hearing."

Acute hearing. Golden eyes. A sleek and muscular body. Like a jungle cat, and somehow that didn't frighten me, though a weak voice in my brain said maybe it should.

"There's no reason for you to fear me." Strangely, his reading my thoughts didn't frighten me, either.

"I know."

That was the last time either of us mentioned fear. Instead, we talked as easily and happily as if we'd known each other for fifteen years instead of fifteen minutes. What did we talk about? Honestly, I couldn't have told anyone later. I do remember we were nattering on about Baroque architecture, the subject of my thesis, when the alarm on my cellphone went off. Oh, crap. I'd parked in the public lot behind The Sleepless and was only prepaid to five-thirty a.m. Reluctantly, I slid off the stool and picked up the two goblets on the counter. Mine was empty. His was still mostly full. Both were stone cold.

"Sorry." I meant it with every cell in my body. "My boss is a tightwad. I think he has the a/c and the lights monitored. If he finds out I was in here after closing..."

Dal stood. "I understand completely." He bowed—*World, are you watching?*—and touched his lips to my inside wrist above the goblet I was holding. "I have enjoyed this evening immensely. I look forward to next Saturday."

That was my cue to say something equally charming, or anything at all, but I was so jaw-locked with shock and excitement, I couldn't have shouted "Fire!" if The Sleepless were burning to the ground. I just watched Dal walk to the door and out of it.

The Sleepless is upstairs in a converted 1920s warehouse. The stairs are steel and noisy as a bucket full of scrap metal. I listened for Dal's footsteps going down, but didn't hear a thing. He not only looked like a cat, he moved like one.

Later, I hoped I washed the private reserve goblets and put them away, but it was all pretty fuzzy after he left until I woke up the next evening.

Sleep. The week after my first conversation with Dal, it was as though I'd taken some sort of time-release, no side effects, sleeping pill, one that kicked in the minute the sun came up and lasted until sundown the same day. The whole year I'd been working at The Sleepless, I'd battled chronic insomnia. No melatonin, no self-hypnosis, no anything, convinced my metabolism I could be nocturnal, like a bat or a ferret.

After meeting Dal, I sawed logs all day and woke fresh as a daisy in just enough time to shower and dress for my shift at the café. If I never saw Dal again, would I still be able to snooze the bright hours away, or would I go back to fighting the bed between dawn and dark? I wasn't about to spoil my mood by thinking about that. I just focused on Dal's promise, "I look forward to next Saturday." After that, the future could take care of itself.

Saturday came around right after Friday, the way it always did. It began at sundown for me, and I skipped breakfast. I hadn't felt hungry all week, a change from my usual cravings for Oreos and grilled cheese sandwiches, but one I attributed to sleeping better. After I showered, I started dressing for the night. My choices were limited by Artie's "barista uniform" rule: black, or, if you're feeling creative, black.

I had always thumbed my nose, safely, at Artie's rule by wearing black with ultraviolet stripes, black with white cuffs and a collar. On this Saturday, however, black on black seemed just fine. Silly to match my clothing to a man I'd just met, but the way Dal wore black made me see it as elegant and worldly, not teen witch pretentious. By eight in the evening, I had poured myself into the blackest black thing I had, a sleeveless, ankle-length velvet sheath with corset lacing front and back. I pulled my long ash blonde hair into a more elaborate up-do than I would normally bother with and thrust an ebony chopstick through it.

My make-up got a half-hour of careful attention instead of slapping on some foundation and a smear of lipstick. I checked out the look in my bedroom mirror, satisfied.

This girl's ready for anything.

Nobody was outside the door when I opened The Sleepless. It was another sign of how slow trade had gotten in the past few months. At the start of the year, there had always been a half dozen customers waiting for me to open.

"Just you and me, kid," I said to a roach that scuttled away from the threshold when I unlocked the heavy faux Tudor oak door. Lights went on, kratom batch got started, skull mugs were readied. I was counting spoons when Tamara came in.

"Hey, Tea B—Romagene," she said, then froze and gawked. "Wow. Great dress. And I love the hair. Something special tonight?"

"No, just felt like, you know, dressing up a little."

Tamara's raised eyebrows showed she didn't buy it, but she went to her table and started staging it for customers or, as she called them, "clients." She flung a purple silk shawl over the two-top and followed it with a crystal ball on a stand, a statue of Isis, and her packs of Tarot cards (Aquarian, Rider-Waite, Celtic, GoT.)

As she worked, her eyes kept veering sideways toward me. Mine didn't veer back since, frankly, I had enough to do without engaging in a staring match with the house fortuneteller. Finally, Tamara had her props arrayed the way she wanted. With a critical glance at the clock over the door, she settled into her chair with a sigh and took her dinner out of her tote bag. She always ate before her first client.

"Blood sugar," she'd told me once, solemnly, as though imparting Universal Truth. "It's all about glucose."

I didn't care either way, but what I did know was Tamara seemed to think blood sugar required strong foods, ones that filled the room with a special fragrance called Tamara's Eats. Pita stuffed with garlic-oozing hummus, chicken breasts redolent with pesto, shrimp curry. Luckily, the smell dispersed after a while, but I got its full impact for the first hour. It was really powerful tonight. What was that pungent bowl she was digging into? Gumbo filé? Four Alarm Chile? I thought I'd better light a scented votive on the table next to her.

I didn't get that far. I had the candle in one hand and a lighter in the other when I crossed the room and got close enough to see Tamara shovel a full spoon of some smelly, beany, stew-y stuff into her mouth when a wave of violent nausea hit me.

I dropped everything and ran like hell for the restroom.

I barely made it. In between heaves, I tried to figure it out. I have a strong stomach and rarely get the upchucks, even after several hours of tequila shots and a midnight hotdog from a cart. Last time I was this sick, this suddenly, was...

Damn. I didn't want to think about that now or ever. Despite my aversion, it shoved its way into my brain, and I had to deal with it, right there in the grungy restroom at the end of the landing outside The Sleepless.

After the museum jobs had thumbed their noses at me, I spent three months job hunting without success. One hard day, after two employers dismissed me as "over-qualified" and a third wanted to know if I spoke Polish, I drifted into a bar. I had enough cash for one double vodka martini before my resumé and I went home to cry ourselves to sleep. Halfway through the drink, a man who leaned on the bar next to me had other ideas.

He was only my second one-night stand, ever. I'm not sure the first one counted since it was with my grad school Renaissance Painting study partner and we both fell asleep halfway through. Then, the study partner and I had been sharing a bottle of schnapps. That time, I was sure I had only one drink after the martini, a Bloody Mary my new friend at the bar had bought me. Had there been something besides vodka and tomato juice in it? If there had been, it went into the drink when I'd stupidly visited the restroom, since when I came back, the Bloody Mary was there at my place.

"Oh, I don't think I should..." I began, but he slid the drink over, insisting.

"Just this one. It'll be weak. You know they always short the liquor in cocktails."

We clinked glasses, and the next morning, I woke alone in a strange bed.

Lucky I didn't wake up dead, I'd thought at the time. I'd rubbed my aching head and hunted for my clothes—easy, since there was no furniture in the small apartment besides the bed and a chair. My clothes were folded on the chair. There was a note on top.

Hey, sweet cheeks! Drop by my place around ten p.m. The Sleepless Café on 3rd St. Beverage on me. I've got a job for you, too!

No signature, and God help me, I couldn't remember his name. Drop by his place? Not in a month of Sundays. I'd crumpled the note and threw it on the bed. Then, I put my clothes on and left, pulling the door hard after me so it locked. My car was parked in front of the apartment building. I had no clue how it got there.

Righteous indignation had lasted exactly two weeks, until my electricity was shut off for non-payment. Florida, summer, no a/c, no money, no prospects. I propped open the sash windows in the two-room studio I'd rented at the back of an old house and considered my options. They boiled down to one—take the damn job from the damn date rapist. I drove to the address he'd given me.

My drive-by lover was there, leaning on the bar from the back side. All bonhomie and cheer. I'd rehearsed what to say, but in the moment, I could only hand him my resume and blurt, "Hell of an interview."

He seemed to think I was being delightfully witty. Still with no idea of his name, I followed him mutely around the café as he pointed out its attractions (were those photos of dead people in that case?) and walked me through the equipment and menu. The whole time, he was reasonably professional. No unwanted touching or sly innuendos. At the end of my "training," he handed me a business card from a resin yoga posed skeleton at the end of the bar.

The Sleepless Café
9:00 p.m. to 5:00 a.m. Monday—Saturday
Artie Barsoonian, Owner/Proprietor

So, that was his name. I asked when I should start, and he said that night. Then he winked, the only sign he had ever met me before, and left. Thankfully, he returned to the café only on the rarest occasions. The first of those was bad, though, and it had happened a week after I'd started work.

It was a few minutes after nine p.m. on a Saturday. Tamara, whom I'd liked at first sight, even though I've never been a devotee of the crystal ball game, had her table set up and, thankfully, hadn't yet unpacked her evening meal. There was a burst of noise from the doorway and three people came through—Artie, a woman, and two children.

I wasn't introduced to any of them. The kids, two girls about six and eight, flitted around the café, laughing. The woman was quiet, exotically pretty in a dark-haired, olive-skinned way, and very pregnant. Artie was the solicitous husband, trying to get her to sit, pressing something to drink on her. She shook her head at everything. She was smiling, but had a faintly hunted look, as though she just wanted to leave. Artie waved to Tamara and made some stupid joke about psychics. Then he gathered up his family and herded them out the door. He didn't look at me, speak to me, or even appear to see me.

Tamara waited until the clatter of the Barsoonian Brood on the stairs died out before she said, "Makes me sick."

"Was that Artie's wife and kids?"

"Yeah, that's them. The wife, Sofia, she's an angel. How she got tangled up with Artie—well, we all do stupid things."

Yes, we do. We do really, really stupid things. "Do they come in often?"

"No, hardly ever. Might cramp Artie's style, if you know what I mean." Tamara shuffled the Tarot cards with a kind of vengeance. "He doesn't spend a lot of time here, either."

"Yeah, well, that works for me. I wouldn't mind seeing him, oh, how about once every Leap Year?"

Ha, ha, ha, laughter from both of us.

But it wasn't Leap Year, and it turned out I needed to see Artie a few nights later, because that's when the vomiting started and the little testing stick came up pink.

"Congratulations," Artie grinned. "I love kids."

"Yeah, I can see that. You've got three of them. That you know of."

"Look, I'm sorry for your trouble, but you need to talk to your boyfriend."

"I don't have a boyfriend."

"Then you should get one. That way you won't do any more dumbass single girl stuff like   a few weeks ago. You were so drunk, you couldn't tell a cab driver where you lived. I drove you in your car to an apartment I own. Then I had to pay a cab to take me back to my car."

I was speechless. With shame, yes, and with rage so hot, it was coming out of my eyes. I couldn't believe the man I was glaring at didn't burst into flames. He may have driven me to an apartment, and he may have left me there, but other things happened in between the two. I knew it, and he knew it.

Despite my flame-thrower eyes, Artie wasn't burning. He was cool and collected. He pulled a roll of money out of his trousers pocket and peeled off three hundred-dollar bills. He actually smirked as he handed them to me. "Never let it be said Artie Barsoonian doesn't help a woman in need. You know what to do."

Yeah, I knew. I made an appointment at a clinic, but before I could keep it, I woke in the middle of my daytime sleep, doubled up with terrible cramps, and that was the real end of the "dumbass single girl stuff." I went into work that night even though I felt like I'd been kicked in the abdomen. I knew exactly whose foot was in the boot. I knew, I was working for him, and I hated it and him. I also hated myself, but there was nothing to be gained from that or the rest of it. Other than Artie's three hundred dollars, which I'd kept.

I'd focused on finding another job, easier said than done as I knew from my rounds of failed interviews in the past months. There was a recession. Jobs, even "hospitality sector" jobs as bad or worse than the one I had, were as rare as the museum jobs I'd already found didn't exist.

Artie never mentioned the incident. I expected sexual harassment, but no, not a hint of it, which was worse for two reasons. One, I could've nailed him legally. Two, it would've meant he had felt something, however low and carnal, during our one-nighter. Well, who was I to throw stones? I had felt so little, I couldn't remember it at all.

Because of the drink, I reminded myself. The spiked drink waiting for me on the bar, the one he'd encouraged me to drink because "you know they always short the liquor in cocktails." True, most bars did. But they didn't make up in Rohypnol what they held back in vodka.

I'd get him for it. I didn't know how or when, but I would.

When I finally got back to The Sleepless after my trip down Memory Lane in the toilet, Tamara had finished her odoriferous supper. She put the trash from it in a plastic bag and thoughtfully knotted it tight, then buried it in the waste can behind the bar. She also lit the scented candle I had dropped and put it in the glass skull holder on the table next to hers. I wasn't sure if Pineapple Ylang Ylang was any better than the food smell, but at least it didn't trigger my nausea. I absolutely, positively knew I wasn't pregnant, so maybe I had a touch of stomach flu or had developed food allergies.

Note to Self: *go home and throw everything in the fridge and the pantry out.*

I forgot all about the bad start the night had gotten off to as soon as Dal came in, which he did at four a.m., sharp. As before, we had the café to ourselves. There hadn't been a customer since three. This Saturday, I paid for an extra hour in the municipal parking lot behind the café, so Dal and I wouldn't be interrupted by any cellphone reminders. The talk over tea was even better than the week before and went on longer. I barely made it home and into bed before I fell sound asleep.

On the following Saturday, the light wars started. There hadn't been a war during the week   because Tamara wasn't there to complain about my turning the dimmer light switch to nearly off. When it was where it was usually set, at a lux level about that of a confessional, it literally hurt my eyes, so I dimmed it. A few customers complained briefly when they walked into furniture before they got adjusted, but pain shot through my eyeballs when I turned the lights up. The customers would just have to enjoy the noir. They did, until Psychic Saturday.

"Romagene!" Tamara wasn't quite shouting, but she was definitely raising her voice.

I went over to her table, all set up, and earlier than usual. Thankfully, no *arôme de chili*. After my flight-to-the-loo episode, the psychic ate her dinner in her car before she came into the café on Saturday evenings.

"Sit down and give me your hand," she said the second I got close enough for her to grab it.

I pulled my hand back. "I don't have time for this, Tamara, I've got—"

"Do it or I'll call you Tea Baby every five minutes as long as I work here."

"Bee-yatch," I grumbled, and sat.

"Palm up. You know the drill."

I put my hand on the table and flipped it over begrudgingly. Because of the low light, the psychic was using a penlight for her readings. She clicked it on and reached for my fingers, but barely touched them when she jerked back like she'd brushed a hot stove. My eyesight's been very sharp lately. Tamara probably thought I didn't see her wiping her fingers on the edge of the silk table cover. Instead of taking my hand again, she leaned over it, frowning and peering at my palm under the penlight.

"Girl, you are halfway to hell."

"Isn't that a song? Halfway to hell, I'm only halfway to—"

"It's *Highway to Hell*, funny girl, and if there *is* one, you are barrelin' down it at ninety miles an hour. I don't know what you're doin', but you need to stop it. Now."

I stood. "What I'm doing is really none of your business, Tamara." It wasn't rude, but almost. I glared at her and she glared back, and then I walked to the bar.

After that, we just stopped having anything much to do with each other. The only exchanges we had in the three weeks after she saw Satan in my palm had to do with the lighting in The Sleepless.

She'd yell, "You do know I'm reading palms over here, right?" Or "I can't tell if this card is the Hanged Man or the Six of Pentacles! Turn the lights up!"

The lights went down and up and down and up, and after four Saturdays of that, Tamara left and didn't come back. I actually wondered whether the psychic had handed in her notice after the hell-in-the-palm reading. Tamara went, and if Artie was head-hunting psychics to take her place, I guess none of them passed. Or maybe he couldn't find an applicant as stupid as me to take the interview.

None of that mattered, not to me. The weeks went by, weeks that, for me, had only one day—Saturday. Actually, two days, since Saturday night was Sunday morning while Dal and I sat at the bar and talked. After Baroque architecture, we chatted our way through the Pre-Raphaelites and Bauhaus and World War One. I marveled at him. His history knowledge wasn't just encyclopedic, it was intimate and entertaining. He had me laughing so hard, I nearly fell off the barstool when he talked about Queen Victoria's swimming arrangements, and how Regency dandies padded their calves and buttocks—and crotches—to look better in tight trousers.

We progressed to touching. Even that had an elegant, Old World quality. Having been chafed and squeezed and pinched and rough-housed by boyfriends over the years, it was the height of sublimity to be touched with restraint and courtliness.

"Do you enjoy it when I stroke your cheek like this?"

"Would you care to put your arms around my neck?"

"Will you permit me to place my hands on your waist?"

And the compliments!

"Romagene, your mind is a delight to me. It is like a beautifully furnished chateau and I long to live in every room."

"Ma chère, your scent is like a green wood in summer, a Devonshire wood, full of wildflowers."

If American men had any idea how that sort of courting affects a woman, they'd be lining up around the block to take lessons from Dal. Not that I planned to share his charm with anyone else. I was more and more sure every week that I wanted Dal to myself—forever, if possible.

In between glorious Saturdays, I felt cross-training fit all the time, even though I hadn't seen the inside of a gym in months. I no longer got tired standing behind the bar in The Sleepless for hours. After my shift, I fell into bed for a full twelve of dreamless, popping up at sunset, ready to do it again. I hadn't seen the sun in weeks, and didn't care. As for eating, I didn't replace the food I'd tossed after my nausea episode. All I'd kept were a couple bottles of good wine and some teas. Somehow, that seemed like plenty.

Until the seventh Saturday. That whole week, I'd been feeling hunger, a strong but peculiar kind that didn't just growl in my stomach the way hunger usually did. This was a whole-body thing, a yearning for sustenance that came from my cells and spread outward until I felt hungry in my skin, my hair, my eyes. Dal saw it that Saturday.

"You're not eating." Not a question, just a statement of fact.

I cringed a little. I didn't want him to think I was harboring some condition like anorexia nervosa or bulimia. People with food disorders make poor romantic partners.

"Yes, I am. Well, no, not a lot." I looked pleadingly into his deep, topaz and brown eyes. "I just don't seem to care about food. But I feel good! I feel great! I—"

He took my hands in his, and his touch was like a cool river washing over my nerves. "It's perfectly fine, *ma belle*. Normal, in fact."

Normal? For whom, a fasting yogi? "What's happening to me, Dal?"

For once, he didn't ask my permission to touch me. We were sitting at the bar, facing each other as always, and he took me by the waist with both hands. Then, as though I weighed five instead of a hundred and five pounds, he simply lifted me off my bar stool and sat me on his lap. I was briefly alarmed at the display of strength I'd never seen in him, but he held me with his eyes, his incredible eyes, and all the fear went out of me at once. I sat quiet and trusting, like a child. He thrust one hand into my hair and held my head upright, carefully, so our eyes stayed in contact. His fingers gently massaged the back of my head while he spoke.

"You're nearly there, my precious Romagene. You are balanced like the beautiful dancer you are, on the knife edge between life and not life, sun and moon, light and dark. Your blood or my blood. It's up to you now. Only you can say which you choose."

"If I say mine, I won't see you again, will I?"

His other hand snaked around my waist. He pulled me closer to him. So close, I could feel his breath on my face, his erection hard against my thigh.

"You'd better hope not," he said.

He removed his hand from my waist and barely, *barely* stroked my jaw with his fingertips. I let my head fall back, exposing my throat. With a low growl, he nuzzled it, nipped at it. His teeth dragged lightly from the underside of my jaw to the hollow of my collarbone, grazing the skin, but never breaking it. He was tasting me, I knew, his lips and tongue gliding possessively, hungrily, over the tender flesh, his mouth pressing against pulse points and lingering there to sense the heartbeat surging just underneath.

I felt suspended, an aerialist twisting at the end of a rope high in the air. So high, I couldn't see where or to what the rope was attached above. Below, there was nothing but mist, the tail of the rope disappearing into it, turning and quivering as I twirled.

"Yours," I whispered. I closed my eyes and parted my lips. The last thing I heard was Dal's deep groan as he bit his wrist and held it over my mouth.

That was the beginning of the change, but nowhere near the end. Dal was a wise and patient teacher. Since my condition was delicate and needed close monitoring, he came into The Sleepless every night it was open, always very late so no one would be present to interfere with our private lessons. Lessons that included as many embraces, gentle nips, and kisses as they did words.

"For many centuries, we were accustomed," he told me in the first lesson, "to turning warmbloods all at once, within minutes, even seconds. Sometimes, it was necessary, of course, when life trembled on the precipice of death. But such sudden turnings were...traumatic. They caused months, sometimes years of transitional fury. Uncontrolled hunger, violence, loss of control, even madness." He shook his head sadly. "Drop by drop is wiser and, for the warmblood, yields better results, though it requires great discipline and patience on the part of the *faiseur*, the maker."

Revelation glowed in my brain. "The tea. You've been putting it into my tea."

He nodded, and we both smiled, sharing a secret joke. He kept explaining.

"With patience comes reward. To watch, day by day, week by week, as the thing is done?   Ah, my little nightbird, that is joy of a very special sort." He kissed my fingertips. "You have given me this gift, this exquisite pleasure, and I am eternally grateful."

He bit me then, and every night. Many bites, many times, but gentle ones, from my upper arms to my shoulders and across my upper chest, leaving tiny red crescent marks. I had begun wearing the same thing every night, a strapless bustier covered by a short jacket until Dal arrived. Then I peeled off the jacket and bared everything from my fingertips to my cleavage.

I longed to bite him back. The second week, after I had chosen his blood, was the first time I felt that urge. It was so strong, it nearly lifted me off the bar stool. I leaned in, lips parted, fixated by the slow throb of the vein under his jaw. He watched me closely, as he always did. So careful, my darling was, so protective.

"Not yet, Romagene, not there," he crooned, "but I can help ease the hunger." He undid the gold cufflink on one sleeve of his black dress shirt, then placed it on the bar. Rolling up the sleeve, he slowly turned the silk under in measured folds. Without once taking his eyes off my face, my mouth, he bared his strong pale forearm to my hungry gaze. His finger touched a spot on the inside of his arm, where a thin blue vein pulsed under the skin.

"There," he said softly, and I dove for it.

I lost track of time after that night. I think perhaps two more weeks went by, maybe three. One night, after we had kissed and nuzzled and lightly chewed each other's lips as we always did when we greeted, he said, "Before, you were half in shade, half in the light. Now, you are whole."

We stood, our hands joined in the middle of The Sleepless. It was like a wedding, and I was full of emotion. Pride, excitement, gratitude, deep love for my teacher who was now my heart, the blood of my blood.

Dal smiled. He was an indulgent mate. "What is the first thing you want to do, my jewel?"

Before I could answer, Artie came barging into The Sleepless. I couldn't imagine what he was doing in the café at that hour until I saw he had a girl with him. The girl was obviously inebriated or drugged. She was also obviously a teenager, no more than sixteen, maybe less. Even though it was my shift and I was supposed to be there, Artie, who was clearly hammered himself, started yelling and ordering me out.

"What the hell are you doin' here on a Sunday night, you dumb bitch?"

"It's Saturday night, Artie. Or Sunday morning, if you want to get technical. I work here, remember?"

Apparently, Artie didn't remember, or he was so tanked he couldn't remember the days of the week. I've been able to see amazingly well in any light recently, including total dark, so I saw Dal take the teenager's hand and pull her away from Artie. Dal was smiling and looking into her eyes, and she followed him as meekly as a kitten. He maneuvered her out the door, and I heard her uncertain steps, though not his, as they went down the stairs.

Artie hardly noticed the girl was gone. He was weaving and shouting in the middle of the café, calling me every disgusting name to call a woman. I would have been just fine walking out and letting him fall face down on the floor, or jump out a window, or whatever else popped into his rotten brain, until he grabbed a candleholder—one of the heavy glass skull ones, matching the mugs on the tables—and came at me with it.

There was no explosion of rage on my part, no fountain of anger sending a black plume into the sky. One second, I was standing there in the path of Artie's oncoming charge. The next second, Artie was on the floor, and I was kneeling over him. I had torn open his throat and his jugular vein.

With my teeth.

I had my right hand in his hair, holding back his head. My left one was on his heart so I could feel it slowing. His eyes were blank with shock and fear, but I hardly noticed. Slowly, almost casually, I bent to his throat again, and drained him while I let my memories flood his dying brain. The abuse, the shaming, the harassment, the insults, the Bloody Mary, the three hundred dollars, the girls. I drank and drank and drank, for the girls.

"And this," I said into Artie's dulling eyes just before I took the last long pull, the one that stopped the heart beneath my hand, "is for Tea Baby."

"Better now." It wasn't a question from Dal, more an observation.

I nodded, shy but resolute. "The girl?"

"I sent her home in a taxi. She won't remember this night at all. She was just fifteen."

I nodded again. "I did what had to be done."

He took my hands and kissed them, first the right, then the left. The left had a bit of Artie's blood on it and Dal smoothly, sensuously, sucked it off my fingers. When they were clean, he folded my hand against his heart and looked deeply into my eyes.

"Whatever you did, whatever you will ever do, is fine with me. I will love you forever, Romagene."

Forever. "That's a long time, Dal."

"It is." He put his arm around my waist and pulled me to him, tight. "We should get started."

Holding each other, we walked into the night.

24

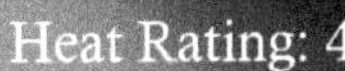

Dream Logic

Harris has just been fired from his job, and though he sees this as a fresh start, he's questioning his life choices. Desperately alone, he slips into slumber to tackle his problems another day, only to find his dream woman waiting for him. However, upon waking, he realizes she may not be a dream, after all.

Isaac Sher

DREAM LOGIC

Isaac Sher

Isaac Sher

Part One:

"We know this is an emotional time for you, Harris. This was not a decision we arrived at lightly."

Harris stared down at the oversized envelope in front of him on the table, and pulled out a stack of documents, feeling strangely numb.

Kevin from HR continued on with his rehearsed speech. "In recognition for your ten years with our organization, we have put together this severance package for you, which I think you'll agree is pretty generous."

Nodding silently, Harris allowed him to finish the presentation without interruption. After reading through the agreement carefully, he signed his name and walked out of his now former employer's building with a copier paper box full of his personal belongings, and a cashier's check in his pocket.

Moments later, he climbed in his car.

"They *fired* you? For what?"

Driving away from the bank, Harris shook his head as he listened to his friend, Shondra, on speakerphone. Call it shock, but he was strangely unaffected by the happenings. "Not fired, laid off, along with at least thirty other folks. I just deposited a huge severance check from them. I've got more coming from my unused vacation time, and there's some other

"

benefits, besides. Hell, I even qualify for unemployment now. Honestly, it's not so bad."

"At least you're out of there. I still say you were a saint for putting up with their BS as long as you did."

"Well, it's done now, Shondra, and it's time I start over. I've given my blood and sweat for a decade, and now it's time I take care of myself for a bit. And I can afford to."

"Gonna buy that PS5 you were drooling over? I wanna watch your pale-ass face when you kill your first robot dinosaur."

He laughed as he pulled onto the highway. "Hell yes. I already placed the order online. It'll arrive by Thursday." Carefully easing into the midday Chicago traffic flow, he took a deep breath. Skyscrapers lined the horizon under a thick layer of smog and exhaust. "But for right now, I'm going to go home, take a hot bath, and maybe turn in early. I didn't sleep well last night, anyway."

Shondra's voice deepened with concern. "I only ask that you take at least a few days off before you start your job hunt. Give yourself a chance to process all of this, y'know? This was your first job out of college. Losing it is going to sting, even if you don't feel it yet."

"Yes, Mom," Harris said through a laugh. "Actually, I already have a plan for tomorrow. I'm going to finally get that gym membership I've been putting off. I always said I was too wiped out after I got home from work to get any exercise in, so now I don't have any excuses."

He'd put off his health too long and had tacked on too many pounds as a result. Time he fixed that.

"Good plan, Harris. Get your flabby butt on an elliptical, and watch the straight girls line up to see the results."

"Yeah, right. I just need to get my doctor off my back about my 'good cholesterol' levels, and see if I can get back into last year's jeans." He slowed down to let someone pass him and get into his lane. He wasn't in any hurry. "Sex is the last thing on my mind right now." Too much drama and too many complications.

The dream was unusually vivid. He was walking down a nondescript hallway, the walls and ceiling a plain white, the floor made of unpainted wood. He knew it was a dream, it had that slightly off-balance feeling of unreality, like a haze around the edge of his vision. But he could think clearly enough, and even control where he was going.

He opened the door at the end of the hallway, and stood inside what looked like someone's half-empty living room. There was a kitchenette off to his left, a small table and four chairs directly ahead, and then, off to his right, was a large and comfortable-looking white sofa, facing away from him.

He approached the sofa, and as he reached the side, he found a woman lying there. She wasn't wearing a single stitch of clothing—and he realized, in that moment, neither was he.

Lying on her back, the woman had a toned and athletic physique, very unlike his. Her long blonde hair was pulled into a single braid, but the shape of her eyes suggested partly Asian heritage. Her breasts were a pretty sight, perfectly proportional with her five-foot-nothing frame, with gravity's effects suggesting they were real and not the result of implants. She looked to be in her late twenties or early thirties, and she had one hand between her thighs, languidly rubbing in circles around her hairless pubic mound.

For a long minute, he just stood there, watching this mysterious woman making love to herself. Her eyes were closed as she issued little gasps of joy, and her back arched as part of a long, full-body stretch. When she slipped a finger inside herself, Harris spoke without even thinking.

"My God, that's beautiful."

She slowly opened her eyes, a smoldering dark brown color. One eyebrow rose in unconcerned surprise, and her voice was relaxed and languid. "Is this a sex dream? That's cool." She spread her legs, her fingers toying with the beautiful folds there. "Maybe here, at least, I can get someone to lick me." She met Harris's gaze. "Hey, big guy. Help a horny girl out?"

He chuckled. "Maybe I had sex on my mind more than I thought if I'm dreaming something like this. Sure, pretty lady, I can, ah, help you out."

He dropped to his knees in front of the couch, and she obligingly shifted to be in easy reach of him. He kissed her inner thigh, marveling at how real everything seemed. Her skin was soft against his lips, her salty sweat coated his tongue, and her rich natural perfume of arousal invaded his sinuses.

Every muscle in his body grew taut with tense need as his skin heated to boiling and his heart thundered.

She murmured immediate approval, her fingers toying with his thick black hair. "Never had a dream this real before. Goddamn, your lips are warm."

"Real?" He laughed, pausing briefly to lap gently at one side of her mons, pulling another gasp from her. "I'm licking the pussy of a stranger I just met five seconds ago. Nothing...mmm, you taste good...nothing about this makes sense."

Her fingers tickled the shell of his left ear, and then she gently pulled him closer to her heat. "Dream logic. Doesn't have to make sense, it just is. Do that again, but on the other side. Oh yeah, right there, stranger. Make me scream your name."

His lips pursed around the hood of her clit for a moment before he looked up. "Hard to do that if you don't know my name, pretty lady."

She looked down the length of her body to meet his gaze again. "True. Tell you what. Put a finger in me first, *then* tell me your name." She rested her head back on the sofa again. "Not that I'll remember it again after I wake up..."

He obligingly slid one finger between her flushed lips, marveling at the way her body reacted to his touch, and desperately wanting relief of his own hardening problem. "Harris Kaminski, at your service."

He bent his head and closed his lips over her hood once more, his tongue swirling in a circle around the hidden nub there.

"Fuck, that's good. Harris, Harris... Did I know a Harris in school or something? Where is this coming from? Yes, right there." Her grip transferred back to his hair, clenched tight with spasming pleasure. "I'm Kyrie, Kyrie Saito, and if you don't finish making me cum, I'm gonna hunt you down and take what I need by force." She moaned again from deep in her throat.

He wordlessly obliged, holding her legs open with one hand as he slipped a second finger inside with the other. Since she enjoyed that last tongue motion so much, he decided to keep at it, his open mouth covering her clit entirely as he continued his deliciously wet task.

After a few moments and another series of little gasps from her, the mysterious Kyrie's thighs suddenly clamped tight around him, a long wail echoing through the unfamiliar room as she drenched his fingers with her arousal.

Her voice gave out, her legs relaxed, releasing him as she murmured aloud, "Holy shit. I just came in my dreams. Can people even do that?" Her body went limp, but her lips were wide and smiling. "I needed that, thank you."

He stood, licking her essence from his lips, and climbed onto the large couch next to her. There shouldn't have been enough room for the two of them to lay side by side, but dream logic prevailed again, and he was now curled up behind her, one arm gently wrapped around her flat belly. Strangely, his needs were forgotten, though he was still hard.

She snuggled in and guided his hand to cup one of her breasts. "All of you is so warm, just like that masterful mouth of yours. I'm gonna have to dream about you again, Harris." She turned her head and kissed the tip of his nose. "You even knew that I like to cuddle afterward. Dream men are the best."

He inhaled deep, taking in the scent of her silken hair like a drug. She smelled like an intoxicating mix of rich ginger and saffron laced with sage. "Dream women are pretty awesome, too." He nibbled the edge of her ear, and she purred happily in response.

"I'd love to be someone's dream woman, Mister Figment-of-My-Sub-conscious. I'd like that very..." She paused and looked over her shoulder at where her backside met his waist. "Now that is inconsiderate of me. Harris Dream-Tongue, I've left you high, hard, and dry, haven't I? Would you like me to take care of you like you did for me? Sit up for a second."

He moved upright, and his dream lover turned around on the sofa so that she laid on her side with her face in his lap.

"Let's see if I remember how to do this," she said with a chuckle before her mouth descended on him. Taking every inch of him inside her, her tongue performed some insane miracle of sensuality around him, the suction threatening to make him erupt too soon—

VEET! VEET! VEET!

His eyes flashing open, he looked at the glowing display and bleating alarm of his bedside clock. He'd forgotten to turn off his usual alarm, even though he no longer had to go into work. With a multi-layered groan, he hit the off switch with a closed fist, perhaps a bit harder than necessary, and got up to sit on the edge of the bed.

"Kyrie," he murmured as his length stood at rapt morning-wood attention.

A moment later, as the cobwebs in his awareness cleared, he realized he'd remembered his dream, something that didn't often happen to him. Usually, the details of his dreams would evaporate like mist moments after waking up, but not this time. He remembered Kyrie. He remembered every little detail—the sound of her gasps, the smell of her hair, the feel of her wetness around his fingers. It had felt so strangely real that he lifted his fingers to his nose to check for her scent. To no avail, sadly.

"Damn." Muttering further curses under his breath, he stomped out of his bedroom and into his shower.

As he sat in his car in the gym's parking lot, Harris stared out at the building's huge front window. Even at this early hour, it was full of people, pedaling, lifting, and exercising their way through levels of fitness he had never attained in all his life.

What if they laughed at him? He didn't want to be some freakshow outsider, the strange whale swimming among sleek sharks, who might all whirl around and descend upon him en masse for daring to invade their territory. He'd only been sitting here for a minute when his phone rang with Shondra's unflappable grin shining on his caller-ID screen.

With a sigh, he picked up the call. "Hey, Shon—"

"You're just sitting there in the parking lot, aren't you."

He looked at his phone in awe and horror. "Do you have a camera in my car or something?"

"No, but I know you, Harris, maybe better than you know yourself. I remember what happened when I dragged you to my old gym five years ago, and you better believe I am still kicking myself for not realizing sooner what those assholes were pulling on you. Most gyms aren't like that place, and you might recall me and many of my friends all quit our memberships there when the managers refused to do a damn thing about it."

He winced, remembering the fake friendliness those guys had presented, only to change the settings on his exercise bike when he wasn't looking so he could barely even move, making him think he was even more inept than he'd believed. Their laughing had been the worst.

"Yeah, I remember."

"I'm telling you, that sort of crap isn't tolerated at most places. In fact, most gyms will actually be really friendly to larger folks because they know you're motivated to work really hard. But I don't blame you if you don't exactly want to have strangers offering to help you out this time around."

He looked up from the phone, watching the indistinct silhouette of some perfectly-formed woman running on a treadmill. Poetry in motion. "I just don't feel like I belong there."

Shondra was silent for a moment, and he could easily envision her sitting in her office, staring thoughtfully out her window as her hands furiously crocheted a new blanket or scarf for someone.

"Would it help if I was to join that gym with you? Be your workout buddy?"

He shook his head, forgetting for a moment she couldn't see him. "I should go in by myself today, at least. Make sure they're actually friendly to those who aren't already Practically Perfect In Every Way. If they're assholes, fuck 'em. I'll just leave and go somewhere else."

"You're gonna go in now?"

"Yeah. The longer I stew in the car, the worse it'll get."

Shondra's smile could be heard in her voice. "Attaboy. Here's a little something to help." The email notification tone went off on his phone. "I just emailed you a coupon that place is offering. If you let them give you a tour, they waive the usual sign-up and processing fees, and just charge you the first monthly dues, and give you a gift card on top of that.

Probably take you no more than half an hour, and you get to keep the gift card even if you don't become a member."

"Thanks again, *Mom*."

"Think nothing of it, Harris. We got each other through high school, and we'll get each other through the rest of this life, too. You helped me meet Delilah and get my head on right about her, so helping you out with this is just the tip of the iceberg. Now, get in there and get yourself a gift card, okay? I got a meeting in ten, so I need to go. You going to be alright?"

He stepped out of the car. "On my way inside now. Thanks, Shondra. Lotsa love."

"Lotsa love, Harris. Bye!"

Slipping his phone into his jeans pocket, he crossed the lot and entered the gym. As he stepped through the second set of automatic doors, a chime sounded and signaled the woman at the front desk to turn around and begin her usual greeting to their customers. But she only got as far as "Good morning! Welcome to..." before she completed turning around and stopped dead in her tracks.

His jaw dropped. It was Kyrie from his dream in the flesh, wearing a matching set of black and gold sports bra and yoga pants, and a nametag attached to the former.

Five-foot-nothing—a perfect athlete's physique with beautiful feminine proportions.

The same blonde hair, pulled back into a long braid.

Those same beautiful brown eyes.

She was staring right at him, her cheeks growing redder by the second, and her expression was full of so many emotions at once—surprise, confusion, fear, and even lust.

His mind was racing, and he could only imagine how his face showed much the same.

For a long moment, nothing was said, their silence filled with the background noise of the gym and its many customers or machines.

Her mouth opened again, and after a false start, she seemed to find her words. "I need to see your ID, sir. Please."

He could only nod, reaching into his pocket for his wallet, and handing it over for her to see.

She took a deep breath, looked down at it, and her eyes bugged out of their sockets. "Harris Kaminski. Oh, my God."

He tried to swallow the lump in his throat. "Kyrie...Saito, right?"

Her eyes got even wider. "My nametag doesn't have my last name on it."

"Yeah. You told me your name yourself. Last night. I know, I'm kinda freaking out right now, too. Dream logic shouldn't apply here." This was utterly impossible.

Her stare was intense, boring right into him. "Did you know I worked here?"

He should his head fervently. "I swear on everything I hold dear, you were the last person I expected to meet here. I was just coming in to get a membership." He gripped the countertop, his knuckles turning white as he lowered his voice to a whisper. "I didn't think you were real."

He was wondering if he'd actually woken up this morning.

She leaned in, whispering as well. "This is going to sound really stupid, but I actually feel really guilty right now."

"Guilty?"

She leaned in closer, her lips right by his ear. "Because you made me feel so good, but I woke up before I could make you cum in my mouth." She eased back, a new blush forming on her beautiful face.

He held out one hand to her. "How about I buy you a drink sometime, and we can...discuss that?"

She shook his hand, and squeezed it gently. "I'd like that." She looked down at his hands and smiled. "Now I know this is real. Your hands are just as warm as I remember. Nice to meet you again, dream man."

Part Two:

"And over here, we have the hydromassage chairs. Their use is included in your membership, and they're great for relaxing after a long workout."

Harris made appreciative noises, and dutifully paused to look over the chair. Despite everything else going through his mind at that moment, he was actually very impressed with the gym he was touring. "Very nice. What's next, Kyrie?"

His guide turned and smiled, her grin most definitely lighting up the room as far as he was concerned. "I think we've covered about everything, Harris." She gestured around her, drawing his eyes away from her and back to the assortment of other customers and workout machines scattered throughout the gym floor. "We've only been open for a year, but we've already created a thriving community, ranging from fitness professionals to those like you who are just getting started. It's important to us that all of our members feel welcome at all times, so definitely let us know if you ever have any problems along those lines, or about anything at all!"

He nodded. "That's actually really good to hear. I've had some problems at other gyms who seemed to think it was funny to have bigger people come in try and lose some extra weight."

Her eyes narrowed. "Seriously? That's horrid!"

"I'm afraid so. Put me off going to a gym for years, a lot of time lost."

"Well, I'm really, really glad you came in today." She glanced around again, her gaze lingering for just a moment on an older woman in a company-branded hoodie sitting off to one side, twenty feet away, her head bent over a stack of paperwork.

Kyrie met his gaze and nodded toward the woman, silently mouthing the words "my boss," and gritting her teeth nervously for a moment. He glanced in that direction and nodded back to show he understood.

Kyrie went back into "saleswoman" mode. "So, should we pull the trigger and get you signed up?"

"You really sold me on the place, Kyrie. Let's do this!"

"That's great! Just follow me back to the front desk, and I'll work through your forms as fast as possible."

As she turned to head in that direction, he couldn't help but take a deep breath and boggle at everything going on this morning. Kyrie was an absolute knockout, unquestionably the hottest woman he'd ever had a direct conversation with. She was sculpted and fit in all the ways he wasn't, five feet tall and every inch of her a woman of legend. Her long golden hair was tied into a braid which reached the small of her back, and her dark eyes burned like coals, full of life and passion. Between the shape of those eyes and her last name of Saito, he guessed she was partly of Japanese descent, not that it really mattered. She carried herself with utmost confidence and poise, reveling in the fact no one would ever mistake her for anyone else. She was her own person, and he could tell she loved being who and what she was. That sense of self was, if anything, even more attractive to him than the flawless curves barely hidden under her gym-wear.

I want to find whomever invented this yoga pants trend and shake their hand, he thought to himself, taking in a deep appreciation for the way Kyrie's backside moved underneath the tight fabric.

As they reached the desk and sat down on either side of it, he took a deep breath to try and calm his libido. In most circumstances, he'd be idly wondering what her body really looked like without those tight clothes while trying not to be obvious about undressing her with his eyes. But today, things were different. Last night, they were strangers who had somehow shared a dream where they not only saw each other completely naked, but fell into a passionate embrace almost immediately. When they ended up meeting each other in person this morning and recognizing one another from the dream, they both were shocked the lover was all too real.

In his dream, he'd brought her to a screaming oral climax first, and then woken up just as she was getting started on returning the favor. And she'd dropped hints today her dream had gone exactly the same way. Once the official tour had started, she'd been very careful to be a complete professional, but there were moments when he thought she might have been looking at him with a very thoughtful expression.

"So, Harris, you're not just getting this membership because I'm the one selling it, I hope."

"Absolutely not. I mean, I'm..." He paused, trying to find the right way to phrase things. "I'm really glad to have your company, but I'm very serious about trying to get into a real exercise routine. This gym seems like the best place for that."

As she was writing something down on her clipboard, he decided to go for broke. "But that being said, I really would like to buy you—"

Kyrie held a finger to her lips, and pointedly glanced back in the direction of her boss. She tore a sheet of paper off her pad and set it down in front of him.

He looked down at the note.

STRICT COMPANY RULES. NO FRATERNIZING WITH C USTOMERS...

Well, damn.

She saw his sad expression, and held up one finger again in a "wait for it" gesture before returning to writing another note, which she passed to him a moment later.

ON COMPANY PROPERTY. OTHERWISE, I WOULD HAVE BLOWN YOU IN THAT SAUNA ROOM, BELIEVE IT!

The exclamation point had a little heart for the dot, and was followed by a doodle of a slyly grinning smiley face, licking its own lips.

She quickly traced a fingertip across her clothed nipple as her eyes locked with his. She then quickly produced a third note.

YES, I WOULD LOVE FOR YOU TO BUY ME A DRINK. MY SHIFT ENDS AT 3:00 PM. HINT: I LOVE FLOWERS AND COF-FEE.

He was still thinking about that hypothetical blow job, but he managed to carefully fold up the three notes and put them into his pocket. "Thank you, Kyrie." He glanced over in the manager's direction, thankfully still distracted by her paperwork, and then back to the vision in front of him. "Once we get my membership sorted out, I was planning to go shopping for some workout clothes, and then come back this afternoon. I'm thinking I'll be back around 2:00, and then head out around 3:00. Maybe I'll see you around then?"

She gave a small laugh. "I've got a training session from two to three, so you'll see me on the floor, but after I'm done, I'll help you out with some cooldown stretches. Sound good?"

"Absolutely."

As Harris stepped out of the locker room at 2:00 that afternoon, clad in a brand new pair of loose shorts and t-shirt, he stopped and looked around the gym floor. While not excessively crowded, there were still a large number of people around, each absorbed in their own routine or working in small groups.

He spotted Kyrie off in one corner, helping a pregnant woman work through some stretching routines, and decided to find his own patch of floor to do some warmups of his own.

It was still nerve-wracking making his way through the aisles, passing by all these people sporting definition and muscle tone that a professional wrestler would envy. He knew it was irrational to think they even registered his presence at all, much less had some sort of nefarious plan to humiliate him, but all the same, he still felt like he was walking around with a giant "Kick Me" sign pinned to his back.

Eventually, he did find an empty spot at the edge of the room, and after a few moments of indecision, he started doing jumping jacks. A minute later, a man's voice coughed politely behind him, and Harris stopped to turn around.

The man had the face of a grandfather, but the wiry and muscular arms of Bruce Lee. His hair was silver, his face full of laugh lines, and he bore a full mustache that clearly received as much hard work and maintenance as his arms.

"Are you Harris? Kyrie asked me to look out for you." He wore a plain white tank top and a pair of purple sweatpants, his face wide and smiling.

Harris let out a held breath at the mention of Kyrie's name. "Yeah, that's me. I just joined this morning." After a moment's hesitation, he held out his hand. "Harris Kaminski."

The older man accepted the handshake, and thankfully felt no need to exert any strength into his grip then, which put Harris even more at ease. "Roscoe Jacobsen, pleased to meet'cha."

"Thanks, Mr. Jacobsen, I appreciate that. I feel out of my element here."

"Hogwash! And call me Roscoe. I retired from teaching high school ten years ago, and left the whole 'Mister' nonsense behind with it."

Harris gave him a thumbs-up. "Roscoe it is, then. What did you teach?"

"American History. Lord knows we're living in some weird times now, though. The history books on the early twenty-first century are going to make for some intense reading, no two ways about it."

Harris remembered his own history teacher and the big poster she'd mounted on the classroom's back wall. "My history teacher had a favorite saying: 'Those who forget the past are condemned to repeat it.' George Santayana, I think."

Roscoe's smile got even wider, his gleaming white grin showing below his mustache. "Oh, I know we're gonna be friends now. You went to West Ridge and sat in Mrs. Russell's class, didn't ya!"

"Guilty as charged." He smiled as a few memories flitted through the back of his mind. "She was one of the best teachers I ever had, hands down."

"Damn straight, and God rest her soul. But we can waltz down memory lane another time. We're in a gym and this is workout time. I saw you doing jumping jacks just now, and I gotta tell ya. Don't. Wreck your knees with that shit, 'specially being a hefty fella. Smart you wanna warm up, but let me show you some better stretches. Sound good?"

In spite of himself, Harris looked around the room again, and thankfully, no one else seemed to be watching him and Roscoe. He knew in his head he wasn't being set up to be some sort of show with Roscoe as the instigator, but even so, the old fears were still there. Roscoe's kindness still felt suspicious.

At that moment, his gaze fell again to where Kyrie was working with her client. Somehow sensing he was looking her way, she glanced up, waved, and when she saw who he was standing with, she flashed him a big okay signal, making a circle with her thumb and forefinger.

His last doubts fading away, he turned back to the older man next to him. "If you're willing to spend the time on me, I'm willing to learn."

Roscoe patted him on the back. "Son, I'm a retired widower with a fat pension, a healthy diversified stock portfolio, and more free time than I know what to do with. I got in on the ground floor with this new place, and I damn near made it my second home." He stood opposite from Harris with his legs slightly spread. "Now, do what I do. Feet shoulder width apart, keep 'em flat, and reach up and over with one hand. Stretch like you're trying to grab a ceiling light. Yeah, just like that."

An hour later, Roscoe and Harris were getting dressed in the locker room, having washed off a layer of sweat.

Roscoe bent over as he sat on a bench, slipping on a pair of dress shoes. "So, I got a question for you. If I'm outta line askin' you this, Harris, you just say the word."

He lifted up one arm to sniff himself, and put on another bit of gel deodorant, just in case. "Fire away, Roscoe."

"How'd you and Kyrie get acquainted?"

He paused as he replaced the deodorant's cap. "A series of strange coincidences, I guess you could say. We, ah, bumped into each other briefly last night. I apparently made a good first impression, and then it just so happened she was working at the gym I planned to join." That seemed as safe an explanation as any. "Blew both our minds when I walked in to see her behind the desk."

Roscoe nodded. "She said much the same." He looked up from his shoes, and straightened his collar. "You sweet on her? Because her eyes were all lit up when she asked me to help you out. I'd hate to think she's making something out of nothing."

Shaking out his jeans as he pulled them from his locker, Harris gave a lopsided grin. "Let me put it this way. Yesterday, I had zero intention of looking for a date anytime soon because I've had a lot happen this week, and I'm still figuring things out. But Kyrie..." He paused to collect his thoughts again as he stepped into his pants. "I'm really glad this happened. I've known her less than twenty-four hours, but I definitely want to keep on seeing her. So yeah, 'sweet on her' sounds about right." As he pulled on a clean black golf shirt, he raised a playful eyebrow in Roscoe's direction. "Why, am I going to have to fight you for her?"

Roscoe gave a hearty laugh at that. "I may be single, but I much prefer the fine wine of ladies my own age, thank you very much. Naw, Kyrie's a sweetheart. We've been good friends this past year, and I want to make sure her next boy's a kinder sort than the last couple of dolts she picked out."

Running his fingers through his hair, Harris cursed himself for forgetting to bring a comb. "Probably best I leave that last part alone." He still didn't like the drop in his gut. "Hey, does my hair look okay?"

His new friend just laughed. "You look fine, ya big bear. Now, get on out there, and show her a good time."

"Look at you, Harris! Fresh out of the shower, just the way I like 'em."

They stood just outside the gym's front door, their breaths misting in the cold afternoon air. Kyrie wore a pair of jeans almost as snug as her yoga pants, and a blue winter-weight jacket.

"I didn't get to say before, but you look really good in that coat. Where did you find it?"

He grinned, rightly proud of his favorite item of clothing. "I was in Los Angeles for a business trip about four years ago, and spotted it in the window of a store as I walked past. I knew immediately I had to have it. Glad you like it, and may I say, you look lovely, as well." He gestured to the lot. "I happened to buy something for you while I was out today. If you'll follow me, it's in my car."

She sashayed alongside him, smiling at her much taller companion. "Should I close my eyes?"

"No need, we're right here." He hit the unlock button on his keychain and pulled a loosely wrapped package from the backseat of his four-door Toyota.

As he held it out to her in both hands, she carefully ripped off the paper to reveal a small flowerpot containing a single orchid with dark purple and white petals, the long stem wrapped around a thin metal rod sticking.

"Oh my, Harris, are you on point or *what*?" Her eyes lit up anew, and she squeezed his hands. "You are *so* perfect. I can't believe it, but we have to get in the car right now. You're going to drive me home before this gorgeous blossom freezes to death." She carefully plucked the pot and what was left of the wrapping paper out of his hands, and walked around to his passenger side door, climbing in without pause.

"I figured it would be okay to leave it in the car a bit longer while we got coffee, but this works, too. What about your car?" He slid into the driver's seat and held the flower again for a moment while she fastened her seatbelt.

"I live three blocks from here, so I just walk to work every day. I've got a car, but I don't use it too much." She took the plant back and pointed out his route. "Left out the driveway, then left again at the light, and then left at the second stop sign."

He shifted the car into gear and made his way out into the afternoon traffic. "If you like, I can just wait in the car while you take the flower inside, and then we'll head to the restaurant I had in mind."

"Where did you want to go?"

"One sec." He watched the oncoming traffic for an opening, and then eased his car through the major intersection. "Okay. Ever had Ethiopian coffee?"

She shook her head. "I don't think I've ever had Ethiopian anything. Do they make it strong?"

He couldn't help but chuckle as he approached the last turn. "From what I've read, Ethiopia *invented* coffee. This place roasts the beans right in front of you, then grinds them and brews a fresh pot on the spot. And yes, it is very strong."

"Holy shit, I have to try... Wait! That blue house on the right. Park there."

Pulling up to the curb, he left the engine running and unlocked the doors. "Orchid Home Delivery, at your service. I'll wait right here, and Kyrie?"

"Yeah?"

"Thank you for trusting me, letting me drive you home. I really appreciate that."

She blinked in surprise, and seemed to absorb that for a moment in silence. "Call it intuition, but I feel like you deserve that trust, Harris. Really." She looked down at the flower in her lap, and then raised her eyes back to meet his again, a new resolve shining in her smile. "Come on inside. It's too cold to wait out here." She opened her door, and turned back to look at him. "Are you coming, or what?"

His jaw dropped, but he turned off the car, grabbed his keys, and followed her up the side staircase to her second-floor apartment.

"I live by myself. The landlord lives on the first floor, but she travels a lot, so we worked out a deal where she knocks a little off my rent if I pick up her mail, shovel snow, mow the lawn, that sort of stuff." She immediately placed the orchid on a front window ledge so it could get some sunlight, and then grabbed a keychain hanging on a pegboard by the door. "In fact, I need to check that mail now before I get, ah, distracted. Hang your jacket up, have a seat. I'll be right back."

Putting his coat on an empty peg, he took a look around. The apartment's living room had a medium-sized flatscreen TV mounted on one wall with a large rug and unrolled yoga mat in front of it. There was also a large sofa facing the TV, but it was not the same pattern as the one in their shared dream that seemed to shift in size to accommodate their cuddling. The dream-sofa had been white with gold flowers on it, while this one was a solid mocha color.

He sat down, feeling his muscles unwind after the short but intense workout with Roscoe, and looked around again. The walls were painted a soft sky blue color, and a host of framed photos or prints hung around the room. A young man with the same blond hair and facial features as Kyrie appeared in most of them, either with Kyrie or on his own. A brother, perhaps. One picture showed her and the man standing between an older Japanese gentleman in an expensive business suit, and a middle-aged Caucasian woman in a casual summer dress with Kyrie's smile and a thick mane of wavy blonde hair, presumably her parents.

His inspection was interrupted by a large cat who suddenly jumped onto his lap.

"Whoa! Hey there." The silver-gray feline was larger than most housecats, stocky and muscular, with gold eyes and a well-groomed soft coat of fur. The cat looked him up and down, and then reared up on his hind legs to put his front paws on Harris's chest. "And what's your name?" The cat responded by butting his forehead into Harris's chin. He scratched gently on the cat's ears, which led to more headbutting and a loud purr that echoed through the room.

"I've never seen Buster warm up to someone so fast!" Kyrie replaced the keychain on the pegboard as she closed the door behind her. She pulled off and hung up her jacket to reveal a snug light blue babydoll t-shirt and plopped down on the couch next to Harris. "Normally, he won't even come out when new people come around, much less get all lovey-dovey." She reached out and scratched Buster's other ear, leading to the cat kneading his paws back and forth into Harris's chest. "Oh, he's in a *good* mood." She pointed to Buster's paws. "Kittens do that to get more milk out of their mother's breasts, so if you see a grown cat doing that, that's their body language for major happiness."

"Aha!" Harris gave Buster's forehead a playful *boop* with a gentle fingertip, and Buster responded by rubbing his face all over that finger. "I always wondered about that. My neighbors had a Russian Blue just like Buster, although not as big, and she would do this now and then. Yes, Buster, I like you, too."

She watched him and Buster play for a few moments before speaking up again. "I am firmly of the opinion that cats and dogs are really good judges of character. I once had a boyfriend who, in hindsight was, shall we say, kinda toxic. Every time I brought him here, Buster would go after him like a buzzsaw. One time, he literally shat himself in terror and hid in the closet for hours." She frowned, and then stroked Buster's back. "That last incident is what had me look at that asshole in a new light, and finally pay attention to everything my friends were saying about him. I dumped him three days later, and right after that, he got banned from the gym for threatening one of my coworkers after she wouldn't tell him my work schedule."

"Yikes. Glad you're okay now, though."

"I dodged a bullet. Three weeks later, he'd picked up some new girl, and then got thrown in jail for breaking her nose and her arm when she wouldn't put out for him on their second date." She shivered. "That could've been me."

He reached out and gave her hand a squeeze that he hoped was comforting. It didn't seem right to say something like, *I'm glad it wasn't you*, since he didn't want to sound like he didn't care about the other woman.

She squeezed his hand back and offered a faint smile.

Buster chose that moment to give an indignant meow, batting at Harris's free hand and headbutting it with his forehead to demand more ear-scratches.

They both laughed, and Kyrie stood. "Okay, now I'm starting to get a little jealous, Buster. Into the kitchen with you, and it's time for your dinner, anyway. She scooped the large cat, who gave a token sound of protest, but happily draped himself over Kyrie's shoulder as she walked away with him. "Can I get you anything to drink, Harris?"

"Water would be great, thanks! Roscoe must have pulled a few gallons of sweat out of me today. Thanks for introducing me to him, by the way. He seems really nice."

Kyrie giggled as she scooped cat food for Buster. "He's really hardcore about his workouts, but he's only hard on himself. He doesn't judge anyone else at all. That's why I thought he might make a good workout buddy for you." She returned from the kitchen with a glass of water in hand. "Heeeere you go. Water Home Delivery, at your service."

He chuckled and gladly accepted the glass, taking a huge sip of it right away. "Thank you, I needed that. I didn't realize how thirsty I was until just now." He took another gulp, and then turned to set the glass aside on the small table next to the sofa.

As he swiveled back to face Kyrie again, she'd moved to kneel on the sofa, directly facing him. Her t-shirt had come untucked from her jeans, and her fingers were fidgeting with the shirt's hem.

"I know exactly what you mean, mister." She was leaning forward just a tiny bit, her chin lifting as she spoke.

He firmly told his brain to stop trying to overthink everything, and took his cue to lean in and kiss her.

A gasp and a small whisper of "thank you" passed her lips just before their lips touched, and their first kiss lingered for a long, sweet moment. Without letting their connection break, Kyrie climbed into his lap, straddling him and wrapping her arms around his shoulders. He caressed her cheek, and she leaned into his hand, murmuring a little purr of affection as their kiss ended.

They silently stared into each other's eyes for a long time, both smiling all the while, a connection tethering.

She eventually spoke first. "Did you make reservations at that Ethiopian place? Do we have to leave soon?"

"Nope." He leaned in and placed a kiss on her cheek that drew another dazzling smile from her. "They're walk-in only, and I have nowhere else I want or need to be other than right here, right now."

"Good answer, Harris." She reached down and peeled off her shirt, tossing it aside to reveal a simple white cotton bra. "I can still feel how you touched me last night. I don't care what it was, a dream or... You know what? Never mind, it doesn't matter how it happened." She nipped gently at his earlobe. "All I know is that you make me feel sexy, you make me feel beautiful, and you make me feel safe."

"Me, too, Kyrie." She looked up in surprise, but he continued. "I was terrified to walk into that gym today. I almost didn't do it because I didn't feel safe. You made it safe for me, pretty lady. You made it okay for me to be...me. I can't ever thank you enough for that."

She lunged forward, devouring his lips with another kiss. Where their first kiss had been tender and gentle, this one was hungry and urgent, their hands eagerly holding each other together as tightly as possible.

"You...you have to cum down my throat tonight, Harris. I left you high and dry last night, and I need to feel it, taste it from you."

He reached behind her and managed to smoothly unhook her bra one-handed, and she tossed away the garment to reveal her body to him. Her naked breasts looked exactly as they had in their dream, and she moaned as he cupped one in his large hand.

A loud, irritated meow rumbled from behind the closed kitchen door.

They both dissolved into a fit of giggles.

"Fuck off, Buster! You can't have him, he's mine! I don't care how nicely he scratches your ears—'"

He started nibbling along her ear and stiffening her nipples into hard points against his chest.

"Goddamn, Harris, you're making me so wet."

Squeezing her denim-clad backside, he continued his playful kisses along her ear. "Mmm. Show me."

Grinning, she stood, one hand caressing her flat stomach as her smoldering eyes burned bright. "Not until I've blown you so hard, you scream my name. I have a promise to keep. Unbutton those pants, mister. We're just getting started."

Moments later, she was on her knees before him, and he watched in awe as his length disappeared into her mouth, inch by deliciously slow inch, her eyes never leaving his.

If I'm still dreaming, he thought to himself, *I don't ever want to wake up.*

Part Three:

Kyrie's mouth engulfed his length, and the sensations that rushed through him were exactly like what she'd done to him in their shared dream. Harris stared down at his new lover in disbelief as she knelt before his comfortable seat on her couch.

"Mother of God, that's intense! How are you doing that?"

She let his length pop from her lips and smiled up at him as she squeezed the base. "It's my 'secret technique', but you can thank my college roommate for teaching it to me." She made a show of sliding her tongue up and down the underside of his straining erection. "You deserve the best I've got, Harris. And I want you to cum hard down my throat."

He reached out to caress her hair, his fingertips trailing along the length of her single braid. "Guys like me," he said as his free hand gestured to his out-of-shape body, "don't usually hear that from beautiful women like you. Not that I'm taking my luck for granted for a second."

She took him in her mouth again, but as she did, she reached up with both hands and caressed the front of his shirt-clad body from his chest to his waist. When both hands reached his groin for a two-handed stroke, she came up for air again.

"I don't want some muscle-obsessed gym-junkie anymore, Harris." She kissed his belly, and then briefly sucked at the glistening tip of his rod before she looked into his eyes. "Been there, learned that lesson. All they want is trophy pussy to go with their six-pack abs to show everyone how manly they are." Very carefully, she cupped his balls in her hand, and licked them.

He took slow breaths, trying not to let the pure pleasure he was feeling cause him to burst too soon. "You're not going to have that problem with me, beautiful."

"I know that." She laid a trail of kisses across one thigh as she stroked him. "When I first saw you, all I could think about was how much of a sweet warm teddy bear you were, and how much I wanted to feel your big body on top of me, around me..." She engulfed him anew, using that same mysterious trick again as she deepthroated him and buried her nose in his pubic hair. A moment later, she came up for air again, her voice getting deeper and quivering with lust as her gaze burned into his. "And inside me." She held eye contact as her skilled hands continued stroking and caressing his shaft, his balls, his body. "I hope you don't mind me thinking of you like that?"

"I'm glad to be your teddy bear, Kyrie. I've never wanted anyone as much as I want you." He caressed her cheek, and she leaned into his hand with another warm smile on her lips.

Her tongue slid from his root to his tip. "I can't wait to taste you, to feel you throb and gush in my mouth." She gave his tip a dainty little kiss, and then looked back up at him, running her palm in a slow caress down his chest. "While I've got my mouth full, I want you to tell me about what you want to do to me afterwards. Or better yet," she grinned, and reached under his black shirt to give one of his nipples a light pinch. "Did you touch yourself this morning after you woke up? Because I sure did, thinking about that amazing dream of ours."

"God, yes. I came so hard, thinking about this amazing new fantasy girl I'd dreamed up." He flashed her a wink, and she giggled in response. "She tasted so good when I licked her into a screaming river of joy."

She grinned. "And you're going to stick your tongue in her again soon, I hope?"

He could only nod, licking his lips at the thought.

"So, how about this." She kissed the back of his hand, still gently working up and down his length with her grip. "Tell me what you imagined about me when you were stroking it this morning. Tell me how you fucked me in your fantasy because, before you leave this apartment, you're going to do it for real."

"Well, it all started when you dragged me away from the sofa and onto a proper bed—"

She had taken her cue to resume blowing him, and it took him a moment to regain a semblance of coherent thought.

She got her wish of his cum down her throat, and his desire to taste her again became reality. He was still wrapping his mind around the reality part. How had she jumped out of his dreams or how had he climbed into hers? None of it made sense, but he chalked it all up to destiny. The whole thing.

Through the years, they never learned the mystery of their strange meeting, but they never took one another for granted. He remained her teddy bear, and she was his everything.

And their love-making? Still hot. Every time, while in the throes, she would tell him, "You're better than any dream, Harris. I'm so glad I met you. Don't ever stop."

He didn't intend to.

Penelope's Problem

Lance has a huge problem. His mother is
about to be kicked out of her rehabilitation facility,
and no one else will take her. At his wits end,
he hires his last resort, Penelope, who reminds
him of a sexy elf. They couldn't be more opposite
if they tried, yet sparks fly at one of his dinner
parties, and they both learn the heart wants
what the heart wants. Opposites attract or not.

Julie Castle

PENELOPE'S PROBLEM

Julie Castle

O^{ne}

Lance Harrison looked through the large picture window of Aunt Penelope's Home Help Agency and frowned. It was definitely on the shabby side. Ordinarily, he would've picked another agency to help him with his mother, but he was desperate. Besides, all the others who knew about his whimsical mother had turned him down. The place was clean and cheerful on a side street off the French Quarter in a dilapidated building. That was, if one went in for tie-dye and beads. He certainly didn't.

The receptionist stood in the center of the room and seemed to be having some fit. Jiggling her nicely curved derriere to and fro, she threw her hands in the air. Long red curls bounced on her shoulders as she moved. Flattening his hand on the plate glass window, he felt the vibrations on the glass and realized she was dancing. This was no way to run a business, but he didn't have time to be picky.

He leaned closer and listened to "Respect" blaring from a boom box on the receptionist's desk. Inappropriate or not, he had no other choice. To pick up his mother before they ejected her from Shady Acres Rehab Center, this sexy hippy chick was his only hope. It couldn't have happened at a worse time because he was hosting a party tonight after becoming Assistant District Attorney for the parish of New Orleans. At this late date, he couldn't cancel it. He'd have to grit his teeth and get through the evening unscathed.

The woman sang along off-key. Her dress was too short and made of soft fabric that clung to her figure. When she spun around, he couldn't help noticing how attractive she was in a hippy, free-spirited sort of way. Not his type at all. Her eyes a sparkling green, she reminded him of an elf—a highly improper elf.

Aunt Penelope had better brush her staff up on office etiquette if she wanted to stay in business. He couldn't have his mother dealing with a bunch of flakes.

Penny Brown kicked off her platform shoes and danced toward the file cabinet. Time to get this going-out-of-business party started, good and proper. Ferguson had been filed under U for Uptight. No doubt Uncle Harry's idea of a joke. God love him, she wouldn't trade one of her unique relatives, even if they were a handful at times.

At least Aunt Penelope's had lasted longer than her other start-up businesses. Aunt Eudora's morning tea-leaf reading had been correct—things were looking up. Soon, Penny would find her destiny. According to Eudora, she'd know her fate because her desire for him would overwhelm her common sense, and everyone knew she was the most common sensical member of the clan.

Doing a slow shuffle, she turned to lay the file on the desk, only to notice she was being watched. A tremor went through her that had nothing to do with fear. A man with his nose practically pressed against the windowpane stood gazing at her as if bemused.

Welcome to the club, buddy, she thought, staring back at him.

Good gracious, he seemed well dressed for a Peeping Tom. He looked like he'd just stepped off the pages of *GQ* in his black suit. His hair, a dark brown, caught the glow of New Orleans's setting sun. His eyes flashed a determined navy blue. She couldn't help noticing the stern look on his handsome face. It all but screamed bill collector.

Oh, merde!

There was only one way to find out for sure. She flashed him a come-hither smile and winked at him. She was darned if he didn't look shocked instead of enticed. He wasn't your run-of-the-mill Peeping Tom, which left collection agency goon.

When he pushed open the door and started to walk inside, his presence carried such intensity, it rocked her back on her heels. She took a step away, instinctively reaching for the can of mace in the file cabinet.

His mouth tightened in blatant disapproval. "I would like to speak to the manager. Now." He shot a pointed glance at the boombox, adding gruffly, "And I would appreciate it if you'd turn that music down."

Anger rapidly replaced her fear. If this would-be bill collector expected to cash in on her misfortune, he'd find himself out of luck. All she had was twelve dollars in her bag.

"Sorry, we're closed. You'll have to come back tomorrow."

He ignored her statement, sitting in the chair in front of her desk while fixing her with a determined gaze. "I'll wait."

Sighing, Penny blew a wisp of hair out of her eyes. What would it take to get rid of the man? "Fine, what can I do for you?"

He frowned at her. "I'll wait to talk to the manager."

Leaning forward, her hands flat on the desk, she glared at him. "I *am* the manager. I'm Aunt Penelope. So, state your business."

His eyes darkened and frown lines crinkled his forehead. She decided she'd shocked him again. She didn't add up to his idea of an honest businesswoman. Then she noticed he wasn't staring at her face anymore. He stared at her cleavage, where her full breasts almost tumbled out of her unbuttoned sundress. She straightened, her cheeks heating as she hurriedly closed the top button.

Breathing deeply, his nostrils flaring, he flashed a distracted gaze back to her face. "I need to hire some home help."

So, he wasn't here to collect on one of her extended family's many unpaid debts. Wonderful! Here was a chance to save her business.

Overjoyed, she beamed at him while his eyes narrow in response. "Well, why didn't you say so? Sit still, and I'll get you some coffee."

· ❤ · ❤ · ❤ · ❤ · ❤ ·

"That isn't necessary, ma'am." Lance scowled after her as she rushed into the back room, ignoring his protest.

She called out, "Would you like cream or sugar?"

He looked at his watch. "I take it black, but coffee isn't necessary. I'm in a hurry." He thought he heard her mumble something like, *"Whatever, you yuppie jerk,"* but he couldn't be sure.

She returned a minute later. Looking at her quizzically as she handed him a mug of what appeared to be badly hand-painted unicorns, he wondered if he was really this desperate. Maybe a bribe would keep Mrs. Rockwell, the Shady Acres Rehabilitation Center administrator, from ejecting his mother. Even thinking about it, he rejected the idea. As an officer of the court, that sort of bribery was beneath him. But, damn it all, he was tempted.

Unfortunately, it wasn't all he found tempting. He looked "Aunt Penelope" over again.

She rushed to take a seat behind the desk. "What kind of help are you looking for, Mr.—"

"Harrison, Lance Harrison," he said, watching her fish a stack of new forms out of the recycling bin.

"If you are so kind as to fill this out, we'll get started."

Grabbing a pen off her desk, he quickly filled out the form, scrawled his signature across the bottom, and thrust it back at her.

Her eyes widened. "You *are* in a hurry! I'll fill in my part, and you can be on your way."

"Fine. I'm due to pick up my mother from the rehab center in half an hour. I need a home companion who can keep an eye on her and assist my housekeeper with the extra work involved in my mother's daily care. I'd need the home companion to live in."

She nodded, smiling. "When do we start?"

He glanced at his watch, noting how much time had ticked by already. If he left now, he could barely make it in time. "Right away."

"Okay. Let me lock up the shop, and I'll meet you outside."

His eyebrow lifted at her excited tone, and her words sunk in. "You?"

Her smile faded, and he wondered why it bothered him so much.

"Yes, *me*. As you peeped in the window, what you witnessed earlier was my official business closing party. I'm the only one left. So, take me or leave me."

Maybe it wouldn't be so bad until he could make other arrangements. The thought of keeping Aunt Penelope around was more appealing than he wanted to admit.

Rising to his feet, he said, "I don't have any other choice. I'll take you."

Two

Penny got into his car, wondering if dealing with such an opposing energy force was terrible karma.

"Buckle up, Penelope," he said just before peeling away from the curb.

She clicked her seatbelt in a hurry. "It's Penny. Penny Brown. Only my Aunt Eudora calls me Penelope. You're in quite a hurry?"

"Yeah. Sorry for the strong-arm tactics back there, but I'm in a bind."

"Oh." The hint of desperation in his voice intrigued her.

She looked at his grim expression when he didn't elaborate. What kind of trouble was he in? She recalled the hungry look in his eyes when he'd ogled her cleavage, and frowned. He didn't seem like the kind of man who habitually hit on the help. Only time would tell, of course.

She turned on the radio for something to do with her hands. She was surprised it was tuned to a country music station. Knowing her new client listened to "Friends in Low Places" made this uptight yuppie seem more human to her.

She leaned back and gazed at him. "Tell me about your mother."

He sighed. "Mother is unique."

"Good. I like unique."

He cast an amused glance at her dress. "So, I noticed."

"Thanks for the fashion slam, Mr. Blackwell," she shot back at him with little heat in her retort. She recognized a man on the horns of a dilemma, so she could probably excuse his bad manners.

"Sorry. I'm a little tense. No need to take it out on you."

"How unique is she?"

"Well, she started out normally. She and Dad were married for fifty years and raised three kids. My mother said she got bored after Dad died and took up all these kooky pastimes. Now she runs around the countryside with her other widow friends to casinos. I even heard them talk about going to a bar."

"That doesn't sound weird to me. Your mother is probably having the time of her life."

"You're wrong. It's getting out of hand. The last straw was when she went skydiving."

His mother sounded like a hoot. She'd fit right in with Penny's clan of free spirits. But, with Lance's stern tone, she could tell he disapproved of his mother's pleasure-seeking activities. Had he put her away to control her? She didn't like working for a person like that, but desperate times called for desperate measures. "So, you locked her away in a rest home?"

He shook his head. "You don't know my mother, Penny. Nobody pushes her around. She landed wrong and badly broke her wrist. I talked her into going there for rehab. And now they're bouncing her out. That's why I needed your help, pronto. I wonder if Mom's starting to lose it, between you and me."

She was surprised by his sudden openness. Maybe he was warming up to her. She decided to withhold judgment until she'd met his mother. "What happened?"

"Mother started a food fight."

She stifled a laugh. "What? That's outrageous."

"That's what I said, but not in that amused tone. Mrs. Rockwell, the administrator, said she was 'saving the damages'—whatever that means—for me to see."

"Oh, my."

He pulled up to the rest home, a large building, which looked more like a country club. "Come on, let's go get her."

Penny got out and followed him up the walk.

Catching up with him, she could almost feel his tension building by the stiffening of his shoulders. Was his mother really that difficult?

·❤·❤·❤·❤·❤·

Lance held the door open, waiting impatiently for Penny to join him. She was too busy looking around to hurry up. He tried to temper his irritation as she slipped in beside him. Two men in wheelchairs, another man with a walker, and a woman with a cane were eyeing them with open curiosity just inside the entryway.

"Hello," Penny greeted them warmly.

"Howdy," said the man who used a wheelchair and wore a cowboy hat.

"You think that's them?" the lady with the cane said in a loud whisper.

"Looks like it," said the guy with the walker.

It seemed like he and Penny were the focus of entertainment for the group.

"Follow me." Lance directed Penny, heading down the hall without waiting.

Near the end, he stopped dead in his tracks in a large open doorway and stared. Jell-O, spaghetti, and salad were everywhere—in the drapes, on the walls, even dangling from the ceiling fan. Noodles whirled around, flapping in the breeze.

Beside him, Penny let out a whoop of laughter.

"Oh my, it's priceless!" she said with great enjoyment.

He cast a repressive glance her way, stifling his brief amusement at the comical sight. His mom was a corker, he had to admit. "It's not funny. Come on, let's get this over with."

He turned and headed toward the administrator's office. The first thing he noticed was Mrs. Rockwell, a plump middle-aged lady in a scratchy-looking pink suit standing behind her desk, scowling at someone in the corner of her office.

Once he entered the room, he realized his mother was receiving said unrepressed scowl. Sweet-looking with gray hair, his mother wore a spaghetti-stained cast on her wrist. She grinned unrepentantly at Mrs. Rockwell. At their approach, his mother glanced up, her gaze curiously lingering on Penny.

Lance tapped on the doorframe. "I came as quickly as I could, Mrs. Rockwell."

The administrator sniffed, her frown replaced by a relieved expression at seeing him. "Mr. Harrison, thank you for your prompt arrival. Did you see the damage?"

"Yes, I'm sorry. Feel free to send me the bill."

"Indeed, I will. The drapes will have to go to the cleaners."

"Fine." He turned. "Are you all right, Mother?"

She smiled. "I'm just fine. Hello, son." She stood, picking up a suitcase with her good arm. "Take my bag. I'm all packed."

"I'll have the others brought to your car," Mrs. Rockwell said.

He took his mother's luggage and, once more, offered a lame apology. "Sorry for the trouble, Mrs. Rockwell."

"Stop apologizing to Old Rockslide and tell me who this cute girl is you've got with you." Mother brushed past him and started down the hall.

He hurried after his mother, Penny following behind.

"She's a home helper who will keep you out of trouble."

Mother stopped in her tracks and turned to scowl at him. "Another jailer?"

Penny smiled and stepped forward. "Do I look like any jailer you've ever seen?"

Mother looked her over warily and then smiled. "No."

"Good. Then we can concentrate on being good friends."

As a group, they began walking again. The same four residents in wheelchairs, and the two with a walker and canes, flanked the entry.

"Yeah, Elly," they yelled when they saw his mother.

"You struck a blow for all of us," another shouted, adding, "Old Rockslide will think twice about serving us that crummy spaghetti again."

"Thank you, thank you," Mother said, sweeping past them like a queen. "You really must do something about the sub-par food, Lancelot dear. I can't tolerate it, and neither will they."

He opened the door. "When you came here, you said the food was good."

"That was when I thought you would make your romance work. Didn't want to get in the way, you see." She turned to Penny. "My son muffed it, so I'm back."

"Great," he grumbled, getting everyone loaded in the car. Now he was stuck with a matchmaking mother and a sexy elf. What other disasters would fate throw his way?

Three

Penny gazed, wide-eyed, at Lance's home. It looked like it'd been lifted from *Gone With The Wind*, a two-story classic colonial. The guy was loaded.

She glanced at his striking profile, noting the capable movements of his big hands as he parked the car. It seemed funny that he'd remained unattached. She wouldn't have thought a man like him would be alone. Women probably flung themselves at him left and right, but from what Eleanor had said, he missed catching them. And Eleanor sounded like an even pushier matchmaker than Penny's Aunt Eudora.

Maybe he was gay. No, the look in his eye when he'd ogled her cleavage earlier said otherwise. Perhaps he had a little trouble with his equipment.

When the car stopped, Penny jumped out and opened Eleanor's door. Time to start earning her keep.

Penny gazed at the older woman with concern when she leaned heavily on her arm. As she helped her out of the car, Penny couldn't help noticing her charge's eyes sparkled with mischievous amusement. Eleanor obviously reveled in her victory, but the effort had taken its toll on her energy. She seemed frail and too worried about her son's lack of a love life. Penny would have to see what she could do to remedy the situation. Maybe she could have Aunt Eudora whip up a love potion or charm to help the clueless man find a mate.

She put that scheme on the back burner as the front door opened. A tall, austere man stepped out onto the porch. "Good evening, Mr. Harrison, and it's good to see you, as well, Mrs. Harrison."

"None of that snooty stuff, Bains." Eleanor breezed through the door. "Penny, meet Archie Bains, my son's butler. He and his wife, Rosie, run this place. If you want anything, ask them. Archie, this is Penny. She's Lance's new girl."

Lance frowned at his mother. "Please spare me any more of your matchmaking attempts, Mother. I'm still living down the last one."

She shrugged. "I don't know what you're talking about."

His eyes narrowed. "Oh yes, you do, Mother. Signing me up for a dating service was crossing the line. You have no idea what kind of proposals I got."

She shook her head. "Oh, pish. You're a stick in the mud, Lancelot dear. Look at your engagement with Liz. I set it up for you, didn't I?"

Penny felt sorry for him. She knew what it was like to be badgered by a determined matchmaker.

"My point exactly," he murmured, his expression worried.

Eleanor sighed. "She was an idiot and not good enough for you, son. I would never have hooked you up if I'd known how fickle she was."

So, there *had* been trouble between Lance's sheets. If he couldn't hold a fiancée, maybe he would need one of Eudora's love potions.

"Oh no, you don't," Lance grumbled. "You're not drawing me into this conversation."

Walking into the house, Eleanor stopped to look at several servants bustling around, setting up a buffet table and bar. "You having a party, son?"

"As a matter of fact—"

"Political?"

He shrugged. "Job-related."

Penny looked at him curiously. "Are you a politician?"

"Assistant District Attorney."

Penny's knees buckled. Because of her family's history of trouble with the law, maybe working for an assistant DA wasn't a bright idea. Time to come up with Plan B to get out of this job quickly. Fortunately, Lance was too focused on his mother to notice Penny's distress.

"Count me out," Eleanor added, "but Penny might like to go."

Socializing with his political cronies sounded horrible. She'd keep her distance until she figured a way out of this. "No, thanks. I don't have a thing to wear."

"That's right. I did hustle you over here," Lance said. "I'll take you home to pick up some of your things."

She didn't want him rubbing shoulders with her family or even knowing where she lived. "No, thanks. I'll call to have a bag dropped off."

"In that case, I'll leave you two to settle in. Miss Brown, your room is at the end of the hall, two doors down from my mother's."

Penny helped Eleanor move back into her room, relieved to see the lady relax. Eleanor seemed touched as she looked around her bed and sitting room.

"He kept it just as I left it." She picked up a framed photo showing Lance with an elegant blonde, sighed, and lobbed it in the trash. "Liz comes from our social set. I thought they'd be perfect together. I was wrong. I think perhaps he needs someone down-to-earth like you."

"Me?" Penny couldn't have been more shocked. "Honestly, Eleanor, I barely know your son."

Eleanor just smiled.

After she unpacked Eleanor, Penny found the guest room Lance had given her for the duration of her stay. It was lovely, with a private bath and a vast empty closet, reminding her she didn't have a change of clothes. She pulled out her cell and waited for five long rings. Cousin Michael should be home from school by now. The most mainstream of her relatives, he'd cause the least hubbub here.

"Astrophysical Hotline. This is your medium, Eudora speaking."

Penny sighed, feeling two worlds collide. "Hello, Aunt Eudora. Is Michael there?"

"No, baby girl, I'm afraid he's not. I thought you were a client. Sophie's supposed to call and tell me how her love charm worked."

"Love charm?"

"Yes, dear. She's hoping to spice up her love life."

"Oh."

"What's wrong, baby girl? I'm picking up a disturbing vibration over the phone. Are you in danger?"

Penny couldn't deny the of intrigue in Eudora's voice at the prospect. She didn't want the cavalry charging up here. "No, nothing like that. You must be picking up on my excitement. I got a job, so I won't have to close the agency."

"How wonderful!"

"Yes, isn't it? The problem is the job is a live-in. I will need someone to pack a bag for me and bring it here."

"You can't pick it up?"

"No, I'm on duty now."

"What kind of home help is it?"

"I'm caring for a man's elderly mother."

"Hmm, and what about the man? What ails him, baby girl?"

"I think he might need one of your special brews."

Eudora chuckled. "Needs a little help in the romance department, huh? I'll get right on it."

Penny pictured herself slipping one of Eudora's love charms under Lance's mattress or a potion in his tea, and her face heated. "On second thought, we'd better forget it. He's not the love potion type."

"A non-believer, then. He sounds interesting."

"You mean dull as dishwater."

"No. Don't forget, baby girl, opposites attract."

"Not going to happen," she said. Lance could stay in a romance rut for all she cared. "Could you have Michael drop my bag off? I'll be waiting outside."

"Of course. Give me the address and watch for it this evening around eight."

Four

Penny hustled down to the kitchen after six to make a light supper for Eleanor before Lance's guests arrived. Hopefully, she'd be able to steer clear of them. The oversized kitchen was bustling with kitchen staff on full alert.

She smiled. "Something smells good. What are you making?"

The cook, a tall older man, frowned at her. "And you are?"

"I'm Penny, the home help worker. I came to fix a tray for—"

"Not now. I'm much too busy."

Shocked, she shook her head. She knew Eleanor was starving, having tossed her spaghetti lunch in the food fight. Penny's empty stomach tightened, but she wasn't about to ask him for something to eat after this rough reception. Eleanor, however, was a different story. She wouldn't have her charge go hungry.

"Listen, Chef Boyardee..."

Before she could finish, the feeling of someone watching her made her fall silent and look around. Lance stood at another entrance into the kitchen looking drop-dead handsome in a tux.

"Trouble?" he asked.

"No, that is, um…I'm just getting some food for your mom and…" Her stomach growled.

Lance turned to frown at his chef. "Well?"

"Right away, sir."

To her amazement, a plate was quickly assembled with mouth-watering food.

"Make that two plates, Fritz," Lance insisted.

Penny flashed him a grateful smile.

Lance picked up the tray before she could reach for it. "Did you make your call?" he asked.

She hesitated for a moment. Gallantry came as a surprise to an employee. "Yes, my luggage will be dropped off later." She followed him down the hall to his mother's room.

The housekeeper, Rosie, and Eleanor looked up when the door opened, and both fell silent. For some reason, they looked guilty.

"Dinner is served." Lance placed the tray on a side table. He glanced at the photo in the trash and winced.

"You don't have to stay and eat with me, Penny, dear. Rosie and I are going to have some quiet time. Why don't you go down to the party."

Penny knew Eleanor was determined to play matchmaker, but she wouldn't be pushed into anything. "No, thanks."

"Well, there's a gazebo in the courtyard. It should be lovely this time of night."

That did sound like a good idea. She'd noticed the gazebo on arrival. It faced the driveway. When Michael brought her things, she could intercept him there.

She picked up her plate with a smile and a nod of agreement. "Sounds good," she said before beating a hasty retreat.

Five

Lance mingled with his guests, greeting political cronies, thinking he'd much rather tackle the work he'd brought home with him. He glanced through the French doors at Penny sitting in the gazebo on the east lawn. Now, there was something else he'd like to tackle. He wondered where that thought came from, telling himself to get a grip. Still, she looked tempting in the moonlight.

He returned to greeting his guests when the evening turned disastrous.

Liz, clinging to Carl Anton's greasy arm, walked into the room. His gut clenched. Who'd invited them? His party planner undoubtedly, seeing as Anton was at the hub of state legislation.

Gritting his teeth, Lance smiled when Liz and Anton looked his way. He reminded himself that socializing with people he despised was part of the game, one he was heartily sick of doing. It was the main reason Liz had dumped him, claiming he wasn't ambitious enough.

Suddenly, all he could think about was getting away for a moment before he said or did something he shouldn't. His gaze fell outside on Penny like she was a lifeline for him. He picked up two glasses of lemonade from the bar and went outside.

Nobody seemed to notice his departure as he walked away. He strode across the flagstone path to the pavilion. Penny kept watch on the driveway, probably still waiting for her suitcase. Her plate looked empty, he noticed. She had been starved earlier, yet she hadn't asked for anything for herself, had only thought of his mother. It spoke volumes about her character.

She turned to glance at his approach. "Something wrong?"

More than you know, lady, but he shook his head. "I thought you might like something to drink." He handed her one of the lemonades.

She smiled as she accepted the glass. "Thanks, but you didn't have to do that."

"No problem. I needed a breath of fresh air." He sat next to her, his stress abating. There was something about this woman that got to him, touched him.

"Is the party not working out?" She eyed the house.

He shrugged. "You're very perceptive. The party is about what I expected, except for a few unanticipated guests."

"I understand that. We usually have a few moochers glom onto our family barbeques, too."

He chuckled, his mood lightening. Moochers—that described Liz and Anton to a T.

"Is that why you ran out here, away from your guests?"

He winced at her dead-on reasoning. "My hangers-on, you mean. They're so busy schmoozing, they won't even notice I'm gone."

He settled back in the wicker chair, but the tinkle of a silver bell rent the air. Penny gasped beside him, making him wonder who or what was coming.

"Oh no," she murmured

"Something wrong?"

She sighed. "Nothing. I know who's coming. It just isn't who I was expecting. Like you said, an unexpected arrival."

He couldn't help being intrigued. Who could shake up this hippy chick? "I don't see anybody."

"Just wait and listen."

A bell tinkled again, louder, as a shape slowly came into view down the long driveway. While it drew closer, the exterior lights around the house highlighted a bike rider's blue dress and matching net hat.

He gazed at her in surprise. "Wow. Who is that?"

"My aunt Eudora. She doesn't drive, as you can see."

Eudora came to a halt a few feet away. Her bicycle bell jingled joyfully. "Penelope, there you are."

Penny stood and walked toward her aunt. "Nice to see you, Aunt Eudora."

Eudora used the bike's kickstand and brushed dust off her white gloves. She pecked Penny on the cheek on her way toward the pavilion. "And is this your employer?"

Penny pulled her suitcase from the saddlebags and then rushed to apparently head off her aunt. "Aunt Eudora, meet Mr. Lance Harrison."

"Nice to meet you, ma'am." Lance rose, taking in the pair. Eudora was about his mom's age, and she bore a strong resemblance to Penny. Why did the prospect of him meeting her aunt shake Penny up? He took Eudora's arm to help her up the gazebo steps.

"I'm pleased to meet you, too, Mr. Harrison."

He escorted her to a chair. "Call me Lance. Have a seat. Would you care to join us for a glass of lemonade? I can fetch another glass."

Eudora batted her false eyelashes. "That would be so lovely, young man."

As he went to head inside, he overheard, "I see what you mean. Excellent manners, but shy."

"He's not shy. More like reserved," Penny said in his defense.

He appreciated her sticking up for him.

On his return, he overheard more of their conversation.

"And don't get any ideas. I don't need one of your love charms, after all."

He darn near dropped the glass. What was all this about love charms?

"Fiddlesticks. Young people never know what's good for them."

Eudora pulled a small brown paper sack out of her enormous handbag and thrust it at Penny. "Even if it's not you who graces his bed, this will be good for whatever ails him."

He couldn't believe what he was seeing as Penny grabbed the sack, stuffing it in her luggage as he entered the pavilion. Both women turned to him as he filled the glass, then handed it to Eudora. "Here you go."

She smiled. "Thank you very much." She sipped and studied Lance. "So, my niece tells me you're single."

He choked on his lemonade. "Yes."

She patted his hand, then turned it over to look at his palm. "Someday, you'll meet the right one."

Bemused, he let her examine his palm.

Penny watched him warily. "Aunt Eudora…"

"Yes, baby girl?"

"I forgot to mention that Mr. Harrison is the Assistant District Attorney."

Eudora's lips puckered. "Oh, really." She dropped his hand.

He glanced from Penny to Eudora at this seeming bombshell. "Is there something wrong with that?"

"Of course, not. Somebody's got to do it. It just takes a bit of getting used to, that's all." Eudora stood abruptly. "Well, my children, I must be off. I'm late for a reading."

Penny waved her off. "Goodbye."

Lance stood by Penny's side, watching Eudora ride away.

"Reading?" he asked, already dreading what she might say.

Penny nodded. "Tea leaves. She's one of the clairvoyants people from your office keep trying to run off the square."

"Good grief," he murmured. He couldn't get involved with them. He sure as hell didn't believe in psychics.

"I take it you're a non-believer?"

"I'd sooner show up on Fat Tuesday in an Elvis suit singing "Burning Love" than go to one of them."

"Too late, Mr. Harrison. You just had a palm reading, free of charge."

"Ah, so that's what that was about."

A noise from the party drew his attention to the house once more. "I guess I can't avoid it much longer."

He made his way back to the party, trying to put thoughts of palm readers, love charms, and sexy hippy chicks out of his mind.

Liz and Anton were still there, holding court before a group of people. Her icy blonde looks didn't charm him any longer, but she moved like she was the lady of the manor. He decided to toss her and her current lover out, to blazes with the consequences.

Moving toward them with a purposeful stride, he was brought up short when Penny's arm slid through his. The gesture was casual yet intimate. Surprised, he went stiff for a moment as her touch caused a tingle through him. Maybe she'd dosed him with some love potion unobserved.

"Hi, honey. Sorry I'm late." She smiled. Under her breath, she whispered, "Need a rescue?"

He could hardly believe she'd do this for him. Falling into the spirit, he smiled at her. "You're just in time, sweetheart."

"Aren't you going to introduce me, Lance?" Liz said.

"This is Penelope Brown. Penny, Liz Reynolds."

"Oh yes, your ex." Penny glanced at Lance and said softly but audibly, "Or should I say your *why*?"

He chuckled, giving her an appreciative smile. Penelope Brown was good for his ego.

"I don't believe it," Liz hissed.

Ignoring Liz, Penny smiled at him, raised herself on her tiptoes, and kissed him.

He pulled her into his arms, and the entire room faded. He lost himself in her kiss. God, she had the softest mouth and the most incredible taste. He stifled a groan, deepening the kiss. He wasn't sure how much time had passed as he eased away. He only had eyes for her, kiss-swollen lips and the sultry look in her eyes drew him to her.

Her brows rose. "Lance, honey, I need a word with you. Alone."

A glance told him Liz looked positively furious, but he couldn't care less. She'd faded from significance in his life. Wondering if he'd been love-charmed, he ultimately decided he didn't mind. He followed Penny to a quiet nook, turning his back on everyone who watched them.

"Feeling better?" she asked, stepping back into the corner by her suitcase.

"Yes." She was feminine perfection in her sunflower dress. Unconventional as she might be at first glance, he wouldn't change a thing about her. "Thanks for the rescue."

She grinned. "You're welcome. All in a day's work for Aunt Penelope."

Her smile was enough to brighten his world.

When she bent to reach for her suitcase, he stopped her, putting a hand on her arm. "No. Stay, Penny. Please."

Six

Penny mingled with Lance's guests, but couldn't keep her gaze from returning to him. She was starting to fall for the guy.

Was that so bad?

When she'd spotted trouble brewing with his ex, it'd been instinct to jump in and save him. Maybe she should, but she didn't regret her actions. To his credit, he'd taken her quickly improvised role-playing well. Heck, he hadn't even freaked out when Eudora read his palm. There was much more to Lance Harrison than met the eye. He had a wicked sense of humor, and the man could kiss. Her toes curled each time she remembered.

Her feet were killing her as the party ended. When finally the room cleared out, only the two of them remained. She was suddenly a little shy, not quite knowing what to say.

He took the problem from her by striding up to her with a smile on his face.

"Come with me." He her hand and led her out into the garden.

She let herself be towed along in bemusement. Maybe Eudora had slipped some of the love potion to both of them. It might explain her growing romantic feelings toward Lance Harrison.

At the pavilion, she smelled an intoxicating aroma. Café au lait and beignets for two were laid out on the table.

"I had them delivered from Café Du Monde's," Lance said.

The Café made the best beignets in New Orleans. She could hardly believe it. He'd gone to such lengths to plan this moonlight snack for them. His sweetness turned her to taffy.

"How did you know?"

"Know?"

"My weakness for these," she murmured.

"Any other weaknesses I should know about?"

There was hope in his tone, and she grinned at him. "Keep this up, and you might find out. Are you sure you and Eudora didn't lace my lemonade with a love potion?"

He laughed. "I've been thinking the same thing. I didn't spike yours. Did you spike mine?"

She shook her head. "I thought about it., but...."

"Somehow, I don't think we need it." He'd spoken the words in her own heart.

Her mouth watered as she reached for a delicious beignet. She bit into the confection, letting it melt on her tongue while the powdered sugar coated her lips.

His hungry gaze focused on her mouth, and she couldn't look away from him. "Try some." She held the beignet out to him.

"Love to," he murmured, but instead of bending to take a bite of the donut, he bowed to taste the powdered sugar on her lips.

"Yum." He growled in a sexy tone.

She thought the same thing as he swept her into his arms, and the donut fell from her hand, forgotten.

The hunger overwhelming her senses told her she'd found her destiny.

Male Seeking Male

When Greg's best friend places a personal ad on his behalf,
he doesn't know whether to be angry or grateful.
Though bisexual, he's only ever been with a woman.
But when Jack, his sexy neighbor across the hall
answers his ad, claiming to offer the experience he seeks,
Greg jumps at the chance.
But as things heat up in the bedroom, a trust
builds in their hearts. Now they must see past their
differences and future plans or lose a once in a lifetime love.

Kathleen Lee

MALE SEEKING MALE

Kathleen Lee

Greg slammed the newspaper down on the coffee table in front of him and stared at his best friend of nearly twenty years.

He'd give her credit, Rachel looked nervous. She was biting her recently applied lipstick right off and a crease formed between her pale eyebrows. She flipped her long, strawberry blonde ponytail over her slender shoulder and combed her fingers through the fine strands while bouncing between foot to foot.

"What were you thinking?" he barked.

"I was trying to help," she said, her voice taking on an uncharacteristic whine.

"Trying to help..." He pinched the bridge of his nose and stared out the picture window of their shared apartment, where he knew their quiet Seattle neighborhood bustled with the morning rush one story below their brownstone. The view of the park across the street, teeming with bigleaf and vine maples, did little to calm him, nor did the rare rays of sunlight streaming through the bright green foliage.

"Look, Greg, you're out of the closet. Our friends know. Your family's known for years."

"That is hardly the point."

He leaned back on the sofa. He'd told his family back in high school that his door swung both ways. Though disappointed at first, the news didn't seem to surprise them. And because he'd dated women—only women—his friends hadn't a clue until a few years ago. He'd lost a couple of friends at that announcement. More than a couple. The good ones, like Rachel, had stayed. Then again, Rachel knew before his family.

"You said you wanted a male relationship, that you wanted the experience."

Greg leaned forward and picked up the newspaper. "I didn't mean for you to place a freakin' ad on my behalf." He read aloud. "'Recently out 28 yo male seeking male for experience. Must be tested clean. Pics please.'" He sighed. "End quote. And whose email address is this for them to reply?"

She came around the table and sat next to him. "A new address. I set it up just for this." She opened her laptop on the table, and he watched her sign into a Gmail account. Twenty-two new messages.

Criminy.

Rachel took his hand in hers. "I kept your privacy. If this doesn't work out, you just delete the email account." When he just stared at her, she plowed on. "You don't go out to bars. All our friends are straight. It's been three years, Greg. You want this. You want to meet someone."

Over midnight margaritas one night—an idea Rachel had from watching the movie *Practical Magic*—he'd told her how lonely he'd been feeling. An obvious mistake.

Truth be told, his only experience with a man had been in a closet—the irony was not lost on him—his freshman year of college. He'd attended a frat party, and after five beers, a guy he didn't know shoved him in a closet, went down on him, and left him shaking against the wall afterwards.

He'd never seen the guy again. But it did confirm that Greg's attraction for men went beyond photos and thoughts to a physical, visceral reality. True, he wanted a relationship with another man. True, he wanted the experience. But to go about it like this...

"Rachel, I know you mean well, and I love you for it, but I can't. Not like this."

Ignoring him, as she was often apt to do, she opened the first email. A picture of a man in drag looking very much like 80s Madonna filled the screen. 'Like a Virgin' was typed below the picture.

Greg's balls shrank inward.

Rachel pressed her lips together in an attempt not to laugh. She stared at him through her blue mischievous eyes and finally gave in to laughter. "Okay, maybe not this guy." She deleted the email.

He swiped a hand down his face, his chest rumbling with surprised laughter. "Definitely not." Though he had nothing against drag or transvestites, it just wasn't his thing. He'd never found the flaming guys to do it for him, either.

The next twenty emails were more of the same, aside from a scattering of men who looked old enough to be his grandfather or young enough to earn jailbait status.

He glanced at his watch. "I have to get to work. We will talk about this later."

"Are you mad?" she asked.

He glanced from her to the laptop and back again. He loved Rachel more than life itself. They'd been close since they shared the monkey bars in grade school. To this day, they'd never slept together or ever thought to cross that friend zone line, even when they'd become roommates five years ago. There were times, dark times, when he wouldn't have made it through without her.

He kissed her forehead and rose. "I'm not mad."

"Promise? I really was trying to help." She stood. "You deserve to be happy, Greg."

Funny, his ex-fiancé didn't seem to think so.

"Promise. I'll see you tonight."

Greg grabbed his suitcase and keys before heading down the stairs and out into the summer heat. The accounting firm he worked for was only a few blocks away, so he decided to walk. It would give him time to think over Rachel's idea.

And the possibilities.

How great would it be if something came from her ad? He was twenty-eight and had zilch experience with men. The opportunity had never arisen, and at this point, he was much older than the age when most came out. After years, he'd almost given in to the fact he may never know what it would be like to have sex with a man. To see if he preferred it to women. Hell, to even know if he enjoyed it.

He crossed the street as a trickle of sweat beat down his back beneath his polo. Seattle was in a monstrous heat wave, exuded by high humidity beyond measure. Walking to work was a mistake, but he'd needed to clear his head. He passed several pretzel and hotdog venders near the park and turned south toward the small business district.

Whatever happened, he needed to choose his first lover with care. He'd need someone patient, someone who wasn't overzealous or rough, who would take things slowly. Of course, he'd have to be somewhat attractive, too. Males were not gentle by nature, but he'd need that. At least for a little while. Someone to teach him the ropes, which was close to the story he'd given Rachel on midnight margarita night a month ago.

He shook his head. As if that would ever happen. He'd never find such a man.

They didn't exist.

After the overnight shift from hell, Jack opened the exterior door to the brownstone where he lived and made his way up the stairs to his apartment. Being an EMT was exhausting, and most days, he loved his job. Not today. Today they'd lost a kid in a three car pile up, and this was after they'd responded to an elderly woman's house and found her not only dead, but rotting in the heat.

Shit. It would take him years to get that image out of his head.

He flipped his keys, absently finding the one for his apartment door, and inserted it into the lock. Yelling from across the hall had him turning.

He'd had the same couple living across the hall for almost five years. Because they were day-shifters and he usually worked third, he rarely saw them. And he'd never heard them raise their voice. If anything, they were insanely considerate knowing the paper-thinness of the walls. He'd never even heard their TV.

He walked across the short hall to stand outside their door, then shook his head. This wasn't his business. Yet he stared at the door, hesitating. He was ingrained with the need to help, something his friends claimed he'd probably been born with. It felt like a curse caring about humanity so damn much when, really, most people didn't give a rat's ass. He kept his gaze on the door.

If their argument got ugly...

The male neighbor was talking, something about a newspaper ad. When he started reading the ad aloud, Jack took a step back. Raised his brows. Made a note to close his mouth.

He'd just assumed the couple across from him were married. At best, in a committed relationship. The few and far between times he'd seen Greg, the man never gave Jack the impression he was gay. Not that Jack's gaydar was noteworthy, but Greg just didn't give off that vibe.

The man was hot. And, apparently, gay.

Realizing this wasn't domestic and he wouldn't need to step in, Jack walked back to his own apartment and let himself in. Stripping off his uniform coveralls in route to the bathroom, he smiled.

Greg. Gay.

He turned on the shower before shucking his tee and boxers and stepping in. Even though the heat index outside was scorching, hot showers after a shift was a luxury he refused to give up. For that reason, his energy bills were high in summer, but he dealt. The hot spray helped to wash away the grime from his job and soothe his sore muscles. He made quick work of washing before thoughts of Greg came back in his head.

They'd moved into the building around the same time and had introduced themselves. Since then, Jack could count on one hand the number of times they'd run into each other. In those instances, Greg looked the same. Short, sandy-blondish hair cut in a simple style. Pressed khakis and a polo was his usual attire. His body was more athletic than muscular, and he stood in height that matched Jack's six feet by inches. There wasn't anything exceptional about his bluish-gray eyes except the criminally long, thick eyelashes. His jaw was wide and clean-shaven, and his mouth...

Yeah, the mouth. Wide smile, lush lower lip.

Jack was semi-hard just thinking about what he'd like that mouth to do. Before he realized it, he was stroking his length and groaning. He pressed his hand against the white tile for balance and pumped his hips, jacking himself off to images of Greg. The orgasm was short-lived, probably due to exhaustion, so he rewashed and stepped out of the shower.

Normally, he'd fall in bed right about now and sleep a solid six hours. Except, now his brain was whirling with possibilities. It had been some time—more than a year, he thought—since he'd taken a lover. The fact that there was a candidate right across the hall, and one he was obviously so attracted to, had him grinning again.

Instead of climbing in bed, he walked into his living room and booted up the computer. Greg had read aloud from a newspaper article, but Jack didn't subscribe to any. He went onto the website for several Seattle papers until he came across the personal ad that sounded like Greg's.

The placement said 'recently out' and 'seeking experience'. As much as he was interested in the specifics, Jack wouldn't get his answers unless he emailed Greg. He pulled up a blank email and typed.

Greg took a long pull from his beer and hit delete. Delete, delete, delete.

This was getting stupid. He'd come home from work, and after eating a quick bite, logged into the email account Rachel had set up. Fifty emails. Not a promising guy in the bunch. Most of the pics were cock shots. He got down near the bottom of the list and saw an email with the phrase 'Across the Hall' in the Subject line. Wondering what that was a euphemism for, he opened the email.

Heard you arguing with Rachel this morning. I didn't want to intrude, but was worried because you two are usually so quiet. I overheard part of your conversation and read your ad. I had no idea. I'm out and interested. I work third shift and sleep when you're at work. If interested back, come over and knock on the door anytime after five. Open invitation. I'm not seeing anyone currently. I get tested every six months, always use a condom, and haven't been with anyone in a year. If not interested, no harm done.

Jack from across the hall

Greg's finger hovered over the Delete key. As the shock receded, his pulse jumped.

He tried to remember what his neighbor looked like and couldn't draw much more than tanned skin, jet black hair, and kind blue eyes. They'd hardly run across each other at all. To think, all this time, he'd been living in the same building from a potential date.

Jack seemed like a normal guy. Quiet, polite. He'd attached no picture to the email, but then, Greg wouldn't need one. Of all the hits off Rachel's ad, Jack was the only decent one.

He leaned back on the couch and swallowed hard. He'd been wanting this for so long, the idea of being with a man within his grasp had his heart pounding. And nervous because, yeah, he had no experience. He hadn't been this wound up over his first time with a girl, and he'd been sixteen then. What if he did something wrong? What if it hurt?

He stood and paced the floor, stealing glances at the door as if he could see right through the hollow birch.

Three days later, he hadn't checked his email and hadn't yet knocked on Jack's door. He'd blown Rachel off when she asked about any promising leads. Hell, he was a coward and knew it. And the only way he'd find out what he wanted was to go after the opportunity.

Pocketing his keys and cell, he walked across the hall and knocked on Jack's door. Several seconds ticked by before the door opened.

Jack stood on the other side, one hand on the knob, the other on the frame. The black t-shirt he wore stretched over the lean muscle of his chest and shoulders, and his jeans were strung low on his hips. He looked like the vague memory Greg had of his encounters with him. About his height, close to his build. His black hair, a touch too long and waving at the ends, made his blue eyes the focal point of his face. His nose was thin and straight, his jaw had a slight shadow, and his lips were thin over a half-cocked grin.

"Thought you weren't interested when you didn't knock," he said, his voice like gravel and damn sexy.

Greg cleared his throat. "Took me time to gather some nerve first." He wasn't sure why he admitted that, as it didn't provoke any confidence, but the words couldn't be taken back.

Jack opened the door wider, a silent invitation to come in, so he did. The door closed behind him.

"Have you eaten?"

"Yes, but you go ahead."

"I'm good. Want something to drink?"

Because he didn't know what to do with them, he shoved his hands in his pockets. "Sure, whatever you have is fine."

"You look like you need a stiff drink," Jack said, a hint of amusement in his tone.

A surprise laugh escaped. "I think I do, no offense. Don't you have to work tonight, though?"

Jack shook his head. "I'm off the next three nights. On four, off three. That's my schedule. Captain and Cola okay?"

Greg nodded and looked around when Jack walked into the adjoining kitchenette. The living room was clean. The walls were a gray tone and the floor a bare maple. The floorplan mirrored his and Rachel's apartment. In the corner was a fifty inch flat screen and a decent Blu-ray collection of war movies. The pictures on his walls were landscapes, mostly of the ocean, and all in matching black frames. He had a recliner adjacent to a brown leather sofa and not much else but two glass end tables.

Jack returned from the kitchen and handed Greg a glass. "Sit and relax. I won't bite unless you ask."

Another nervous laugh escaped as he took a seat. "I'm sorry. I'm new at this."

Instead of sitting next to him, Jack took the recliner, probably to give him space, for which Greg was grateful.

"Your ad said 'recently out' and looking 'for experience'."

Greg stared into his glass before taking a huge gulp. It burned all the way down. "Rachel placed the ad, therefore the argument you overheard."

Jack's posture radiated calm. "How long have you been out?"

"My family's known a long while. My friends a few years back." He looked at Jack. "I'm bi, so this really hasn't been an issue until..."

"Until you wanted to test the other side."

"Yeah," Greg said through a sigh. Feeling a little better after his liquid courage, he leaned back against the couch cushion.

"Have you been with a man?"

There was no insinuation or patronizing to Jack's tone, which made Greg loosen up and breathe a little easier. Greg told him about the one brief college experience he had.

"So, you enjoyed it?" Jack asked. "You're positive you're into guys?" Greg must've given him a strange look because Jack continued. "I knew I was gay before puberty. I'm just trying to grasp if you're certain. I've never been with anyone bisexual."

"I'm sure." Greg debated how much more to say before deciding to be completely honest. "I jerk off to men and women."

Jack nodded and sipped his drink. "If we do this, if we hook up, I'd ask for exclusivity. I don't share. That includes women."

"Sounds reasonable." Greg studied Jack's large hands, wanting to ask questions. Jack took in Greg's exploration as if it didn't bother him. "I don't know how this works. I mean, I understand the basic fundamentals..." Greg laughed nervously and swiped a shaking hand down his face. "God, I'm an idiot."

For the first time since sitting down, Jack looked irritated. "You're not an idiot. You're inexperienced and curious. There's a difference. I wish I'd had the courage to do what you're doing when I first started dating."

Greg sucked in a breath, wondering how Jack was able to calm his nerves with such ease. He'd been a wreck when he'd walked in. He still felt nervous now, but it seemed more like anticipation than anything else. "Thanks for that. For understanding."

"You're welcome."

Greg took another sip of his Captain and Cola, mostly Captain. "I guess I'd want to know if we'd be in a relationship. Like...dating?"

Jack appeared to mull that over. "I'm not into one night stands, if that's what you're asking." He leaned forward and rested his forearms on his thighs. Very, very muscular thighs. "But this situation is a little different. We'll get intimate at a pace you set, when you're ready. If something becomes of us after you get the experience you want, then we'll see."

Jack had just relayed everything Greg was hoping for. Someone to teach him at a pace he could handle. Everything about Jack radiated confidence and gentleness. He had a worldly way about him that emanated trust. But this deal felt one-sided. "What would you get out of this arrangement?"

A seriously sexy lopsided grin spread over Jack's face. "Besides sex and companionship, you mean?" Something dark came over his expression, settled in his eyes, as his smile fell. He set down his drink on the glass table and glanced out the window before returning his focus to Greg. "Like I said, I wish someone had done this for me. Wish I'd had the courage to ask."

Greg didn't feel courageous. He felt like an idiot. And something horrible had obviously happened to Jack once before, but they weren't at a place to go there, so Greg dropped the subject for now. Instead, he asked, "How often would you like to get together?" Man, he sounded like he was interviewing a job recruit.

"The nights I'm off seem like a good idea. The shift difference might be difficult, but I sleep when you work and vice versa. Three nights a week work for you?"

"Yes, sure." Three. Nights. A. Week.

"Are you attracted to me?"

Caught off guard, Greg whipped his gaze to Jack. "Yes, of course. I wouldn't have..."

Jack lifted his hand, cutting him off. "Just checking. I find you very attractive."

"Yeah?" *Brilliant, brilliant response.*

"Yeah," he muttered in a low timber, raking a shiver through Greg.

Jack rose and moved over to the couch to sit beside Greg. He took the glass from his hand and set it on the table. Every move was slow, deliberate, and had Greg in a cold sweat. Greg swiped his damp palms on his jean-clad thighs and waited.

And waited. And waited.

Out of the corner of his eye, Greg watched Jack, aware of how close they were sitting, hip to hip. Aware of Jack's hand now on his thigh, of his other hand behind Greg's head on the top of the couch.

After what seemed like eons, Jack leaned forward and brushed his nose under Greg's ear. He smelled vaguely of antiseptic and a spicy soap. "When you're ready, turn your head and kiss me."

Jack stayed where he was, not rushing, not pressing him for more. Greg eased his head back, offering Jack more room and forcing himself to relax. Another shiver tore through him, followed by an igniting of his nerves. Jack continued to stroke the sensitive skin on his neck with his nose, his mouth, until Greg was so hard, he groaned.

Instinct had him turning his head for a kiss. Sheer pleasure kept him there.

Greg could taste the alcohol on Jack's tongue as he thrust deep in his mouth. Kissing him was so very different from kissing a female. For one, there was brute strength, a sense of equality, and no need to hold back. Greg lost himself in the act, and soon the need to touch warred with his nerves.

Jack's hand fell to the back of Greg's head, massaging and tangling his fingers between the strands. When Greg moaned, Jack's other hand slid up his thigh to cup Greg's erection. He thrust up from the cushion, tightening Jack's contact.

"That feels good," Greg muttered, breathless from the kiss.

"You can touch me, too," Jack said, staring into his eyes. In them, Greg saw how turned on Jack had become. Saw the primal lust Greg was feeling also.

Greg reached over and cupped Jack's fly. Jack hissed in a breath.

"I want you so badly right now." He claimed Greg's mouth once again and dominated the kiss. His palm stroked him through his pants and Greg nearly came. "Can you lay down? Are you okay with that?"

In answer, Greg lay back. The position automatically spread his thighs and Jack nestled between them. He leaned down, and they continued the fevered kissing while rubbing their cocks together through their pants. The friction was intense, slightly grating, and hot as hell. Greg gasped in much needed air as his spine tingled with a looming orgasm.

"We'll keep the clothes on tonight," Jack said, nipping Greg's lower lip. "You come with me through our clothes and then go home. We'll go a little further tomorrow night if you still want to."

"I still want to."

Jack smiled wide. "Sleep on it, anyway."

Greg thrust his hips, forcing another hiss from Jack. Greg worked his hands down the hard planes of Jack's back to cup his ass. Jack's low, deep moan told him he liked what he was doing, so he slid his hands inside Jack's jeans. The skin to skin contact had Greg's erection straining to the point of pain. Jack's muscles were wrung tight, his skin smooth and soft beneath Greg's hands.

"You're playing with fire," Jack said and crushed his mouth to Greg's. The incessant rubbing began anew, this time with enough friction to have Greg at the brink. "Come, Greg," he ordered, his voice breathless.

He didn't need any more cues. Between the feel of Jack's ass in his hands, the deep kissing, the cock grinding, and Jack's voice, Greg blew his wad, shuddering beneath him. Jack's release was made with a feral sound against Greg's mouth and a firm thrust of his hips.

They lay there for several minutes until Jack finally lifted his head. "Go home and get cleaned up. I'll see you tomorrow." He kissed Greg's mouth lightly and smiled before standing.

Greg sat up and watched Jack's retreating back as he walked down the short hall to what Greg assumed was the bathroom. Over his shoulder Jack said, "Oh, and Greg? I can't wait."

Jack sat at the edge of his bed and scrubbed his hands down his face. He'd jerked off so many times after Greg left last night that his dick was raw. He wasn't a prude. He enjoyed sex, usually, but he hadn't come in his pants since he was a horny confused teen. Greg had needed that barrier the first time, though. Jack needed to take it slow for Greg's sake.

Hell, he never wanted to be buried so deep inside a man before. After Greg's initial hesitation, Greg had relaxed and heated up, gave back and responded with vigor. It took more restraint than Jack thought he had not to rip their clothes away and sink himself deep.

He wondered what was different with Greg. Normally, Jack was all about the tease. Foreplay was better than the act.

He glanced at his clock. Greg would be over in a little under an hour. It had been a long damn time since he looked this forward to an evening.

If Greg showed, that was.

Jack rose and made himself a ham and cheese omelet, wolfing it down in record time. He'd just finished dressing and brushing his teeth when the knock sounded at his door. He grinned.

Greg stood on the threshold looking significantly less intimidated than the night before. "Hi," he said with a hesitant smile.

Jack's bones melted. "Hi." He ushered him inside and offered him a drink, which Greg declined. "How about a movie?" Jack suggested.

Greg glanced at the Blu-rays across the room, almost looking disappointed. "Uh, sure."

"Pick one and I'll meet you in my bedroom. Second door on the right."

"Bedroom?" Greg said, and to his credit, without a hitch.

Jack didn't answer, just walked down the hall and into his room with a smile cracking his face. He waited next to his dresser almost ten minutes before Greg came inside the room to meet him.

Greg held up a case. "*We Were Soldiers.*"

"Hmm. Good choice. Come over here," Jack said, trying to keep his voice even.

Greg closed the distance and handed over the movie. Jack loaded it into the player and turned on the TV.

Greg's swallow was loud in the aftermath when they stood inches from each other, not touching. Jack let the tension hum as the previews started to roll. Then, he bunched the neckline of his shirt, yanking it off. As Greg watched every motion carefully, Jack unbuttoned his jeans and slid the zipper down. Greg swallowed again. Jack let his pants fall around his ankles and kicked them away, leaving him only in his boxers and a semi-hard erection.

"Did I mention we're watching the movie naked?"

Greg's gaze was focused on Jack's crotch. "No, you didn't mention that part."

"Disappointed?" he asked, stepping into Greg's space. Heat radiated off him in waves. His musky scent of arousal filled Jack's nose.

Greg shuddered a breath. "No."

He could tell Greg was aroused, but he couldn't read if he was afraid. So, very slowly, he palmed Greg's polo and slid it up, revealing a washboard stomach and defined pecks. His skin was paler than Jack's, and a light dusting of hair covered his chest. He wanted to bury his face in the soft curls. Instead, he removed Greg's shirt completely. He lifted his arms in compliance, leaving his hands to rest on top of his head while Jack worked on his fly. Greg's eyes drifted shut. Jack grinned, sliding a finger down his chest, around his belly button and to his waistband. The pants fell. Jack's gaze drifted to Greg's package, stirring his own lust. Greg kicked away his khakis and opened his eyes.

Leaning in, Jack brushed the sensitive skin below Greg's jaw with his lips and slid his palms into Greg's briefs, nudging the material down. Again, Greg kicked them away without a word. His erection jutted out toward Jack as if begging to be touched. And he would. Later. For now, Jack built up the tension until Greg was wanting this so bad he ached, too.

Jack pulled away and dropped his boxers. He walked over to the bed, climbed in with his back against the headboard, and waited. Greg stood next to the dresser, the title screen of their movie popping up behind him. After several seconds, Greg joined him in bed, assuming the same position. Jack covered them with the dark blue comforter and clicked Play on the remote.

Greg's stunned silence was amusing and lasted until the rolling credits two hours later. "Good movie," he said absently, eyes still trained on the screen, his dick still hard by the way it tented the sheets.

Jack turned off the TV and lay on his side, propping his head in his hand.

From under the sheet, he palmed Greg's calf and slowly worked his hand up until it rested on his hip.

"I thought you'd never touch me," Greg moaned.

"You want me to touch you?"

Greg slid down and lay facing Jack. "Yes."

Jack reached over and grabbed lube from the nightstand drawer. Greg watched him with rounded eyes. "No penetration tonight, Greg. I promise."

Jack put the lube on the comforter and watched as Greg relaxed again. Jack placed his hand back on Greg's hip, working his way up over the smooth muscles of his chest and back down. When he could feel the tension drain out of Greg, Jack leaned in and kissed him. A slow, steady tease of licking and nipping. Greg's fingers dug into Jack's asscheeks, urging him closer.

Jack uncapped the lube with a resounding click and poured a generous amount onto his hand. He rubbed both their cocks until they were slick. He mounted Greg and stared down at him. "You okay?"

"Very."

Jack palmed their dicks, his hand barely able to hold both together. He rested his other hand next to the pillow by Greg's head so he could raise up and watch him. Jack thrust, sliding their slick, hard cocks together.

"Oh, yessss," Greg hissed, his pelvis jutting up in a plea for more.

Jack thrust again, slowly at first, working them at a slow pace, until Greg was so intent on speeding things up that Jack went right along with him. Their hips rocked, their balls slapped together, their cocks ground until Jack could feel the tickling at the base of his spine. Greg's muscled chest beneath him, the hard planes of his hips, felt so damn good. Greg's hands fell from Jack's shoulders to cup his ass, propelling Jack to go faster. Harder.

Greg's back arched. A moan rumbled through his chest. "Gonna come, Jack."

"Me, too," he managed.

Greg's hot seed spurted between their bodies. Jack's joined. Greg made the sexiest sound in his throat when he came, part moan, part whine. Jack's orgasm racked through both their quaking bodies. When he came back down, Greg was still having residual tremors.

"Holy orgasm, Batman," Greg said, breathless.

Jack dropped his forehead to Greg's chest and laughed. "Never had that response before." He reached over and took a clean washcloth from the nightstand and wiped them both down. Then grabbed a baby wipe to finish the job.

Greg looked sated. And Jack liked the sight of him in his bed way too much.

"What now?" Greg asked.

To lesson the blow, Jack kissed him before answering. "Now you go home and anticipate tomorrow night."

·♥·♥·♥·♥·♥·

"So, where have you been the past couple nights?"

Greg tore his glance away from the TV and looked at Rachel. "If you can believe it, across the hall."

She sat down next to him on the couch and propped her feet on the table. "At Jack's? Why?" When he just stared, a long "Oh" popped out of her mouth. "So, you two...?"

"Yeah," Greg said, smiling like an idiot.

"Huh. Didn't know he was gay. How's it going?"

"Really good." Greg crossed his arms and looked back at the TV and ESPN's coverage of the Mariner's game.

"Just good?"

He glanced at his watch, counting the hours until five when he could see Jack again. Being as it was Saturday, Greg didn't have the distraction of a long workday to pull him through. "No, I believe I said 'really good'."

Rachel grinned. "I want details."

"Since when? And no." Greg smiled. "I'll just say he's very patient and taking it slow, which I appreciate. Except..."

She dropped her feet and adjusted her position to rest her head in his lap. A gesture they did often and Greg found comfort in. He combed his fingers through her hair as she prodded, "Except what?"

Jack had worked Greg to an orgasm two nights in a row. And both nights he all but shoved Greg out the door afterwards. It's not like he was expecting a cuddle or anything, but Greg's trek back across the hall felt like a walk of shame. "He's not really into the snuggle thing. Makes me feel like a slab of meat."

"Maybe he just doesn't like overnighters."

"Yeah," he agreed. But a little something more than 'go home' would be nice.

"Why aren't you over there now?"

"He works third shift. Can't go over there until five." He glanced at his watch again, seeing that it had only been a minute since he last checked. He still had a half hour.

"How about I make you a grilled cheese before you leave?"

Greg grinned down at her. "Promise not to burn it this time?"

"No," she said lightly and rose.

He listened to her clanking around in the kitchen and shut off the game to join her. Greg usually did the cooking in their unit, since Rachel only mastered canned soup and cereal. She set two slices of buttered bread on the skillet before unwrapping the cheese. He winced and turned the heat down so she didn't scorch the bread. She moved aside to let him finish and then they ate quickly together before Greg headed out and knocked on Jack's door.

Jack answered with a towel around his waist. Greg's gaze followed the water droplets down his sculpted chest and swallowed. "You should answer the door this way every time."

Jack laughed and stepped back to let him in. When the door kicked shut behind him, Jack pointed toward the hallway. "Should I get dressed?"

Taking the initiative for once, Greg stepped over to them until they were chest to chest, thigh to thigh. "I'd rather you didn't."

Jack's eyes widened a fraction before primal heat filled the depths. The man had amazing eyes. "Okay then."

Greg leaned in and kissed him, loving that they were the same height, the same build. To him, that made for equal footing. Jack's lips were firm, his tongue soft and wet. The man knew how to kiss, too. Their tongues warred until Greg couldn't take the tease anymore.

He removed his shirt and cupped Jack's neck to draw him back into the kiss. Jack moaned and dropped his towel. With their mouths welded, Greg stripped the rest of the way and brought them hip to hip. The friction of their dicks together was so freakin' good. He ran his palms down Jack's bare, damp chest, causing a shiver in response. He loved the feel of his soft skin over tight muscles.

Jack brought his arms around to cup Greg's ass. "I want you so bad. The past two days I haven't slept thinking about you, hoping you'll show up."

Greg looked into his eyes. "What were you worried about? I told you I like this. Like what we're doing."

"You might change your mind."

Greg studied him a minute more, surprised by the spark of vulnerability. "I haven't. And if I do, I'll tell you." He ground his hips. "To be honest, Jack, I just don't see that happening."

Jack's fingers dug into the skin of Greg's ass, pulling the cheeks apart. "Lock your knees, Greg. And hold onto something."

Jack dropped to his knees and fisted Greg's cock. Greg sucked in a breath and slammed his palm on the front door to keep him upright. Sensing his weakness, Jack grabbed Greg's hips and turned him until his back hit the door.

Then his mouth closed over Greg's swollen dick, taking him all the way in until Greg's tip hit the back of his throat.

"Holy shit," Greg muttered. He grabbed a fistful of Jack's hair and held him in place.

Jack eased his mouth back, swirling his tongue. Cold sweat broke out over Greg's body, a stark contrast the heat fueling inside. Jack's hot, wet mouth fucked him at a mind-numbing pace, both drawing out the pleasure and torturing him alike. Jack bobbed his head, deep-throating him. Every time Greg's tip hit Jack's throat, he got closer and closer to climax. Greg felt Jack's finger along his asscrack, and he enjoyed what he was doing too much to protest. Jack's finger massaged his hole, never penetrating, never applying too much pressure, all while his mouth worked his dick. The combination was dizzying. Greg's balls tightened.

"Jack, I'm coming. Pull out."

Jack didn't stop. He firmed his lips around Greg's shaft, holding him deep and swallowing his tip while continuing to knead his hole. Greg exploded into Jack's mouth, down his throat, until there wasn't a drop of cum left and every shudder had run its course.

Greg slid down the door, reaching for Jack. Jack grinned and sat between his legs, chest to chest, and rested his head on Greg's shoulder.

"That was freakin' amazing, Jack."

"I usually don't like giving head that much." He looked at Greg. "But your reaction made that damn enjoyable."

Greg noticed Jack stroking his own cock and realized Jack hadn't come, too. "I've never gone down on a guy. I don't know if I'd be any good at it."

"When you're ready," he murmured against his mouth.

Greg stilled. "I'm ready now."

Jack eased back. "You sure?"

Greg nodded, placing his hand over Jack's to stop his stroking.

Jack studied him for a moment before nodding. "The trick is to loosen your jaw and throat. It makes your gag less sensitive. Use your hands until you get used to it."

"Okay."

"Let's go in my room. This floor is hard and cold." He stood and held his hand out for Greg. He took it and followed Jack into his bedroom.

Jack crawled onto the bed and lay on his back, his dick pointed toward the ceiling. Greg crawled in after him and straddled his chest, moving in for a kiss before working his way down.

Greg licked Jack's tip, swirling his tongue over the head and sliding his tongue into his slit. Jack sucked air through his nose and threaded his fingers into Greg's hair. Encouraged, Greg opened his mouth wide and sank his lips around Jack's shaft. He could only get half of him inside his mouth, so he used his fist to pump Jack's base.

"That's so good, Greg," Jack moaned.

Greg drew back, earning a grunted protest from Jack, before he repeated the motion and took him just a bit deeper. He couldn't get him to his throat, but he loosened his jaw like Jack told him to do and was able to breathe a little better through his nose. His saliva made Jack's dick slick and easier to glide. In no time, Greg bobbed his head and worked his hand. Jack moaned, and Greg could tell he was restraining himself from thrusting into his mouth.

Taking a move from Jack's playbook, Greg worked his other hand under Jack's hips and slid a finger into his crack. Jack's fingers tightened in Greg's hair and he spread his thighs wide. Greg massaged Jack's hole, remembering how good it felt when Jack had done the same.

"So, so good, Greg."

He sucked harder, applying more pressure to his hole.

"Coming. I'm coming."

Greg appreciated the warning. Jack's hot seed spilled into his mouth, hitting the back of his throat. Greg swallowed before he could choke, and tasted the salty sweetness of cum. Greg continued his motions until Jack's tremors stilled and his dick went flax in his mouth.

"Get up here," Jack ordered, breathless.

Greg complied, crawling up his body and nestling next to Jack's side. He rested his head on his chest and licked his lips. "Wasn't expecting the taste to be sweet."

"Pineapple juice," Jack murmured. "Drink a glass a day and it makes the cum taste better."

"I will have to buy pineapple juice then."

Jack laughed. "You okay?"

"Very," he said, placing a kiss on Jack's chest and burying his nose in his warmth.

Jack shifted onto his side and looked at him. "For a guy who's never given head, you're damn good at it."

He smiled, loving that he made Jack feel as good as he did. "Is this the part where you kick me out?"

"What?"

Greg shrugged. "You've been in a hurry to get rid of me the past two nights."

With tenderness, Jack ran his hand down Greg's side and linked their fingers. "I didn't mean to make you feel that way. You're new at this, and I'm trying really hard to restrain myself. Having you here, sleeping here or anything afterwards, would snap the control I have." He brought their hands up and kissed Greg's fingers linked with his. "I'm working the next four nights. How about when you come back on Thursday, I make us dinner? You can spend the night."

Greg felt liquid warmth pool around his heart. "That sounds great."

Jack nodded and glanced over Greg's shoulder. "For tonight, you should..."

Greg quieted him with a kiss. "I know, I know. I should go home."

As Greg dressed and left, he realized just how far away Thursday was.

·♥·♥·♥·♥·♥·

By the time Thursday rolled around, Greg was bursting at the seams. Not only excited about more physical contact with Jack, he was looking forward to dinner and what happened after the physical stuff. For the first time, he'd get to share a bed with Jack.

He was also nervous as hell. They hadn't had anal sex yet, and though Greg really wanted to go there and experience it, the possible pain had his heart pounding. Jack was well endowed, as was Greg. They weren't enormous by some comparison, but Jack's size would surely not fit. Would it? Would he get used to it? Like it, even?

Greg knocked on Jack's door and waited. He could smell something Italian lofting into the hallway from whatever Jack was cooking, making his stomach rumble. Jack opened the door wearing jeans and nothing else.

God, the man was hot.

"Hey," he said and stepped inside.

"Hey yourself," Jack said and surprised him with a quick kiss. "Hope you're hungry."

"I so am." Greg followed him into the little kitchenette and sat down on a stool by the counter. "It smells good."

"I should've asked you if you were allergic to anything."

"I'm not," Greg said, enjoying the view of Jack's wide shoulders and muscled back as he stirred a pot.

"Working as an EMT, I see all kinds of allergy responses. I know better than to not ask." He spooned angel hair pasta onto two plates. "What do you do for a living?"

"I'm an accountant."

Jack threw his head back and laughed. "Should have known. Between the casual dress clothes and that little look you get, like you're trying to solve something, it should've been obvious."

"Are you saying I'm a nerd?" He asked in jest.

"Not even a little," Jack said, spooning an amazing-looking sauce over the noodles. He added a slice of fresh Italian bread to their plates and brought them over. Jack sat on a stool next to Greg.

"This looks good," he said, twirling a forkful. He took a bite and moaned. "Tastes even better."

"Veggie marinara sauce. Homemade."

"I'll have to return the favor next time."

"So, you like to cook?" Jack asked, taking a bite himself.

"Yes, though I'm no chef. Mom taught me a few decent recipes growing up." They ate in compatible silence for a few minutes until Greg asked about Jack's family.

Jack wiped his mouth on a napkin and set his fork down. "I don't have any family."

"None?" he said, shocked. He didn't know what he'd do without his. Sure, they were loud and opinionated and quirky, but they loved each other.

Jack picked his fork back up and moved his food around his plate. "They disowned me when I came out. Very religious."

Greg's stomach turned sour. He set his hand on Jack's thigh. "That's terrible. How long ago was that?"

"I was seventeen. I hitchhiked here from the Midwest." Jack stared at his plate. "All a long time ago. Doesn't matter."

"It does too matter. You matter." Greg tilted Jack's chin until he looked at him. "Were you close before you came out?"

"I'd rather not talk about this, if you don't mind."

He nodded, understanding. This was still painful for Jack, no matter how long ago his family had disowned him. They didn't know each other all that well.

Greg looked at his plate and forced himself to take another bite. "I'm sorry."

"Don't be. It's not your fault."

"It's not yours, either," he said, swallowing hard.

Jack shoved his plate away and swiveled on his stool until he faced Greg completely. "I don't talk about this with anyone," he said quietly. "I have exactly two close friends, both I met through work, and they think my parents are dead."

Greg pushed his plate away, too, appetite gone. "You don't have to say anything you don't want to, Jack. But if you want to talk, there's no judgment here."

Jack stared at him with an unreadable expression for several minutes until resignation shone in his eyes. "They called me a pervert when I finally got the courage to tell them. Said I was an abomination and I was going to hell. I'm from a small, Midwestern, god-fearing town. I don't know what I was expecting, but I thought they'd love me anyway." He rubbed the back of his neck and looked away. "They threw me out that night with the clothes on my back and ten dollars in my pocket."

Greg blinked back angry, bitter tears. He waited until he knew he could speak clearly before talking. "Hate only breeds more hate. These religious fanatics should pay closer attention to the Bible before they judge what they don't understand." He grabbed Jack's hand. "Look at me," he said with more ferocity than he intended. "There's nothing wrong with you. There's nothing wrong with being who you are."

Jack's mouth thinned into a straight line, most likely an attempt to stop the quiver. "I know that now, but thanks for saying that."

Greg kissed him, trying to illustrate the gentle kindness Jack hadn't received and should have. "It's their loss."

Jack's eyes slammed closed as he rested his forehead to Greg's. "I ruined our dinner. I don't know why I talked about them now."

"Because you needed to."

They stayed in that position for several heartbeats until Jack kissed Greg's cheek. Then his jaw. His throat. "Would it scare you if I said I wanted you inside me tonight?"

Greg swallowed. His heart rate jumped, then stopped. "Yes. And no."

"Then we'll wait."

"No, you misunderstand me. Yes, I'm nervous, but I want to be close to you. I want to be deep inside you, have you deep inside me." He cupped Jack's jaw, worked his thumb over Jack's dark shadow.

"Are you sure?"

He nodded. "Very sure."

Jack eyed the plates and then Greg before sliding his hands up Greg's thighs to rest on his hips. "I guess we could save this food for later. Work up an appetite."

He grinned, feeling more resolute in his decision. Jack had been gentle up until now. He'd never rushed Greg or pushed him into anything he didn't want to do. Jack wouldn't hurt him, so he'd enjoy this experience like he had all the other ones.

"Good thinking."

·♥·♥·♥·♥·♥·

Together, they cleaned up the kitchen and stored the leftovers in the fridge before finally making their way to Jack's bedroom. Jack pulled out two condoms and a tube of lubrication and set them on the nightstand.

He turned to Greg and pulled him into his arms, wanting him so bad he ached. "If for any reason you need me to stop, you just tell me, and I will."

Greg looked at him with the utmost faith and trust that Jack would do as he promised. "I will."

He closed his mouth over Greg's and worked the kiss slowly, leaving no area of his mouth unexplored. Greg's erection grew between them, telling Jack he was ready. They undressed each other slowly, kissing every inch of each other's flesh until standing no longer became an option.

At some point in his life, Jack figured Greg had to have seen a gay porno or read how this was done. But because Jack couldn't be sure of that, he felt the need to explain the steps. In their past encounters, the act of telling Greg what he was going to do seemed to put him at ease.

He directed Greg down onto the mattress on his back so that his legs dangled off the side. Jack nestled between his thighs and leaned over him. Greg's erection brushed Jack's stomach. "I'm going to stretch your hole a bit with my fingers, just to get you used to me, show you how, so you can do it to me. After, I'll let you fuck me first."

Greg's eyes darted back and forth between Jack's. He nodded, closing his eyes as if resigning himself to an unwanted task. He wasn't even breathing. Jack grabbed the lube and popped the top. Greg flinched. Jack put a decent amount of lube on his fingers, because as he remembered from his first time, there was no such thing as too much lube. The pain of Jack's first experience lingered in his head, his heart. Jack would not allow Greg's experience to be anything like his own.

He knelt between Greg's thighs and placed his hand without lubrication on Greg's chest. Greg grabbed for it and held it, eyes still tightly closed. Because Greg's muscles were rigid, Jack kissed and licked Greg's thighs, earning a sharp intake of air. When he started to relax, he nudged Greg's thighs further apart with his shoulders and took Greg's balls in his mouth. Greg's dick, which had lost some of its stiffness, sprang anew.

His head shot off the mattress. "I love your mouth."

He grinned, releasing Greg's balls and licking his way up Greg's cock. He took Greg deep into his mouth until Greg's head slammed back and his hips thrust upwards.

He slid his lubed fingers along Greg's crack and massaged the hole. When Greg was loose enough, he slowly slid his index finger past Greg's tight ring of muscle and sank it inside him. Greg fisted his free hand in the sheet, the other still tightly holding Jack's hand.

"Don't stop," Greg panted.

Jack slowly slid his finger out and then back in, working it until he thought Greg could handle another finger. In the next thrust, he slid two fingers inside and felt Greg contract around him.

He held his fingers still and released Greg's cock from his mouth long enough to say, "Relax against my fingers."

Greg did as he asked and moaned.

"Too much?"

"No," Greg said. "Keep going."

Jack eased his fingers out and thrust back inside, this time crooking the tip of his finger to hit Greg's gland.

"Yes," he groaned and bore down on Jack's fingers.

He fucked Greg's ass, without the need to touch his dick, which Jack took as a good sign. He slid his fingers out completely and stood between his thighs. Greg groaned a protest until Jack rolled a condom down Greg's length and applied a proper amount of lube.

He leaned over Greg and kissed him deep and thorough. "I want you inside me. Just go slow, I haven't bottomed in awhile." He helped Greg to his feet and cupped the back of his head, bringing him in for another kiss. "Want you so bad."

Taking the initiative, Greg grabbed Jack's hips and spun him around. He gently pushed Jack's face into the mattress and nudged his legs farther apart. Jack ground his dick against the sheets, needing to be fucked. To fuck.

The cold sensation of Greg's lubed fingers worked Jack's crease. Jack groaned and pressed back into Greg's hand. Greg slid one finger inside, knuckle deep. Jack thought he'd die from want.

"More."

In the next thrust Greg inserted two fingers, lightly stretching Jack's hole. "Do you need another?" he asked, his voice strained with lust.

"No."

Greg's fingers slid out and Jack felt Greg's tip nudging his hole. He gripped the sheet, pressed his face into the mattress and sucked in a breath, prepared for the first onslaught of invasion. Greg eased inside so carefully, Jack felt a wedge in his throat. Halfway, Jack forced his muscles to relax and accept Greg's cock. Greg thrust balls deep and paused.

"God, you're so tight. You feel so good. This is so different than... Does it hurt?" he asked.

Jack reached behind and grabbed the back of Greg's thighs, shoving his face further into the bed so that he had to turn his head to answer Greg. "A little at first, but then you get used to it. You just have to relax and let it feel good. I promise you, it does feel really good."

Greg leaned over and clutched Jack's shoulder, the other hand kneading his hip. He placed a kiss to Jack's neck as he eased out so that all that remained was his tip. Greg lightly bit the tendon on Jack's shoulder and thrust inside. The new position allowed Greg's dick to touch Jack's gland.

"Don't stop, Greg. Just like that. You can go harder now."

Greg didn't hesitate. He drew back and rammed back in, setting a maddening and delicious pace. Jack worked a hand between himself and the mattress to grab his own cock and squeeze, stopping his climax for now. When he came, he wanted it to be inside Greg if he could handle it. Their balls slapped together, and Jack bore down, accepting every thrust from Greg.

"I'm going to come," Greg grunted, pounding into him from behind, his fingers digging deeper into Jack's flesh.

Jack clenched his inner muscles, tightening for Greg to make his orgasm even better. That pushed Greg over the edge. He roared, jerked twice more, and stilled. Jack could feel his seed filling the condom inside him. He slipped out when he collapsed on Jack's back, panting.

Jack remained motionless, allowing Greg time to recuperate. It took a few moments, but Greg straightened and disposed of the condom. Jack crawled in the bed, laying on his side and rested his head on the pillow. He patted the mattress beside him. Greg joined him so they lay facing each other. Greg fluffed the pillow and stared at Jack, locking their gazes in the low lamplight.

"How do you feel?" Jack asked.

"Amazing. I never knew it could be like that."

Jack smiled and leaned in for a kiss. He thrust his tongue against Greg's, slow and sweet. He'd never been with a man he felt like he could kiss all night and still be satisfied. The act of kissing Greg was a sensual one, made even more intimate by the feeling Greg put behind the action.

Jack wrapped his free arm around Greg, slid his hand up and down Greg's back. He loved touching him. All his smooth skin and lean muscle contrasted the hard ridge of his narrow hips. Jack groaned and tugged him closer, wanting inside him so, so bad. From the first time Greg knocked on his door to answer his invitation, he wanted inside him.

He eased back to look him in the eye. "Are you okay to try bottoming?"

Greg worked a swallow and kept his gaze level. "Yes. I want to feel you inside me."

Jack rolled him to his back and reached for a condom and lube. With Greg watching, he rose up on his knees and sheathed himself, then applied more lube than he'd put on Greg's condom before. "Turn on your side away from me. Bring your knees up to your chest," he said.

Greg rolled onto his left side so Jack could spoon his back. Jack kept the lube within easy reach and kissed Greg's shoulder, working his palm over Greg's chest in the process. He slid his hand lower and cupped Greg's balls, noting the life in Greg's dick had returned. Jack worked him until he was hard and straining and bucking into Jack's fist.

Jack applied a generous amount of lube to his fingers and rubbed it between Greg's cheeks.

Greg sucked in a breath. "It's cold," he said.

"But my cock is hot."

Greg moaned, bearing down on Jack's fingers in invitation. When he was able to get two fingers inside, Jack scissored his fingers to prepare Greg's hole. "You okay?" he asked, his voice radiating the calm he didn't feel.

"Yes. Now, Jack."

Jack withdrew his fingers and grabbed the base of his throbbing dick. He played with Greg's opening, rubbing the tip around and massaging the tight ring of muscle before easing into the first penetration. Greg made a sound, half cry, half moan, and clamped around him. Jack kept his invasion slow-going. Halfway inside, he met so much resistance, he couldn't go any deeper.

Jack released the hold on his own dick and reached around Greg's hip to stroke him. Greg's dick had gone lax, so Jack fondled his balls until he became semi-hard again. The lube in his hand made his cock slick and easy to manipulate. Jack rubbed Greg off, feeling his hard, thick length pulsing in his hand.

Jack was still halfway inside Greg, and in time, his muscles released their vise. "That's right," Jack said against the shell of his ear. "Relax against me." Jack licked a trail over Greg's shoulder and up his neck. Greg groaned and tilted his head for better access. Jack latched on to the sensitive skin below Greg's ear and thrust the rest of the way inside.

Greg's muscles tensed, but only for a moment. It took Jack an obscene amount of restraint not to pound. He eased his hips back, applied more lube to his shaft, and shoved back inside, then halted his movement.

Jack stroked Greg's cock again, waiting for the okay to continue.

Greg hissed out a breath. "You were right, this does feel so good."

That was all the invitation Jack needed. He withdrew and plunged inside Greg's tight, sweet body. Hell, he'd never felt anything better. Though he restrained himself from the pounding he wanted to give Greg, going carefully through Greg's first fucking, Jack felt the beginning of his climax. His hand stroked Greg's dick in time with his thrusts, sliding down to Greg's base as Jack reared up.

"I'm going to come in a second," Jack warned through gritted teeth. "Come with me. Come again, Greg."

"Yes," he groaned, bearing down and meeting Jack thrust for thrust.

The tingling traveled from Jack's spine to his balls and right up his cock. He buried his face in the crook of Greg's neck, spurting his cum into the condom. Greg spilled over the hand stroking him and they quaked through the orgasm together.

·❤ · ❤ · ❤ · ❤ · ❤·

Greg's ass was sore, but in a very good way. Jack had taken it slow and used a tender amount of gentleness. To think, he'd been so afraid of this. Yeah, it had hurt at first, but then the ache eased to an uncomfortableness. And then it was great. Beyond great.

He rolled on his side to face Jack. Jack stared back at him with a smile. "Are you okay?"

He loved that Jack asked. Was still asking. To him, it showed he cared. "I'm wonderful. What about you? Was I...satisfying?"

Jack's laugh held no humor. "You were beyond satisfying." He snagged his arm out from under the comforter and tugged Greg flush to his chest. "I can't get enough of you, it seems."

Greg felt the same way. He replayed their sex in his mind and decided to ask the question he'd been wanting to since day one. "That first night I came over, you said you wished someone had done this for you. What did you mean by that?"

Jack rolled onto his back and braced his arm over his face. "You've got work in the morning. We should get some sleep."

"Nice subject change."

"I like talking about this even less than discussing my family." Jack swallowed. "In fact, I've never talked about my family or my first time with anyone."

Greg let the subject go. When and if Jack wanted to talk about it, he would. He didn't need pressure from Greg. But whatever happened must've been bad. It made Greg's chest ache. He closed his eyes. "Thanks for tonight."

Greg felt Jack's arm hit the mattress and heard his head turn on the pillow, but he said nothing. He'd just about fallen into an exhausted sleep when Jack spoke.

"When my parents kicked me out, I told you I hitchhiked."

Greg opened his eyes, finding Jack's face flush with his. "I'm listening."

"I stuck with truck stops, thinking it would be safer. The first guy who picked me up asked if I sucked dick. I needed the ride, and hey, I was gay." Jack grew silent for a minute, his eyes glazing. "The guy was a fat slob. While on the interstate, he unzipped his fly and shoved my face down. Longest five minutes of my life. I threw up in a fast food bag after." He laughed without mirth. "He handed me a stick of gum. Anyway, at the next stop, he asked if I take it up the ass." He shook his head and looked over Greg's shoulder.

"You don't have to say anymore."

Jack looked at him, jaw clenching. "He directed me to the back cab, and I willingly shoved my pants to my ankles. I had no money and..."

"You don't have to explain yourself to me."

Jack stared at him, the seconds ticking by before he finally nodded. "The guy's pecker wasn't very big, but for a virgin, it sure felt enormous. He didn't use any lube, but at least he wore a condom. My ass bled for two days."

"God, Jack." Greg thought about the tenderness Jack had shown him, thought about how uncomfortable the first penetration felt, and could only imagine what Jack went through. No prep, no lube...

He reached over and pulled Jack's arm, rolling onto his back so Jack was partially sprawled over him. Jack rested his cheek on Greg's chest. He swallowed hard and fisted his hands in the soft, dark strands of Jack's hair.

"What happened after that?"

"My plan was to head to California. Being a more liberal state, I figured I'd fit in better there. But most of the truckers I came across were heading to Washington, so I ended up here. I worked at a coffee house and lived in this fleabag apartment until, one day, this group of paramedics came in and told me about this EMT program. I've been doing that ever since." He lifted his head and kissed Greg's chest. He rested his chin and stared at Greg. "I've managed to put some money into savings and I'm hoping to buy a small house by this time next year. It sounds stupid, but I really want a dog. I think that's the only thing I miss from home. My dog."

If it was possible for a heart to break, Greg's just did. "What kind of dog?" he forced out.

"Sandbox was a golden retriever. I want one who looks just like him."

Greg wasn't the type of queer who cried often, if at all, but damn if tears didn't well behind his lids. He rolled them over and covered Jack's body with his own. Seeking out his hands, Greg linked their fingers and kissed Jack with everything he couldn't say until the moment passed.

"Do you want kids?" Greg asked.

"No," Jack said through a sigh. "Being gay, my partner won't have the right equipment."

"Smartass. There's adoption or surrogacy."

Jack vehemently shook his head. "If something were to happen to me or my partner, custody laws get funny. The kid suffers. Besides, I don't have a grandma's house to take them to and spoil them on hugs and chocolate chip cookies."

Greg's heart sank. Just when he thought he was getting somewhere, connecting with another person, reality slammed in. "I want kids."

Jack tossed his mail on the counter and ended his call with his boss. The offer just made to him was hard to pass by. But he didn't want to get his hopes up, change his life around for a man who didn't want the same things.

He and Greg had been going strong for a month now. They were great in bed together and Jack had told him things he'd never told anyone else. The trust Jack didn't give easily was there.

But Greg was bisexual. He also wanted kids and loved baseball. Not that Jack hated kids or baseball. The kids thing was a pipe dream he let go of a decade before. And baseball, well, he just couldn't get into it the way Greg did.

He was on shift tonight, which meant Greg wouldn't be coming over for another four days. Jack didn't feel like he could wait that long to talk to him.

Jack pocketed his cell and walked across the hall. Rachel and Greg's laughter spilled out into the hall. They'd had dinner together with Rachel a few times, just the three of them. Jack liked her a lot, though he questioned Greg and Rachel's platonic relationship.

He knocked.

"Come in," Greg yelled. This was proceeded by more laughter.

Jack opened the door and took one step inside the apartment before stopping short in his tracks.

Greg was on his back on the sofa, Rachel sprawled over him laughing, as Greg held the TV remote out of her reach.

She giggled and blew her pretty strawberry blonde hair out of her gorgeous blue eyes. "Thank you, Jack. Tell Greg he's outnumbered now. He has to turn off the baseball game."

Jack's gaze flittered to the TV and back to the couple on the couch. *How cozy.*

And just like that, every insecurity he'd spent years banking rushed to the surface and choked him. His stomach rolled, feeling very much like the first time he'd been fucked in the ass.

Platonic, his ass. Serious denial was more like it.

And damn, he hated how much this hurt.

He forced his legs to move and closed the apartment door behind him. His own apartment door slammed in satisfaction a second later. He hadn't even had time to swipe his hand down his face before Greg was pounding on his door and letting himself in.

"What's wrong? What was that about back there?"

Needing distance, Jack walked to stand behind the sofa and rested his hands on the back, leaning into them. "You told me there was nothing going on between you two."

Greg flinched like he'd been sucker-punched. "Me and Rachel? There isn't."

Jack raised his brows.

"Look, I don't know what you think you saw, but Rachel and I are close. We touch each other a lot. We have never nor will we ever sleep together."

Jack didn't speak, didn't move, because damn his legs felt like they'd give out.

Greg took a step closer. "I haven't been with anyone else since you. I don't want to be with anyone else."

Jack refused to feel hope with those words. "For how long?"

"What?"

Jack straightened, keeping the couch between them. "For how long will you want to be with me, Greg? You're bisexual. You want kids. Hell, if I were you, I'd go the easy route. Marry a woman and have beautiful children together. Why subject yourself to ridicule and be the butt of jokes when you can have a normal life?"

"I had a fiancé once," Greg said calmly, steel ringing through. "I figured I owed her the truth, so I told her my door swung both ways. She was so disgusted, she threw the ring back at me and walked out. She took several of my close friends with her. The easy route isn't who I am, Jack. Love is love, no matter the gender. And I've never felt about anyone the way I feel about you."

Jack sucked air slowly through his nose, trying to inflate air back into the lungs that Greg just knocked the wind out of.

"Why did you come over to my apartment?" Greg asked in the silence. "You're on shift tonight."

Jack's brain was too numb to filter his response. "My boss called and asked me if I wanted to move to days. Seems a few of our new recruits want the third shift pay differential, and I don't need the extra income anymore." Jack looked at Greg and laid everything out in the open, pain be damned. "Since you got the gay experience you were after, I was wondering if you wanted a relationship. Moving to days means more time with you."

Greg took a step forward. "I..."

Jack held up a hand to stop him. "But we're too different, Greg. This will never work. Better we end this now."

"I want you."

Jack closed his eyes. Shook his head. "Bye, Greg."

"So, that's it?" Greg barked. "Our time together meant nothing to you?"

Jack ground his molars to dust to get the next phrase out of his mouth without turning into a sob queen. "We had an agreement. It's over."

·❤·❤·❤·❤·❤·

His last four shifts on third before making the transition to first was hell, putting it mildly. Jack was exhausted, aching, and hungry.

And he missed Greg something fierce.

He climbed the stairs to his apartment and found Rachel sitting on the floor, her back against the apartment door, and holding two coffees.

She rose and offered him one of the cups. "Can we talk?"

Jack looked across the hall at Greg's door.

"He's at work," she said.

Jack accepted the coffee, muttering a *thanks*, and invited her in. She glanced around briefly before settling in on one of his stools by the kitchen counter. Not knowing what to do, he stood there waiting for her to speak her piece.

She patted the stool next to her. "Relax. I don't bite, unless you want me to."

His gaze whipped to hers, recalling he'd said the same thing to Greg their first night.

"Yeah, he told me," she said. "Crazy, but that's how he knew he could trust you."

He shook his head and took the stool next to her. "What can I do for you, Rachel?"

"You can get over yourself and call Greg like I know you want to. He's miserable. You're miserable."

"I appreciate the advice, but..."

"I'm not done," she said, humor lacing her tone. "He told me about your argument. Greg and I have had many opportunities to hook up. We never have. You can hear this straight from my mouth. We're more like siblings. There's no spark."

Hearing it from her mouth did help, but there were more things between them than her. "Okay."

"There's something dark about you, Jack. I can see it in your eyes. Whatever caused this pain, I'm sorry, but Greg won't hurt you." She smiled to soften the words. "You're insecure, and that's normal. But let me tell you, I've seen him with women. Many women. He never looked at them the way he looked at you."

She hopped off the stool and walked to the door, coffee in hand. He opened his mouth to speak, but she whirled around.

"Still not done," she said. "This having kids issue? You'd be great parents, and Greg's family would accept them. Have children or don't. If you don't, you can spoil the shit out of mine." She took a bow. "That is all."

Rachel marched right out the door before Jack so much as blinked.

Truth settled into his gut, his mind. His heart.

If Rachel had any romantic feelings for Greg, she wouldn't have come over and said what she did. And Greg told Jack he'd known her since they were kids, so the whole looking at Jack differently thing rang with sincerity.

He knew all along what he'd been feeling for Greg, he'd just used the easy excuses to end things instead of taking the chance. Hell, he knew that first night Greg was different. Not just the physical connection, but the emotional one. Jack never allowed a connection. Not since the day his parents kicked him out. It was the real reason none of his relationships lasted.

He never missed any of his lovers after they'd left, either.

He missed Greg.

Dammit. He was a fucking idiot.

A week after Jack ripped Greg's heart out and stomped on it, Greg was in no better shape. He went through the everyday motions in autopilot, barely eating, and sleep just a distant memory. He knew he was acting like a drama queen, but Rachel, bless her, never called him out.

He made a pot of coffee, content as shit it was Saturday. He wouldn't even have to get dressed. Once the brew was going, he stepped out his door to grab the newspaper. Technology meant he could have the news right on his phone, but he liked the feel of paper in his hand. Plus, the newspapers were taking a hit, so why not support them?

He looked down and frowned. The newspaper was out of order with the Personals laying on top of the front page. A bright green circle was highlighted around one of the ads.

Rachel trying to meddle again.

He picked up the page and read.

Male Seeking Male: Must live across the hall and be willing to accept apology. Must be open to a house in the suburbs and want a dog. Kids negotiable. Baseball is not. Miss you.

Holy shit.

Jack's apartment door opened, and Greg looked up to find him leaning against the frame, crossing his arms. "I hope that's the last ad either of us has to place."

Greg's hands shook. His heart stopped. "Do you mean it?"

"Yes. Every word. Especially the 'miss you' part."

Greg cleared his raw throat. "The ad says something about an apology."

Jack grinned. "So it does. Well, then. I'm sorry, Greg. For everything." Greg just stared, so Jack went on. "I'm sorry. I'll say it a thousand times."

"No," he murmured. "I heard you. Just give me a minute."

"Give me forever."

Greg's heart chose now to start beating again. Loudly. "I could do forever."

Jack smiled and closed the distance between them. He cupped the back of Greg's head and brought his mouth over his, igniting the flame between them and sealing the gap.

Greg drew back and smiled. "You could have just walked across the hall. You didn't have to place an ad."

"Nah. This was more romantic."

Moonlight Magic

Years ago, Sam broke Dabney's heart, and neither of them have gotten over it. As she casts a spell for security for her and her sisters, things go terribly wrong, and Sam comes to the rescue. Now in the same orbit again, can they overcome their differences and breach one another's walls to find a true, lasting love, or will they let the magic fade?

Katie O'Connor

MOONLIGHT MAGIC

Katie O'Connor

One

Dabney Booth scraped her hands across her eyes. They burned like someone poured acid in them. She was exhausted, but it was too late to quit. If she was going to meet the conditions of her grandfather's will, she had to be married by the end of the month.

She'd tried all the usual routes, blind dates set up by friends and neighbors, dating apps, she'd even humiliated herself by going on a Three Moon Falls cable television show called *Falling for the Bachelor*. She'd been punted from the show when she'd kicked their chosen bachelor in the junk for getting handsy. The man was a pig. What option did she have left, except for magic?

If she didn't meet those conditions, two point two billion dollars would be given to her cousin Hector, and he was a drug addict. She didn't want the money for herself. She wanted it to fulfill a family dream to open an animal sanctuary with her two younger sisters.

The rules of magic said you couldn't cast a spell for personal gain. Magic didn't work that way. It wasn't something for nothing. Magic had a cost. Casting for yourself either ended up failing or rebounding badly. But this wasn't for her. It was for her sisters, and the animals. And if that meant she needed to conjure a temporary husband in order to inherit, so be it. This spell would benefit so many people and injured animals. That made it for unselfish purposes. Right?

She leaned on the gazebo wall to gather her strength. They were renting a small acreage outside of town. The gazebo was private and well out of sight from the nearby road. She couldn't tell her sisters about the spell. They'd pitch a fit. She had already managed twenty-seven nights of magicking. One more wasn't going to kill her.

From full moon to full moon. The spell she'd dredged up on the magical web took a full lunar cycle to complete. Tonight was the last night. The moon was full again, and as a bonus, it was a full blood moon, and that alignment only happened once every two and a half years. If she missed this one, she'd still be single when the will conditions came due. When she received the funds, she'd make sure Hector got into rehab and that he wanted for nothing. If he cleaned up his act, she'd give him a fair share.

Anger at the ridiculous condition rippled down her spine. *Ugh. Grampa, you're a butthead.* Her paternal grandparents had died before she was born, and she hadn't been close to her maternal grandfather. He had disowned her mother when she had married a man he hadn't approved of. Her parents had been dead for nine years before she'd even learned of his existence. They'd been able to spend some time together during the last year before he'd succumbed to cancer.

Inhaling several long slow breaths, she pushed away her ire. Strong emotions could negatively impact a spell, and she could not risk messing this up. This last repetition had to be perfect.

Struggling to warm up, she moved closer to the small brazier she'd lit earlier. She had all her spell ingredients lined up on the side bench. Enough delay. The moon was at peak fullness at 9:24. She had to be ready to drop the final herb at exactly that time. Her phone buzzed in her back pocket, reminding her there were only five minutes left.

Walking clockwise, or deosil, around the charcoal brazier that served as her ritual fire, she called Goddess and her consort to aid her in her quest. Candles in lantern shields sat at north, south, east, and west. She rang a small bell in time to her steps. Music helped build the final energy the spell would need. She sprinkled the herbs one at a time into her cauldron, her concentration intense. She recited the ritual words over and over as she worked. She dropped in a heart-shaped anthurium blossom. As she reached for the last ingredient, her alarm vibrated in her pocket. Perfect timing.

"As I will it, so mote it be!" she called to the heavens.

Something sparking a bright red screamed through the air, nearly hitting her in the face. It landed with a thump on the brazier.

"What the..."

The brazier exploded in a shower of sparks, throwing her backward, out of the gazebo, and onto the grass. Everything went black.

Sam "Sparky" McKenna crouched beside Dabney. His heart beat over-time. What was the crazy witch doing this time? She'd blown up half her backyard. Her straight black hair was singed on the ends, and one eyebrow was missing. Luckily, she didn't appear to have burned her skin. His chest hurt looking at her. She'd stolen his heart years ago, but after they'd broken up, she'd refused to speak to him. She'd probably be mad he was here, even though it was his job.

"Dabney, can you hear me?" He grasped her hand in his. "Don't move. Lay still. The ambulance is on its way."

She didn't open her eyes. "Back off, Sparky. Don't touch me." After a beat, her lids lifted, and her glare gouged a hole in his chest.

"Are you hurt?"

The fire hadn't amounted to much more than a grass blaze, but the explosion had left one hell of a divot and totaled the gazebo. Everything smelled of ash. Whisps of smoke still rose from the gazebo's rubble. His crew sprayed it one more time and poked at it with a shovel to be sure the flames were fully extinguished.

"I could be bleeding to death, and I wouldn't accept your help. Go. Away."

He bit back a laugh. It was that stubborn independence he loved most about Dabney. "What happened?" She'd done some crazy magic, but this took the cake.

"None of your damned business."

"I'm the fire chief. You blew up half a block and burned your gazebo down." A slight exaggeration, but he still had to investigate. "It's my business to investigate all explosions. Tell me, Miss Booth, exactly what happened."

"It wasn't my fault."

"You have to be the least coordinated witch on the planet. I told you to go see the Hawk sisters. They can help you hone those skills."

"It. Wasn't. My. Fault." Her eyes narrowed. Fire danced in their gray-green depths. They looked like the Pacific after a storm.

"Were you, or were you not, casting a spell?" He kept his voice low. Not all of the firemen and paramedics were aware of magic.

He looked around. She *had* been doing magic. Her brazier was sitting halfway across the yard, just on the edge of the blast radius, and her cauldron had flown nearly as far. "Seriously, Dabs, you could have been seriously hurt. You probably have a concussion as it is."

"Yeah, my head hurts like Loki was pounding on it with Thor's hammer."

He chuckled. That sense of humor was another of her irresistible traits. "Come on, Dabs. Take it from the top."

"Yes, I was magicking. I finished my spell, and just as I dropped in the last herb—which was a bay leaf with the thing I am trying to manifest written on it—when something sparking came shooting from over there. It landed right in the brazier, like an arrow hitting the bullseye."

"Something sparking?"

"Yes, Sparky, something flew at me that was trailing red sparks. It came from there." She jabbed her finger to the north, behind him. "I think it was that little brat playing with fireworks or something."

Sam sighed. That brat was her next-door neighbor, Hank Green, a twelve-year-old hooligan with a drunken father and over-worked mother. The police had picked him up with fireworks more than once.

"Fireworks?"

"Yah, but big." She spread her hands about eighteen inches apart. "Big. There was no real noise, though, just the hissing of sparks, then boom." She slapped her hands together. "Ouch. That hurt my head." She tried to sit up.

"Step aside, Sam, I've got this." A medic nudged Sam to the side and knelt in his place. "Hey, I'm Damien. How do you feel?"

"I feel like I got hit by a bus. Mostly my head. I think I hit it when I landed."

"Okay, let's check you out." He spooled off a list of questions, and Dabney answered them perfectly. "How long were you out?"

She nibbled her lip, and Sam wanted to sooth it with his thumb.

"I don't know. It went boom, then Sparky was pestering me. Where are my sisters?" She struggled as she again tried to sit up.

"Stay still until I'm done examining you. If you were out the entire time it took the fire department to arrive, you could well have a concussion."

She managed to settle into a seated position.

Sam placed his hand on her shoulder. "Your sisters are over there on the back step, Dabney. They're fine. They called 911 for you."

She looked up at him, and the vulnerability in her eyes nearly crippled him. "I swear, Dabs, they're okay. Do what needs to be done. I'll stay with them until the doc checks you out."

A crow screamed in a nearby tree as Dabney looked at Sam. Why wasn't he ugly? Why hadn't his betrayal turned him into a pock-marked weasel? Or a skunk. He was a skunk for sure. He shouldn't be the studliest man she'd ever met. His green eyes shouldn't make her heart skip a beat. If he wasn't a rat-bastard, she'd be totally into him.

By the Goddess, she missed him. She'd been certain he was going to propose on their two-year dating anniversary. He hadn't.

"Can you check on them, please?" She swallowed her fear for her sisters. Suddenly, inheriting billions didn't seem so important. Bridgette and Emerald were just kids. Emmy was only fifteen and Bridge thirteen. With their parents long dead, Dabney, who was now thirty, had been their guardian for a decade. She was more mother than sister. She'd struggled to keep them fed and clothed. The only reason they weren't homeless was their parents' insurance. Sadly, those funds were running out.

"If you sit still for the medics, I'll check on them." Sam's smile was almost as reassuring as seeing the girls for herself. She couldn't tear her eyes from him as he jogged toward the house.

"How's the head? Where does it hurt?"

She blinked rapidly and turned her attention back to the paramedic. What was his name? Damien. Right.

"It hurts everywhere." She finally managed to focus on the question. "Mostly at the back and the right temple." She touched the sore spot. Her fingers came away bloody. She wobbled sideways. "Oh, I'm bleeding." She hated her own blood. She could fix a gash on her sisters without blinking, but a papercut on her own hand made her woozy.

"Dabs, don't look," Sam demanded. "I brought the girls."

She turned toward them. They had fire department blankets wrapped around their shoulders and were huddled together. Their tear-streaked faces broke her heart. Sam stood behind them with a hand on their shoulders.

"I'm fine, girls. It's just a bump."

"That's not true. Your aura is messed up. I can see the lie and the pain," Emerald snapped. "Don't tell lies."

Behind her, Sam shrugged?

"She's going to be fine," the medic said. "We'll take her to the hospital for a quick checkup, just to be sure. Do you have someone to stay with you while she's gone?"

"We're not infants," Bridgette grumbled.

"No, you aren't," Dabney agreed. "But you are shaken up. Heck, I'm shaken up." She managed a laugh. "Sam, will you sit with them? Maybe order a pizza and watch a movie? I won't be long."

It was beyond wrong of her to ask the favor of a man who had dumped her on their anniversary. It was a wonder he even cared how she was doing. No, that wasn't fair. He'd never treated her badly, even after the breakup. It was the abrupt dumping that had her stumped.

"You got it. I've got a craving for a barbecued chicken pizza. What about you girls? Maybe dessert, too?"

He instructed his second-in-command to take over ensuring the fire was out and then starting the paperwork. He slung his arms around her sisters' shoulders and turned them toward the house.

As easy as that, they went inside with him. They adored Sam. They had from the first time she'd brought him home to meet them, back when she thought they'd be together forever.

The trip to the hospital was fast, and Doctor Carter met them there. A short time later, Hyacinth Hawk arrived. Most people thought Hyacinth was a midwife, but she was a magical healer, as well. She was the go-to person for magicals in town when they needed medical care.

The doctor watched without comment as Hyacinth healed her wound and dropped, exhausted, into a chair.

"Juice?" she mumbled.

Casting magic was a lot of work and took a physical toll. Hyacinth had spent her energy on healing the internal damage to Dabney's head. She left the cuts and bruises alone. Because so many people were aware of the accident, news did travel quickly in Three Moon Falls, it was best if conventional means were used to close her head wound.

After Hyacinth had eaten a tray of high calorie food, she turned to Dabney. "What happened? There's magical residue all over you. White magic."

"My spell was finished when something hit my brazier, and it exploded. I suppose that means my spell was for nothing." Dabney wanted to weep. Now that she was fine, and her sisters were in good hands, her need for money jumped forward into her mind. "I spent a month on that spell. Every single night."

"You should work with a coven for big spells. Why don't you swing by the shop and we'll help you out. But if the spell was finished, maybe the magic was complete and will work."

"Do you think..." Dabney shook her head. "Never mind."

"Do I think what? Don't be shy. I'm from long line of witches. Salem witches. I've had help at my beck and call my entire life. Not everyone is as blessed as my family. I know you come into the shop. You're a solitary, right? You work alone?"

"Sometimes I work with my sisters."

"Oh, honey. Half of this town is magic. Come by and we'll help you. If we can't, we'll find someone who can. Now, what were you going to ask me? I know Celtic, Scottish, Cajun, and Irish witches. Hedge, kitchen, and candle witches. I even know hoodoo and voodoo practitioners. Someone will be able to help you hone your skills. Your sisters', too."

Something in Hyacinth's voice was reassuring, almost as calming as seeing Sam when she'd opened her eyes earlier. Only, this calm didn't come with the undertones of having lost something important.

"I'm in a tight spot." She sighed. "I need to be married by the end of next month. I was trying to catch a man. Not a specific man, that would be wrong, but a man to marry who would care for me. If I'm not married, I'll lose my inheritance to my cousin. The girls and I need that money for our animal sanctuary. Okay, we need it to survive." She explained the will and conditions, and their plans for the sanctuary, and how they were being evicted in sixty days. "Do you think the spell went wrong because it was for selfish purposes?"

"Was it, though?" Hyacinth asked. "I mean, my grandmother would know more than I do, but to me, it feels like this was more for the animals and your sisters than for you. I think this was either a freak accident, or someone was deliberately trying to scare you."

Maybe it was an accident, but what if that firework had been magical rebound?

"I hope you're right." Dabney needed that money. Her cousin would still get a share, but she and her sisters would get the bulk of it. She felt greedy, and at the same time, she knew her grandfather would be in favor of the sanctuary. They had discussed the idea when Emerald had started bringing home wounded animals and nursing them back to health. When he passed, his enormous house was sold and the money put into the estate. Now, nearly a year later, she was running out of time.

Hyacinth patted her hand. "Come by the store and talk to Gramma Pearl. Maybe she can help. Nobody knows more about magic than my grandmother."

Two

It seemed silly to be babysitting kids as old as Emerald and Bridgette, but they were obviously distressed over Dabney's condition. They sat on the floor in the living room, chowing down on pizza, soda, and cheesecake. They were still chatting when Dabney got home.

"Hey, guys. I'm back." She strolled into the living room like nothing had happened, and as if her clothing wasn't charred and dirty.

The girls leaped up and rushed to her, buzzing with questions, demanding to know she was okay.

She tolerated it for a moment, and then thrust up a hand. "Whoa." When they calmed down, she said, "I still have a headache and probably will for a while. It's late. You girls should get to bed, okay? Sleep late tomorrow. It's Saturday, we'll skip housework for this week."

They thanked Sam for the pizza and hurried off as if they were afraid she'd back down on her promise. She watched them go, and he watched her watching them.

Slowly, she turned toward him, her normally straight spine slumped, and she slid to the floor beside him. "Any food left?"

"You know it." He pulled the box he'd been saving from under the table. "Pepperoni, pineapple, bacon, and mushrooms." He pulled out a smaller container. "With fresh tomato to go on top." Dabney loved cold pizza.

"Yes! You do know the way to a woman's heart, don't you."

"Apparently not." He'd messed up by breaking up with her instead of telling her the truth. Learning she was set to inherit so much money had scared him. "I am sorry for dumping you."

"Water under the bridge. I've moved on." There was a slight tremor in her voice that belied her words. As far as he knew, she hadn't dated since they split up.

"Have you? I haven't. I still love you." He sipped the last of the beer he'd taken from the fridge.

"Sparky, you never loved me. If you had, we'd still be together."

He didn't argue. The only thing that would convince her otherwise was the truth, and he could never tell her that.

He changed the subject. "Tell me about tonight's magic." He kept his tone light and conversational when really, he wanted to shake some sense into her.

"The explosion wasn't my fault! It was that stupid firecracker." She jumped up, groaning before heading to the kitchen and returning with two beers.

He frowned.

"Don't give me that look. I haven't taken any pain meds, nor do I plan to. I hate drugs." She gave him one, popped the top on hers, and took a couple sips. "It was a simple spell. Sort of."

One thing about Dabney? She never lied. Ever. She'd walk away in the middle of an argument rather than tell an untruth. Her fib to her sisters earlier was the first lie he'd ever heard her utter.

"Tell me about it. What were you working on?"

"A moon phase spell. Twenty-eight days of magic, all toward one result." She snatched up a slice of pizza and took a huge bite like she was using food to stop her words.

"That doesn't sound simple." He knew better than to push her. She'd clam up and shove him out the door. He was too content to be here, looking at her, being with her. He wanted to stay in this moment forever.

Gods, he was a lovestruck idiot. Still.

"I needed something. I found the spell and worked it. Tonight's the full blood blue moon. There's enormous power there if you know how to tap into it."

He didn't say anything. They'd worked magic together before. Their power magnified when they cast as a duo. It wasn't simple addition, one plus one equals two. It was more one plus one equals five. Magic could be funny that way.

"You could've asked me for help. We might not be dating, but we're powerful together." His butt was cramping from sitting on the floor, so he stood and offered his hand. She rose with him, and they sat side-by-side on the couch like they used to. He rested his arm on the back of the cushion, his fingertips just brushing her shoulder. "Maybe we could try as a duo?"

"Give it up, Sparky. It was a one-woman spell."

She wouldn't meet his gaze. That meant it was something she didn't want him to know about. Interesting.

"I saw you outside Barnaby and Sons. How was the visit to the lawyers?" He was curious if there was a way out of the clause that withheld the money. He didn't want her money, but if they were still engaged, she might think he did.

"The meeting was fine. Good and bad. I miss Grampa so much. We didn't visit him enough. We barely got to know him, and now we'll never see him again." She sniffed, and he handed her a tissue from the side table.

"He was a good man. He did a lot for this town."

It was a story kept from non-magical people, mundanes, but a decade ago, just before her parents passed, her grandfather had nearly died fighting a sorcerer bent on using magic to steal all the property in town. He'd triumphed in the end. She hadn't known about the fight until she'd moved to town because she'd lived in Grande Prairie at the time. She'd been in Three Moon Falls for just over three years.

He'd fallen for her the moment his cart bumped into hers in the grocery store. He'd asked her out immediately. Lucky for him, she'd said yes.

They sat in silence for a moment before he asked, "How bad was the damage to your head?"

"Pretty bad," she admitted. "Hyacinth came to the hospital and healed the internal damage. We let the doctor give me stitches. Too many of the firefighters aren't magical. It would be weird if I didn't have stitches. Besides, half the town probably heard the explosion. My ears are still ringing a bit."

Sam was barely magical, though his paternal grandmother had been one of the best. Magic was like that. It often skipped generations if both parents weren't magical. Abilities were passed down by the mother. Men could be magical, but didn't have the gene to pass it on. Nobody quite understood the contradiction of how someone's magic was stronger if they had two magical parents, and yet a man couldn't pass it on if his child came from a non-magical mother. It had only been a couple years, a decade maybe, since the genetics of magic had come under official and serious study.

It turned out that many more people were magical than anyone suspected. Intuition was often ignored, as was foresight. Over the years, witches had hidden their magic even from their own children until it had faded away. Often, extreme circumstances brought it back in unexpected ways.

"You should get to bed," he suggested. Despite her magical healing, she had deep purple swollen circles under her eyes. Her hand trembled as she sipped her beer. "Do you want some tea first?"

"I have work to do."

"Not tonight, you don't. Your spell has been destroyed. Tea?" he repeated.

"Fine."

He loved how she could put a full reprimand into a single syllable. "Which one?" She made her own teas, or purchased them from Four Seasons Metaphysical, a shop owned by Hyacinth and her family.

"Top shelf. Blue and white tin patterned with roses."

Her memory was exceptional. If she put something away, she'd know exactly where it was, and how much remained. This told him she hadn't made a mistake in her spell, despite her obvious exhaustion. While he waited for the kettle to heat, he checked his messages. Nothing. He wondered if the police had found Hank Green yet. Something had to be done with him before someone else got hurt. In Alberta, you had to be eighteen to use fireworks. Hank was only twelve.

He carried the tea to the living room. Dabney had stretched out on the couch. Her eyes were closed, and her hands curled up under her bandaged head. She had a few small burns on her arms. No doubt, Hyacinth had taken the pain of those away while healing Dabney's head. Magic was a wonderful thing when used correctly.

No sense waking her. By her own admission, she hadn't slept properly for a month. What in the world was she magicking that took so long? It must be important. And why was she excluding her sisters? Though all three were novices, they often worked spells together. Something was up here, and he was going to find out.

He draped a soft star-patterned quilt over her shoulders and tucked her in before clearing the empty food containers. He carried the cardboard ones to the compost bin and washed the plastic ones for reuse. Working quietly, he hand-washed the dishes and put them away.

A whisper caught his attention. He turned to find the oldest of Dabney's younger sisters, fifteen-year-old Emmy, standing in the doorway.

"Shouldn't you be sleeping, Emmy?"

"Shouldn't you have gone home by now?" While Dabney's sister, Bridgette, was quiet, Emmy definitely had Dabney's spunk and sass.

"I thought I'd stay in case she needs anything tonight."

"Thanks." She walked up to him and leaned against his chest. "Her aura is better, but it's still damaged and weak. I'm so scared."

"I'm worried about her, too, munchkin."

"Ugh. I'm an adult." She stepped back and looked at him. "If you ever loved her, you have to fix this."

"You know I love her. We were practically engaged." *She'd have dumped me when she learned my secret.* "Wanna tell me what's wrong? What do I need to fix?" Tonight had been torture on his heart. He ached for Dabney's pain, and for her sisters' fear and worry.

"Outside."

They went out the back door onto the covered deck. The air was warm and reeked of fire. He was still in his uniform. He'd shed his protective gear, but the stench lingered on his clothing. Outside was much worse. The acrid smell redoubled now that they were close to the remains of the gazebo. He sat in one of the padded wicker chairs. Emmy sat on the matching loveseat, feet folded crisscross, a blanket slung over her shoulders.

"Tell me what's up."

"You can't tell her I told you," Emmy warned.

"I swear on the Goddess that your secret is safe with me."

"She never told me, but I found her notes in her personal grimoire. She's doing a spell to attract a man."

"What? Why?" Personal gain spells were a no-no and destined to have unintended negative consequences.

"Not for her sake, for ours."

"Explain." A thousand questions danced on the tip of his tongue, like fire lapping at the edge of a timber.

"When Grampa died last year, a condition of his will was that Dabney had to be married in order for the sisters to inherit. Otherwise, our cousin Hector gets everything. Even with all three of us working, we're barely making a living. Remember before, when you came around, we talked about an animal sanctuary?"

He nodded. It was their dream, and one he supported fully.

"Dabney didn't say anything, but she...*we* can't open an animal sanctuary without a lot of money. Three Moon Falls doesn't have an animal shelter since the old one closed, and it needs one. Stray animals are increasing. I'm probably a healer. Bridge hasn't found her skill yet. Dabney is our guardian. She didn't say how much money it was, just that it was enough. Grampa left enough money to open a sanctuary, send Emmy to university, and for us to live on. It's win-win. So, she didn't try magic for herself, she did it for us."

He'd heard rumors about the will. The local lawyer's receptionist had a loose tongue. She sucked at keeping secrets. Dabney's inheritance was why he'd broken up with her. He couldn't bear for her to think he had ulterior motives for dating her. He'd been stupid. He probably should've explained his situation. Now he couldn't because she rarely talked to him, and certainly not about anything personal. Last night had been the exception.

"You have to do it, Sparky. Marry Dabs so we can get the money. Bridge really needs to be able to afford university. The animals need help, and Dabney is miserable without you."

There was a lot to comprehend in Emmy's urgent statements. Finally, he said, "I don't see what you think I can do."

"Marry her, you idiot." She made a sound of absolute disgust. "You love her."

"I do. She doesn't love me. She barely tolerates me." He'd propose again in a heartbeat if he thought she'd accept.

"She does love you. She's been miserable since you broke up. Just ask her already."

"It doesn't work like that." How could a teenager even begin to comprehend the complexities of adult relationships? "Marriage has to be between two people who love and respect each other. Maybe, at one time, Dabney loved me. Now, she has no respect for me, and I can't say I blame her. I dumped her. I fully understand she can't forgive me."

"She would if you would apologize." She spat the words out like she was stamping her feet in a temper tantrum.

He stared out into the moonlit night. His gaze skipped over the gazebo's burnt husk and landed on the trees which shivered under a light breeze. He had little magic of his own, but easily recognized the magical residue lingering under the light of the full moon. Mundanes would never notice it, but magicals would. The residue needed to be cleaned up.

"I'll apologize again, but I promise you, it won't do any good." *God, what he wouldn't do to marry Dabney. If only his secret wouldn't destroy their love.*

She jumped up and kissed his cheek. "Thanks, Sam. You're the best. I can't wait until you're my brother-in-law." She hurried toward the back door.

"Don't get your hopes up," he called as the screen door slammed.

He scrubbed his hands over his face. He'd just committed himself to total humiliation. First in his apology and convincing Dabney he was truly repentant, and then in a proposal. Maybe he could do it all in one shot.

The question was, was Emmy right? Did Dabney still love him?

He stared out over the yard. It was time to gather the lingering magic before someone with ill intent put it to a nefarious purpose. It was a testament to the severity of Dabney's injury she hadn't thought to clear it herself. She obviously hadn't realized it had been more than traces of magic cast, but also lingering unused magic, which had gone unspent in the spell, or in this case, interrupted.

Though his magic wasn't strong, maybe he could use it to help her.

He walked back and forth across the lawn, north to south and south to north, pulling the magic shards toward himself. He repeated the action in an east-west direction. Though the shards were invisible to a mundane, he saw their glimmer easily. He hummed as he worked.

He traced the outline of the yard, pulling what he could from beyond the fences, murmuring under his breath as he walked and pulled the shards to himself. "Mother Earth, take this unspent magic, use it for the purpose it was intended. Use it to fulfill the needs of Dabney and her sisters." He held the gathered shards in his cupped hands and raised them skyward. "As I will it, so mote it be!"

The bits brightened and glowed in his palms before spiraling upward and out of sight.

Three

Absolute silence greeted Dabney when she woke. Her ears had almost stopped ringing. Even Hyacinth's healing hadn't quite silenced the bells in her ears last night. The current near silence was a blessing. She listened for sounds of her sisters, glad the ringing had quieted. Were they awake yet?

She struggled to sit up. Her entire body ached. Magical healing was too costly to the practitioner to heal needlessly. Minor ailments were best left to heal naturally. She was grateful that her concussion had been healed, and she could live with a few aches and pains. She hurried to the washroom. Her bladder was bursting. How long had she slept? It was daylight, so a few hours, at least.

Her sisters' beds were made, their rooms were unusually tidy, and there was no sign of them in the house. Bridge probably went to the library, and Emmy would be out at the shed checking on her animal charges. Dabney trusted them enough that she didn't feel the need to chase after them. They'd call if they needed her, and they knew what time supper would be.

She was so proud of her sisters. Each had a different personality, and a different future, but they worked hard and strove to be better every day. As she did. Like Bridge, Dabney wasn't extremely magically gifted.

She had some innate skills, but needed proper training. She'd barely started that training when her parents were killed. She'd persisted on her own as best she could because her parents had always said it was best to keep training within the family. Her magic came from her mother. Her father had none, nor did her grandfather.

Now, with only her sisters left, it might be time to admit defeat and seek the help of more experienced magic casters. The magical web had good information, but nothing beat one-on-one training. She had some time tomorrow to visit Four Seasons Metaphysical and look into it.

But first, food. Despite last night's pizza, she was ravenous. Casting big magic did that. It sucked energy right out of a person Contrary to popular television, magic always had a price. And after twenty-eight nights of casting, her body was drained.

She would make herself eggs and toast. The perfect breakfast. But first, coffee. Coffee was her weakness, and she had to limit herself to two cups a day, or she'd be vibrating like a jackhammer, but there was no way she could avoid it all together. It was part of her soul.

She sighed. Yeah, Sparky had been part of her soul, too. Her soul mate.

To her surprise, the coffee pot was prepped and ready to go. All she had to do was push the button. A sticky note stuck to the top said, *I've taken the girls out for a while. Relax this morning. Get some rest. Sam.*

She frowned. He used to sign his notes, Sparky. The impersonal note hurt.

"Huh," she mumbled to herself. "Wonder where they went." As the coffee brewed, she prepped her breakfast. With food and drink on a pretty wooden tray Bridge had painted, she headed out onto the back deck and instantly wished she hadn't.

"Gross." The scent of ash and mud was almost overpowering and reminded her of last night's failure. "Pixie sticks." She pushed out a breath.

First order of business was to clean up the mess and figure out what it would cost to have the gazebo replaced. Would insurance cover it? That would probably depend on whether or not they charged the little jerk next door. And she'd have to let her landlord know what happened, if he hadn't heard it through the gossip grapevine already.

Out in the center of the grass was a rough unburned spot. She trembled knowing that's where she'd lain. Even unconscious, her magic had kept the fire from reaching her body. She'd been damned lucky. The Goddess was with her last night, even if it hadn't seemed so at the time.

She turned her mind to the issue of finding a husband. What kind of jerk makes marriage a condition of inheritance? Her old-fashioned grandfather, that's who.

"Oh, Grampa. Why did you have to do this to me? I want love to come naturally, not through a spell or having to hire someone to marry me." She ate because she needed the energy to deal with her day, and with the rubble in her yard, not because she was hungry. Her appetite had fled at the first sniff of ash.

She scrolled her phone, searching for an alternate way to solve her problems. If she didn't get that money, she'd never be able to afford to send Bridge to university. Dabney was a nail tech, and she loved her job and working with people, but it did not bring in the big bucks.

Being thrust into parenthood at twenty hadn't left her any time to get the degree needed to make more money. She was happy in her job, but expenses were mounting, and she had no savings.

She kept scanning her newsfeed. "Speed dating?" She read the article on the local digital notice board. That was one way to meet men in a hurry. She signed up for the event taking place that night. Crossing her fingers, she whispered a prayer to the universe that tonight was the night she met the man of her dreams. Ruthlessly, she pushed Sparky's image aside.

She checked with the fire department to be sure it was safe to start removing the debris of the gazebo. They gave her their permission, but told her to check with the police. An hour later, a duo of officers arrived and conducted their investigation, complete with a thousand questions and hundreds of pictures. Lucky for her, one of the officers was Leticia Stone, who was a Voodoo Priestess and understood magic. A complete mundane might not have been so understanding. Investigation complete, they gave her the go ahead to demolish.

She took her own pictures and salvaged her hurricane lanterns, though they'd need new glass. Her cauldron was dented, but still whole. That was a relief. It had generations of magic seeped into its cast iron. It would be a shame to lose that legacy. Her brazier was toast. She'd definitely need a new one. She grabbed her hammer.

"Let the demolition begin." If she wasn't so exhausted, she might have used a bit of magic to help clean the yard, but after a month of nightly magic, and last night's disaster, she thought manual labor might be the better option.

"I don't want to do this," she muttered as she stared down the ruins of the gazebo.

A crow called from the trees, his tone harsh and mocking.

"Ya, ya. I get it." She blew him a kiss. She was never outside without a crow or raven appearing nearby. They were her spirit animal.

She was knee deep in ash and detritus when Sparky showed up.

Somehow, she couldn't call him Sam. Sparky suited him so much better and not just because of all the sparks his touch set off.

He'd moved to Three Moon Falls shortly before they started dating and had been doing a fire safety talk at the school on career day when they'd met. It was the only time she'd ever heard him stumble over words. He'd meant to say, "Always be aware of where your sparks might land," but had ended up saying, "Be aware of your sparkies." It was a slight slip that nobody else even noticed. She'd called him Sparky on their first date, and later, it caught on at the firehall.

Manners dictated that she greet him despite being busy with demo. "Sparky."

"What are you doing?" he asked, hands on his hips.

"Baking cookies."

"Funny. Don't give up your day job. I told you last night I'd help with this. Let me get my truck and tools."

She swung her hammer again, knocking the remains of two boards apart. There was more structure left than she had imagined, but nothing worth salvaging. If she had a firepit, some of it might have been burn-worthy.

Muttering under his breath about stubborn women, he strode away.

She opened the RV gate in the back fence, and he backed in. Her sisters hopped out of the truck.

"Hey, you two," she greeted them. "How was your morning? Where did you go?"

"On the coolest tour of the lake," Emma declared. "Sam knows a guy with a boat, and he took us to look at the place where the falls blew up last year. It looks so different from water level."

"Nice." She'd seen the view a couple weeks ago. The damage was incredible, but the falls flowed on. She refused to think about the man who had blown it up. The magical community said he was looking for a sacred item, but nobody could, or rather, *would* confirm the idea. Rumor also said the Magic Council had dealt with him.

She smiled at Emmy and Bridge. "Don't forget you both have your studies. Summer vacation doesn't mean no studies." All three of them spent time each day perusing magic books and trying to hone their skills. Her sisters would probably benefit from taking a class or two, as well. She was fast learning that just being born with magic wasn't enough. Someone had to teach her what to do.

Grumbling, they walked inside, leaving her alone with Sparky.

He immediately starting pitching board remains into his truck. "I'd shovel that ash into buckets or boxes. Something you can seal for disposal."

She saluted. "Yes, sir." With an eyeroll, she went into the garage for some old boxes. He was right, but that didn't mean he should be ordering her around.

"Make sure they're stone cold," he said when she came back.

"They're not just cold, they're cold and soggy. How much water did you guys dump on this thing?

"Enough to put the fire out. How's the head?" His voice was laden with concern and tenderness. A tiny crack split her heart, making it ache.

"It's okay. A bit sore, but not too bad, actually. The bruise is ugly and the stitches are brutal. It'll probably scar."

He walked over to her and shed his work gloves. "Let me see." He cupped her chin gently between his calloused fingertips and tipped her forehead into the light. "It's actually not bad. The bruise will fade, and the stitches are straight and even. No redness. I'll bet Hyacinth Hawk has a concoction that'll help with healing. You should go to the shop."

"Tomorrow. I'm busy today." She waved at the disaster in her yard. The gazebo was gone, the grass singed or trampled near to death by the emergency crews. Everything was sloppy and mucky from the drenching it took. Except for the spot where she'd lain. She shuddered.

"They're open late," he advised with a hint of censure.

"I'm busy tonight."

"Oh?"

"Yup." She was not telling him her plans. They were none of his business. He'd lost any right to know anything about her when he lied to her.

"Okay, don't go. It's your face." He shrugged and went back to work.

Her chin was cold now, and her heart wept. Why did he have to dump her without a good reason? He was perfect for her, except for that one wee flaw. His refusal to tell her why they had to break up was a lie, of sorts. He knew why, he just wasn't going to tell her.

She'd accepted a lot of odd behavior from other people, but lying was the hard line. Sure, she understood white lies. Saying a dress was pretty when it wasn't, or saying she liked someone's ugly new haircut.

Even saying she had other plans to avoid a dreary function. That one was borderline. If it was an important event, she went anyway. But when it was cousin Cicily's third husband's fifty-sixth birthday at a dive bar, staying home to read *was* other plans. But you never lied about the important things.

Sparky's lie of omission was beyond acceptable, and she'd never forgive him.

Annoyingly, his comment about it being *her face* bounced around in her head, and she redoubled her motions to get finished sooner. Maybe she could get to the shop before the speed-dating event started.

She shoveled and shoveled until her back ached and her fingers could hardly hold the handle.

"Take a break," Sparky said. "I had Emmy make lemonade. Have a drink."

She dropped her shovel and took off her gloves. Even through them, her hands had blisters. Crap on toast. "Thanks for the drink. I didn't realize how thirsty I was."

"You know me, always taking care of my gal."

"I'm not your gal."

"You know what I meant." He drank deeply from his glass, his Adam's apple bobbing with each swallow, and his brows pinched together in a frown. Why did that make her want to kiss him?

"How do I get rid of the mud?" She stared at the devastation to her once lush grass.

"Let it dry and give it a good raking. The grass should spring back quickly. It usually does after a fire. It's not supposed to rain for a couple days. That'll help. We'll be able to smooth the dirt back into the hole. I stopped at the insurance agency. Based on my report, they'll cover the rebuild."

She couldn't help but smile. "Thank you, I appreciate that. I can't afford to replace it myself." Dang, he was such a nice guy.

He bowed. "All part of the service." His wink went straight to her libido.

"Ha ha." With Sam's help, they had the yard cleaned in a couple of hours.

"I'll run this to the dump for you." He waved at the debris in his truck. "Want to come along for the ride? I'll buy you a latte afterwards."

"Make it an ice cream and you've got a deal. Let me grab my wallet."

"No need. Fire department has free dumping."

"Sweet deal." After she told the girls where they were headed, he pulled slowly out of the yard. She shut and latched the gate behind him.

The landfill was ten miles outside town. They drove through town without conversation. Tension mounted in her shoulders. She shouldn't have come. Being with him and not talking was tearing her apart.

"Dabs?"

"Yeah?"

His audible sigh clawed at her sanity.

"I really am sorry."

"It's just a gazebo." She pretended to misunderstand his apology.

"I'm not talking about the gazebo. I'm talking about us."

"There is no us." She wanted to dive out of the truck. If she tucked and rolled, it shouldn't hurt too badly, right? They did it in movies all the time.

"There could be."

"Get this straight, right here and right now." She glared at him. "There is no us. There never will be an us. Not now. Not ever." She crossed her arms over her chest and stared out the side window. "That magic fizzled long ago."

He matched her silence for a full minute. "Yeah, but it was magic, wasn't it?" The words were so low her ears barely picked them up. But her heart heard them loud and clear.

Though she didn't know the fellow manning the entry to the landfill, he'd heard all about the damage to the gazebo. "That kid has to be stopped," he muttered. "When you start rebuilding, give me a call. I've got tools and I love a good project."

"Thanks, I appreciate that." One thing about smaller towns like Three Moon Falls, everyone knew everyone else's business. Sometimes, like today, that was a good thing. Other days, not so much.

He handed her a slip of paper with a phone number. "See you then," he declared, waving them through the gate.

Was he dateable? He seemed nice. She shoved the idea away for later consideration as they drove down the gravel road toward the pits.

Painted, the wood wasn't reusable, so everything went into the landfill, not the recycling bins, and they headed for Hot and Cold, a small shop near the beach specializing in french fries and ice cream. Neither of them was particularly dirty as the ash had been more mud than anything else. They brushed themselves off and went inside.

"What'll you have?" he asked as they stood in the short line waiting for their turn.

She debated doing the polite thing and having a simple cone. But the effects of her month-long magic spell and the morning work were dragging on her. "I think I'll have the mega banana split."

"That has six scoops of ice cream, five syrup toppings, nuts, marshmallows, a full banana, gummy worms, and sprinkles. No way can you eat all that."

"I've been *working* hard." She put a slight emphasis on working so he'd know she meant magicking.

"Maybe we should go eat a real meal first."

"Nope. Bridge is making her famous barbecued ribs for dinner."

"She's thirteen."

"Yup, but she's an amazing cook. She started learning when she was six. I think her *skills* might lay in the kitchen as well as with animals." Kitchen witches were definitely a thing. Many were unable to cast big magic, but could infuse everything they made with subtle magic of all different sorts. Dabney, on the other hand, couldn't cook to save her life. She'd tried, and her meals were edible, but only just. How her sisters had survived on Dabney's limited cooking skills was anyone's guess.

They placed their orders, and once the food was ready, they carried their laden trays to a corner booth. She stared down at her enormous dish with a grin. Silently, she said a prayer of thanks to the Goddess and the universe for the blessing in front of her. Gifts like food were always acknowledged in her home. Small blessings were important.

They chatted idly about the fire, the girls, and how they'd done in school this year. Both were excelling and had many strong friendships. Emmy was getting into boys, though Bridge had no interest yet.

Dabney indulged herself on food and conversation, doing her best to ignore the fact that she and Sam weren't friends, they were enemies.

"What's up for tonight?" he asked.

"Speed dating," she replied without realizing she'd planned to keep her evening a secret.

"What? Why would you do that? There are plenty of men in town interested in you."

"First, none of them want a built-in family. Who wants to take on two teenage girls? Nobody, that's who. Second, I'm picky about who I want to spend the rest of my life with."

His frown at that statement was gratifying, though she hadn't been referring to him.

"Still..."

"Leave it, Sparky. It's not your concern."

"It is when it might eventually involve Bridgette and Emerald. I love those girls like they were my own."

It was a blow to her heart he'd given up on her, but there was comfort in knowing he'd always be there for her sisters.

"Seriously, my dating life is none of your concern," she hissed. "Do you think I'd do anything to put them in jeopardy? Stuff it up your firehose." It was a darn good thing she'd finished eating because her appetite and all of her good humor vanished in a magical puff of ire.

What she wouldn't give to turn him into a toad right now.

Four

This might be the biggest mistake he'd ever made. Sam sat in his pickup outside the Stardust Hotel, working up the courage to go inside.

After he'd opened his big mouth about her dating life, Dabney hadn't said another word to him. Not one. Not even thanks for the help. He'd like to be mad, but it was entirely his fault, and that was why he was sitting here, outside the hotel, working up the courage to go inside for this stupid night of speed dating.

He couldn't let her marry just anyone. Not for money.

If it was for love, he was all in, because all he ever wanted was for her to be happy. Having that inheritance wouldn't make her happy, she wasn't about money. It was about a comfortable life for her sisters. He knew her too well to even think otherwise.

Someone tapped on his window.

"You going in or what?" Hyacinth Hawk grinned at him.

He climbed out of the truck. "Are you?"

"Yeah, I am. I don't know why." She sighed. "Hazel signed me up. She thinks that since she and Amber have found men and are blissfully happy, I need one, too."

"Typical sister," he said, though he didn't have one of his own. He had three brothers, though, and they could be total pains.

"Yup. Why are you here? Aren't you still pining for Dabney?"

"Does everyone know?" They ambled toward the doors, virtually dragging their feet.

"Not everyone. I'm more sensitive than most. Your auras mingle when you're together," she said as if everyone talked about auras.

"She's here. I'm hoping to convince her I'm not all bad."

"She'll come around," Hyacinth reassured him.

"Didn't I hear something about you and Earl from the bookshop?" he asked gently, not wanting to poke an old wound, but trying to deflect the conversation.

"Years ago, we dated. Highschool. That's ancient history. Nothing there now." She avoided looking directly at him.

"Here's to two wounded lovers finding new happiness," he declared with a mock toast. If he was a praying man, he'd be down on his knees, begging God, the universe, the Goddess, and all the other deities that were ever written about, for help.

"Well," she said as he opened the door for her, "let's do this thing. Best of luck to you." She leaned close and whispered, "I could give it a small magical shove, if you wanted me to."

"I appreciate that, but I think it's best just to go where the universe leads me."

She nodded approval. Her family didn't cast magic lightly, even though they were some of the most magical in town.

·❤·❤·❤·❤·❤·

The hotel's owner had rejigged the tables in the lounge to lay in straight rows. The lights were on, but it wasn't a daylight kind of bright. The illumination hovered right at that spot that took away hard lines and made people look their best, without it being too dark to see easily. Mood lighting.

The scene reminded him of a high school dance. Boys on one side of the room, girls on the other. Everyone sipped drinks and nervous chatter filled the room. Their tension rolled over him in waves.

"Holy crap," he whispered to Hyacinth. "This place is a zoo." There had to be sixty people from their thirties to their fifties. Who knew Three Moon Falls had this many single people?

"Holy busted wands."

"Hey, isn't that Earl."

"What? No stinking way." She pivoted on her heel. "I'm out of here."

"Stop." Sam ordered. "He's looking this way. Don't let him know he's scaring you off. Maybe you won't even get to him." He did some mental math. "At five minutes a person and one minute to shuffle between tables, and breaks, you're looking three hours minimum. You could get lucky."

"I'm not interested in Earl."

"Friends don't lie to each other." He patted her shoulder. "We've got this. You can handle Earl, and I can try and win Dabney over. This is our chance."

"I hate you right now." She grinned at him, and they fist-bumped. "Let's do this."

His first date was a fifty-four-year-old Sagittarius with six cats, no job, and entirely too much cleavage. It practically sat on the table. No, thank you.

The next was a sweet woman, a nurse at the seniors' lodge. She would have been a potential date if he was looking for a date. Guilt slammed him hard for wasting the other daters' time.

Numbers three through six didn't even make an impression on him. With each chime of a bell, the men moved to the next table. Three more stops, and he'd have his chance.

"Dude, look at me," the woman in front of him hissed. "If you're so hung up on that one," she stabbed her finger toward Dabney, "Why are you even here?"

"I am so sorry." He sighed. "We had a thing once." He smiled an apology. "I'm Sam. I apologize, and it is nice to meet you…" He left a space for her to add her name.

"April Mendez."

They chatted for a few moments. She was a very nice woman.

The bell rang, and he apologized again.

"If it doesn't work out with her, call me. I work at Tresses Hair, on Sixth."

"You are very gracious, and kinder than I deserve. If I strike out, I'll call." Under different circumstances, he would be interested. But tonight, and every night, his entire being was wrapped up in the beautiful Dabney Booth.

Two more rounds, and he stood beside Dabney's table.

She leaned back, glared, and growled, "Why are you here?"

"I'm here to talk to you. May I join you?" He did his best to keep from sounding like he was begging for her time.

"Whatever."

"Thank you." He slid into the seat and leaned forward to place his clasped hands on the table. "Hi, I'm Sam McKenna. Nice to meet you."

She rolled her eyes. "Dabney."

"Did you know Dabney means judge, or one who imparts justice?"

Her eyes widened in shock. "I did. I just didn't think you did." Her brows furrowed and her shoulders rose.

"I know everything about you. I know your middle name is Adelaide and that means noble or kind. I know your hopes and dreams. I know how big your heart is. I know you need to get married." Her glare deepened with every word. He swallowed hard. "I'd like a chance to explain myself to you."

"Ha. I have no time for more lies of omission. Or were you going to flat out lie this time?" Her voice rose and the people at the closest tables stared.

"I'll gladly accept every bit of that anger if you'll give me ten minutes of your time." He waited five seconds, then ten. His stomach roiled and twisted. Her stony expression was the toughest, scariest thing he'd ever faced.

"Tomorrow morning. Sandpiper Park. Third picnic table in. Eight a.m."

"Thank you." He couldn't stop a smile from forming.

"One chance. Ten minutes by the clock. Don't mess this up."

She shook her finger in his face, so he grabbed it and kissed the tip. "You won't regret this," he promised.

"I better not."

The bell rang again.

"Thank you, Dabney. I know I don't deserve another chance." She looked like she was going to change her mind, so he nodded and stepped away. Saved by the bell.

If he could've left at that moment without looking like a jerk, he would have, but that would've left one woman unpartnered. He was not that type of person. Instead, he stayed and tried to focus on the women he met.

Time and time again, his gaze found Dabney. More often than not, she was looking at him. Each time their gazes collided, she frowned and turned away. She wasn't as unaffected as she tried to appear.

Dabney stared at Sparky as he chatted with a pretty redhead. She looked enthralled. He seemed distracted. Good. He'd better not be enjoying other women's company if he expected to get back in her good graces.

"Did I mention my Lamborghini?" the man across from her—Bobby?—said.

"I believe you did. How do you feel about porcupines for pets?"

"What?" He reared.

"Well, they are cute." She was looking for a husband, but had no interest in a man whose entire conversation was centered on his money and material things. Aside from being able to help her sisters and the local stray animal population, she had no interest in money.

She winced. That wasn't entirely true. She appreciated money. Who didn't? But it wasn't the be-all and end-all of her life. She cared about people and the environment. Billy, or whatever his name was, had mentioned at least six high-end cars.

"I was thinking about giving up all my possessions. You know, donating them to charity, and going to live off the land in the woods."

"Lady, you're nuts."

She stifled a laugh as the bell rang. He nearly tipped his chair over in his haste to flee.

"Dabney, how are you?" Earl Cooper slid into the chair. "You haven't been into the bookshop in ages."

"Too busy. And I'm saving for Bridge's university tuition."

"Isn't she like twelve?"

"Thirteen last week."

"Everything good with you?" he asked her, though his gaze kept darting across the bar.

"Pretty good. Except for—"

"Yeah, I heard about that. I heard the police were talking to Hank about the fireworks. His mother is beside herself."

"I feel for her."

His eyes flicked away and stayed fixed on something, or someone.

She turned. "Hyacinth is pretty, isn't she?"

"I have no interest in her," he blurted.

"It's okay to be attracted to someone you can't have," she offered.

"Like you and Sam McKenna?" He smiled weakly. "You guys were in the bookstore together quite often."

"Well, that spark faded. The magic is gone."

"Magic is utter nonsense, but I'm sorry you lost what you had." He seemed genuinely compassionate.

"What's your ideal date?" Maybe she could date Earl. He was decent, except for his dislike of magic.

"A nice dinner and a movie." He stared at his hands.

"Seriously? That's what you're going with? Don't you rock climb for fun?"

"I do, but it scares women away. I do better if I tell them about that later."

"Earl, trust me on this…maybe we can't have the one we want, but the least we can do is be true to ourselves and the people we approach by being honest and upfront."

His sigh was audible. "I suppose."

They chatted for the rest of their time.

"Good luck with Sam," he said as he stood to move on to the last table. "He's a good man, and you deserve someone special. Take care now."

The next woman to sit with Sam was all hands, touching her shoulders, patting her palms on the table until she hid them on her lap. Dabney fumed as she watched.

Then came Damien, the medic who had looked after her after the accident. He didn't seem bothered by her lack of attention. "He misses you."

"No, he doesn't. He dumped me."

"Maybe he had a good reason," Damien suggested when she turned her full attention on him.

"Let's talk about you. What do you do for fun?"

"I like bungie jumping, long walks in the woods, polishing rocks, star gazing, and riding wild buffalo." He smirked.

She laughed. "You do not." In the next row over, she could just make out Sparky's glare.

"Well, the rock part is true. Once upon a time, I thought I wanted to be a geologist." He shrugged. "But somehow I ended up a medic."

"I wanted to be an engineer, but life changed that for me."

"Do you like your job?"

"I do. I like working with people. I probably would've hated cubicle work. What about you?"

"I love being a medic. Trouble is, medics, like doctors, have a bad rep for being cheaters. It scares a lot of women off."

"Firemen get that, too, from what I hear."

"Sam's not like that. He's true-blue. He hasn't dated anyone since you. He gets razzed about it all the time. You know how guys are."

"Yup. Men are pigs."

"Hey, I resemble that remark. You aren't wrong. Without a good woman to help civilize us, we're animals." He leaned back and smiled.

"Look, if this thing with you and Sam ever gets fully settled, I'd be happy to buy you dinner."

"Thanks, Damien. I think I'd enjoy that." He was definitely going on her list of potential dates. He was sweet and kind and seemed honest.

In the end, after way too long of a wait, she was given a list of fifteen men who found her suitable. Damien and Sam were both on that list. She barely remembered who the others were. Admittedly, with Sparky in the room, she hadn't paid full attention to her other dates. She'd done them a disservice.

"Can I drive you home?" Damien asked as she headed for the door.

"Oh, thank you. I'm good. I drove tonight. I'm not far away." She chuckled. "But you knew that, you've been there."

"Drive safe."

She drove home, headlights in her rearview mirror all the way. Judging by the height and distance apart, they were Sparky's. He'd followed her home more than once to ensure she arrived safely. Tonight's attention irked her as much as it softened her heart.

By the Goddess, she missed him.

Five

"Where are you going?" Emmy demanded.

"I have a meeting." Technically not a lie. She didn't want to get her sisters' hopes up for nothing. The chances of her working things out with Sparky were less than none.

"In a sundress? At seven-fifteen on a Sunday morning?" Her eyes bulged. "Are you going to church?"

"I'm not going to church, but what if I was? Witches and magic practitioners can be Christians, too."

"Where are you going?"

"I'm meeting with someone from at speed dating last night."

"Don't go. You should be dating Sam. He's a great guy. I love him." She dashed away a tear.

"Oh, honey. It isn't that easy. Sam and I broke up." Okay, he'd dumped her out of the blue. "You can't always come back from that. Look at how many of your friends' parents are divorced. Relationships end." She hugged her sister close. "No matter who I date, you and Bridge will always come first. Each and every time. I love you both."

"You love Sam, too."

"Yes, I did. I'm not sure what I feel now. Go back to bed. Have a lazy day. I promise to be home by noon. Don't forget, this is the first Sunday of the month and that means Sunday brunch." She saved her tips every week. They went for brunch once a month, the leftover funds were squirreled away for Bridge and Emmy's education. They didn't have much, but she managed to fund this one luxury every month.

Emmy trudged away, muttering under her breath. Dabney was glad she didn't understand the words, though she thought she caught *stupid* and at least one cuss word. She'd let it go today. Some battles were best left unfought. Her sisters deserved to be able to vent their emotions rather than bottle them up.

With one last sigh, she headed for Sandpiper Park. It was twenty minutes away, around the side of the lake. It was a quiet picnic area that few tourists ever discovered. Locals considered it their private beach.

She was early. Way too early. Nervous, she paced the length of the beach, sandals in hand. It was still cool, though the day promised to be a scorcher. Light clouds skittered across the sky. Seagulls squawked on the sand and flapped out of her way. She laughed at their antics, and the fact she found *sea*gulls at the lake.

High in a tree, a raven squawked. She mimicked its cry, and it flew close over her head. Emmy wasn't the only one with an affinity for animals, though mostly Dabney connected with birds, particularly crows and ravens.

She sat on a long driftwood log that must've been pushed on shore when the lake had frozen over. Spring always meant debris on the beach. Two crows perched on the end and squawked an enquiry.

"Waiting for a man," she answered, feeling silly.

The closest one squawked a second time and inched toward her.

"He dumped me," she confessed. "He broke my heart. I don't know why I agreed to meet him. It's going to bust my heart open again."

The crow tipped its head left, then right.

"Don't look at me like that. I don't still love him."

The bird cawed and it sounded exactly like he'd said, "Ha."

"Hush, you."

Her timer beeped. It was time. She stood and piled a small handful of sunflower seeds on the log. She always brought birdseed to the lake. It was a tradition her mother had started, and today, she needed to feel her mother close by. She walked away, reluctant to leave her friends.

The birds cawed and she looked back. They were pecking away at the pile.

She rounded the last corner, her feet soundless on the sandy path. Sparky stood beside the picnic table, hands stuffed in his pockets. He looked left and right. She was slightly behind him. He'd have to turn almost fully to see her. She took a moment to stare at him. Her heart ached. She blinked furiously to keep tears at bay.

Two crows landed in front of him and cawed a loud warning.

A giggle escaped her. *Were they the same birds? Were they protecting her?*

Sparky whirled around. "You're here. I thought you might stand me up."

"I keep my promises." She kept her voice cold, though she wanted to rush into his arms.

He nodded. "I brought you a caramel latte and a cheese croissant."

"Thanks. I could use a coffee." If her stomach would keep it down. She was ridiculously nervous. She couldn't shake the feeling that everything was at stake.

"Come sit, please." He waved toward a red plaid blanket on the bench. "You look pretty. I like that dress."

The dress was a light lilac with deep purple irises and rich green leaves scattered over it. It fell to just above her knee. It had delicate straps and a scooped neckline. It flattered her neck and jaw. She'd chosen it because she always felt put together when she wore it. Especially when she paired it with pretty underthings and a hand-knit lacy white cardigan. Right now, deep inside, she was trembling and on the verge of cracking. She needed the strength of looking her best to keep from shattering.

"Thank you." He looked good, too. He'd shaved and, unless she missed her guess, he'd managed to get his hair trimmed after last night's dating event. Apparently, being well known and popular came with perks.

She sat on the bench, feet planted firmly on the ground, hands knotted together in her lap. She pushed down lightly to keep her knee from jiggling up and down.

Sam paced back and forth in front of her. At this moment, he wasn't her Sparky. He was pure Sam. Straight, solid, serious, and too handsome for words.

She waited, growing impatience clawing at her insides, while he composed himself.

Finally, he stopped and faced her. He jammed his hands in his pockets and said, "Dabney…"

The crows cawed and hopped up on the table behind her.

Sam leaped back.

"Relax. They're just birds."

"I…I forgot your family has an affinity for animals."

"Ignore them. They're harmless." She wanted to rush away, but she was held fast by her need to know what was on his mind. Was he going to explain why he dumped her? She cleared her throat, wordlessly encouraging him to speak up.

"Dabney." He paused. His hands clenched and unclenched in his pockets. "Okay. I don't know where to begin."

"How about starting with why you dumped me. On our anniversary, at that." She hadn't meant to snap at him, but the harsh words just exploded out of her.

He winced. "Okay. I deserved that." He scraped his left hand down his face and jammed it back in his pocket. "There are things about me you don't know. Things that happened before either of us came to Three Moon Falls."

"I assumed so. Everyone has a history. Most of us have baggage. I try to judge people by their actions, not their past. I'm friends again with my high school bestie, even though she told lies about me." She snapped her mouth shut. He was confessing, not her.

"I moved here from Ontario. Barrie to be precise."

She nodded. Nothing new there.

"At one time, my family was very wealthy." He paced back and forth, staring at the ground and kicking little rocks and pinecones out of his way.

She'd never seen him so tense, and the statement only brought up more questions. If she had persuasion magic, which was incredibly rare, she'd zap him and make him spit out whatever he had to say faster. Sadly, she was a very low-level witch with almost no magic. Look at the disaster her catch-a-man spell turned into. She could've been hurt much worse.

Or, it could have been amazing if Hank hadn't blown her up, her mind whispered.

"My father was the CEO of a trading firm. He got greedy and starting skimming money. Eventually, he was caught." He looked at her as if he was expecting a reaction.

"And?" She couldn't understand what this had to do with their relationship.

"He was sued. We lost everything. Shortly after that, Mom and Dad died in a car accident. At least the police had ruled it an accident. I don't believe it was." He paced faster.

"That's so tragic." She went to him and placed her hand on his shoulder. "I'm sorry you went through all of that."

"That's not the end of it." He stepped away from her touch. "I have massive unpaid debt from Dad's legal bills."

She knew there had to be more. Most people had debt.

"And my uncle was similarly charged. He's in prison for life for embezzlement."

"What are you saying? I don't understand what this has to do with you. You aren't your family. You are you. All that matters is what *you* do."

"I know about the money." He swallowed hard. "I've known since your grandfather died."

"Dammit, Sam. Get to the point. What has that got to do with you, or us? So, I've got money, or might get some. Isn't that a good thing if I can remove that debt from your shoulders?"

"No!"

"What?" She wanted to beat her head against the picnic table. Getting the truth out of Sam was like pulling teeth.

"I love you. I've loved you since I met you, but I can't be with you. What if I'm a crook, too? What if I stole from you? I can live with my debts, but I can't live knowing I might do you wrong."

She cradled her head in her palms and shook it. Idiotic man. "Oh, Sparky. I don't care about that. I trust you. You're the Fire Chief. They wouldn't have given you that promotion last year if you weren't trustworthy. You've never been dishonest with me. Except when you dumped me," she added dryly. "You should have just told me."

·❤·❤·❤·❤·❤·

Sam paced back and forth. A glimmer of hope grew in his chest, like a spark fanned by the wind. She wasn't running in fear. Then, to his absolute horror, she burst into laughter.

"What the hell is so funny?" He'd just bared his soul and revealed his fears. Inherited genes were a thing. Didn't she understand that?

She leaped up and cupped his cheeks in her cold hands. "Oh, Sparky. I adore you. I wasn't laughing at you. I was laughing at me."

He didn't see what was funny about their situation.

She laughed some more and kissed him firmly on the mouth. He didn't have the strength, or the will, to stop her.

"I was laughing," she chuckled, "because I was casting a spell to bring me a man. Someone I could marry to keep the money out of my drug addict cousin's hands. I thought I failed."

He shook his head. Had she met someone at date night?

"But I woke up, and there you were. The man of my heart, right in front of me. Begging me to be okay. The magic worked. It brought you back. Maybe I'm not a failure, after all."

He backed away. "I'm not the man of your dreams, but, if you want that money for the girls, for your animal shelter, to help your cousin heal, for whatever, I'll sign a prenuptial agreement and marry you."

She laughed. "Oh, you'll sacrifice yourself for me, will you?"

Heat flooded his face. It was all he could do not to turn away. He'd skipped the truth when he dumped her, then spent months wishing he was with her and hadn't put that sad look on her face. He wasn't going to lie again.

"Okay. It's no sacrifice. I love you. I want to be with you. I want to marry you. I don't want your money. I dumped you because I didn't want you to think I was after your inheritance. And because I'm afraid I'll steal from you. My genetics run to thieves and liars."

"Have you ever stolen from me? Or from anyone?"

"No! Not since I stole a chocolate bar when I was ten."

"Have you ever lied to me? Or to my sisters?"

"Except for not telling you why I broke up with you, never. Not one white lie." That was the bold, unvarnished truth. While his father had preached honesty, he hadn't practiced it himself. Still, the value had stuck with Sam.

"Then get over here and kiss me," she demanded. "After that, we're getting married."

"But..."

"Zip it, Sparky. I trust you. My heart trusts you. And if you do anything stupid, I'll zap your ass. I'm going to visit the Hawk sisters and take some magical classes. I need to bring my magic up to its full potential."

"But the money..."

"Sparky, I'd rather have you than the money, but I'm blessed. I can have both. Are you going to kiss me, or what?"

She looked adorable with a pretend pout on her face and hands on her hips.

He swooped in and drew her into his arms. "I was such an idiot," he whispered.

She pressed her mouth to his, and for the first time in way too many months, he kissed her. He kissed her until his knees went weak and he was breathless. Tendrils of happiness and arousal coursed through him.

"Whoa." He leaned back and looked down at her blissful face. Her gray-green eyes shone. "You pack a punch."

"You might say...I'm magical." Laughing, she ran from him. "Race you to the beach."

He grabbed their coffees, the snacks, and the blanket. He hurried after her, the crows calling encouragingly overhead.

She waited for him, hands on her hips. "What took you so long?"

"I brought your breakfast. I know how you are without coffee. I didn't want you to zap me," he teased back, but she had already zapped him. She'd zapped his heart at first sight, and he was lost. Thank the Goddess she'd let him back in.

Six

Dabney stared up at the clouds skimming across the sky. It was a beautiful day. A perfect and gorgeous one for a wedding. She had a rare day off that coincided with Sparky's. It was the perfect day to bring their lives together. Warm air, a light breeze, and bright sunshine. Good omens, all of them.

"Are you ready for this?" Emmy asked her. "I can't believe you're getting married."

"Me, either," Bridge declared, smoothing the lace of her new dress.

"Me, either," Dabney laughed. "I'm so glad Sparky and I worked things out."

"You never told us what happened," Emmy said.

"And I never will. Our relationship is our business. Suffice it to say, we made up and we'll be happy together. And," she giggled, "we're set for life. Bridge can finish school and go to college or university without worrying about money. We can open our sanctuary. I can open my own nail salon if I decide that's what I want to do. I can go to university, or take night classes, or quit work. We're free to do whatever we want." She paused. "But we're not letting the money ruin us. We're not wasting it." She grinned. "Life is wonderful, but most wonderful is that I get to spend the rest of my life with Sparky."

"You do know my name is Sam, right?" He wrapped his arms around her.

"Not to me. You'll always be my Sparky. Let's do this."

Bridge and Emmy ran ahead to the beach where the minister and their friends waited.

Hyacinth waited beside her sisters, Amber, Lazuli, and Hazel. They'd become close friends in the two weeks since she and Sparky had made up. The girls from the beauty shop stood alongside Sparky's firefighter friends and his brothers. The mayor was there in her weird sandals, red shirt, and purple floral pants. Who knew she was magical, too? She was supervising the wedding on behalf of the magic council. While the council had no say in marriages, they did keep track. Sort of a magical version of public records.

Hand-in-hand, Dabney raced across the sand with Sparky.

They paused in front of a minister. First, a traditional marriage, then a Wiccan hand-fasting.

Sparky turned Dabney to face him. She smiled into his shining eyes, absorbing the love that glowed in their depths.

"I love you." He leaned in and kissed her passionately. Liquid heat ran down her spine and her entire body sprang to life. She lost herself in the kiss until the small crowd cheered.

"Ahem," the minister cleared his throat. "You're supposed to kiss her after the ceremony."

Dabney laughed.

"Sorry, I couldn't wait." He kissed her again.

Someone in the crowd called, "Get a room."

Everyone laughed.

She slipped her hand into Sam's, and their life together began with crows calling overhead.

This novella is connected to the "Three Moon Falls" series by Katie O'Connor.

Lucky Me

Declan's family is cursed.
For the past one-hundred years,
bad things happen if they fall in love.
So he lives his life one woman at a time.
Until he meets Lily, and finds himself
wishing for a forever that can never be.
Yet their fate encounter and one week of bliss
just might be enough to turn his luck around.

Kelly Moran

LUCKY ME

Kelly Moran

Day One

The first time I saw her was in late summer. St. Louis had been at the tail end of a blistering heat wave, so hot the asphalt radiated like a cast iron skillet and merely blinking was enough to land you in the hospital from too much exertion. She was sitting on a bench in the park next to the library, a book in her hand and back to me. I'd had my eight-year-old nephew Liam with me. I'd thought to let him run through the wading pool before we headed back to my apartment after our lunch. One look at her, and she'd stopped me dead in my tracks.

I'm still not entirely sure if it had been her dark hair trying to break free of the orderly knot at the back of her head, the pencil skirt and white blouse that had made her seem so sophisticated, or the shamrock tattoo on her elegant nape that had first drawn my attention. Probably the ink. Clovers had been a bone of contention in my family since my great-grandfather had thrust us into our one-hundred year curse. Irish or not, myth or not, the shamrock was not a lucky charm in the O'Leary clan.

Regardless of what had drawn me to her, the sizzle in my gut and pull on my balls had been something akin to impact. Sending my nephew ahead to the playground within sight, I'd rounded the bench and said something brilliant like, "Hot one outside today."

Which was interesting because beauty didn't typically strike me stupid. I'd had women before, had basked in their loveliness, had taken many to bed. All had been left satisfied—screaming my name, mewing their post-coital pleasure, panting for breath...and wishing for more. That's not arrogance, it's fact. Due to my family's...bad luck, picket fences and ever-afters would never be in the cards. So, I'd learned long ago to take—and give—pleasure and happiness where I could. Practice made perfect. I was a master at foreplay, verbal or otherwise. I did not get tongue-tied or flustered in a female's presence.

She'd glanced up from her book and had struck me blind with a pair of cerulean blue eyes. Framed by thick black lashes, they were the kind of eyes that made a man notice that particular feature before all others. Even an ass like myself had been trapped by them for what seemed a good hundred years before I'd taken in her slight curves, full breasts, and long holy-hell legs. Fantasy after fantasy had pummeled my brain as I devoured her.

I said I was an ass.

With a tilt of her head, those bow-shaped lips of hers had started moving. It had taken concentration, but I'd focused on what she'd said. And that had proved fruitless because whatever wonderful insight had drifted from her perfect mouth had been spoken in another language. French, I believe.

My gaze had dipped to the book in her lap. *Wuthering Heights*. I should've lost interest at that point. Any woman who read Bronte for fun was dangerous. Alas, it had only peaked my curiosity. The edition had been in English. Which meant she'd been trying to brush me off by responding in French.

With a dip of my chin and smile tugging my mouth, I'd said, "Have it your way, *a mo rún*." Irish Translation: my secret. I hadn't planned on giving up. I'd figured I'd let Liam cool down in the pool and swing back that way to see her again. Much to my errant discontent, she'd been gone when we'd returned.

To say she'd crossed my mind in the ensuing months would be like saying the Atlantic Ocean was a puddle. I'd drifted to the same park countless times and had never spotted her there again.

One week before Christmas, however, I'd just stepped out of the office building where I worked after a staff meeting I'd wished I'd called in sick for, and there she'd been. Across the street from the newspaper headquarters, she'd worn a red peacoat, white scarf, and black pants as she walked with purpose on the sidewalk. Her dark hair was loose around her shoulders and trailed halfway down her back. In her hand had been a to-go cup of coffee from an independent bean house I loved. I'd done a double—and then a triple—take, not believing it had been her. Frozen in my spot, I'd stared as she'd gotten farther and farther away.

Then, she'd turned her head as if someone had called her name. Her blue gaze scanned the area, landed on me, and stalled. The breath left my lungs in a whoosh, expelling frost before my face that had been carried away by a bitter wind. She'd tilted her head, much like she'd done a few months prior, and smiled.

Then, she was gone. Again.

Kicked into gear, I'd crossed the busy street, nearly gotten myself killed in traffic, and chased after her for several blocks. With no sign of her, I'd ventured into the coffee house to ask around and had received not one stitch of information. I'd even visited the shop every day for a week at the same time each morning, and nothing.

A few weeks later, while attending the mayor's annual New Year's Eve party at the St. Louis Art Museum on Fine Arts Drive, champagne halfway to my mouth and five minutes until midnight, I'd glanced across the crowded room. And saw her. Alone in a corner, she had on a strapless emerald dress that enhanced her hourglass curves and dipped low enough in the front to draw my attention from her eyes to the creamy white swell of her breasts. Her hair had been loosely pinned off her neck in some elaborate feminine style.

Champagne flute in her hand, a wistful, distant smile on her lips, her gaze drifted from the people dancing to the caterer's table and, finally, to me. For a moment, her brows arched, as if she'd realized running into each other had become an epidemic, too. Slowly, her mouth widened into a grin that had me dizzy and grappling for stable ground.

One of the men I'd been chatting with tapped my shoulder to say his goodbyes, and I'd reluctantly torn my gaze from her to extend courtesy. I'd shaken the banker's hand as the crowd started counting down the new year.

Ten, nine...

I'd turned, ready to head to my mystery woman's corner to, at the very least, get her name. Are you seeing the pattern? Can you guess what happened next?

Eight, seven...

Yeah, luck had never been on my side and, combined with the family curse, I'd been screwed from the first blink of her baby blues. She was destined to be an elusive, intangible blip in my life—a cock and mind tease to the nth degree.

Six, five...

I'd set my glass on a passing waiter's tray and strode to where I'd last seen her. Pissed off, I'd turned three-hundred and sixty degrees.

Four, three...

I'd woven through the bodies. Checked the hallway and front foyer.

Two, one...

Gone, baby, gone.

Happy New Year it was not. I'd searched the grounds, the street, asked the doormen. She had dissolved into the night like she had vanished the last two times I'd encountered her.

Three plus months had passed since then. Little more than a week before the dreaded St. Patrick's Day holiday, and I sat in my brother's pub at a high top table with two of my best former college buddies, scaling the joint for my next conquest. My heart wasn't in it. Truth be told, I hadn't had a woman since the second time I'd encountered *her* right before Christmas. Hell of a dry spell for me.

Heath was married and had kid number one on the way. He was ensnared in Josh's tale of Valentine's gone wrong. A perpetual bachelor, like myself, Josh relayed his credence to never date on Cupid's day. I pretty much chalked the hearts-and-shit holiday to an excuse for greeting cards to sell more baubles.

I sipped my whiskey, half-listening to my mates. The place was pretty busy for a Friday night. It was ladies' night and there were plenty of them.

Only a few open tables remained, coupled with a handful of bar stools. Desperation clung to the air. Ice clanked in glasses. Laugher rose over the Celtic music playing through the speakers.

My brother knew how to run a great pub, that was for sure. Gleaming, polished wood, green leather seats, a stone hearth in the corner. Brass fixtures reflected the old-world lanterns. Irish Eyes had been quite the success in the ten years since Aiden had opened.

The familiar jangle of the door, followed by a brisk, cold blast of air, barely registered in my head. I swirled the ice in my glass, ready to call it a night, despite the early hour and me not needing to work in the morning. I'd turned in a few articles at the newspaper this morning, so I was good for a couple weeks.

"Serious potential, nine o'clock," Josh said.

Sighing, I lifted my head, glanced at the door, and stilled. No goddamn way. "Son of a bitch. It's her."

"Her who?" Heath asked, following my gaze.

"The woman from the park." Edging forward, I watched as she stripped out of a blue raincoat and set it on the back of a stool. Leaning over the bar, she kissed my brother on the cheek and took a seat. Tonight she had on a red T-shirt and a pair of skinny jeans that did fan-fuck-ing-tastic things for her legs. I couldn't make out what the shirt said from here. Her hair was in a high ponytail, little wisps floating around her face.

"Are you serious?"

Unwilling to lose sight of her again, lest she disappear, I nodded for Josh's benefit.

Something strange took hold of me, made me unable to move. Everything inside my head screamed to stay right where I was, not to engage. My strange fascination for her was unlike me and not healthy. Despite my mind's two cents, my body wasn't listening to direct orders. She was pulling me into her orbit without her even knowing I was in the pub. She hadn't looked my way.

"Damn. Does that mean she's off limits?"

I growled. "Fuck, yes." Apparently, she made me territorial, too. My buddies and I had an unspoken rule. We didn't sleep with the same women and we didn't step in when the others were interested. Period. I trusted Josh to get the hint, yet... The thought of someone else touching her had red-hot flames licking under my skin and my temples pounding. Standing, I grabbed my glass. "Dibs," I said, like we were back at the University of Missouri at a frat party.

Blood roaring, body vibrating, I made my way across the hardwood floor. With every step closer to her, my heart pounded. I was finally going to talk to her. Learn her name. More...

Three, two, one.

Leaning an elbow on the bar, I faced her. "Of all the gin joints in all the world, you walk into mine." Cheesy? A little. I didn't use lines to pick up women, didn't need to, but part of me wanted to test her. At twenty-eight years old, most of my generation had not seen the movie *Casablanca*. In the barest glances I've had of her, I noticed she had a world-weary way about her, a grace rarely seen nowadays. I was more curious than anything whether she recognized the film. Besides, it broke the ice.

She turned to me, those shocking blue eyes widening in surprise for a flicker of an instant before returning to aloof. "Seeing as this is an Irish pub, wouldn't it be more prudent to say 'of all the whiskey joints?'"

Even as a flare of disappointment hit for her not acknowledging the nature of the quote, I smiled. "Witty." I sat on the stool next to her.

Smiling, she dropped her chin in her palm. "And technically, this is Aiden's bar, not yours."

"Touché." But how did she know that, or my brother, for that matter?

As if summoned, Aiden made his way to us, wiping a glass with a white towel. "Declan. Need a refill?" My brother, four years older than me, was a good-looking guy, but eight years of raising Liam as a single father had worn on him. Or perhaps, it was just time that crinkled the corners of his eyes and had gray weaving through his black hair.

"I'm good." I turned to my mystery woman.

Ah, the head tilt. I couldn't tell yet if she did this out of interest or acknowledgement. "Does using Bogart quotes from *Casablanca* typically work for you when trying to pick up women?"

Fuck me. My interest in her notched to all-consuming. I shrugged with a nonchalance I didn't feel. "Don't know, *a mo rún*. I've never tried before." I held out my hand. "Declan O'Leary."

"Lily Durand." She didn't hesitate in shaking my hand. Her grip was firm and delicate at the same time. Her skin, smooth as glass and warm as a good ale hitting my gut, sent my pulse thumping hard. I wondered if she was this soft everywhere and intended to find out.

"You, Lily Durand, are a hard woman to pin down."

Amusement lit her eyes, curved her lips, and I wanted to kiss that sexy little mouth until she felt something else entirely. "Am I?"

I gave her a grunt of agreement. "Three times I accidently run into you, and three times you escaped me." No way in hell was it happening again.

Her eyebrows arched. "We'll always have Paris."

My fingers tightened around my glass. My balls ached in pure, unadulterated desire. The combination of her quoting *Casablanca* back to me and her teasing me over speaking French the first time we'd met was so...fucking...hot. "One might call this encounter fate."

She took a sip from her pint in response, eyeing me over the top of the glass. Her curious—and interested—gaze swept my face.

My family didn't carry the typical Irish fair skin and hair, but rather the Celtic end, or Black Irish, as some would say. My eyes were as green as summer grass in the old country, so I've been told, and I had a perpetual shadow on my jaw either from being unwilling or not interested in shaving. I once dated an artist who said I had perfect symmetry to my face and high cheekbones. I take care of myself, eat right, and work out three times a week at my home gym. I had the defined arms and wide shoulders, along with the six pack abs, women found attractive. Again, not arrogance, fact.

I appreciated women, all sizes, but those who took care with their appearance turned my head first. Not out of a sense of vanity, but because it reflected confidence in themselves. To me, this didn't mean makeup and designer clothes. In honesty, I could care less what a woman wore or what size jeans she filled. It was how they carried themselves that roped me in, and appearance played a small part in that. Curves were so much more of a turn on than a slender rail who had nothing to hold onto. A woman who wasn't afraid to eat and then play to work the calories off did it for me. And a sharp mind was as sexy as killer legs.

Attraction be damned, those were the kind of women I stayed clear from. A matter of survival. And all those traits Lily seemed to possess. Yet here I was, playing with temptation.

Now that I was up close, I read the phrase on her T-shirt. *I'm not Irish, but you can kiss me anyway.* Hmm. In time.

I dipped my head, indicating her shirt. "Is that an invitation?"

She set her pint down, keeping her long fingers on the glass, and drew a deep breath. "How do you know Aiden?"

Was she trying to get details from me or assessing whether I was safe to concede? Didn't matter. "He's my older brother."

She glanced at Aiden, still standing behind the bar, as if to ask, *Is this guy legit?*

Aiden's gaze slid to me and back to Lily. He nodded, smiling as if reassuring her. Who knew my big brother could be a decent wingman? Aiden hadn't dated since he'd met his wife, who had died delivering Liam, her death a result of the O'Leary curse, Dad said. Our age gap had desisted us hanging out in the same circles until I'd graduated college. Either way, whatever Aiden's connection to Lily was, it wasn't sexual.

"You are quite the vision, Lily." I liked the way her name sounded when I said it. And she was quite lovely. Pale skin, dark hair, long lashes. And her eyes? I couldn't wait to see them clouded with lust as I drove into her. In this light, her hair had the slightest hint of reddish highlights and would look perfect wrapped around my hand.

"Thank you." Smile. "You're not hard on the eyes either, Declan."

I groaned. It couldn't be helped. The way she said my name had me past half-mast. She had a soft tone that drifted like smoke and clung to everything within range.

I raked my gaze over her, loving her hourglass shape. She either had great genes or worked out regularly. Her hottest asset wasn't her rack or her legs, though. It was her understated self-assurance. She didn't flaunt her intelligence or shy from a compliment. And her sense of humor? Needless to say, I had to adjust myself on the stool.

Impatient, I dialed my voice to hoarse. "Would you like you take this conversation to a more private venue? My apartment, for instance?" My fingers clenched my glass again. I never took women to my place. It was theirs or a hotel. I didn't like the invasion of privacy or the possibility of one of my lovers going stalker. It hadn't happened, but call me paranoid.

And without hesitation, I'd invited her as if I hadn't set that rule for a reason. By the look on her face, she was considering.

Her gaze skimmed the tats on my right arm that disappeared under my white tee—a sleeve of writing in Gaelic. "I don't date men with tattoos." She said it without any criticism or condemnation, as if she was testing me, not being judgmental.

A rough laugh dragged from my throat. Remembering the shamrock tattoo on her nape, I lifted my hand and skimmed my fingers over her neck. A caress. Light. Sensual. "Said the woman with her own ink." I ran my fingertips in a slow circle, teasing her hair and eliciting a shiver from her. "And, *a mo rún*, I never said anything about dating."

I dropped my hand, and she sucked in a breath, pink tingeing her cheeks. I swallowed another groan at her responsiveness.

Aiden stepped away to take care of a customer. I waited until he was out of hearing range, then asked, "How do you know my brother?" I knew Liam's teachers and babysitters, and she wasn't one of them. Aiden didn't get out much. He lived at the bar, and I would've recognized if she was a regular, so I was more than curious.

"We..." She brushed away a strand of hair from her face and gave a slight shake of her head, as if deciding not to divulge the information after all. "I've known him a couple years. We're friendly acquaintances."

I nodded like that was enough for me, which it wasn't. "Have you slept with him?" I was pretty certain she hadn't, since Aiden didn't date or screw. I didn't share and, despite wanting her more than was wise, I'd slam the brakes right now if she'd been with Aiden.

Her gaze whipped to mine, wide. Appalled. "No."

I nodded again. "Are you married?" She didn't wear a ring.

She shook her head, and I was nearing the end of my rope. For seven months she'd been in my head, one way or another. I wanted her under me, on top of me, bent over the nearest hard surface.

"Then there's nothing stopping us, *a mo rún*." The huskiness in my tone wasn't deliberate, but my cock twitched against my zipper as her pupils dilated.

Her teeth sank into her lower lip. "What does that phrase mean? You keep using it."

I knew I had her. Instinct and her signals told me. It was all I could do not to stroke myself through my jeans. I leaned close to whisper in her ear, making sure my lips caressed the shell. "It's Gaelic and means *my secret.*"

She shivered and I smiled in satisfaction. We were gonna be so fucking good. I nuzzled my nose against the soft spot behind her ear, breathing in her light perfume, before easing away. She looked at me through heavy lids, her lips parted with shallow breaths.

Fuck, yes.

I tucked a piece of hair behind her ear, letting my touch linger on her cheek. "Hand me your phone."

A tiny wrinkle formed between her brows. "What?"

"Your phone. May I see it?"

She blinked and reached for her purse on the bar, pulling out her cell and handing it to me. She seemed more than a little confused and too turned on to realize what she was doing.

I swiped the screen and sent myself a text. I wasn't taking any chances in not getting her contact info. I tapped into her settings and spoke as my thumbs went to work. "I get regular health exams, never have sex without a condom, and I've never been arrested. Talk to Aiden. He'll tell you you're safe with me." Finished, I gave her back the phone and retrieved mine from my pocket, thumbing a text. "I put my address and phone number in your contacts."

Her gaze jerked to her cell as it pinged.

Her text to me, which I'd sent, said: *Hello, Declan. I want you.*

My response: *Hello, a mo rún. You have me.*

Slowly, her cautious gaze slid to mine. Held. In the span of seconds, we stared at one another, her pulse beating hard in her neck and my heart thumping against my ribs. Anticipation coiled in my gut, tightened the base of my spine.

After an appropriate amount of time, I smiled. "I'm going to head back to my place now. Talk to Aiden. Come to me afterward. I'll be waiting for you."

It was a gamble, walking away from her. But this time, I had a name and a number. If she decided not to meet me tonight, I'd keep at her until I changed her mind. This was going to happen. She wanted me. I wanted her.

Heading to the table, I grabbed my coat, said goodnight to the guys, and walked back to the bar while shrugging into my jacket. One hand on the counter, the other on the back of her stool, I brought my face to hers until we shared the same air.

My lips feathered hers. "I'll. Be. Waiting."

Day Two

I stood at the wall of windows in my apartment two hours later, staring off into the distance at the Eads Bridge and Mississippi River. The night was clear, stars winking against the inky blackness. Lights from other buildings flickered. Cars passed. Still, I stood, calm everywhere but inside me.

It was past midnight and she hadn't showed. Disappointment flooded me, made me ache. And I was more than a little shaken it wasn't just a physical tug I felt toward her. Her mind was fascinating, at least what I'd gathered from our short conversation. I found myself wanting to know more about her. What she did for a living. If she had any family.

Sighing, I slammed the last of my whiskey neat and headed toward the kitchen. The drink hadn't soothed my tension. I'd given more than ample time for her to come to me. Though I wasn't tired, it was best I head to bed. In the morning, I'd call Aiden and find out what he knew about her. Maybe drop her a text to remind her I was around.

Desperate, much?

I rinsed my glass in the sink when the ding from the elevator alerted me someone was on their way up. The only one with a key was Aiden and he'd still be at the pub. I'd told the doorman it would be okay to let Lily up, if she showed.

Heart hammering, I jerked my head around. The lights above my entrance indicated the car would stop in seconds. Frozen, my gaze riveted to the elevator doors, I waited.

Ding. Swoosh.

Aiden stepped into my apartment with...Lily behind him. My gaze went right past my brother and latched onto her like a man starving. The familiar punch to the gut at seeing her nearly knocked me back a step. She offered me a weak smile and looked around, while I breathed for the first time in what seemed like minutes.

Aiden squeezed her shoulder. "You all set?"

She nodded, her smile encouraging. "Thank you."

"Anytime. Why don't you head inside? I need to talk to Declan before I head out." Aiden waited until she'd walked deeper into my apartment before turning to me. "She wanted me to bring her," he said in a quiet tone. "I had to wait until another bartender could fill in before leaving."

I nodded, respecting her caution. After all, she barely knew me.

"Listen." Aiden stepped closer and leaned against the counter, crossing his arms. "I don't get involved in your affairs. If you want to start something with her, that's fine. None of my business. But you can't fall for her. Hear me? You have to keep her away from the curse. I like her. She's a nice—"

"I got it." It wasn't as if I didn't know the consequences of falling in love, hadn't had it rammed into my skull from birth. It was exactly why I lived my life the way I did. No strings, no commitments. Part of me often questioned whether our family's bad luck was mostly hysteria, the belief in the supposed curse so strong it gave it validation. But the facts made that argument null. History was proof. "You know me. I don't get attached."

Aiden studied me a long minute, his gray-blue eyes weary. "All right." He shoved off the counter and wrapped me in a brief hug, slapping my back as he pulled away. "Love you."

"Love you, too."

After Aiden left, I turned toward the living room. Across the space of my vast apartment, she stood by the bank of windows in the same spot I'd vacated a few minutes before. Her back to me, she faced the view, still in her blue raincoat, purse clutched in her hands by her chest. I shook my head, wondering why she looked so right standing there. She'd never been here before. I'd never had a woman here that wasn't family. Yet, there was my mystery woman, looking like she was home.

I cleared my throat. "Would you like something to drink?" I moved around the open kitchen and into the living room, keeping distance between us.

She turned her head. "No, thank you. You have an amazing place. It's so big. I love the view."

I glanced around, trying to see it from her perspective. Because the windows let in a lot of light, I'd been able to paint the walls a dark green. My leather sectional was navy, my tables black walnut. The pine hardwood floors ran throughout the apartment, including the three bedrooms, except in the kitchen where I had earth-tone granite. My cabinets were white, the countertop marble. The art on my walls was mainly enlarged photographs from my visits to Ireland.

"It's home." I shrugged.

"Do you rent or own?"

"Own. Since I graduated college. The top five floors are privately owned. The rest of the building is rental units." We O'Learys weren't rolling in pots of gold, but we were comfortable. We were good with our money. Our women, not so much.

"That explains why Aiden needed a key for the elevator."

I nodded. "Can I take your coat?"

"Oh." She breathed a laugh that had me closing my eyes to savor the sound. "Yes." She slipped out of the jacket and passed it to me.

I was tempted to hang it in the hall closet, but strangely didn't want to move that far from her, so I set it on the coffee table. She placed her purse on top and stared at it, her expression unreadable. I wanted to touch her so badly my hands flexed.

"I didn't think you were going to come."

She smiled, the gesture not quite reaching her eyes, and met my gaze. "Honestly, I wasn't sure I would, either. I don't typically do this kind of thing."

If that was true, and I had no doubt it was, then talking out her anxiety might be a good move. "Don't do what sort of thing?"

Her eyebrows quirked, her expression pure *duh*. "Go home with strange men. Have one night stands."

Her straight-forwardness made me realize she wasn't anxious or nervous, just out of her element. I gestured to the sofa and took a seat a foot away to give her time to adjust.

"I'm not strange," I said to lighten the mood, and her grin had me biting back a groan. Christ. I don't think I've ever desired a woman the way I did her. "What made you decide to come then?" Not that I was sorry she had, but everything about her had me curious, wanting to probe into that beautiful head of hers. Such an enigma.

Taking a deep breath as if to fortify herself, she lowered her lashes. "About ten months ago, I...decided to take more chances. Not play things so safe. Live a little."

"What sparked the change?" She didn't strike me as the type to not go after what she wanted or someone who played it too close to the vest. She wasn't pushy, but she was direct. Just how had she thought she wasn't living?

She opened her mouth as if to speak, but then pressed her lips into a line and shook her head once. Her striking blue eyes glanced away, more than a trace of grief in them.

Okay, so that wasn't up for discussion. Disappointment shoved around in my chest, but I couldn't blame her. I was shocked at how badly I wanted to know. Veering around the why, I focused on the how. "What sorts of things do you want to try with regards to your change? I'm assuming sex has something to do with it, since you're here."

Her head tilted, and I fought a grin. She could go from aloof to hot to adorable faster than a downshift of my Mustang.

She lifted her hand and dropped it back in her lap. "Sex has been unsatisfactory."

Not for long, but I kept mum on that. I propped my elbow on the back of the couch and rested my head in my hand. "Have you had a lot of partners?" I should really stop with the talk and get right to the action. Her backstory and reasons shouldn't matter. I should rock her world and send her on her way.

Her gaze direct, she shrugged. "Enough, sure. I'm just not very good at being assertive when it comes to the bedroom. I've only slept with men who I've been in a relationship with and they've controlled the act."

I was incredibly turned on she wasn't afraid to be honest, that she could look me in the eye and state her issue. No looking away or shyness. "Sex isn't about control, unless you're in a Dom/sub situation, which I'm not into. I prefer my lovers to give and take." Though, truly, I'd been with all types. A lot of my encounters had let me do all the work. I was good with that, just not all the time. There was nothing sexier than being fucked by a woman, and I was man enough to admit it.

"I'm not a prude or anything. I just want to try something besides... missionary."

Christ. I could show her all kinds of positions. A dozen ran through my mind right now. "First, I never said you were a prude." The fact she was here and having this conversation proved that. "Second, are you telling me you've not made love other than in missionary?" Because, hell. Ten more positions popped in my filthy, filthy mind.

Her blue gaze studied me. "Not really, no. I..."

I gave her a second, but she didn't finish the thought. "What happens when you're with a guy? Do you freeze up?"

She sighed. "Not at all. I enjoy sex. I don't always get off, though." She paused and looked at me, really looked, as if trying to phrase her words just right. "I want to experiment a little. I want to be..."

Ah ha. And there we have it. She wasn't apprehensive or shy about sex. She just didn't know how to ask for what she wanted. Her experiences had been boring as shit and unsatisfactory for that reason, coupled with the fact her lovers had sucked. So, she'd settled for tedium. Until, for whatever reason, she decided to change that. Go after a better O and came to me.

My cock stirred from half-mast to want-her-now. "You want to fuck and be fucked in return."

Her cheeks went crimson, but her eyes never left mine. Her lips parted, breaths shallow. "Yes," she whispered.

When her gaze dipped, exploring my body, I groaned. Heat fanned my skin as if she'd touched me. She bit her lower lip, gaze halting over my fly.

That's right. Look at what you do to me.

"What you're referring to would take more than a night. You're not going to be comfortable using assertion after a few hours. I'm good, but I'm not that good. There's only so many hours in one night." I'd put them to good use. But come tomorrow morning, she'd be gone and seeking new ventures with different potentials. The thought sent a tendril of unease through me. She was no virgin and gave off every indication she could take care of herself, but not every guy handled his lovers with respect like I did. The thought of someone hurting her made my jaw clench. Hard. And yeah, I didn't want anyone else touching her. Which was a problem. "Stay the week with me."

Fuck. That *was* my voice and those words *had* just left my mouth. Fuck again.

Her head reared, blue eyes wide. She licked her lips, and the image of that mouth wrapped around my cock had me stroking myself through my jeans for relief. And, suddenly, I didn't care that she was in my apartment where no other woman had been. Didn't care that I'd just offered to keep her here for a week, which was exactly six days longer than I'd ever promised another.

I was so screwed.

Lifting my hand, I traced a finger along her collarbone over the edge of her shirt. "Look at it this way. You can experiment with being open with no risks. Relationships aren't my bag. I don't date. One week. I'll get what I want and give you what you need, so when you get involved with your next boyfriend, you'll be less concerned about taking initiative. We'll count tonight, or last night, as day one."

Grabbing my hand, she stilled my movement. "Are you sure about this?"

No. But I wanted her, and one night would never be enough. "Positive." I kissed her fingers and set her hand down on my lap. "I have rules, though."

A sexy as hell slow grin curved her mouth. "Is this the part where you tell me your tastes are very singular and you slide a contract in front of me? Unlock your red room?"

My breath caught and my cock jerked. The woman had read *Wuthering Heights* and *Fifty Shades*. What an interesting conundrum she was. Swear to God, if she started quoting *Lord of the Rings*, I'd come right in my jeans. "I told you I'm not into BDSM. The occasional hand restraints are fine, but that's where my interest ends."

"Okay." Grin remaining, she blinked. "What are these rules?"

"First, honesty at all times. If you don't like something, if I get too rough or not rough enough, or if you want to try something, you tell me. No matter what."

Mirroring my pose, she set her elbow on the back of the couch and rested her head in her hand. "Agree."

"Second, condoms are non-negotiable. I don't fuck without them."

She nodded. "Agree."

"Third, and lastly, no falling for each other. I'm dead serious on the no relationship thing."

Her eyebrows lifted in amusement. "Agree. That's all?"

I wondered just what she thought my rules were going to be, but she agreed quickly, so I nodded.

"I have two rules to add to the...verbal contract."

I fought a grin. Damn. She was something. "Shoot."

She held up a finger. "You don't date, so having a lover suddenly underfoot will be an adjustment for you. I want you to tell me if it's too much. I can sleep on the couch or at my place if that happens. We can still hook up, minus the roomies." Up came another finger. "And when this week is over, no awkwardness. Aiden is my friend and your brother. It's likely we'll run into each other again."

She just might be the perfect woman. "Agree and agree." My gaze roamed over her curvy body. "We done talking?"

"Yes." Her smile was a cross between endearing and naughty.

"Good. Come closer."

Scooting over, her hip met mine. "Better?"

As an answer, I cupped the back of her neck and brought her mouth to mine. Impact. There's always that moment of anticipation when kissing a woman for the first time. Part heart tripping, part tightening in the gut. How a woman kissed said a lot about her. More than sex, kissing was an intimate act. It told a story.

My lips brushed hers, testing, cajoling. A sigh fluttered from her, and I dipped my tongue in to taste her. Dark ale and a trace of mint. Jaw wide, she stroked my tongue with hers, no retreating, no tease. She went right after me. Long, languid caresses that were neither pushy nor aggressive. Lily's kiss was a mirror to what I knew about her personality thus far. She was careful, but willing. Sensual and sweet. She liked exploring versus rushing.

What I'd planned to be a slow seduction—we had time, after all—quickly morphed into a devouring. Warm, wet, her lips sealed around mine, closing the gap and upping the game. I threaded my fingers in her hair and the scent of her light perfume swirled around me. Like her, the fragrance was warm and inviting. A mix of musk and something fruity, like an aged sweet lambrusco wine.

I eased back to whisper against her lips. "What do you want?"

Her hooded gaze locked onto mine. It reminded me of blue ice melting in a tumbler. "You."

I groaned. I ached. "How do you want me? Tell me." This was about her, but I couldn't wait much longer. Months of curiosity and insane interest were coming to a head. We could do more discovery later, learn one another better after the first taking was out of the way. "Better yet, show me."

A slight hesitation, then her leg slid over mine and she straddled me. My hands immediately went to her hips and I thrust against her through our clothes. They needed to go. A strangled cry parted her red lips, and she cupped my jaw, closing in for another kiss.

Before we both lost our fucking minds entirely, keeping her mouth fused to mine, I lifted my hips and withdrew my wallet from my back pocket. Fumbling by touch alone, I located the condom, tossed it next to us on the cushion, and threw my wallet on the floor.

Her fingers raked down my chest, nails dipping into the indentations of muscle, before she stopped at the hem of my shirt.

"Do it," I encouraged.

She shoved the material up and over my head, then skimmed her heated gaze over me, stopping at my tattoo sleeve. Tracing the letters with her fingers, she licked her lips. "I'm assuming this is Gaelic. What does it say?"

No one had ever asked me that before. Most women saw the foreign language and handwritten scrawl, nothing more. I don't know why, but uneasiness ratcheted in my chest. The tat was something I'd done for myself, not for anyone else, but would she think me a sap?

Clearing my throat, I recited the poem from memory. *"When you are old and grey and full of sleep, and nodding by the fire, take down this book, and slowly read, and dream of the soft look your eyes had once, and of their shadows deep. How many loved your moments of glad grace, and loved your beauty with love false or true, but one man loved the pilgrim soul in you, and loved the sorrows of your changing face, and bending down beside the glowing bars..."*

She recited the last part with me. *"Murmur, a little sadly, how love fled and paced upon the mountains overhead, and hid his face amid a crowd of stars."* Swallowing, her gaze met mine. "You tattooed a Yeats poem on your arm?"

I couldn't read her right now, and it was pissing me off. I don't think I'd ever felt more vulnerable in my life than I did in this moment, and I had no fucking clue why. Added to that, the fact she knew the sonnet enough to quote with me had to be one of the sexiest things I'd ever encountered.

"He was a great Irish poet, what can I say?"

She nodded slowly, gaze distant. *"Oui, il était un brillant poète. Et vous me surprenez, mon secret."*

About the only word in there I understood was *oui*, meaning yes. She needed to speak French while I was driving into her. It just became a new fantasy. "What does that translate to?"

"Yes, he was a brilliant poet. And you surprise me, my secret."

I sucked in a lungful of air, my cock so hard it was bound to bust my zipper. I don't know what had come over me, calling her *my secret*, but to have her use it in return was...fuck. I didn't know what.

"Do you speak fluent Gaelic?"

I shook my head. "Enough phrases to get by. You seem pretty good with French."

She nodded. "It was my elective in high school, and I kept learning from there."

Brains were hot. Grabbing her by the hips, I lifted her off my lap and set her on the floor. I had both of us stripped bare, condom in place, and her straddling my thighs before she even knew what hit her.

The sight of her stalled my lungs. Pale, creamy skin. Rosy pink nipples budded to hard points on the most amazing breasts, too full for a handful. Flat stomach, narrow waist, and hips that flared in a perfect hourglass. A small triangle of dark hair covered her mound, but she was bare below it.

"You're beautiful, Lily." Leaning forward, I feathered my lips across her neck, her throat. "Tell me something else in French. I don't care what." My hand closed around one breast, kneading, while the other held her hip, fingers digging into her soft flesh.

Breathing ragged, she gripped my shoulders. *"Qui se sentent si bon.* That feels so good." A delicious little humming noise escaped her throat. "Don't stop."

I almost laughed. "Not a chance." Sliding my hand from her hip to her inner thigh, I grazed my knuckles over her center, and she shivered. Hell, I goddamn loved her responsiveness. "Keep going, *a mo rún*. Tell me what you want. In French."

With a mewl of frustration, she jerked her hips. *"Touchez moi.* Touch me."

"With pleasure." Mouth clamped on the tendon in her neck, I spread her folds and groaned. "So fucking wet." My cock twitched. My balls pulled taut. I inserted a finger into her heat, and she clenched around it, drawing another moan from me. I added a second. She was tight, but she could take me. I wouldn't have to be gentle when I thrust. Which was going to be soon or I thought I might expire. I pressed my palm to her clit, circling, while I curled my fingers inside her.

She tipped her head back, a strangled cry filling the room. *"Oui. Maintenant. Je te veux maintenant.* Yes. Now. I want you now—"

No translation needed. I gripped her hips, and she rose on her knees to assist. Aligning myself to her entrance, I guided her onto my shaft. She sank slowly, and though a bead of perspiration trailed down my temple and it nearly killed me, I let her set the pace. Tight, wet heat enveloped me. I threw my head back on the couch, watching her take me, while my hands clenched her thighs.

When I was fully rooted inside her, I hissed through my teeth. So...f ucking...good.

She held my jaw in both hands, eyes wide. Surprise and revelation shone in all that blue, as if she was feeling the cataclysm, too. Dropping her forehead to mine, she rocked her hips.

A roar ripped from deep in my throat and I lunged forward, sucking her breast into my mouth to tame the sound. I pressed my palms to her back, adoring the smooth skin and delicate muscle shifting underneath. She wrapped her arms around my head, holding me to her. Swirling my tongue around the rosy pink areola, I rubbed her other nipple between my thumb and forefinger, and thrust. She rolled her hips, and I came undone.

I'd never been this desperate. I couldn't hold a lucid thought, pin down a thread of sanity. I was barely keeping my release in check.

Slumping onto the cushion, I eased out of her as much as the position allowed and, with my hands holding her hips and her fingers clenched around my forearms, I thrust into her as I brought her down. Our bodies slapped in the silent room. Our haggard breaths joined the fray. Her breasts bounced as she rode me, and I didn't know where to look first. She was a goddamn vision. Flushed skin. Red, swollen lips parted in pleasure. Hooded blue eyes lost in the moment.

My gaze dropped to where we were joined, my cock slick from her as it pumped. "So...beautiful... *a mo rún.*" The base of my spine tingled, the sensation dancing up my back. My balls grew heavy, tight, and I knew I was too close. I brought my thumb over her clit, pressing, circling. "Come, Lily," I ordered, my voice hoarse.

She bit her lower lip, eyes closed in pleasure. "Almost there," she whispered, breathless.

I shifted my hips the slightest bit and grabbed her ass, spreading the cheeks. Increasing my thrusts, I urged her down to my chest so my pelvis could hit her in the right spot. She slid her arms between my back and the cushion, grinding down as I drove up, completely in sync as if we'd done this a million times.

The roll of her hips became more frantic and her inner walls fisted me in a vise. She tensed above me, pressing her face into my neck. Her cry of release was muffled by my skin, but mine tore through the room as I pumped, stilled, and pumped twice more. Bowing against her, I shook as I emptied into the condom.

She went limp on top of me, face still buried, breath hot and ragged. I could do little more than thread my fingers in her hair and struggle for air. Sweet Christ.

After a moment or fifty, she lifted her head to sleepily smile down at me.

Grinning back, I tucked her hair behind her ear and placed a gentle kiss on her lips.

Day Three

After crashing hard, we slept in late on Sunday. At least, I had. I awoke to cool sheets on her side of my bed and was shocked at the trip of worry in my chest. I found her fully dressed in the outfit from the day before, standing in front of my living room windows.

She turned. "Regrets?"

Strangely, my only regret had been not waking up beside her. I'd shaken my head as answer, she'd mumbled something about needing to get some of her clothes, and off to her apartment we went.

She lived in an older part of the city in a complex dating back to the turn of the century. Once inside, I casually glanced around. Her carpet was threadbare, but unstained. She had a few chairs, no couch, and a thirty-inch flat screen. And books. Tons of books. Wall to wall bookshelves encased the living room. Plants and glass bottles decorated the small space between the ceiling and the top shelves. The place was cozy, inviting.

"Like to read, do you?" My grin slowly fell when my gaze landed on her.

She bit her lip as if...nervous. "I want to answer you, but I feel you'll look differently at me. You'll think I'm boring."

I was pretty sure she could tell me anything and boring would never enter into my thoughts. "Try me."

She crossed her arms and looked at her feet. "I'm a...librarian. That's what I do for a living." Her face twisted into a please-don't-laugh-at-me expression as she peered up at me through thick lashes.

I stilled, every inch of me except my cock, which twitched to life behind my fly. My brows lifted so high I was sure they were near my hairline. "Two words, Lily. Librarian. Fantasy."

A laugh breathed out of her bow-shaped lips. "Oh, come on."

"Completely serious." My gaze took her in, as if looking at her for the first time. This explained how she knew the Yeats poem so well, and her eclectic taste in reading material. How oddly ironic we both made a living by words. "I'm a columnist for the St. Louis Post."

She blinked. "Really?"

"Really. Do you have a pair of reading glasses?"

"Uh..." Confusion marred her brow. "Yes."

I groaned. "Bring them along when you pack your bag."

She stalled for a beat, shook her head as if amused, and disappeared into a bedroom down the hall. Twenty minutes later, she reappeared, having changed into black leggings and a blue sweater under a leather jacket, and mentioned something about it being a nice day for a drive.

I shrugged. Late spring was hitting St. Louis, and though the temperatures fluctuated, today was nearly sixty and sunny. Buds were blooming on the trees and the grass was recovering from winter, almost an emerald green.

We made our way outside and she set her bag in my trunk. Then, she took my hand and led me to an underground parking structure, tearing the tarp off a...Harley.

My heart did some kind of twisty pounding thing inside my chest. I stared at the bike, not ashamed to admit I was turned on to the point of pain.

"Yours?" Just when I thought I had a handle on her, she turned the page. A librarian who owned a motorcycle and fucked like a wet dream. Screwed didn't begin to cover the magnitude of what I was to become.

"Yes." She grinned, sending my heart into cardiac arrest. "Want to go for a ride?"

"Fuck, yes." As she pulled out two helmets, I stared at her. "I haven't been on one of these since college." A buddy of mine had owned one. I'd never had any inclination to buy a bike, though.

She handed me a helmet and put hers on. "Hold onto me and lean into turns. I got the rest." Straddling the bike, she turned the key and glanced over her shoulder at me. The roar of the engine bounced off the concrete structure.

Kicked into gear, I donned my helmet and climbed on behind her, cradling my inner thighs along the outside of hers, bringing my erection snug against her ass. We fit. The vibration from her revving the engine only made me harder.

Without a word, she heeled the kickstand and tore out of the structure. She played it safe as she wound through the city and then really let go as we neared the state park. Wind whipped around us, her hair flying wild. I kept my hands on her hips the whole ride, wanting to explore her body as she drove but not wanting to distract her. After a couple of complicated turns through a thickly wooded area, she parked on what resembled a private trail and cut the engine.

I removed her helmet and mine, setting them to dangle on the handlebars, and breathed in pine. Birds called overhead and the scurry of squirrels crunched in the distance. I wrapped my arms around her from behind. She turned her head to meet my kiss. Effortless, as if knowing what I wanted without direction. Everything with her had been easy so far.

"Nice spot," I said casually, noting the seclusion. "Any reason in particular we're here?"

With her face so close to mine, it was simple to take in her reservation, but I gave her time. She wanted to learn to take initiative, and I was a patient guy. Dark navy flecks infused the cerulean in her irises as her long lashes blinked slowly.

After a few beats, she turned to face me, straddling me as I straddled the Harley, and brought the heat between her legs in direct contact with my straining cock. "I've always wanted to have sex on a motorcycle. I bought the bike a few months ago."

Another check on her things-she-wanted-to-do list. Again, I wondered what sparked the change. I pushed her dark hair away from her face and grinned. "I'm all yours."

She nudged my jacket off my shoulders and tossed it to the ground. Following her lead, I did the same with hers and groaned when she reached for the snap on my jeans. The teeth of the zipper sounded, and I sprang free. Her warm, soft hands wrapped around me. I bucked into them. She used the perfect amount of pressure as she stroked me. When her thumb caressed my slit, I put my hand on her chest and eased her down to recline against the handlebars.

"I'm obviously ready for you, *a mo rún*. Are you ready for me?"

My gaze never leaving hers, I inched her leggings down her thighs, taking her panties along. Instead of stripping them off her, I left them around her ankles, lifted her legs, and brought them to either side of me, so she caged me in. Her ankles crossed low on my back.

Removing a condom from my wallet, I ripped it open with my teeth and rolled it down my length, all without taking my gaze from hers. Ensnared by her, my chest ached as I placed my palms on her belly under her sweater and splayed my fingers. Her breath caught in her throat, her eyelids lowering in lust.

Wanting to see her, I dropped my gaze to the small triangle of dark hair on her mound. I ran my hands up her thighs, parting her folds, and groaned louder than the rev of her Harley when she'd let it rip on the open road. Beautiful just didn't cover it. I hadn't had a chance to really look at her the night before. Her pink flesh was saturated for me, her clit swollen. I pressed my thumb to her hot little button, and she arched her back, her breathing ragged. I wanted to taste her so bad, but I'd do that later. Tonight.

"You're more than ready for me. Look at you."

Seeing her spread out on her motorcycle, core inches from my shaft and teeth working her lower lip, had the blood in my veins streaming like lava. I wanted to stay in this moment an eternity, hovering in that fragile space between heaven and torment, anticipation tightening my balls.

She grabbed my thighs. "Take me. Please."

I sank a finger into her heat. "Take you where? Here?"

A mewl, and she nudged my lower back with her feet. "*Oui.*"

Done.

Fisting the base of my shaft in one hand, I slid the other under her ass to raise her pelvis to me. I filled her slowly, my gaze darting between where she stretched around me and her lust-lost eyes. When I was as deep as I could go given our position, I stilled. Hell, she felt so goddamn good, it took too much restraint to keep it together. "How do you want to be fucked, *a mo rún?*"

A cry whimpered in her throat. "Hard. Fast."

Done and done.

Hands on her hips, I dragged her off my cock until only the tip of me remained inside, and then pulled her back onto my shaft fast, hard.

At her more intense cry, I put two of my fingers in her mouth to give her something to latch onto. We were alone, but there was no sense in drawing attention to what we were doing if anyone was close by. Her sound would carry. She sucked my fingers, swirling her tongue around the knuckles, and I pulsed inside her.

Rolling my hips, I retreated from her hot, tight sheath and pounded back inside. She bit my fingers as another holy-fuck sound moaned around my digits. Leaning slightly forward so I could hit her clit when I thrust, I repeated the motion, again and again, picking up speed and urgency. I grabbed the handlebars above her head with one hand for balance and momentum, sinking deeper. Her ragged breaths escaped between my fingers, her teeth clenching so hard I was sure she left permanent marks. My thrusts more animalistic than human, I drove inside her, sweat beading down my temple.

My balls grew taut, my spine stiff. Fuck. I kept my pace, but whispered a coarse order near ear. "Come, *a mo rún*. I'm so fucking close. You feel too fucking good. Come...hard...for...me...Lily." I punctuated each word with a fast thrust, dizzy with need.

"Declan..."

Hell. I loved the way she said my name.

Her back arched off the bike and she screamed. I had just enough wherewithal to clamp my hand over her mouth as she clenched around my shaft, jerking me to an explosion. Light danced behind my lids. Air trapped in my lungs. I buried my face in her soft sweater to contain my grunt as I finished. Shuddering, I cupped the back of her head and attempted to keep my weight off her while I regained a semblance of normal breathing.

Her fingers wove tenderly through my hair. I shuddered again at how thoroughly even the simple caress rocked me. From the inside out.

Lifting my head, I kissed my way up her jaw. "I will admit, sex on a motorcycle is on my list of top choices now."

Her throaty laugh shook us both.

We cleaned up and redressed, then brought her bike back to her apartment and headed to my place. The rest of the day, I coaxed more fantasy ideas from her, adding in my own twist and promising her we'd get to them all.

After the supper rush, we headed to my favorite Italian restaurant for dinner. I preferred less crowds and she didn't seem to mind. After we ordered, we picked at our salads, the conversation never going stale as the scent of garlic and merlot swirled around us. The lighting was low and our table small, intimate. We discussed everything from politics to religion to sports, and though we didn't agree on a lot of the topics, there was respect in the light debate.

Wiping her mouth on a napkin, she leaned forward. "Okay, so I have a question. Not that it's any of my business, but why don't you date? To be honest, you're pretty good at it. Do you have a crazy ex-wife who milked you for every penny? Long lost love you're pining for?"

I smiled because it was rather difficult not to around her, even though my answer was sure to send her running. If I answered honestly, that is. Outside of the family, no one knew. Choosing my words carefully, I pushed my salad plate away. "I'm afraid it's a little stranger than that. I need to tell you a story."

Sipping her wine, she eyed me over the rim. "I like stories."

I laughed and wiped a hand down my face. "One hundred years ago, back in Ireland, my great-grandfather fell in love with a girl from a neighboring farm. She was promised to another, so they kept their love secret. For luck, she gave him a four leaf clover and told him to come to her the night before her wedding, and they'd run off together."

Her eyes narrowed. "This doesn't end well, does it?"

I sighed. "No. My great-grandfather got cold feet, ran late with his chores, and lost the clover. Ashamed, he didn't do as she asked, and she was forced to marry the guy she didn't want. On her wedding night, she snuck out to see my great-grandfather one last time, and told him since he threw her luck and love away, he and his ancestors were destined to never have either for as long as they lived. The only way to break the omen was to redeem themselves one day."

Her head tilted, lips twisting in thought. "Interesting. What does that have to do with you?"

The waitress arrived with our meals, chicken alfredo for Lily and lasagna for me. After the waitress left us alone, I lifted my gaze to Lily, wondering if she would think I was a whack if I finished the story. To anyone outside our family, it would seem crazy wrapped in more crazy.

It also happened to be true. To my knowledge, not one O'Leary had ever told another soul about the curse.

I took a few bites of my meal, waiting for her to do the same, before I continued. "So, for the past hundred years, the men in my family have been cursed. We can't fall in love or something bad happens."

She appeared skeptical. "Like what?"

Hell, I was all in now. Why not? "Ever since the curse began, not one generation has had a female born. To add to that, every male who has fallen in love has lost them to divorce, illness, or death. Even as recent as my brother, Aiden. His wife died delivering Liam."

A tiny wrinkle formed between her brows. She opened her mouth, but nothing came out.

I swallowed my bite of lasagna. "You don't believe me."

She pushed her food around her plate, appearing to choose her words. "I believe you believe it. Many cultures hold merit to curses, rituals, and spells. I just think your family is putting so much credence into this one incident that you're making the curse true, or at least twisting it to believability."

See, this was one of many reasons why she was so damn fascinating. Instead of outright thinking I'd gone over the cuckoo's nest, she took into account my heritage and the facts presented. "Part of me always felt that way, too. But it's hard to argue with history."

She nodded. "Why hasn't anyone tried to break the curse?"

I shrugged. "Many have. My grandfather married for convenience, swearing he never loved my grandmother. She died anyway. One of my uncles is gay. His lover emptied his bank account and fled. My mother lasted the longest. My father, before proposing to her, spent hours scouring fields for a four leaf clover to present to her, thinking he had to pick it himself. After months of searching, he found one. She died in a car accident a year after having me."

She set her wine aside, her lips pouting. "Has any woman tried to give one of your relatives a clover?"

"Not that I'm aware."

She set her chin in her hand. "It might make the difference. Just a thought, should you meet a woman one day who sweeps you off your feet." She grinned, the candlelight illuminating her warm, yielding eyes.

"Regardless, I understand your hesitation. I think scorned by a lover is more romantic personally. Go Hemingway style next time you tell your tale."

I stilled, shaking my head. My chest swelled to capacity with some foreign sensation that both hurt and felt oddly good. I just didn't know what to make of her. Our conversations never lagged, we had obvious chemistry, she was sweet and sassy equally, her mind was sharp as a blade, and we shared similar interests. She wasn't just the perfect woman, as I'd thought earlier, but the perfect woman *for me*.

Fuck. I knew I should've left her on that park bench in my memory.

I nodded toward her plate. "Let's eat."

Another notch in her perfect column? She ate everything. No bitching about carbs or whatever. She ate and enjoyed the food. And I enjoyed her. Too much.

Day Four

I awoke in the middle of the night to an empty bed. By the coolness of the sheets, Lily had been up awhile. She'd done this the night before as well, but I hadn't chased after her, figuring she'd wanted some privacy. Even when we fell asleep wrapped in each other, she was a restless sleeper. I wondered what haunted her. Sometimes, when she thought I wasn't watching, a lost, gutted expression filled her eyes that had my stomach bottoming out. Little did she know, I was always watching her.

Scratching the stubble on my jaw, I rolled to check the time, noting it was only two. I debated leaving the bed, but curiosity got to me. Shoving the covers aside, I padded barefoot down the hall, wearing nothing but my boxers.

I found her facing the bank of windows in the living room, a blanket wrapped around her. Moonlight lit her pale skin. The vastness of the city beyond made her seem fragile. Though she appeared lost in thought, the weight of the world sank her slender shoulders.

I rubbed the ache in my chest. "I guess two orgasms weren't enough to knock you out. I'll have to try harder." After dinner, we'd barely made it inside the apartment before I'd taken her on the kitchen counter and then again up against the wall in the hallway. We'd also watched a movie.

I'd let her pick and had been pleased to learn she liked variety. Action, sci-fi, comedy. She was game.

She turned her head, offering a sweet, sad smile that had the ache in my chest spreading to my gut. "I'm sorry I woke you."

"You didn't." I stepped deeper into the room and eased behind her, resting my chin on her shoulder. "You have work tomorrow. You should come back to bed."

She hummed her agreement and leaned into me, gaze back on the city. "I don't sleep very well."

Skimming my lips over her neck, I said, "Are you uncomfortable here?" She always smelled so good. Her light perfume combined with her unique scent.

"No." She sighed, and even that sounded weary. "It's not you. I don't sleep well anywhere. Layover from my childhood, I suppose."

Icy tendrils of dread wove up my spine. I slid my arm around her belly, the other held her jaw, turning it toward me. I should've tugged the blanket off her and taken her up against the window, which had been one of the fantasies we'd worked out together. Instead, I said, "Explain," like I had any right to her life.

Her gaze swept my face, finally settling on my eyes. In the dark, her irises looked more like twilight than blue.

She swallowed. "I grew up in foster care. Constantly moving around, I never got into a good sleep rhythm."

The breath stalled in my lungs. She had no family? Hell, fucked up as mine was, I didn't know what I'd do without them. A thousand questions pounded through my skull, never making it to my mouth. Because I wanted to know more, to hold her in my arms and coax the ghosts from her past, I did the only thing I could. I gave her my body instead.

Dipping my finger between her breasts, I yanked the blanket from her hold, finding her naked underneath. Christ, I loved her body. "I'll just have to find clever ways to wear you out. Any suggestions?" Cupping her breasts, I licked the pulse in her neck and groaned when it thumped wildly for me. Some of her earlier ideas swam through my mind, and I tried to fit one to this moment.

Arching into my touch, she moaned low in her throat. "Declan."

I growled. "Again." Stepping out of my boxers, I kicked them away and pressed my cock into the crease of her ass. "Say my name again. See what happens." A dare, one I hoped she'd take. I knew exactly which fantasy of hers I'd fulfill tonight. Sliding my hand down her belly, past her mound, I parted her folds. Fuck, I loved this about her, too. She was always so drenched, so ready for me.

She brought her arms up and fisted her hands in my hair, thrusting me deeper into her crevice. "Declan."

Checkmate. Grabbing her hips, I spun her around, bent her over the couch, and kicked her legs apart. I paused just before taking her, my body shaking with feral need. My cock pulsed in my hand as I stared at her wet folds, the delicate curve of her spine. This was one of her top choices. To be taken from behind, roughly.

"I'm on the pill. I'm safe, too." She turned her head to pin her wanton, needy gaze to mine. "Or go get a condom. Up to you."

Air rasped in my lungs. I'd never had sex without a condom, never intended to. And I was safe, as well. A strong part of me trusted her, was more intimate with her than anyone else. I wanted this so bad my balls pinched with a sharp pang. To claim her, no barriers, no walls, spoke to me as if an unforeseen force was driving me.

I looked from her eyes, to where we would join, and back to her eyes again. Her gaze pleaded, begged.

I thrust inside her, hard, deep, and clenched my jaw at the bombardment of sensory overload. She was so fucking tight in this position. Her cry of delight hit my ears. Her warm, giving flesh under my hands trembled in satisfaction. And her hot, wet sheath enveloping me without anything between us was the closest thing to heaven a guy like me would ever get.

Claim...her...

Wrapping her dark hair around my hand, I gently tugged her head back. Her palms met the cushion before her, the knuckles white. I withdrew and drove into her, our skin slapping.

She cried out, desperation leaking from the sound.

My chest heaving, I stopped, just to be sure. "Too hard?" She'd said she'd wanted this, and though she'd taken me before, I had to be certain our tolerance was on the same level. Rough wasn't typically my style, but when the mood called for it, I could go barbarian.

"No," she panted. "More. Please."

Fuck. Yes.

I ground against her perfect, round ass, moved inside her until my eyes rolled to the back of my skull. I pulled out, shoved back in. Repeat. She met me each time, pushing her hips back into my pelvis. Her supple walls wrapped around every rigid inch of my cock. *Yes, yes, yes.* Each thrust was delivered with more force. Her breasts swung over the couch. Her ass reddened as we slapped together. She made the most fucking unbelievably sexy sounds, muttering my name over and over.

When I was getting close, I brought my fingers to her swollen clit and pinched. That sent her spiraling into an orgasm. Her inner muscles closed around my shaft as she vibrated beneath me. I thrust twice more, air trapping painfully in my lungs as pleasure assaulted the rest of me. My release was so jarring, tears filled my eyes and my throat closed, blocking my roar of pleasure. Jaw wide, I emptied inside her.

When my lungs worked again, I leaned over her, curving my body around hers. "You undo me, *mo milis*." My sweet.

Too satisfied and happy to care that I'd shifted endearments, I carried her to bed, tucked us in, and pulled her back flush with my chest. After she drifted to sleep, I buried my face in her hair and closed my eyes.

The next morning, when sunlight through the blinds woke me, I was alone again. Rolling to my back, my gaze automatically landed on her clothes hanging on my closet door and her bag on a corner chair. She hadn't left me. She'd just gone to work.

My heart rate calming, I blew out a stream of air and scrubbed my hands over my face. I was getting in too deep if Lily being gone brought a surge of panic. I couldn't keep her. I knew that. I'd always known forever wasn't an option, not with anyone.

Climbing out of bed, I relieved myself in the bathroom, avoided my reflection, and strode into the kitchen. Next to the coffeepot was a folded piece of pink paper. It did not make me stupidly happy to see she'd left me a note. Okay, it did.

So screwed.

I snatched the paper and opened it.

I made coffee. I'm going to swing by my apartment after work to get my car. I should be back by six. I can pick up dinner, if you like. Text me with requests. I had fun this weekend. xoxo

My gaze locked onto the Xs and Os scrawled in her neat, willowy writing. Hugs and kisses. A simple inflection. Nothing to indicate she'd gotten attached.

My hands itched to text her. I ignored them.

I read the note twice more, the fucking pathetic sap I was, and poured myself a cup of coffee. I drank it in front of the windows, the very spot in my apartment that seemed to be her favorite, and rinsed the carafe out when I was done.

Still didn't text her. Progress.

Taking the note, I tossed it in my nightstand drawer and stepped into a pair of nylon shorts. I needed a good workout to expel her from my mind. This wasn't healthy, her constantly being in my head. Under my skin.

I headed into the spare bedroom I'd turned into a home office and booted the computer. I'd turned in a few articles at the Post, but checked to make sure my editor hadn't emailed with revisions. He hadn't, which was disappointing because that would've at least kept me occupied.

I looked at my phone, scowled, and didn't text. Go me.

Task complete, I made my way to the other spare room to pound out my frustration the old fashioned way. Scrolling through my playlist, I set my iPod station to hard rock and started on the treadmill. By the time I'd completed three miles, I was drenched in sweat and it had very little to do with the workout. The entire trek, I'd envisioned all the things I wanted to do to her when she got home from work.

Home. This wasn't her home. She was temporary, the situation a fleeting blip in my life.

I wiped my face with a towel and moved on to the rowing machine, then lifted weights. Muscles tense and strained, I headed toward a shower. I knew I'd overdone the workout when it hurt to turn the water on.

Letting steam fill my bathroom, I shifted to drop my shorts and froze. On the gray marble vanity, next to a small bamboo plant, was Lily's toothbrush. Next to that, her cosmetic bag. She'd cleaned up after herself, had put her things in a tidy pile off to the side, but she was in here.

In my space. The room still smelled like her shampoo from her shower this morning.

I got a rare sense of what it was like to live with another person, and I was shocked at how much it didn't scare me. I had no idea if that was because of Lily or the deep-rooted part of me that wanted things I couldn't have. I liked women, but there was something uniquely satisfying about belonging to someone. One person to share everything with. Years ago, I'd shut down that desire. A few days with her and it all came flooding to the surface.

Closing my eyes, I placed my hands on the counter and leaned into them. I took a few calming breaths, but anxiety coiled in my gut and tension tightened my chest. Every male in my family had tried and failed to defy the curse. One hundred years, nothing but loss and regret. I couldn't do that to Lily. I needed to get a hold of myself.

Pushing off the vanity, I popped a few ibuprofen, and turned to the shower. Behind the sheer bamboo-printed curtain, her shampoo bottle sat next to mine.

No...fucking...escape.

And I didn't *want one...*

Two hours later, I sat in my living room, holding my phone in my hand, still debating my text. She'd asked me to give her dinner ideas, not send her sonnets. Yet here I sat, inactive.

Fuck it. I shot off the text.

Me: *Can I have you for dinner?*

There. That summed up our relationship, at least the part I was supposed to be focusing on.

Lily: *You can have me for dessert. What about Greek for dinner? Or Chinese?*

Christ in heaven. Did the woman have a flaw?

Me: *I'd rather skip to dessert.*

Lily: *I can do impressive things with an egg roll and my mouth...*

I sucked a harsh inhale through my nose and stroked myself. Like a teenager. I was goddamn hard from sexting.

Me: *Chinese it is. See you soon.*

Turned out, she wasn't kidding about the egg roll thing. At six-fifteen, she exited the elevator and we ate on the couch facing each other. And she did have a flaw. She didn't like shrimp. I was grasping at straws with that, but whatever. We had something of a food fight when I tried to feed her a bite of shrimp rangoon, and she wrapped her full lips around an egg roll in response. And moaned. Then she went to work eating the thing like she was giving head. I didn't know whether to laugh or cry.

As we were cleaning up, she noticed something was wrong when I winced. My ibuprofen was wearing off, but I thought I'd hidden my discomfort well. Except nothing escaped Lily. Her baby blues seemed to see everything. I don't think I'd ever had someone in my life as perceptive as her.

"I'm fine. I just overdid it in the gym today." *Trying to forget about you.*

A frown of worry wrinkled her forehead. She took my hand. "Come on."

Down the hall we went, to my bathroom, where she ran the bath. I eyed her as she began to strip out of her clothes.

I lifted my brows. "You promised dessert."

She threw her head back and laughed. She had the best laugh. "How about a massage? A good soak will loosen your muscles. Dessert after."

This felt oddly like she was trying to take care of me. And I liked it. So I stayed dressed by the side of the tub while she slipped into the water.

"Did I forget to say full body massage?"

I groaned. Hell, I was already toast where she was concerned. Stripping, I sank in the hot water in front of her, the square-shaped tub accommodating us both, and shut off the faucet.

Wrapping her long legs around me, she eased me back to recline on her chest. "Where does it hurt?"

I thought about saying everywhere, but couldn't get the words past my throat. We'd laughed and played during dinner, and now we were in the bath in a scene that bordered on romantic. I didn't do romance.

"Here?" she said in the silence, and started rubbing my shoulders.

Fuck, that felt good. I laid my head on her collarbone and closed my eyes. Her nimble little fingers kneaded my sore muscles in smooth, even strokes, never pressing too hard. Up my neck, down my shoulders. She worked her way across my back, her hands sliding between our bodies. I couldn't move. My tension released degree by degree, until I felt like I could sleep for a week.

After awhile, she moved from behind me to straddle my hips, massaging my pecs and abdomen. Lazily, I blinked at her and offered a half-grin. She kneeled between my legs and stroked my thighs, which got my cock interested in her proximity, but her fingers headed south to my calves, then my feet. Hell, she even did my arches.

My voice a coarse rasp, I said, "You can stop doing that in about ten years." A beat of silence passed, and I realized what I'd said. We didn't have but three days left, two nights. Years wasn't an option when our time boiled down to hours.

"You feel more relaxed," she said, as if I hadn't spoken. "One muscle is still pretty hard, though." Her fingers wrapped around my cock, and I hissed.

God love her. "I don't think that'll go away anytime soon, *mo milis.*"

Her thumb grazed my slit. "What does that phrase mean? You said it last night, too."

Balls aching, I thrust into her hands. "My sweet."

Her gaze went tender, her smile soft. My chest started to throb behind my ribs in tune with my cock, but more insistent. I held my breath, realizing she wasn't immune to the slight shift in us, either. Perhaps this wasn't all on me. Which only made things worse.

"Well," she said, dipping her head. She licked around the crown of my shaft. "This is dessert, after all. It should be sweet." Her tongue darted out again, repeating the same path with more pressure.

"Fuck me, *mo milis.*" I fisted my hands in her hair and gave it everything I had not to thrust into her mouth. "Lily." From day one, I'd envisioned her lips around me, we just never got there, too insistent, too wrapped up in having each other. I still hadn't tasted her yet, made her come with my mouth, and hell if I was letting our time slip by without doing it.

But she said something in French and swallowed half of me in one fell swoop. The back of my head hit the tub, and I forgot my name.

Day Five

I awoke alone. Again. My gut sank. Logically, I knew Lily had to work and I was a late riser, not to mention a heavy sleeper, but I'd never get another opportunity to spend a morning waking up beside someone, and I wanted to experience it. Just this one time.

Disappointed, I did my usual morning routine, checked my email, and headed into the kitchen. There was another pink note by the coffeepot, and I grinned like an idiot.

Hope you're feeling better today. I'm getting off work a little early. I can make dinner, if you like. Dessert for sure. I've developed a sweet tooth. See you soon. xoxo

I reread the thing a couple times, put it in my nightstand with the other one, and worked out in the gym. The exercise did little to burn off my desire or ease the pressure in my chest. A ball of regret, chock full of what-ifs, had been lodged in my throat for days. I didn't know what to do, if anything. It sure felt like I was breaking my own self-imposed rule. The numero uno one. I should've known—hell, I *did* know—I would fall for her, that we couldn't just be about physical release.

Today was my day to pick up my nephew, Liam, from school. His babysitter had off on Tuesdays and Aiden had the pub. Typically, Liam and I chilled out at Aiden's until he got home from Irish Eyes. We would do his homework, play a few video games, and battle to the death at checkers. But...Lily was a factor this week. I didn't want to bail on her, not with our time running out, but getting her involved with my family pushed the boundaries.

I spent half the day a mess, phone in hand, attempting to figure out what to tell Lily. In the end, I picked up Liam and brought him to my place, never contacting her.

In the elevator, I rubbed my hand over Liam's soft brown hair, mussing the strands. "This okay, pal? My house for dinner?"

He shrugged. "Sure. As long as you get me home by bedtime. I have an English test tomorrow."

I shook my head, sighing dramatically. "Dude, you're eight. Quit being a grown up."

The elevator doors pinged open and the scent of something spicy wafted from the kitchen. I stopped dead in my tracks at the sight of Lily, back to me, cooking something on the stove. Christ in heaven, she was...it was...too *right*. My heart did some kind of stutter-step and headed toward cardiac arrest while the rest of me felt like I was coming out of a deep freeze.

Liam looked between me and her, confusion wrinkling his forehead. "Miss Lily?"

She shrieked, obviously not having heard us, and whirled. "Liam!"

My nephew walked right into her embrace as if they'd been cozy for years. "What are you doing here?"

Her flustered state lasted point five seconds before she waved her hand with a grin. "Making dinner. I didn't know you'd be here. Do you like enchiladas?"

"Heck, yeah." Liam turned toward me—I was still in some kind of shock and holding ground in the entryway—only to face Lily again. "Do you live here now?"

Forget cardiac arrest. I was in heart failure. Black dots swam before my eyes.

She laughed in that warm, husky way that filled a room. "Naw. I just hang out with your Uncle Declan sometimes. We're friends."

Friends. We so were *not* that, or not only that. I blinked and seemed to recover. Somehow. "How do you two know each other?"

Lily wrapped an arm around Liam's shoulders, her smile genuine. "Liam used to be in the story hour group at the library. Now he's in our young adult book club. Aren't you? How far are you on Harry Potter?" She glanced at me. "They just started book one this week."

Liam bounced on his toes. "Harry just got to Hogwarts. You were right. It's better than the movie."

She rolled her eyes fondly. "Books are usually better than the film. They did a good job with the Potter movies, though."

My gaze darted back and forth like a ping pong ball. I scrubbed my shaking hands through my hair. "Hey, pal. Why don't you head into my office to start your homework? I'll be there in a sec." Why the hell couldn't I breathe?

"Sure." Liam gave Lily a fist bump and disappeared down the hall.

I stared after him, not sure what to do, to say. Lily obviously was on friendly terms with Aiden, but I had no clue she knew Liam. And so well. For years, it seemed.

Suddenly, this whole adventure with Lily ground to a halt. The repercussions hit me like a tsunami and pulled me under. Lily and I had agreed to no awkwardness after we were through, but that was before my...*feelings* became involved. Before I had any idea Liam was a part of her world.

I closed my eyes and tried to pull air into my lungs. Futile.

"I-I'm so sorry." She stepped back, creating distance from me, and reached behind her back to untie her apron. *An apron.* Christ help me, even that was hot. "I had no idea he'd be here. I'll go."

In her note, she'd said she'd get off early and make dinner. I didn't realize she'd be home *this* early, though. And it was my fault. I should have texted her instead of avoiding the situation like a pussy.

She started past me, and I grabbed her arm.

"No, don't go. I..." Hell, what? "I have Liam on Tuesday nights. I should've told you."

Avoiding my gaze, she nodded quickly. "I understand. I'll see you later."

"Lily..." I backed her to the cabinets and caged her with my hands on either side of her on the counter. A swift glance over her shoulder told me Liam's eyes weren't on us. Placing my feet between hers, I leaned closer, every inch of me flush with every inch of her.

And *there.* There was my normal pulse rhythm and ability to breathe. The scent of her surrounded me, her warmth enveloping, and the restless energy and panic drained right out of me. She could turn my brain to pudding and my cock to lethal stiffness. She made me desperate and insane with lust. But she also calmed my soul, quieted the crazy.

I dropped my forehead to hers and worked a swallow. "Don't go, *mo milis.*" Brushing my lips across her cheek, down her jaw, I said what I'd never in my life said before. "Stay."

Her uneven exhale skated across my neck. "This isn't a good idea, Declan."

I kissed her in the soft spot behind her ear and closed my eyes. Two more nights and she'd be gone. "I know. Stay anyway." I cupped the back of her head and kissed her mouth gently. No passion, no heat, just a tenderness I didn't know I had in me. She brought that side of me to the surface, and I feared I'd never be able to shove it down when she left.

Wrapping her arms around my waist, she nodded. The concession came with a price. In her eyes, I found the same shattered reality and fruitless hope I'd been battling. No words needed to be said. We seemed to be able to read each other without speaking, a silent language all our own. Right then, holding her in my arms, I never hated my fucking circumstances more.

She was falling, too.

Real love couldn't possibly move at this kind of warp speed, could it? I'd never given much thought to love at first sight, but she had impacted me from the moment I'd set eyes on her all those months ago. But love? No. It never came into play until I got to know her. Having never been here before, I still wasn't sure if this was jacked up lust, infatuation, or the real deal.

I went to help Liam with his homework—I did not miss third grade long division in the slightest—and when we emerged from my office, she was curled up on the couch, reading *The Hitchhiker's Guide to the Galaxy*.

And fuck me dead. I fell the rest of the way. It felt a lot like going splat on the pavement after freefalling ten stories. If the sight of her reading one of my favorite books didn't do it, the way she was around Liam would have.

She kept the conversation going during dinner, encouraging my nephew with compliments and laughing at his jokes. She was cool under pressure. The woman was kind, funny, smart, sexy, and beautiful. Oh, and a good cook. The enchiladas were a mouth orgasm. A part of me always figured once she lost her mysterious quality, once I really got to know her, the allure would wear off. That didn't happen. Not even a little. Lily only got more interesting the longer I was in her orbit.

"Yeah, but she doesn't like shrimp and her feet are always cold." So there. Flaws. She wasn't perfect. I'd discovered after sleeping together the past few nights, her feet were in a perpetual state of arctic. Didn't seem to matter how thick her socks were or how many blankets we piled on the bed. Hell. I didn't mind. I found even that adorable.

I looked up to find Liam and Lily's gaze on me. Twin sets of confusion.

I sighed, realizing I'd said my thoughts aloud. "Good cornbread, Lily."

I really needed to start emotionally backing off, but panic tore at my chest when the thought emerged. Only two more days. It didn't matter what my feelings were, I couldn't keep her. I would have to let her go. Why not enjoy the time we had left? I'd deal with the fallout later.

Before I took Liam home, I dragged Lily off to the side and gave her a quick kiss. "I'll be back late." I had to stay until close to eleven when Aiden's manager was good to bartend alone after the rush. "Please be wearing the apron when I get here. *Just the apron.*"

Her sly, knowing grin was answer enough.

Truth be told, I'd loved my nephew to the moon and back from the first moment I set eyes on him in the hospital. But I'd never had a night drag through eternity like tonight. Worse was after Liam went to bed and I had to wait for Aiden to get home. After solitaire and being unable to find decent television programs, I texted Lily.

Me: *Whatcha wearing?*

Lily: *I'm walking around the apartment naked.*

Great. Now I was hard at my brother's house.

Me: *Groan. Where's the apron?*

Lily: *Can't seem to find it. Wait. There it is. I'm bending over now to get it...*

Did I say hard? I meant granite.

Me: *Vixen.*

Lily: *I'm now wearing the prerequisite outfit aforementioned. Want a picture?*

Sweet Christ. Even her vocabulary was groan-worthy.

Me: *That's not a legit question. Fuck, yes.*

I waited five minutes until she sent a photo. I stared a good long beat before I busted out laughing. In the shot, she was lying on my bed, dark hair spilling around her head, and wearing a smile. The selfie only showed her face.

I broke a few laws getting home. And found her curled up on her side on the foot of my bed, fast asleep. As promised, she wore only the apron. She had her arms crossed over her chest and her hair in her face. Sighing, I squatted in front of her and brushed the strands away.

I came undone. She was so beautiful it hurt to look at her. Actually, physically hurt. Her long, dark lashes fanned her cheeks. Red lips parted with deep, even breaths. In slumber, she didn't have the sometimes haunted expression I'd seen, nor the good humor I'd been privileged to witness, but she still tugged at my chest. My sweet, naughty little angel.

Standing, I turned down the covers and untied the apron. Careful not to disturb her, I lifted her in my arms and set her properly on the bed. After switching off the lights and getting undressed, I climbed in next to her and pulled the blankets up. I barely rolled on my side to face her when she instinctively curled into me, burying her face in my neck. She stuck her cold feet between my calves, trapped her hands between our chests, and wedged our thighs together.

That was us. A complicated knot.

She made a cute noise that sounded a lot like a mew. "I fell asleep."

The rasp of my whiskers scratched against her cheek. I ran my hand down the length of her hair. "You don't sleep much. I disturbed you."

Her lips grazed my throat before she tilted her head to look at me. "Your voice is panty-melting. Low and hoarse and come-hither...ish."

I laughed. "Nice to know."

"Good thing you have a hot body to go with the voice. All ribbed abs and bulging biceps. The way your thighs look in jeans makes me drool."

I laughed again. Someone was feisty tonight. Or she was so tired she didn't know what she was saying. "I'm very fond of your body and voice as well." Understatement.

"You have gorgeous eyes. You know that?"

I'd heard it a thousand times, but coming from her the compliment sounded different. "Like emeralds or grass?" Those were the similes most used.

She hummed. "More like moss. Very unique."

If we were going with unique, her sometimes sapphire, often cerulean, and on occasion twilight eyes won out. "So are yours, *mo milis.*" I felt like shit for waking her. Best I could tell, she got about four uninterrupted hours a night. Why she didn't sleep well still sent chills up my spine. I couldn't get the image of a younger, scared version of Lily out of my head. How bad had her childhood in foster care been? Did she have anyone in her life that served as family? It was none of my business, but yet I couldn't shake the need to know.

I kissed her forehead. "Go to sleep."

Instead of listening to me, her gaze studied my features, her expression unreadable. Usually, she was a wide open book. I hated these few instances when I couldn't read her.

She cupped my jaw, brushing her thumb across my chin. "My experiences weren't bad. I wasn't abused." I had a fraction of a second to be shocked she could read my mind, like she'd crawled inside my head. "I went into the system with my sister at age eight. My sister, Iris, was almost ten. Our parents died in a car accident, and if we had other family to take us in, they didn't step up. I hardly remember them." Her gaze wandered off. "They tried to keep Iris and I together, but it was too hard. We stayed in touch, though. In total, I was placed with three families before I aged out. They were nice people. But none of them felt like home, you know?"

I nodded, even though there was no way I could ever understand what she'd been through. My family had issues, but we loved each other. At least she had a sister. "Lily..."

"Don't feel sorry for me."

My eyes slammed shut as I drew her to me, pressing her face into my shoulder as I fought for control. "I..." Hell. My voice cracked. I lowered my tone to a whisper to hide the emotion. "I don't feel sorry for you." *I love you.* I couldn't say that without putting her in danger, though. I was already walking a thin line. "I'm amazed at your strength."

She didn't say anything more, just rested her cheek on my chest, right over my heart, and drifted back to sleep as if our talk had somehow comforted her.

Me? It was hours before I closed my eyes.

Day Six

My initial waking thought was I wasn't alone. Lily's scent filled my nose first, followed by the realization of the warmth of her soft skin against me. We were spooning, her tucked close, my arm around her. The gentle hum of her breathing had me opening my eyes.

Sunlight filtered through the blinds. She'd stayed in bed the whole night? No restlessness, no rising for work? I glanced at my alarm clock, noting it was nine. She was usually gone by now.

I didn't want to let her go, but I'd hate for her to get in trouble at the library for being late. Burying my face in her dark, silky hair, I breathed deep. I would never forget her scent. An aphrodisiac and turn-on with one whiff. Splaying my fingers over her belly, I whispered her name.

She stretched, pushing her ass right up against my morning wood until I was cradled between her cheeks. Reaching behind her, she wove her fingers through my hair. "I work a half day today. Don't have to be in until noon."

The most ridiculous amount of happiness filled my chest, closed my throat. I swept her hair away from her neck and kissed the shamrock tattoo on her nape. "Best news I've ever heard."

Her laugh was sleep-roughened and made me harder yet. Licking, kissing, and nipping my way down her neck, I moved my hand to cup her breast. She moaned. I tweaked the nipple between my thumb and forefinger. She arched. My erection became painful, so I dipped my fingers between her folds to test her readiness, and found her wet. She gasped and spread her legs for me, and I was more than willing to fill her.

Yet the scent of her arousal hit me, and I wanted to taste her. We'd always been so hungry for each other that little foreplay had been involved. We'd had sex, we'd fucked, but we'd never taken our time. And I was going to make up for that.

I rose over her and started with her mouth, a slow, thorough kiss that had me desperate for air. I could come from her kiss alone. Passionate, endearing, she toppled walls and erected kingdoms with all the power she wielded.

Her body moved under mine, a sensual glide that informed me she was just as lost. Her hands explored me--my chest, my hips, my back, my ass--until fire licked my skin and my heart thundered behind my ribs.

I kissed my way over her throat and to her collarbone, looking up at her when I trailed lower. Her blue eyes watched my descent, hooded and dark. Keeping my gaze on hers, I sucked her nipple into my mouth. Hard. Panting, she dug her fingers into my hair to hold me to her. Swirling my tongue, I eased the ache away and moved to the other breast, giving it equal treatment. She writhed beneath me, chest rising and falling rapidly.

"*Mo grá* likes that." My love. I didn't hesitate to use the endearment because it wasn't an outright admission and she couldn't translate anyway.

"Yes," she breathed, arching into my mouth.

I kissed down her belly, watching her lust transition into slight apprehension. Hmm. She wasn't accustomed to oral? She'd done just fine with my cock in her mouth in the bathtub the other night. Had her previous lovers not been good to her? Their mistake.

Hands on her inner thighs, I spread her legs and blew gently on her wet folds. She sucked a quick breath, the pulse in her neck pounding. I trailed my tongue up one thigh, down the other, and was pretty sure she stopped breathing.

Watching her, I leaned in and sent a long stroke from her opening to her clit. She tasted as good as she smelled. Her eyes closed and she threw her head back as she reached for my hair again, clenching the strands. I groaned, loving her response.

Sliding my hands under her ass, I lifted her to my mouth. I wove my tongue in and out of her, swirled around her clit, and repeated the process. A strangled cry caught in her throat and my hips jerked. I ground my cock against the sheets for relief. Fuck, I ached. I could spend all day between her legs just to elicit her reaction.

"Declan..."

Sweet Christ, my name on her lips. "What is it, *mo grá?* More?" I inserted two fingers inside her, curling them, while flicking my tongue rapidly over her swollen clit.

She came, just like that. Clenched around me, bowed off the bed, and nearly yanked my hair out by the root. My hips pistoned faster against the bed, but it offered no relief. I wanted inside her.

I eased her down slowly and, when her trembling ceased and her eyes slowly opened, I kissed her like I was fucking her mouth.

No way was I done. Rising to my knees, I flipped her over onto her stomach and kissed her back, taking extra time to bite her perfect ass. When I spread her legs again, she gasped and looked at me over her shoulder.

"Ah, *mo grá,* I'm just getting started."

She whimpered and urged her hips back toward me, silently telling me to take her.

Without warning, I pressed my face between her thighs and sucked her swollen flesh. Her broken, pleasured cry was cut off by the pillow when she pressed her face into it. She white-knuckled the blankets and reared back, demanding more. I knew she'd be sensitive from just having come, but I was moments from blowing just watching her. Skin flushed and warm. Musky scent of arousal mixing with her light perfume. Muscles taut, straining to hold on.

I showed her no mercy, since she gave me none. I bit, licked, hummed. She thrashed, moaned, trembled. When she went rigid like she always did right before climax, I rose over her. I crisscrossed my arms between her and the mattress, palming her breasts, and covered her body with mine. One shift of my hips and I sunk deep into her tight, willing body.

I gave us both a moment to adjust, and then slowly rolled my hips. "Declan. *Declan, Declan, Declan...*"

Her breathy moan and chanting almost made me forget to take my time. I wanted to pound, to chase my orgasm inside her like we'd always done. But not this time. I eased out of her, inch by excruciating inch, as her walls clenched like she hated the withdrawal. When only my tip remained, I pushed back in gradually, until a sheen of sweat coated my brow and I was shaking with need. Fuck. Nothing on earth felt better than her.

"Oh, God. Declan."

I wasn't going to last. Not for long. My spine was already tingling and my balls pinched. My arms still beneath her, I cupped her jaw with one hand and her mound with the other, adding pressure to her clit with the heel of my palm. My fingers spread to where we were joined, my cock slick with her arousal.

My groan came from such a place deep within, I was sure releasing it left me partially empty. Keeping my hand right where it was, so I could feel myself thrusting and pleasure her at the same time, I moved, giving her shallow strokes. She was so close I didn't think she was breathing. I increased my rhythm, going as deep as the positioned allowed. I nipped her shoulder. Buried my face in her neck. Rocked into her faster.

We came at the same time, an explosion of light and resonance and utter everything. It was devastating and infinite and cataclysmic. The sounds...the primal, destructive sounds I made didn't begin to encompass my suffering, my bliss. Breaths soughing, I trapped her beneath me, grasped desperately at her arms, hips, neck—too much to hold onto and not enough time.

Frustrated, throat tight, I rolled to my back, reached my arm out, and pulled her to my side. She fit her head in the crook of my shoulder and sighed contentedly. I, on the other hand, was not content. Tonight was our last night, and I was pretty certain I'd sell my soul if it meant not letting her go.

She must've sensed my restlessness, because she murmured quiet phrases in French and stroked my chest. Touches meant to tame the feral. After a while, my heart stopped cracking my ribs and her motions slowed.

Setting her chin on my pec, she smiled at me. "I'm not going to be able to walk at work."

I laughed, damn her, and ran my hand down her hair. "I'll make us something quick to eat. Fuel." I kissed her forehead and got up to step into a pair of jeans. She moved to her back, sheet twisted around her legs, perky breasts thrust forward with her arms over her head. I sighed, leaned over the bed, and kissed her again. "You're beautiful, *mo grá*."

I was halfway to the door when she asked, "What does that phrase mean?"

Shaking my head, I smiled and left the room. I started a pot of coffee while she showered. The eggs were almost done when she emerged, fully dressed in a pencil skirt, blue blouse and...reading glasses.

I groaned and pushed her plate across the counter toward her. "Librarian. Fantasy."

She smiled knowingly and sat on a barstool facing the counter. We ate in silence, and she left for work after kissing my cheek goodbye.

I must've stood a good twenty minutes in a numb state before I kicked myself into gear. Since this was our last night, I figured I'd make dinner. I wasn't great in the kitchen, but I knew a few dishes. I tried to keep myself busy, but the day dragged.

Six days, and I'd become addicted. Not just with the physical aspect of us, but everything. The way she absently played with my hair. The calming presence she brought to my life. How she appreciated food and art. Her maternal instincts, even though she was shown none growing up. The witty comebacks and brilliant mind. She wasn't afraid to learn new things, but she steeped herself in tradition.

The beef roast was finished cooking by the time she strolled in after work. She paused a beat to take in the set table, the flowers in a vase, and the candles. Yeah, I'd turned into a sap. What did I care? It was our last night.

She eyed me as I drew closer. "It smells good in here."

I kissed her until her fingers clutched my tee and she had difficulty standing. "Dinner's done. Have a seat. I'll bring it out."

She hummed and made her way to the table.

We ate, the conversation flowing like the wine I'd bought. She laughed at my holiday stories and I grinned at her tales from work. Every second that passed made me miss her already. I had my family, a good group of friends, but there was no one like her in my life. Around her, I didn't need a filter. It made me wonder, again, who was her support system.

Pushing the plates aside, I reached across the table and linked our fingers. "How often do you get to see your sister?"

Her lips parted, but her gaze dropped to our hands. The grief I often caught in her eyes returned, and my stomach clenched before she even started to speak. "She died last year."

I said nothing—what was there to say?—and absorbed her loss like it was my own. She was alone. Utterly alone in this world. Perhaps she had a myriad of friends and, no doubt friends could fill a void, but it wasn't the same. My throat closed, my chest aching for her. A woman like her should be surrounded by love. If I were in the position to do something about that, I'd give her a litter of kids and sic my family on her until she could only pray for silence.

Her lips pressed together as if trying not to say more, but when our gazes collided, tenderness warmed all the ice in that blue. "We kept in touch growing up, but her foster families weren't as kind as mine. When she aged out of the system, she lived on the streets, got involved with drugs. I think she was just chasing that euphoric feeling they first gave her." She cleared her throat. "She was in and out of rehab a few times, but it never stuck. She committed suicide last summer."

Fuck me. Her voice cracked and I flew out of my seat. Wrapping my arms around her, I carried her into the living room, sat on the couch, and set her in my lap. She curled into me, and though I knew she was crying, the tears didn't break her or turn into sobs.

Helpless, I smoothed her hair and let her be. To lose her parents at such a young age, and then her sister to suicide, had to have created an empty void. And a fault complex in the form of survivor's guilt.

Everyone in her life had walked. Her life had been a series of shit-storms, and I was just another high wind creating chaos.

She sighed. "Iris and I made an interesting pair. She was all out, skated the edge and wasn't afraid to take chances. And I was scared of every-thing. Nothing but the straight and narrow for me, to the point I only existed in the books I read."

Her sudden decision to live a little made sense now. "So, you are venturing out of your bubble."

"Yeah." She adjusted her position and shirt to straddle me, our faces inches apart. Even with red, swollen eyes, she was fucking beautiful. "I came to the conclusion I needed a happy middle. Live, but not reckless-ly." She laughed. "I got the tattoo first. For...luck."

Oh, the irony. I smiled anyway, loving the shamrock on her nape. "Very sexy. What else?"

She shrugged as if shy. How endearing. "I bought the motorcycle and a new wardrobe." Her teeth sunk into her lower lip as her gaze wandered my face. "I took Aiden up on his offer to visit the pub. Before Iris died, I pretty much went to work and back home. I've been trying to get out more."

Her gaze met mine and she sighed, world weary. "Not exactly living on the edge, but I've mapped out a few places I'd like to travel. Made some changes."

I tucked her hair behind her ears and let my fingers linger in the soft, dark strands. "You're doing great. It takes a lot of courage to do what you did. I'm just sorry you lost your sister that way." I paused, but to hell with it. "Do you want a big family? Kids someday?"

She nodded, but the gesture seemed distracted. "It won't make up for all I've lost, but a husband and children of my own would be a perfect way to build a new family." She shook her head as if to clear it and smiled. "What about you? What do you want? A room at the Playboy mansion? A yacht in Cozumel?"

Though her distraction technique was cute, and her smile always pulled one from me, I couldn't do it. I couldn't pretend.

She appeared to recognize my struggle right away, her smile gradually slipping and her eyes sad. Cupping my jaw, she held my face in her hands as if *I* was the treasure. "If there was no curse, if you had nothing holding you back, what would you want?"

"You." I'd throw away every cent in my bank account, do whatever it took. But that wouldn't matter because her and I could never be more than the best seven days of my life.

If she was surprised by my response, and she shouldn't have been, it didn't register in her expression. "Why?"

My head fell back to the couch. It wasn't as if I didn't know the answer, but her wanting one shocked me. Honesty at all times. That was one of my stipulations. At this point, what was one more heap of oh-shit to the pile?

I drew a shallow breath, looking at her and keeping my expression open. "Because I didn't believe in love at first sight until I saw you sitting on a park bench. It's not the basis for a relationship, but you proved to me that feeling can be built upon. You're brave and kind and funny and smart. You don't let the world bring you down and you have an uncanny ability to see beauty in even the ugliest of things. You have an open mind and an even more open heart. That's why."

The regret in her eyes hurt me to the bone. Long, aching minutes, we stared. Somewhere in those ticks of the clock, I'd stopped breathing. Her, too, it seemed. We were at a stalemate and both knew it. The end was here. If I were a more selfish bastard, I'd erase that haunted, hopeful look in her eyes with a promise to keep her, take her all over the world to fill that beautiful mind. But she'd changed something in me, and I couldn't risk her not having the full, wonderful life she deserved. My family's curse would break her. Would, in turn, break me.

Her throat worked a swallow. "We didn't follow the rules."

We, not *you.*

I shook my head. "No, we didn't." And I regretted not one second. Come tomorrow, I'd be sorry as hell, miss her like oxygen underwater, but never regret. She could never be my happy ending, but she would be the only memory of happy.

Determined not to make our last hours together sheer misery, I leaned forward and kissed her. I could take her right here on the couch, against the wall, or bent over the table. We'd completed her fantasy list and mine, had sex in every imaginable position but one. Missionary. It was the way her other lovers had been with her, the reason why she agreed to my offer in the first place. Call me sentimental, but I didn't want the last time we made love to be about position.

Carrying her to the bedroom, I set her on her feet and undressed her slowly, taking the time to kiss every inch of skin I exposed. She did the same for me with lingering touches and gentle caresses, then lay on the bed. I covered her with my body, kissing her for what seemed like hours, days, telling her with my lips what I couldn't say aloud.

And when I entered her, when we came together with gazes locked and hearts pounding in sync, I knew it would be the last time.

Day Seven

I didn't want to open my eyes. If I did, any remnants of Lily ever having been in my apartment would be gone. Not just because she had to go to work, but because she would've thought a clean break would be the easiest. Her things would not be where they'd been the past week. Her toothbrush next to mine in the bathroom, her clothes hanging on my closet door, her shoes in the foyer. Even her scent on my sheets would fade.

Fuck. Moisture burned behind my lids. My throat was raked raw with unshed tears. A black, crushing weight resided where my heart used to be. I could only imagine how my grandfather, my dad, or Aiden had felt after losing their loves. I'd only had mine a week, and I couldn't open my eyes to face her absence.

Last night, I'd fought sleep. I'd stared at her long lashes fanning her cheeks, her pouty lips, her dark hair on my pillow, and tried to commit every detail of her features to memory. As if by any stretch I'd forget her. Eventually, I'd succumbed to exhaustion and had fallen asleep with my arm banded around her. If I imagined hard enough, she'd still be there, tucked to my side.

I laid in bed too long, and when I couldn't take it anymore, I lifted my lids. No Lily. No anything. Gone. Nausea rolled in my gut.

Sucking a harsh inhale, I climbed out of bed. Bathroom. Email. Gym. Shower.

When I finally made it to the kitchen to try to force some kind of food down, my lungs stalled. Right by the coffeepot was a...Little. Pink. Note. A sound like a wounded animal filled my kitchen, and damn. It came from me.

I couldn't bring myself to read it. If she had scrawled something like, *thanks for everything* or *I had a great time*, I just might lose my shit. Permanently.

So, I made coffee and drank it in her favorite spot by the bank of windows. The brew sat like acid in my gut as I stared out at St. Louis, wondering what she was doing right now. If she felt as gutted as me. If it had been hard for her to leave. Somehow, I knew both the answers were yes. I hadn't been alone in this. I saw it in her eyes, felt it in her touch last night. Which only made things worse.

Frustrated, I went for a long walk to blow off restless energy and told Aiden I'd pick up Liam from school. Time with the nephew would do me some good. Except it hadn't. Same misery, different location. Hours later, I wound up right back where I'd been this morning—my state of mind and my body. I hadn't eaten, barely slept, and I missed her so fucking hard.

Sometime after dark, my friend Heath texted me. *Your girl is here at Irish Eyes.*

I stared at the text, torn between anger and remorse. My first instinct was to rush to the pub, fill this maddening hole she left, but the split was too new and circumstances hadn't changed. Plus, Heath and Josh didn't know about the curse. They'd never understand it or my reasons to not be with Lily.

Josh's text came five minutes later. *I love this woman! Why aren't you here with her right now? If you hadn't called dibs, I'd marry her.*

My friends sucked. And, of course—*of course*—Lily would get along swimmingly with them, would win them over with one bat of her eyelashes.

I didn't respond and no more witty commentary arrived from their end.

I watched some mindless TV and tried to read, did some research on a few upcoming articles due next week. Nothing stopped my gaze from shooting back to the pink paper on my kitchen counter. At two a.m., I gave the fuck up and opened the damn envelope.

Inside the folded paper was a four leaf clover, pressed between two thin pieces of glass no larger than a quarter. With shaking hands, I read the note.

Mo Grá,

You called me this in the last days we were together. I am your love, and you are mine. We didn't plan on it, but it happened. I know your reasons for trying not to fall, yet you did. So did I. Leaving you this note, leaving you, was the hardest thing I've ever done. In a strange twist of fate, I picked this clover the day I met you. After you walked away from me at the park, I glanced down at a patch of grass and, mingled in with other clovers, there it was. My hope is that by doing this, you alone can break the curse and be with me. Declan O'Leary, I give you my love and my luck. Please don't throw either away. Meet me on Saturday at Irish Eyes at 7:00. If you don't come, I'll understand and won't contact you again.

Always,

Lily xoxo

Christ. Oh, Christ Almighty.

I looked from the clover to the note. One hundred years ago, my great-grandfather had thrown a woman's luck and love away, sending generations into this mess. No females had been born in our family since. Not one of the men had been able to hold onto forever with their women. To add crazy to the mix, this coming Saturday, the day Lily wanted to meet, was St. Patrick's Day. And she just...just...

Shit. What had she done?

A strangled cry left my throat. My hands shook so violently I had to set the note and clover on the counter or risk dropping them both. My chest heaved. My limbs locked. My heart pounded. Black dots swam in my peripheral.

Shit, shit, shit. What to do?

When my stomach threatened to revolt, I pulled my cell from my pocket and connected with Aiden. I paced, waiting for him to pick up.

"Declan? What are you doing awake? I just closed the pub."

"I need to see you. Now."

"Is Dad okay? Liam?" Panic shot the questions out, lacing my brother's tone. The hum of Aiden's engine filled the quiet. Passing cars zipped, echoing in the phone.

"Yes, they're fine. It's me. I'm not okay. I need to see you."

"Okay, okay." Tires screeched. "I turned around. I'm five minutes away. Be right there."

Disconnecting, I strode to the corner cabinet, poured two fingers of whiskey into a glass and knocked it back. Fuck it. I downed two more. The burn did little to calm my nerves. Pouring another for myself and one for Aiden, I headed into the living room to wait.

A ding of the elevator and Aiden shot out the doors, did a quick visual scan of my apartment, and ate the distance between us. "What the hell is going on?"

I handed him the whiskey. "You'll need it. Sit down."

Impatience making his movements stiff, he shrugged out of his light jacket and dropped on my couch. He held the glass between his hands, knuckles white.

Unable to sit, I paced the length of the floor and back, one hand fisting my hair, the other holding my drink. I didn't know where the fuck to begin, so I started at the beginning. "Last summer, I met Lily in the park."

I told Aiden the whole story, about running into her at various places, then finally the pub. Told him about the one week and how my feelings for her evolved. I left out her reasons for accepting my offer and the sexual shit. With every word, my brother grew more tense, until I was pretty certain he was going to punch me. By the time I was done, I felt like I'd been dragged across asphalt buck naked.

I stopped. Pacing and talking. Then I downed my whiskey and set the glass on the coffee table between me and my brother.

Aiden hadn't moved, but judging by his narrowed eyes and clenched jaw, he was plotting ten thousand ways to kill me. Finally, he set his drink down very carefully and rose. "You stupid sack of shit. I told you not to get involved. I asked you to keep her from the curse—"

"About that." I went into the kitchen, retrieved the note and clover, and returned. I gave Aiden the letter.

His gazed skimmed the note. He stilled, reared, and reread the thing. After a beat, he dropped to the couch as if his legs couldn't hold him. His gaze jerked to mine.

I held up the clover between two fingers.

A gust of air left my brother. He swiped a hand down his face and rubbed his neck. "Shit, man."

"Yeah."

He picked up his drink, tossed it back in one swallow, and slammed the glass down. "What are you going to do?"

I pinched the bridge of my nose. "Would I have called you to come over at two a.m. if I had any idea what I was going to do?"

"Right. Okay, let's figure this out."

I paced again. Hope and anxiety battled inside my chest.

"If you don't go, you'd save her from the curse."

My yes came out more like, *duh*.

"If you do go..."

"I could break the curse or lose her." At this point, our lives boiled down to a flip of a fucking coin. My stomach knotted. I wore the floorboards down to sawdust. Gnashed my teeth. "Hell, Aiden. I love her so damn much it hurts."

His gaze lowered to his hands. "She's been gone less than a day. Try having the best year of your life, bearing a beautiful boy together, only to watch her bleed out in childbirth."

"Christ." I plopped next to my brother and poured us two more fingers of whiskey. "I can't do it. I can't lose her the way you lost Amy. I don't know how you keep breathing."

Aiden nodded. "For Liam, that's how." He sat back and sipped his drink. After a contemplative pause, he looked at me. "You could end it all, right now. In all these years, no woman has done what Lily offered. You could break the curse."

I drank from my glass. Poured another. "And what if it doesn't work?"

Aiden closed his eyes and sighed. "The thing is, if you don't go, isn't that like what Great-Grandfather did? Throwing her luck and love away? Does that start a whole new cycle of curses?"

Sometime between then and the bottom of the bottle, Aiden and I got shitfaced and crashed on the couch, having not solved the great debate.

I awoke midday with my tongue stuck to the roof of my mouth, leprechauns hammering the inside of my skull, and sunlight scorching my retinas.

After a shower, three aspirin, and a bottle of water, I drifted into my office. I uploaded the photo Lily had texted me a few days ago, the one of her laying on my bed, and printed the picture. I put it in an old frame, along with the clover, and set it on my desk. I was still staring at her beautiful face when night fell.

I got drunk. Again. Alone, this time.

It didn't help eradicate her from memory, but it did knock me out clean into the next day, so there was that.

The closer it got to the time Lily asked to meet, the more insane I became. Like a caged animal, I prowled my apartment. Go? Don't go? Risk losing her? Take the chance to be with her? Maybe end the curse? Perhaps start a new one?

I was ready to claw right out of my skin. My head pounded. My gut ached. I was pretty certain a hot poker to the eye would feel better than this limbo. And this wasn't just about me. If the curse wasn't broken by her act, she'd be taken from me in one form or another. There was my family to consider as well. I had the potential to stop years of heartache, end our despair, or start a whole new brand of we're-screwed.

What. The. Fuck. To. Do?

6:30. My heart stopped. I needed to figure it out.

Striding into my office, I grabbed her letter and read it for the millionth time. My gaze landed on her picture, on the clover in the lower corner of the frame sitting on my desk. I looked, really looked at her, and tried to empty my mind of the chaos.

Her blue eyes grounded me, brought back all the times we'd talked, the things I'd told only her. She'd looked at me with intense interest, listened to every word, had been invested in what I had to say. The way her hair spread out over my bed, around her face, had the memory of her scent filling my nose, the calming presence she invoked. I could almost feel those strands through my fingers. Her mischievous smile, a tease, had my body tightening in response. She could make me laugh and pull a groan with her lips alone. I remembered the way she took care of me when I'd overdone it in the gym and how good she was with Liam.

The woman spoke French because she'd read *Les Miserable* as a teen and thought the language would be romantic to learn. She had no family, had been shown very little affection, yet she loved with her whole being. Brave enough to take chances, smart enough to proceed with caution. Selfless, giving, she'd tamed even a guy like me, brought out long-buried desires. We had passion and chemistry. And clever woman that she was, she'd found a way to try and break a curse, to bring hope back in my life.

I straightened. Blew out a breath.

There. My answer. She was it for me. There would never be anyone else, and she risked everything, knowing our family history, to take the chance on us. I had to do the same.

Grabbing my coat, I ran out the door. Rush hour would be dying down, so I took the elevator to the parking garage level and hoofed it to my car. The drive to Irish Eyes was the longest five minutes of my life. My gaze kept darting to the dashboard clock.

6:55.

6:56.

6:58.

At 7:01, I pulled into the pub's parking lot and bolted for the door. Yanking it open, I was assaulted by heat, noise, and the smell of beer. Being Saturday and St. Patrick's Day, the place was packed. Wall to wall bodies.

I shoved my way inside and toward the bar, three rows deep with patrons. Aiden had two additional bartenders working. I tried to see around the crowd and finally spotted my brother on the other side of the bar, talking to some people. I elbowed my way through, gaze scanning the room for Lily's dark hair.

I didn't see her. Panic started to claw my chest the closer I got to Aiden. He'd know if Lily was here, or if she'd been in at all.

A group of guys shouted *cheers*. The Irish music from the speakers could barely be heard over the noise. Female giggling grated my ears.

Where the hell was she?

Finally, I squeezed through the bustle and shouted for Aiden. From a few feet away, he turned his head toward me and stilled. Slowly, he straightened from where he'd been leaning on the bar. His gaze bore into mine, searching, probing. I forced a swallow and nodded, silently telling him I'd decided. And I chose her. Love. Understanding dawned in Aiden's eyes, softening the thin line of his mouth into a knowing smile. With a tilt of his head, my brother indicated the person in front of him.

I shifted my focus and...there she was. Turned halfway on her stool, wearing a light green sweater and skinny jeans, she regarded me through her blue eyes and a carefully masked expression.

The room emptied of noise, everything else fading away. It was just her and me.

I wove through a group of women to stand in front of her, the crowd shoving us in close proximity. I stood between her knees, the height of the stool putting her at eye level with me. Someone slammed into my back, jostling me closer, but I kept my gaze on her. Two days had felt like two hundred years without her. I wasn't even sure my heart was beating.

I lifted a hand to finger the strands of her hair. "Am I too late, *mo grá?*"

Her lips parted, eyes widening. She offered a very slight shake of her head.

"Does your offer still stand? Your luck and love given freely?" Christ, I was dying. Though I'd never been more sure of anything in my life, I wanted to give her an out. There was still a chance her act wouldn't break the curse. To me, a life without her would *be* the curse. Not taking this chance, not having her in my life, was as good as death.

Moisture welled in her eyes, coating her thick, black lashes. Trembling, she nodded. "Yes," she whispered. She cleared her throat and spoke louder. "Yes."

Two things happened right then. One, my heart expanded to fill my chest, so encompassing, the dark crevices sealed. And two, I knew my family's unlucky streak was over. There were no bells and whistles, no signs from the heavens, but I was certain. My soul melded with hers in my brother's pub. Among a throng of people amassed in green, drinking ale and chanting folk songs, Lily and I became one, and I knew.

I cupped her cheeks and stroked her jaw with my thumbs. "I love you. I accept your gift and will never throw it away. You, *mo grá,* have all of me."

She breathed a laugh, tears spilling, and wrapped her arms around my neck. Her lips brushed my ear. "I love you."

I closed my eyes to savor the words. With an arm around her back, I drew her against my chest and kissed her. Her soft lips met mine, tender at first, and then she opened for me. Heat infused my every cell when her tongue met mine, passion and promise with every stroke.

How I'd missed her.

I pulled away to drop my forehead to hers. "I love you, too. So much."

Aiden leaned over the bar, cupping the back of my head and then Lily's. He kissed my cheek. Kissed Lily's. He grinned, happiness and relief and triumph in his eyes. He held my gaze for a moment and nodded, as if he, too, was sure of my decision.

Pouring the three of us a shot, he lifted his. "To love, luck, and the end of bad omens."

Smiling, I tossed back my shot. "*Gach lá ar an saol ar fad tríd.*" Each day the whole life through.

I took Lily home and made love to her. Made love to her every night, in fact. Three months later, I proposed to her in Aiden's pub. We bought a house—a three story old Victorian that she said "had character." Two months after that, we got married in a small ceremony one year to the day we met, right next to the bench where I first saw her and she'd picked our clover.

We didn't talk anymore about curses, not because we were superstitious or concerned, but because we knew and believed there was no more curse.

And if there was any doubt to our truth, one year after we wed, Lily delivered twins. Our twins. Perfect little bundles with dark hair, my green eyes, and her addicting smile. A little boy and...*a girl.*

Lucky me.

Soul's Cruise

Regular vivid dreams of life on a
pirate ship trouble Josh's mind for years.
Then, on a cruise, he meets Heather, a woman,
who not only captivates him, but seems
strangely familiar. She recalls who he is
from another life, another time.
Her Irish ancestry knows of such things, and
fate brought her to the same cruise ship.

Mandy
Eve-Barnett

SOUL'S CRUISE

Mandy Eve-Barnett

An unaccustomed briny aroma invaded Josh's slumber, conjuring dreams of pirates and tall ships in his mind. A large, black-bearded captain loomed over him, shouting orders. The pirate's breath blasted Josh's face, making him reel backwards. It was disgusting a mixture of rotten teeth, belched stomach contents, and rum.

"Get ye up the foremast, boy, and be lively about it!"

Afraid of a flogging, Josh ran barefoot on the wooden planked deck, scurrying past burly, unsmiling men. Their rancid sweat emanated from their toiling bodies. Each man busied themselves with their tasks, keeping their heads low to avoid the captain's stare or displeasure. The salty air and bracing wind assaulted his face and lungs. At the bottom of the mast, he looked up at the rope rigging and the impossibly high climb to the crow's nest. The wet ropes had a pungent smell of kerosene. Fear clawed at his stomach.

I can't do it, I just can't.

A huge swell broached the ship's side, tossing men, rigging, and barrels across the deck. Briny water and debris crashed onto the wooden planks, adding to the unpleasant smell all around him. Josh stumbled, hitting his head on the main mast.

The shock woke him from his dream. Disorientated, thinking the rocking movement underneath him was a figment of his imagination, he opened his eyes. Blinking several times, he squinted through a round porthole at a blue sky and splashing water.

Am I still dreaming that awful recurrent dream?

A knock on his cabin's door and his mother's voice alleviated his bewilderment. *We're on a boat, but not a pirate ship.* A fresh linen scent replaced the buccaneer odors.

"It's time to go to the dining room for breakfast, Josh. Are you awake?"

"Yes, Mom, I'll meet you there."

Once he was dressed, he slipped on his new dark blue canvas shoes. The rubber of the sole has a strong smell, combined with the canvas fabric and waterproofing his mother had insisted on applying. He'd picked them especially for the cruise. At twenty-two, many people would find it odd he accompanied his own mother on such a vacation, but after his father had passed away suddenly of a heart attack three years previously, he felt responsible for her. Especially as his mother's grief took such a toll on her well-being. The cruise was his brainchild, a way to get them both away from home, away from the memories, if only for a short time. The house had become oppressive in the months following the funeral.

He entered the large dining room to the wonderful aromas of bacon, toast, coffee, and fruit. A long serving counter held hot plates at one end and chilled bowls at the other. The hot plates sizzled with fatty fragrance. A long line of people stood choosing their preferences to eat. He found his mother standing to one side, waiting for him.

"There you are. Let's get in line so we can pick our breakfast, find a seat, and eat together."

Their choices made, Josh and his mother sat near the rear of the room by the exit. He spread golden butter generously on his toast, and then opened a strawberry jam sachet. The tangy sweetness of the fruit was unmistakable as the foil peeled off. Next, he poured maple syrup over his pancakes, the aroma a mix of caramel and toffee. He cut into the pancake pile and added a strip of bacon to his bite. Delicious!

A waiter refilled their coffee cups, giving rise to a nutty, smoky fragrance.

His mother's hand covered his own, worry creasing her forehead. "You look rather tired, sweetheart. Are you okay? Is it seasickness?"

He smiled and squeezed her hand. "I'm good, Mom, just that same dream. I think the wave motion brought it on."

"Well, goodness, it's been sometime since you had it, you are probably right. Shall I stay with you?"

"No, of course not I'm not ten! I was going to explore a bit as it's the first time I've been on a cruise ship."

"Well, if you're sure, have fun. I'm going to find a nice spot with a deckchair to read. We can meet back here at one o'clock for lunch."

"Sounds like a plan. I'll see you later."

Josh pushed open the heavy metal door. A whiff of grease wrinkled his nose for an instant before the rush of briny air invaded his nostrils. The ship rocked back and forth like a cradle. He braced his legs and walked along the deck rails for support. Ahead was the lido deck, filled with the sound of excited voices and splashing. Chlorine merged with the stronger brine. He took the metal steps upward and was surprised by a tumbling ball of navy blue string heading towards him. He caught it and began winding the loose thread back around the ball. At the top of the stairs, he was met by a beautiful face surrounded with wavy titian hair, and a hand clasped over her mouth.

"Oh, goodness gracious, I'm so sorry. It just slipped from my hand."

He blinked. She was vaguely familiar; a strong déjà vu feeling overcame him toward this total stranger. He recognized a gentle Irish lilt to her words.

"No worries. Glad I was there to catch it. It could have rolled straight over the edge into the ocean."

"That was what I was afraid of. Thank you for rescuing it."

He shrugged and handed the twine to the young woman. He guessed she was approximately his age, early twenties. Her violet eyes transfixed him, and she smelled so good—a heady mixture of citrus and cinnamon.

"Why do you need string for on a cruise, anyway?"

"Oh, well, you may think it odd, but I use it for macramé. I make wall hangings and art out of it. There're mostly for commissions."

"I don't think that's odd. Sounds kind of cool, actually."

"Would you like to see some of the things I've made? Only if you have the time, I've probably stopped you from something as it is."

"No, I'd like to see. I was just taking a look around. This is my first cruise. I'm Josh, by the way."

"Well, hello to you. I'm Heather. Come this way. I'm all set up on the viewing deck. Might as well have a great view while I craft shouldn't I?"

She had laid out her supplies across two loungers. A delicate scent of cotton and musk rose as she lifted an intricate piece.

"That is so cool. Can you show me how you make them?"

She raised her eyebrows, showing shock. "Are you sure? It's not a thing that interests the men usually."

His smile added to his assurance he was serious.

"Well then, sit here beside me."

As Heather sat and picked up her crochet hook, she could smell his fresh shampoo and musky cologne, so unlike her two brother's body odor and grease. It was a pleasant change. There was a yearning in her chest she could not understand, like he was a long-lost friend, or maybe more. A bizarre feeling coupled with a sense of déjà vu making her pause for a moment. *How did they connect? Who was he?*

She shook the thought from her mind and began to loop, knot, and braid, noticing the keen interest in his eyes. Her fingers worked in rhythm after so many years of practice, almost an unconscious thought.

Josh watched Heather's fingers expertly weave the cotton cord as she explained the different techniques. Before his eyes, the article grew into a complex multi-coloured criss-cross and spiral pattern. When she held up the piece to inspect it, a Celtic-inspired series of knots depicted a landscape.

"Wow, that is the coolest thing I've seen. You must be an expert."

Her laughter caught him unaware. "I'm no expert, that takes many years, but I'm accomplished enough to have my work known in my part of Ireland and some places overseas. My mentor, Mrs. Hainwright, has made macramé for decades, and her designs and deft fingers can produce a piece with such intricate knotting that I feel quite the novice."

He shook his head. "There's no way you can be a novice. Look at what you made!"

"Well, thank you for that. I do my best. Now, I must pack up. I'm meeting the boys for lunch."

He pulled his fingers through his hair, sudden disappointment filling his chest. He queried before he could stop the words. "The boys?"

She tilted her head and gave him a warm smile. "My brothers, Cormac and Liam. They entered a competition and won this cruise. It was for four people, and as neither of the big dolts have regular girlfriends, they asked me. Although, Cormac tried to persuade my Ma, but she has a fear of the water, so then there were three. Maybe we will bump into each other another time?"

He swallowed and licked his lips. *Ask to see her again.*

His courage failed and he replied, "Sure, that would be great."

She folded the macramé piece into a large canvas bag and then placed the balls of cord on top. With a quick smile exchanged, she strode away down the planked deck. He felt deflated. He'd missed his chance.

"There you are. I thought I got the wrong deck or something. Did you have a good time exploring this beast of a ship?"

"Hi, Mom. Yeah, I did." Deflecting his disappointment at losing his chance with Heather, he pointed to the long buffet. "There's so much to choose from. Where do we start?"

His unusual silence over lunch gave cause for his mother to question him several times. His annoyance at the intrusion into his thoughts made him snap, and he was immediately ashamed.

"Sorry, Mom. I didn't mean that."

Tears welled in her eyes, so he took her hand. He knew how fragile she was. He was such a jerk.

"Look, I'll make it up to you. How about we go to the top deck and take a swim?"

With a shuddering breath, and much to his relief, she nodded.

The pool was crowded with kids splashing, multiple floatation devices, and a constant yelling from parents to their little ones. It was not the nice excursion he'd hope for to console his mother.

"Oh, dear, this is frantic. I don't think I can cope with all this, Josh."

"Me, neither. Maybe there's a quiet time when the kids are asleep. What would you like to do instead?"

"Goodness, I'm not sure, but it needs to be less hectic than this." She rolled her eyes.

He took out his phone and clicked the cruise line app. "There's miniature golf, music, or comedy shows. They even have Bingo."

"Oh, now I do like a good game of Bingo, Josh, but I don't want you to feel you need to stay with me."

"Okay, it's on the third level. Come on, it's this way."

As he got ready to leave his mother at the Bingo venue, she turned toward him. "Can you take our swimming gear back to your cabin, sweetheart? I don't want to be carrying that big bag around."

He shouldered both beach bags filled with their towels, suits, and their specially bought water shoes, and headed to his cabin.

Descending a flight of stairs, he was obstructed by a broad-shouldered giant of a man with a shock of red hair and a beard reminiscent of a Viking. Josh had no means of passing by this formidable obstacle.

"I'm sorry, I'll back up."

"That, or I can lift yer over, young'un."

Josh recognised the accent as Irish and stepped backward and upward as best he could without tripping. As the man emerged, a second man similar in stature and with the same bold red hair followed. Then a familiar titian-covered head appeared.

Heather.

So, these were the brothers. He was no match for them in any way, shape, or form. He needed to be careful with his words. By the size of them, they could easily protect their younger sister.

"What a nice surprise, Josh. It's grand to see you again so soon."

Both men looked from Heather to him and back again. Their chests rose as they stood even taller.

She nudged the brother closest to her and gave them both a stern look. "Be off with you, posturing like two roosters. Josh is the one I told you about, him liking my macramé and all."

The men's posture relaxed, and they looked down at their shoes.

Not so tough against their sister, then.

She pointed to her brothers in turn. "This hulk is Cormac, and this one is Liam. Well, where are your manners? Say hello."

Josh suppressed a smirk at her command.

Both men said *hello* in deep baritone and stood to one side.

"Don't stand around like stone columns looming over me. You know I hate that. I'll see you up top in a bit. Off with you."

Josh kept his face expressionless until the brothers were out of sight. "I will keep in line, Heather. If you can control them like that, I'm no match."

"Don't you fret about it. They know not to upset me, as big as they are. I know their weaknesses. Now, enough of brothers. Where are you off to?"

He relayed his failed ploy to cheer up his mother with a visit to the swimming pool. "And now I'm at a loss. I was thinking about trying out miniature golf."

"Forgive me, but that sounds rather sad if you're all alone. Cormac, Liam, and I are going to the bumper cars. Do you want to come along?"

"Bumper cars? I didn't even see that on the app. I'm definitely up for that."

As they walked along the interior corridor, he breathed in her citrus and cinnamon scent. Her hair flowed halfway down her back, and an image of her in a corseted dress with a shawl around her shoulders appeared in his mind.

He shook his head. *Where had that come from?* A pirate ship came to mind. He sniggered. Just that morning's dream echoing for some reason.

Heather turned, and she was that image in full Technicolor—a pirate's moll, down to large hoop earrings, multiple rings on each finger, and a plunging neckline exposing voluminous breasts.

He shook his head, stumbled, and placed a hand on the metal plates of the corridor.

A soft hand touched his cheek, a whispered query.

"Are you all right, Josh?'

He opened his eyes, felt the texture of the carpet underneath his hands. How had he wound up on the floor? He shook his head a third time. There she was again, his titian beauty. There was a deep connection to her, but how?

"I'm not sure. Did I faint?"

"I heard a thud and turned 'round to see you'd collapsed. Do you have seizures?"

"No, I don't. I saw…"

"What did you see?"

He stood up, shrugged, and sighed. "Oh, it's nothing. Maybe I'm seasick, or ate something that didn't agree with me. Come on, let's get to the bumper cars. Your brothers will be getting anxious, and the last thing I need for them to be thinking is I did something I shouldn't. I'm no match for them."

"Don't you worry about those big lugs, I can handle them. Are you sure you're all right?"

"Yeah, sure, really, I am. Come on."

Cormac and Liam gave Josh a disapproving look as he and Heather entered the noisy venue, but were swiftly put right by their sister. For over two hours, they drove, collided, and laughed as they raced the cars around the oval track. At first, Josh tried to avoid the brothers, but soon found out they were just about having fun, no malice apparent.

They sat together to eat burgers, fries, drink sodas, and chat about their lives. Josh learned Heather's brothers were both heavy duty mechanics in their father's garage. It certainly explained their size and muscles. Josh explained his reason for the cruise, and they were all very sympathetic—a reaction he hadn't quite expected. Cormac voiced for his siblings their condolences.

The afternoon turned to early evening, and Josh realized he hadn't told his Mom where he was. He was, after all, her companion on the trip. Quickly tapping out a message, he sent it and waited for a reply. None came.

"Shit! Sorry, I have to go. I abandoned my mother, and now she's not answering me. I have to find her."

"Heh, settle Josh. We'll come and help."

He looked at Liam, surprised at the offer.

"Really, there's no need."

All three siblings stood and chorused, "We would never forgive ourselves if we were at fault. We're finding your Ma."

As the four of them walked along the various corridors and decks, Josh noticed apprehensive and curious glances from other passengers. In truth, he could understand why. He and Heather looked like a couple escorted by two bodyguards. It was like being celebrities, and he couldn't help tilting his chin in an aloof manner just to make them seem more important. Heather must have noticed because she gave him a mischievous wink and did the same.

As they entered the main dining room, he was relieved to spot his mother sitting in a booth chatting to another woman.

"I'm so sorry, Mom, I lost track of time. Are you okay?"

A puzzled expression crossed her face. "Of course, I'm all right. Joan here and I bumped into each other at Bingo. It's a small world. We were at school together, haven't seen each other for decades. We're catching up on all our news." She turned to the gray-haired, lean woman and introduced Josh.

"My son, Josh, is my treasure, Joan."

The woman nodded and said hello, then both women peered behind Josh at his companions.

"Oh, sorry, this is Heather, Cormac, and Liam. I met them all today. We've been on the bumper cars this afternoon."

With introductions made, the Irish siblings left to find a table, and Josh sat with the older women. His mother had tried to persuade him to go with his new friends, but his guilt made him stay, although his mind was turning over. There was something about Heather, a deep core feeling he couldn't explain. And what was that illusion he experienced in the corridor? It had felt so real, so like his recurrent dreams. He was strongly drawn to her, not only physically but emotionally.

·♥·♥·♥·♥·♥·

The ship rocked side to side, freezing wave after freezing wave thrashing the ship's deck. Josh held fast on the rigging. The storm was relentless. Two days of no sail and no land in sight. His fellow shipmates were crossing themselves and cursing in equal measure. He'd heard murmurs below deck.

Never have a woman on board, its bad luck. Now, see what we suffer. We're all for Davy's locker.

As the dream became more intense, Josh tossed and turned in his sleep, his movements limited by the small cabin bed. In the real world, the cruise liner glided across a calm ocean, the opposite of the dream ship's predicament.

Dream Josh staggered across the deck and entered a wooden door, which revealed a set of steep steps. He hung on as best he could as the ship rolled about on the stormy sea. He searched for her in the galley and the small cabin she was restricted to. There was no sign. Panic grew in his chest. A fear born of the glares he suffered from the crew raised worrying thoughts. *Would they throw her overboard, their superstitions getting the best of them?* He shook the dreaded thought away, turned toward the corridor and heard chanting.

Keep safe the ship.
Spare our lives.
Away with the curse and sin.
Bad luck she brings.
Keep safe the ship.
Spare our lives.
Away with the curse and sin.
Bad luck she brings.
Haul her over,
To the depths she goes.
Safe passage for us all.
Smooth seas will follow.

Fear gripping his chest, Josh ran, flying up the wooden steps into salty air and cold water spraying the deck. Her shawl was crumpled on the wooden planks, and then he turned to face the side. There, crowded together, were a group of sailors, knives pulled and held before them. His true love was pinned to the gunwale, tears streaming down her cheeks, fear evident in her wide eyes as she pleaded for her life.

He ran, head down, into the mob and placed himself between them and their quarry. Jeers and shouts rang out, but he stood his ground. The quartermaster stepped forward.

"She goes, or you both go. Make your choice. She's cursed the ship."

There was no choice. They would die together, lost in the deep waters forever.

Josh gasped for air as the dream came to its zenith. He was sinking under the waves, the cold penetrating his flesh, his hands gripping hers, their eyes locked on each other as death claimed them.

A violent shiver rocked his body into wakefulness. The violet eyes followed him from the depths. It was her.

Heather.

He sat up in the cabin bed, warm air around him, and tried to make sense of what he'd seen. Never before had the dream run that far, culminating in the two of them being thrown overboard like worthless flotsam.

How can I, how can Heather, be the people in my dream?

Not waiting for his mother, he hurriedly dressed and placed a note at her cabin door. He had to find Heather, and now.

He went to the dining hall, the upper decks, the bumper cars, and the swimming pool. She was nowhere to be found.

If only I'd asked which deck her cabin was on. I don't even know her surname.

Then, there she was, standing at the railing, looking out to sea, her hair cascading and undulating in the breeze. The sun rising making the horizon blush. Her attire shifted from jeans and sweater to corseted dress. He let the vision remain and felt a change in his clothing, too. A rough cotton shirt rubbed his skin, tight breeches encased his thighs, and leather boots thudded on the wooden deck.

She turned and smiled. "It took you such a long time to find me again, my love."

Their embrace was fierce, familiar, and full of love. Many moments later, eyes locked, he witnessed a shimmering of their images, and they were back in today's time.

He could only utter one word. "How?"

She smiled, drew him to the deck seating, and pivoted to face him.

"Let me ask you, do you have recurrent dreams?"

He could only nod.

"A pirate ship, the high seas, a furious mob, waves swallowing you?"

"Yes!"

Her hands gently cupped his face. "I believe our souls were linked together in our anguish and fear when thrown from the ship. I, too, suffered years of nightmares until I met an elderly Druid." She held up her hand to stall his query. "It seems like so much nonsense in today's technology-filled world, but her reaction to touching my hand sent her into a deep trance. She recalled all my 'dreams' in exact detail. I have never shared them with anyone outside my family. She told me to seek out my heart, my soul mate on the water. At the time, it seemed impossible. We live in central Ireland, a place called Moyvore furthest from the sea. Then Cormac won the cruise. Was it a sign, or coincidence, I cannot tell. I just knew, deep in my heart, I had to come. And then, there you were, just the same. Your eyes, your hair, it was a relief and a certainty in my soul. I was hesitant at first to say anything, afraid you'd think me crazy or insane."

"So, what made you sure?"

"When you collapsed, you murmured my name, my true name, and I knew."

"What do you mean your true name?" A deep frown creased his forehead.

"If you let your mind relax, it will come, my love, my Iosua."

Josh closed his eyes, inhaled deeply, and then exhaled. She stood beside him on a cliff, hands clasped, excitement at the impending adventure thrilling them both. A sea voyage to the Americas, and a new life. He turned to face her... Fraoch, his lover, and soon to be wife.

He whispered it and opened his eyes. "We were to marry?"

"It was another life, long gone. I do not hold you to a promise made in another life, Iosua. I found you, and now we can let go, find new loves, new life in this time."

A rising panic took his breath away. "No! We have another chance, one so precious, so unique, we cannot cast it aside. Why would you let us go so easily?"

"I told you, I do not hold you to your promise. We are different people, live different lives, and miles apart. We were young, impetuous, and naive. I live in Ireland, you in London, it is impossible."

Josh felt her lie as surely as a slap across his face. "You're making excuses. You feel the same as me. This, us, is not to be dismissed, discarded, or made insignificant. The more time I have with you, the deeper I feel our connection, our love. I dreamed last night, that's the reason I scoured this damn ship so early. Before now, the dream always ended at the flight of stairs below deck, but last night, I experienced for the first time our demise. It means something. It means we are free of our past. We can move forward, experience our love the way it was supposed to be. Please don't walk away, please." He gripped her hands, his heart racing and his eyes searching the depths of hers.

Her shoulders sagged. Tears brimmed on her lower lids, and then fell. "I never thought you would feel it so deeply, so completely the way I do. I wanted to give you a way out. After all, we are only twenty-two. Many will say we're too young to commit to one another for life. I had to give you a way out."

He embraced her, allowing her tears to soak into his t-shirt. He'd never felt so at home, so complete, than at that moment. "We belong to one another, now and forever, my darling Fraoch. My promise stands."

They spent every waking moment together for the last three days of the cruise. Reminiscing on their past as memories rose from their unconscious, their home in Ireland, the ravages of the potato famine, all determining their plan to escape the tall ship, not a pirate ship, at all, and their tragic end.

Their obvious intensive and absorbing relationship surprised both brothers and Josh's mother. They covered up the true nature of their love story by explaining it was love at first sight. Josh knew his mother believed it was a 'flash in the pan,' a holiday romance and nothing more, while Heather believed her brothers were wary of his motives, although neither family was particularly rich.

On the last day, the cruise liner docked in Bristol. Josh and Heather clung to one another until the last minute, hurried by their relatives to leave the dockside and head homeward. Plans were made for Heather to fly to Heathrow airport in one week, while Josh used the time to search courses at the Athlone University, which was only a short thirty-minute drive from Heather's hometown. He found a perfect four-year BBus (Hons) course in business and applied.

They were determined this time around. They would be together no matter what.

·❤·❤·❤·❤·❤·

On her visit, Josh took Heather to all the tourist sites. They walked the Embankment, rode the London Eye, visited several museums, and sat together in Hyde Park eating crusty bread sandwiches. They laughed after throwing their crusts to the ducks, swimming and waddling around the pond at the chaos it caused among the waterfowl. The constant traffic noise, the acrid air, and the rush of pedestrians bombarded Heather's senses, so different from the wide-open spaces of her Irish countryside. She found it alarming and claustrophobic. Josh saw their life needed to be lived in a quieter, less rushed place, and knew his path was chosen.

Although he suffered some guilt at leaving his widowed mother, it was alleviated by the appearance of Joan, his mother's old school pal, who upon returning home from the cruise, found her apartment, ransacked by a burglar. It was soon arranged she stay in his mother's spare bedroom until the investigation and redecoration was complete. Seeing the two women together, Josh felt their friendship would be a solace for his mother. Mom, in turn, saw the true and deep love between the two young adults, and gave her reassurances she would be fine. She would not hold Josh to the idea he needed to remain at home.

After months of planning, Josh eventually stepped out of the airport and inhaled the richness and earthy scent of Ireland, and knew he was home. It was stronger than déjà vu. A soul's coupling with place. Heather nearly knocked him off his feet when she ran to him and jumped into his arms, legs around his waist. Their kiss was long, passionate, and observed with kindness, and shock in equal measure. As their lips parted, he gazed into those violet eyes and once again knew there was no other place he'd rather be, or person who meant more.

As the weeks and months passed, he relished the soft Irish lilt, the rolling green hills and farmland, and the welcome of family and friends. It all contributed to him knowing he was where he was supposed to be. It was certainly home and his disconnection with the concrete, stone, and hustle of London became all the more apparent.

They used their original names in secret at first, but a year later, when they moved to Althone, to alleviate Josh having to bus to and fro from the university, they legally changed their names to Iosua and Fraoch prior to marrying. The civil service was small and intimate, followed by supper in a local pub. Josh's mother blessed them with a down payment and refused to take it back, saying it was a gift from her and his father.

Iosua surprised his new wife, his true soul mate, with a week on a tall ship for their honeymoon, and this time, there were no pirates, no chants of discord, but full sails, spectacular sunsets, and the lull of the waves as they slept side by side.

The dreams never returned, their souls at peace, at last.

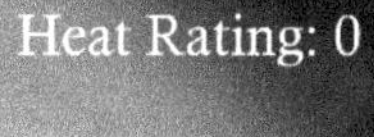

Past, Perfect Polo

Problematic dog, Polo, is in need of rescue,
but maybe he isn't the only one.
Tallulah is learning how to be on her own and
how to spread her wings as an adult.
Polo's owners have dumped him,
and he's now on his way to the pound!
Can she and her boyfriend help him in time?

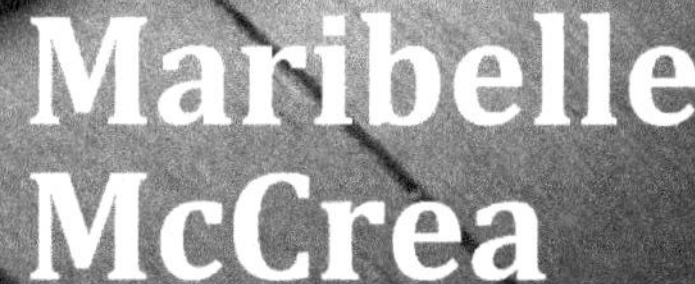

Maribelle McCrea

PAST, PERFECT POLO

Maribelle McCrea

Prologue

"They don't want him. They brought him in for grooming and now they won't pick him up."

The afternoon sun had been shining into the kitchen just minutes ago, but as Lori, our groomer, shares the situation of this poor dog, the clouds cover the sun. It feels appropriate and matches the sadness in my heart.

Momma and I sit beside one another on my parents' sofa, dumbfounded, while Lori gives us the news. Momma has her cell phone on speaker mode so I can listen, too.

"That's awful. I can't imagine doing that ever," Momma says.

Tears threaten behind my eyes. I want to say I'll take the little dog, but I live in student housing in Atlanta. I'm looking for a new place, but I can't have the responsibility of a dog just yet.

"Do you know of anyone who can take him? He's about eight pounds and appears to be a Yorkie mix. If we can't find someone soon, we'll need to take him to the pound, and I just don't feel good about his chances there."

"Yes, I think I do," Momma replies.

"I would take him, but I haven't moved yet," I feel compelled to add.

"Tallulah, honey, I know you have always wanted a dog of your own, but I think Poppy and Nana can take him. They have a special love of Yorkies, and their dog, Sammy, passed away about a year ago."

She makes a good point. Poppy has been looking for another dog, and he's an experienced dog owner.

"I can meet them tomorrow evening if your parents can take him," Lori relays with a sense of urgency.

"I do need to let you know... Polo, that's the dog's name, has been traumatized. Apparently, the family that had him loved him when he was a puppy, but as he got bigger, they started leaving him in the backyard with a much larger dog. He was covered in fleas and showed signs of fear biting while he was here."

"Thank you, Lori. I hate to hear that. Poor pup! We will get him sorted. My dad and step-mom absolutely love Yorkies and have had a few over the years. I will give them a call in the next few minutes. I'm almost positive they'll want him. If they can't drive down from Marietta tomorrow evening, we can keep him until they can meet us."

Momma sounds so calm, but she's slightly trembling beside me. Her heart is breaking for this pup, just like mine.

"Thank you both. I really feel for him and would keep him myself if I didn't already have three dogs at home."

"I'll be in touch soon," Momma says, and there's thickness in her voice. She's about to burst into tears. She's got such a tender heart.

As she hangs up the phone, we each lean into a sideways hug.

"I want to go get him now!" I exclaim. My heart is telling me this dog is meant for me, but how I can make that happen escapes me.

Momma has already dialed the number for my grandfather. She's turned off the speaker phone so I don't hear both sides of the conversation, but I can tell Poppy has agreed to take Polo.

"Can they come down to get him tomorrow?" I ask as Momma hangs up the call.

"Yes. They are super excited and are preparing everything for Polo now."

I know I should be happy, but somehow, I feel uncomfortable, like this is not the right solution. I can't put my finger on why. Maybe I'm just sad or jealous I can't take Polo for myself.

"Momma, I don't know how to explain it, but I feel like Polo should be with me." I know I can share my thoughts and feelings with her, and she'll keep it to herself.

"Well, honey, I agree you would be a better pet parent in general, being younger and having more energy to get the dog out and play with him, but your current living arrangements just don't allow for it."

"I know, and I hope to change that very soon. Parisa and I are looking for an apartment. We can't wait to get out of WestMar. Student housing is the worst!"

I don't mention that I'm also considering moving in with Mason. It's really early in our relationship, but we've been friends for much longer than we've been dating, so it doesn't seem so odd to consider taking it to the next level. Momma and Daddy will not be happy to hear I'm even considering living with Mason, so naturally, I haven't told them.

Momma shakes her head in agreement.

"Let's just pray about it. God will make it clear what needs to happen and when. Don't worry about tomorrow when today has troubles of its own."

I nod in acceptance. Still, I can't shake the feeling that Polo should be my dog, my responsibility. I've never been so certain about anything.

1-Past

"The new apartment is so cute! I can't wait for you to see it." I tell my momma as I juggle boxes and my cell phone on the way in the door.

"That's great to hear, sugar! When does Parisa move in? You mentioned she has to get her things from her parents' house?"

"Yeah, she didn't have much at WestMar since it was fully furnished. Her parents have offered a sofa for the living room with end tables and a coffee table. She will bring that, plus her bedroom furnishings from her house."

"Oh, that's wonderful!"

Momma will want to bring over all the stuff stored in my parents' basement if I don't nip it in the bud.

"Yeah, I probably won't need to buy anything, so that's great."

"Ok, darlin'. It sounds like you are busy moving in, so I'll let you go. Let me know when you have a moment to chat. Poppy called the other day, and he and Nana are having trouble with Polo biting and snarling at everyone."

I put down everything in a hurry and close the door. I need to understand what's going on with Polo. He's been on my mind ever since we got the call from the groomer he was in need of rescue.

"Momma, tell me now. I've got all day today to unpack and stuff."

"Well, I only bring it up because I'm so worried about what Poppy and Nana might do. Poppy sounded really upset, and rightfully so."

"Why, what happened?"

"Polo is not adjusting well, but they've put his crate in the kitchen where all the activity is and so he doesn't have a safe space to get away from people and calm down. All that to say, Polo bit Nana pretty deeply on her hand and she had to go to the ER for stitches."

"Oh, no! I see why Poppy is upset. What else did he say?"

I have a sense of dread, but I need to know the whole story.

"Poppy thinks they should take him to the pound to be put down. He thinks once a dog is a biter, he will always be a biter. I tried to explain about helping a scared dog find security, but you know how old-school he is."

Tears well up and begin to spill over my cheeks, hot and heavy, leaving trails of salt that sting my skin. My chest tightens, constricting like a vice, as a lump rises in my throat, choking back the words I can't say. Each breath feels shallow, the air thick with a weight I can't shake, while my hands tremble at my sides, fingers curling into fists as if to hold onto something solid in this storm of emotion.

"Momma, please call him back. Tell him I will come get Polo today. Please hurry! I can't stand the thought of them putting Polo down."

"Sweetie, can you do that? Not just today, but with school and work? Will you have time for a damaged dog? It's going to take so much patience and work to get him sociable and safe to be around people. I know your heart's in the right place, but I don't want you to take on a burden you're not ready to handle."

"I'll work it out. I need to go get him now." My heart races along with the urge to run to my car this minute and get to Polo, keep him safe.

"Alright, honey. I understand. Your daddy and I will do what we can to help. He's so good with animals. I'm sure he can help get Polo on track to a healthy relationship. I'll call Poppy right now."

"Thank you, Momma. I'll call Parisa and let her know I might not be back for a while, so she's not wondering what happened. She'll have her dad with her, so she doesn't need my help moving the furniture she's bringing."

"That's a good idea. I'll let you know what Poppy says. Love you, bye."

"Love you, Momma. Bye."

I can't focus on unpacking or where I want to put anything in my new room. I wander around the apartment, watching my phone, almost willing it to ring. I need to hear back from Momma that I'm able to go get that sweet pup.

2-Past

After what feels like hours, I've managed to put away my clothes and make my bed, but between fretting and watching my phone, I've done nothing else. I reach for my phone to call Momma and almost drop it as it begins to ring. I snatch the phone off the nightstand, and my heart skips a beat.

"Hey, Momma. Any news?"

"Hey, Tallulah. It took a bit to get in touch with Poppy and Nana, but they can meet us this evening, so you won't have to drive all the way up to Marietta alone. We agreed to meet at that shopping strip right off the exit to Peachtree City up in Fairburn. Can you pick me up on your way? We need to be there by around four this afternoon."

"Yes, that's perfect. That gives me an hour or so to finish squaring away the apartment and getting things ready for Polo. I'll pick you up at three-thirty, okay?"

"Yes, darlin', that works out just fine. I will see you then, and Tallulah?"

"Yes?"

"Breathe. Polo will pick up on your nervous energy and that's not good for him."

"You're right. I know. I already feel better knowing he's coming to us and not the pound. Now, I'm just worried about figuring out how to help him. I have no experience with training a mentally healthy dog, much less one that's been traumatized. I hope I'm not in over my head."

"Take it one day at a time, lean on your daddy, and things will work out. I'm sure of it.

"I'm glad one of us is!"

"You go get finished, and I'll call your daddy to let him know what we're up to. He's got no idea yet, so I need to update him."

"Thanks, Momma. I'll see you soon. Love you, bye."

"Love you, bye."

I send off a text to Parisa, just in case she isn't back with her things before I leave.

Hey! Polo needs a new home. Sorry didn't ask 1st. Emergency. Xplain L8tr. Leaving at 3. Long story. Tell you tonight.

A few minutes go by before I get a notification from Parisa.

Wow! No prob. Love dogs. Don't worry about it. I get it. Can't wait to meet the little guy! C U L8tr. Dad got furniture. On the road soon. XO

I have a few minutes before I need to leave to pick up Momma, and I know I should eat something, but my stomach is still in knots. I know the one person who'll help to calm me down, so I give him a call.

"Hey, Mason. Do you have a minute?"

"Hey, my Lu! For you, of course I do. We're just gearing up for the early dinner guests that show up around four-thirty, so I have a bit of time. What's bothering you? I can feel your stress through the phone."

"I am stressed. Poppy and Nana can't handle Polo, and he bit Nana. It was bad enough she had to go to the ER and get stitches, but Poppy wants Polo put to sleep." The words spill out, but the heaviness in my chest lingers like a weight I can't shake off.

"Gosh, I hate that Nana was hurt, but isn't that an extreme reaction? Aren't there other options?"

"My thoughts exactly. I decided to be that other option." I take a shaky breath, knowing this could change everything. "I know we'd briefly talked about me moving in with you at some point. Would you be okay with me having a dog to bring to that situation down the road? What about Sawyer? Your cat is accustomed to having your space all to himself."

"True, but I feel like you're doing the right thing. That poor dog. Why do you think he's so afraid that he's biting people?"

"The groomer, Lori, said the only details she got from the original owners were that he was in the home as a tiny puppy, but once he was about a year old, they started putting him outside because he barked so much. He was in the backyard with a larger dog, and I guess he was constantly bullied." I can feel my heart racing for Polo, the fear that must have gripped him. "He fear-bites and is protective of his food. I bet he didn't get much to eat with the bigger dog around."

"Man, that sucks. Yeah, I say go get that little buddy. When the time comes, we'll work out something between Sawyer and Polo. It'll be fine."

"Mason, you're the absolute best," I reply with a sigh of relief. I didn't realize how worried I was until he confirmed he was okay with my plan. The knot in my stomach starts to loosen, just a little.

"Lu, honey, I love you and want you to be happy. Let me know how I can help, okay?"

"I will, and I love you, too, Mason. So much." A warmth spreads through me. It feels good to know I have his support. "I'm going to make myself eat a bite before I go pick up Momma. She's going to ride with me to get Polo in a bit."

"Alright, that sounds like a plan. Call me tonight and let me know how it goes, okay?"

"I will. Love you, bye."

"Love you, Lu. Bye."

I finally feel like I can tolerate something, so I grab a yogurt and fresh berries to tide me over until dinner time. At the last minute, I grab a protein bar and put it in my purse. Polo might not give me time to eat tonight if things don't go well. Anxiety tightens my stomach again at the thought, but I push it aside.

I head out the door to go get Momma, my mind racing with a mix of hope and worry about what lies ahead.

3-Perfect

"Mason, I don't know if I can do this." I'm weeping as I try to explain to my best friend how overwhelmed I am. Each sob feels like a wave crashing over me, making it hard to catch my breath. I know he probably can't understand my words between the tears and the hitching breaths as I struggle to speak. My chest hurts, my face is pounding, and the weight of it all presses down on me.

"Slow down, Lu. I'm here. Tell me what's going on."

"I'm late for class, Polo is in the courtyard of the apartment complex off-leash because he needed to go out and I couldn't attach the leash to his collar. Now he won't come back inside." My frustration rams against my temples as panic clutches my airway. "I have to go. I don't know what I was thinking. This is so much more than I know how to handle. Did I make a huge mistake? What am I going to do?" The questions spiral in my mind, amplifying my sense of helplessness.

"Wow, that's a lot for eight o'clock in the morning! I'm on the way, babe. Together, we can do anything. I love you. I'll be there soon, and I'll bring coffee."

"Oh, Mason! Thank you. Daddy is on the way, too. You don't have to come if you don't have the time. I just miss you, and the stress of the last few days has caught up to me." My tears slow, the little hiccups coming less often. I'm slightly mortified I can't handle all this by myself, but then I wonder what would happen to Polo if I didn't have help.

"I don't mind coming to help. If your dad deals with Polo, maybe I can help you feel better. This is a lot, but you've got this. I thought Polo was doing so well. What changed over the last couple days?"

"You're right. The first night and the next morning were fine. I let Polo have free run of the apartment and didn't get near his crate. We just left the door open and put it in a quiet corner of my closet so he could go there if he needed to. He seemed fine. He cuddled right up to me and was super lovey. I didn't need to go anywhere, so I hadn't tried to hook the leash to his collar. Mason, he freaks out if you get close to him with the leash. He almost bit me." My heart aches for him, realizing how scared he must be.

"That's one scared dog. You can tell me more when I get there. Don't worry, babe. I'll be there in ten minutes."

As Daddy and Mason arrive within moments of each other, relief floods through me. I'm thrilled to see the two most important men in my life, but a pang of resignation hits—I'm going to miss my first class of the day. Not a great start to the semester, but it can't be helped at this point. What matters now is getting Polo inside and figuring out how to help him feel safe.

"Daddy, can you coax Polo to come in from the courtyard? I've tried on my own for about thirty minutes and he's still out there sniffing around and ignoring me when I call him. I realize now that I took on more than what I can handle by myself," I said with shame, beginning to course through my heart. "I'm afraid to try and grab him..."

"Give me a few dog treats, and he'll be more likely to follow me."

I hand Daddy the package of pepperoni treats so he can break off small pieces as needed.

"Lori said those are Polo's favorite, so hopefully you'll have better luck than I did."

"Don't you worry, I'll be back with that pup in two shakes of a lamb's tail! These suckers smell so strong, I won't even have to get all that close to him."

Daddy and Mason cross paths as he is going out and Mason is coming in the front door. Mason bobbles the to-go tray holding steaming cups of coffee, but manages to keep them upright.

"Well, hello, Mason! Fancy seeing you here." Daddy raised an eyebrow and grinned. He knows Mason is well and truly smitten, and would do anything for me, including bringing my favorite latte to cheer me up.

"Hi, Grant. Thanks for helping with Polo. If you can wrangle the dog, I'll focus on supporting your daughter."

"I think I have the easier end of that bargain, but you've got yourself a deal!" Daddy heads down the hall to the courtyard door.

Mason smiles at me and shuts the door behind him.

"Quick, before your dad gets back with that crazy mutt..." Mason grabs my arm and pulls me in for a mind-melting kiss.

I know I shouldn't fall for it but, Lord help me, the man can kiss like nothing I've experienced before. My knees go weak, and I reach up to clasp my hands behind his neck for a bit of stability. The peppermint taste of his toothpaste fills his mouth and my sinuses tingle just a bit. It adds to the disorientation since the other part of my brain has recognized the delicious scent of the coffee now perched rather precariously on the kitchen counter.

I pull back just enough to break the kiss and look into his incredible blue eyes. His pupils are dilated and completely focused on me. He always makes me feel like we are the only ones in the room. I mean, we *are* the only ones in the apartment, but he has this way of letting me know nothing else is on his mind and our time together, no matter how brief, is the most important thing to him.

He puts his hands on my hips to pull me tighter to him. This is going to get me very distracted, and soon, very embarrassed.

"Mason, my daddy is going to walk through that door any second, and I do not want to look like two randy teenagers when he does. Besides, I need that latte in the worst way." I reach for the cup and pull it from the cardboard holder. I don't look at him again until after I have the cup between his lips and mine.

"Lu, one day, I'm going to kiss you and not stop. But for now, your dignity is safe. No embarrassing embraces in front of your dad." He is being sarcastic, but it's tempered with his sweet smile, so the sting isn't there.

I put my arm around his waist and turn us both to face the door right as Daddy opens it and produces a wet, stinky Polo. The dog looks up with his tongue hanging out and his breath testifying to the numerous treats he has consumed.

"I brought you some thick suede work gloves, Tallulah. They will be enough protection that you can confidently attach Polo's leash and when needing to crate him."

"Oh, I don't know, Daddy. He snarls like he wants to take my hand off at the wrist. I know he can tell I'm scared, and he just doesn't listen to me. That feeling of shame swells again despite my best efforts to keep it at bay."

"You're right. But don't let it overwhelm you. Let me show you how to handle him. You have to be consistent, so he builds trust with you. He's not had a lot of consistency in his young life. He's stressed and scared because he's having to be the lead dog, and he needs to trust you can be the leader and take that stress away from him. Just watch."

Daddy put on the gloves and slowly squatted to Polo's level.

Polo is backing away from Daddy and growling, but not as loudly as he did this morning. Maybe his hour-long romp has tired him out.

Daddy sits cross-legged on the kitchen floor and pulls the bag of treats out of his pocket. Polo stops growling, his little black nose begins twitching, and I can hear his sniffing from where I'm standing a few feet away. Daddy quietly but firmly calls Polo.

"Polo, come."

Polo takes one step toward him, but stops and drops his head.

"Polo, that's a good boy." Daddy places a tiny pinch of the treat on the floor a few inches from Polo's nose.

The dog snatches up the treat as if he hasn't eaten in days.

"Polo, come," he demands again, and this time, Polo takes three steps before stopping. He's so close, Daddy could grab him if he wanted.

"Now, watch this. It's really important to keep talking to him and tell him what you want from him. No sudden moves and no loud voices."

As he's telling me the steps, he is bringing the leash out of his other pocket. He makes no move to put it on the dog, though. He just puts it on the floor near the wary pup. Polo backs up almost to where he was when they began. He lifts his lip and I see those teeth that have done so much damage, but Polo isn't growling.

"Polo, come," he says once more. This time, Polo walks a circuitous route away from the leash, but gets right next to Daddy's hip and looks up at him.

"Good boy, Polo, good boy." Daddy double treats him and gently pets his head. He holds the leash in the opposite hand and shows it to Polo.

"Walk, Polo?"

With a twitch of his head, Polo seems to be asking Daddy what he means, but he doesn't back away.

"That's a good boy. Yes, let's walk, Polo." And just like that, he has the leash hooked to Polo's collar. A few more comments of praise and another tiny bite of dog treat, and you would never know this dog is a biter. My dad is magic.

"Now, you try." My dad unhooks the leash and hands it to me.

I take a deep breath and slide on the protective gloves in an effort to keep my fear at bay. I sit on the floor a few feet from Polo.

"Polo, come." I have a couple of treats in my hand, but do not offer them yet.

Polo doesn't hesitate and walks carefully over to me. He looks like he could bolt at any moment, but he keeps making progress across the room until he is right in front of me.

"Good boy, Polo. Good come." I offer a small piece of the jerky treat in the palm of my hand, and he takes it much more slowly than the bites he has had before. I wonder if he's just getting full. I take a minute to pet him and talk in low murmurs to him. Then I take the leash from behind my back and follow the same actions Daddy performed—leash loose on the ground, but not too close to Polo's head.

Polo looks at the leash and then actually sniffs my closed hand to see if I have any treats!

"What a smart boy you are! Good, Polo. Walk, Polo?" I'm stunned as I watch Polo walk over the leash and lie down beside it. So much progress so quickly. I would've never imagined. I hook the leash and give Polo another treat to reinforce all this is good, and he's safe.

"Now, it'll be more work to crate him if needed. He's very scared of being shut in the crate, and I imagine it was used as punishment instead of his safe place." My dad gathers his car keys and makes his way to the door.

"Oh, I think we'll just work on building some trust with the collar and leash. I'll leave his crate in the closet and keep it open, maybe even put some toys and treats in there, but we won't use it until he's ready."

"Good idea. Go slowly and reward him with verbal praise and physical attention more than the treats as the days go by. You can do this, Lulu."

"Grant, thanks for the training class! I just learned so much. I've never had a dog, and I know Polo is Tallulah's, but I hope to build a bond with him, too." Mason looks at me and is a bit flushed as he realizes the subtle message his words convey.

"Daddy, you're the best! Thank you. I've got to get to school or I'm going to miss my second class, too. Mason, you and Daddy can see yourselves out while I grab my things. Polo will be fine now."

Both men simply nod and move to leave.

Mason takes a step back toward me and gives me a quick kiss. "I'll come by tonight after the restaurant closes, just to check on Polo, of course."

"Oh, of course, just for Polo. Sure." I smile.

Everything is going to be okay. I hope.

4-Polo

Finally, I think to myself. Saturday mornings take the longest to arrive, but they are my favorite. Polo loves the park, and we're only a few blocks away. It's a gorgeous day and I'm going to spend it with my two favorite boys.

The last few weeks have been a blur. Getting into the routine with Polo hasn't been as smooth as that day with Daddy, but with the help of those thick gloves and lots of extra time built into the morning before class, we have some semblance of a relationship, Polo and me. The snuggles every night and first thing in the morning assure me I did the right thing. Polo has so much love to give, and I'm so grateful I was able to help him.

Mason will be here any minute, and Polo seems to know where we're going. He now will even nudge my hand to get me to hook on the leash so he can go outside. He perks his head and lets out a short bark as we both hear someone walking up to the door.

"Hey, babe! Hey, Polo!" Mason walks through the door.

Polo's little stub of a tail is wiggling furiously. He loves Mason and gets so excited when he gets to go somewhere with him.

"Hey, Mason. How was last night? Polo! Let the man get in the door!" I pull Polo back gently, and he doesn't seem to mind at all.

"It was good. Our numbers are better when the weather is nice. Y'all ready to go? Have you had any other biting attempts?"

"Just let me grab the lunches I packed. Only one biting episode, and it was my fault. I forgot for a moment and went to grab Polo by the collar, and he snapped at me. He didn't skin, but he was immediately remorseful, and we made up quickly."

I hand Mason the picnic bag and blanket, and we head out to his car. It isn't far to the park, but with all the stuff we have to carry, the ride is necessary. In less than ten minutes, we're set up on the grass and relaxing in the sun.

Watching Polo play and romp around in the grass, I can't imagine not having him in my life. I look at Mason and realize I feel the same way about him. Well, same but different, about him, too. I must have a wistful look on my face because Mason raises an eyebrow and stares curiously at me.

"You're pretty deep in thought over there, Lu. Wanna share?"

"Oh, I'm just feeling grateful for the two of you."

"Well, isn't that nice." He kisses me with one of his heart-stopping kisses.

"Yup," I reply. "It's really nice."

Epilogue

"I can't believe they make birthday cakes for dogs," Mason says as he arrives home from work.

"They do! I know our dog-a-versary is not a birthday, but it'll do." I take Mason's work bag and place it on the hall tree so his hands are free to hug me.

He does just that, and I tilt my chin up for a kiss. He doesn't disappoint, and he lifts me off the ground as he deepens the kiss. For a few moments, nothing else exists. It's just me and Mason and this growing heat between us.

"We have so much to celebrate with our little guy," Mason says after he's greeted me properly.

My heart is beating just a bit fast, and I take a quick second to compose myself. It's ridiculous what that man does to me with a single kiss.

"We really do. He's come such a long way, and now you'd hardly know he'd been so skittish. Plus, we're finally able to be with each other all the time. I've wanted to move in with you for so long!"

"So true, babe. I'm glad the timing worked out with Parisa, and everyone is happy with the arrangements. So, I guess we have our dog-a-versary to celebrate, having Polo for two years, *and* our own... What should we call it? Our first cohabitation anniversary? Or maybe first live-together-versary?" Mason laughs at the silly name, but I know he's as thrilled to be living together as I am.

"I don't care what we name it, as long as we have lots more of both celebrations."

"That's something I can definitely promise! You, me, and Polo are a family."

"Don't forget your grumpy old man, Sawyer," I add, not wanting to leave out Mason's cat that he adopted as a tiny kitten. He's not too fond of Polo, but we have hopes that will change over time.

"Yes, Sawyer, too. I love our little family. But, I love you best, Lu."

"I love you, too, Mason. And we are a little family, aren't we?"

I'll take this version of happily-ever-after.

Heat Rating: 2

The Queen

Cole takes a ghost hunting gig aboard the
Queen Mary to find answers on why pictures of his
great-grandfather and Hanna Amery are in an old locket.
Hanna discovers the love she left behind on
The Grey Ghost, housed in the body of Cole.
She just needs to figure out how to get to him.
What happens when they find
each other on opposite planes of the Universe?

Maxine
Douglas

THE QUEEN

Maxine Douglas

One

Well, Cole Masterson, you're in for the adventure of your life, I murmured to myself as my taxi travelled south down the 710 freeway through the mid-afternoon traffic toward the Queen Mary. Now I'd be able to solve the family mystery regarding my great-grandfather, the gold locket, and Hanna. Who was Hanna? By the end of this mission, I hoped to know.

Palm trees, sunshine, and sandy beaches—everything that makes southern California a haven for those who come to play. For me, playing is the last thing on my mind. Ghost hunting occupies it more times than not, and the Queen Mary is the perfect spot to exercise those inclinations and thoughts.

Turning onto Queens Highway—formerly Pier J—at the south end of the Long Beach Freeway, the world's once largest transatlantic vessel loomed in front of me. I knew she'd be large, but I never imagined the magnitude of her presence. It was as if I could feel the past calling to me.

Climbing out of the taxi, I was dwarfed by her shadow, and more intrigued than I wanted to admit, being a skeptic.

I handed over my bags to the bell captain and stepped into the elevator outside the ship. Once on A-Deck, I slowly walked through the door and into another era. An era of 1930s glitz and glamour with a week's worth of ocean as a backdrop. The floors gleamed and the shops glimmered with a long-forgotten style. Okay, so we're basically in dry dock, but we are surrounded by water, and most of it the Pacific Ocean, so it was like I was about to sail away on a transatlantic adventure.

And, strangely, it felt like coming home as I boarded the ship I'd never stepped foot upon until this moment. A chill crept through me as a picture of those glamour years danced before my eyes and the iconic Titanic flitted through my mind—minus sinking into freezing cold water, of course. I was entering another world, and I felt it down to my bones.

I walked over to check in, sure the chill was anything but déjà vu. The smarmy desk clerk beamed at me, no doubt glad of the publicity I might bring to this floating hotel.

"Welcome aboard the Queen Mary, Mr. Masterson. We've worked hard to meet all your requirements, including making sure the other guests will not interfere with your investigation. You'll be staying starboard side in room A105." He handed me the keycard, then pointed toward a hallway just past a small lounge. "Enjoy your stay with us."

"Thank you." I gathered my bags, then walked the short distance to the room. Pausing for a moment at the small hallway entrance to the room door, I gazed in awe of the mile-long corridor disappearing into infinity.

At that moment of anticipation, a delicate shadow caught the corner of my eye, and I smiled. "And so it begins," I muttered, swiping the keycard.

I opened the door and stepped into a long, narrow room. Nothing paranormal in nature jumped out to greet me. Two twin beds lined the wall to the right with a small round table and lamp sitting between the foot of each of them. A television stand sat directly across from the table, leaving barely enough room for one person to pass by.

It was pretty much what I expected. Yes, my room was a bit more meager than the first class accommodations I could've stayed in, but it was exactly what I wanted—simple and cozy, affording me the quiet I needed to work.

"Alrighty then, good thing I opted to room alone, after all."

Tossing my bags on the far bed, I unpacked for the next week or two. Taking the digital camera out of its protective casing, I checked the lens and the amount of space left on the SD card. A quick glance into the bag holding the 35mm affirmed my supply of black and white film was up to par.

When G.H.O.S.T. received a call to investigate the Queen Mary, there was no way I could turn down a chance to disprove the ghost stories surrounding one of the most historic hotels in the country. The entire purpose of this requested investigation was to find a rational reason for what people thought they saw along the ship's hallways, in pictures, or at pianos. Nine times out of ten, a camera will pick up dust particles in the air that implies spirits moving around. With the ship's history of service during World War II, I hated to disprove the theory of it being haunted, but it was part of my job, and I'd perform it to the best of my ability.

This assignment has become two-fold and personal. Not only would I be able to do what I loved—dissecting hauntings—but now I'll also be able to find out if, in fact, the stories about my great-grandfather were true and not the ramblings of a lonely physician treating the wounded during World War II.

According to the tattered journal packed safely between my socks and underwear, my great-grandfather, Dr. William Masterson, fell in love with an English nurse while caring for the wounded aboard this ship called The Grey Ghost during the Second World War. He went on leave, promising to return for the young lady the next time The Ghost came into port.

Upon the ship's return, William found the nurse was gone. Instead, he'd been met by the ship's commanding officer and given a small pouch housing a gold locket. He'd recognized his beloved's locket on sight because it contained precious pictures of them, and his heart had broken. The commanding officer told him Hanna Amery had died of influenza on their return voyage from Sydney, Australia, and been buried at sea. As she lay dying, he'd promised her to deliver the package to Dr. Masterson upon the troopship's return to the States.

After seeing the beauty of the lobby with its art deco and highly polished woods, it was hard for me to believe this luxury ocean liner had ever been a troopship, let alone that great-grandfather was ever aboard her. A ship regarded so highly by Hitler that he'd placed a bounty on her. The first U-Boat commander who sunk The Grey Ghost would receive two hundred fifty thousand dollars, plus instantly become a hero. Fortunately, the Ghost's propellers were so loud, the special sonar equipment on the enemy's U-boats were useless. If not for that, The Grey Ghost and her eight hundred thousand soldiers would have perished in the seas, and I wouldn't be aboard now, spending the next few weeks investigating every nook and cranny.

I hung up the last of my clothes and waited for the ship to quiet down for the night before starting my investigation. The rest of my team wasn't expected to arrive for another twenty-four hours. I'd delayed their trip, not wanting the legend of the haunts to override the reality of their causes. Plus, it gave me a chance to do some digging into the ship's history, and my great-grandfather's role aboard ship during war time.

Glancing at my watch, I was surprised by the late hour. The lobby piano had been silent for some time, but obviously I'd been too lost in my own thoughts to take notice. Now, if the rest of the ship was the same, I'd be able to start investigating without the interruption of the overnight guests. One of the reports was a woman who'd heard the laughter of children coming from the display of the First Class Playroom while on one of the guided tours. Another was the sound of shuffling feet in the Isolation Ward, followed by screaming. The Isolation Ward was one of the exhibits in its original location. So many others had been moved and relocated to the exhibit halls.

I gathered up my camera equipment, and headed out the stateroom door into the hallway. With a black bag containing video equipment slung over my shoulder and my great-grandfather's locket in a pocket, I headed for the Promenade Deck.

I strolled through the lobby and down the portside hall. The weight of my 35mm camera slung over a shoulder, I turned the voice activated digital recorder on, then spoke into it.

"Cole Masterson, portside hall, A-Deck, Queen Mary, approximately 1:30 a.m."

I continued down the never-ending corridor, passing doors closed tightly for the night. Other than an occasionally late-night television show penetrating the silence, all was peaceful...and a bit eerie, even for me. I made sure my footsteps fell lightly so as not to disturb any of the other hotel guests. Not that I have a heavy step. I don't, I just wanted to be sure everyone stayed where they were and out of my hair. For some reason, I have a knack for attracting people inquisitive about ghost hunting techniques. I'm only too happy people want to know, but their questions always come in the middle of an investigation.

I reached the end of the hall and stood at the stern. Again, I brought the handheld close to my mouth. "I've completed the walk down the hall between the outside staterooms and the inside rooms from bow to stern. Nothing appears out of the ordinary." I spoke clearly, then stepped into a small elevator and pushed the button for the Promenade Deck.

The shops are closed at this time of night, so no one should be wandering about, but I have an overwhelming feeling to get out into some fresh air as if I was being crowded. The unusual need to smell the brisk ocean air and watch its inky blackness stretch further into the night, past the Long Beach port of call for Carnival cruise ships, is overwhelming.

My blood rushed through my veins like liquid silver as the small compartment took me slowly up two deck levels. Sucking in a breath to calm my nerves, confusion began to cloud my mind as my head swam.

Why would a simple elevator ride unnerve me like this? This is so not professional, but I can't deny it. Damn, all I want is a breath of fresh air and to check out a good place to settle in for an hour or so. Just me and the ship—that's all I want.

The doors slid open, and I surged forward, trying to get away from whatever bad vibes were haunting me, and jerked to a halt, brought up short by a slight, but noticeable, tug on my camera strap. What the hell? It was as if it was caught on a hinge, but looking back, I see that that's not so. I'm completely alone and unfettered. Damn it all, this is weird even for me. On that thought, I literally charged out of the elevator as a shiver ran through me. Standing and trembling outside the Royal Salon, looking around, I glanced over my shoulder, hoping to catch a glimpse of whatever, or whomever, wanted my attention, but came up empty.

Oh well.

I'm well used to this kind of thing happening on an investigation until I get settled into the rhythm of the site, which was why I always went in a few days earlier than the crew. I'm continuously jittery and on edge at first. I keep telling myself it's the rush of the hunt. Maybe one day I'll actually believe it. Tonight was not the night though. This feeling was totally different. It was personal. Hanna's ghost?

I'm here to get to the bottom of my great-grandfather's journal and the locket that had been found among his World War II belongings packed away in the attic. Granny had said that old chest held secrets of a war well left dead and buried as far as she was concerned. She'd hated the pain reflected in her father's eyes each time he'd gone to the attic and tore through the chest. She'd always found him slumped against it with his war journal spread out in front of him, an opened tarnished locket in his hand, and tears streaming down his face, mumbling something about the war and The Gray Ghost and someone named Hanna. Granny always presumed it was the young woman in the locket, but no one knew for sure, not even great-grandmother.

Faint sounds of voices and music jumble me out of memories as I stepped from the glitz of what was once the first class area onto the deck. *There must be a late night party going on in the ship docked at the Carnival port, but why would they be playing Big Band music unless it's a themed cruise?* I listened a bit closer, but the musical notes dissipated, so I stepped out onto the deck.

The lights cast a yellow glow onto the polished planks and lit my way as I rounded the corner from port to starboard side. Pausing at the stern, I looked out into the bay and tried to imagine what it may have been like for my great-grandfather during those days of war...but can't.

He's come for you at last, Hanna. Bill, my Bill. Here, aboard the ship?

Reluctantly, Hanna Amery kept her distance from him, fading into the background, yet wanting so badly to touch the man she'd given her heart to. Admittedly, he looked a bit different now—his ebony skin a lighter rich tone, his once thin body more muscular—but she could feel Bill's spirit inside him. She ached to reach out and let him know she was here, waiting for him, like she'd promised. From the moment he'd walked onto the deck, heading toward the Isolation Ward, she'd felt his presence. His spirit was as strong today as it was seventy years ago when they'd first met, and it called to her, bringing her back to the present.

The man she loved, here aboard ship, in the spot where they'd declared their forbidden love. She, from a white family and he an African American man. The spot where they'd said their true love vows to God and their shipmates. It shouldn't be possible, yet here he was. Didn't the captain tell him she'd died from influenza trying to heal the sick and wounded on that final trip during the war?

She'd thought for sure he'd feel her near him as he stepped onto the deck, but he walked right by her, and her heart broke. Still, she couldn't help noting he was alone, no wife in tow at all, and it gave her hope. Her mind spun in a thousand different directions!

Why, oh, why doesn't he know I'm here waiting for him?

Hanna continued to watch him, close enough to touch him, but not daring to. If only he'd turn around and really see her things, would be alright.

When he finally stopped staring out into the bay, her heart leapt. Had he felt her? Then, he looked right at her, and she smiled, rejoicing, but he seemed to look through her.

Oh, no.

He headed down into the Isolation Ward.

She was a ghost. He would never see her. She had to accept that.

Two

The steel railing was cold and damp in my warm hand as I strode down the deck, trying to ignore the tingling at my back. Like some spirit was watching me. *Get used to it, it's your job.* Still, it felt deep, personal. A wisp of a chill passed through me at the thought and the soft feminine words, *yes, it is,* echoed forlornly through my mind.

What the hell? Now I was hearing ghosts? I rushed along in a hurry to get below deck.

Peering into the dim, yellowish light cast over the iron steps, I looked back, straining to see the presence that may have touched my soul for a brief moment. The light scent of lavender perfume and the faint sounds of swing music drifted over to me.

Inhaling deeply, I closed my eyes, feeling transported back to the war years, hearing the moans of the sick, the tender voices of the nurses, the motion of the ocean.

Shivering, I opened my eyes, deliberately pulling away from someone else's memories. I couldn't let myself fall into the past or I might not come back.

Where the hell had that thought come from? You're the ghost disprover, remember? Get it together man, I told myself, then turned and descended into what may have been a living hell for some soldiers.

"QM, 2:30 a.m., Isolation Ward," I said directly into the recorder.

Pulling out the camera, I took the steps one at a time, careful my footfalls did not echo through the eerie catacomb of rooms. I turned right at the bottom of the stairs, then weaved through the yellow and green hall. Passing a display of capstan machinery, I paused for a moment at the entrance to the female attendant's room. If my theory was right, this was where Hanna had been billeted. Stepping inside the sparse room, I noted no comforts of home at all for the nurses during war time. A simple room that seemed oddly familiar, housing a bunk, sink, and small bench to sit on. Room enough for two on-duty nurses. While one slept, the other tended to the sick and wounded, and so it went day after day. Modest accommodations at best, but these nurses hadn't been here for a luxury cruise.

Moving on, I hesitated only slightly before stepping into the female ward next door. The faint smell of antiseptic teased my senses, making me slightly dizzy. I hate the smell of hospitals—the scent of death and sterilization don't make for an appetizing cocktail. Follow that up with the always accompanying metallic blood chaser, and I'd be out like a light.

I grabbed the doorframe to steady myself.

"After seventy years, it still smells like a hospital. I can feel the sadness that once filled the Isolation rooms like a leaden blanket weighing me down. Leave it to me, a person who *hates* sterile environments, to pick up on it, but there is no getting away from it."

Continuing through the ward, not willing to let the miasma of pain stop me, I snapped pictures here and there as I ambled along.

The last section of the original ward didn't feel much bigger than the attendant's room, when in actuality, it was. Housing two sets of bunks and two sinks, the narrow room was barely large enough for a nurse and doctor to work magic on their patients. It surprised me the display room had been left open, but then again, they knew I was going to be on board and possibly investigating tonight, so they'd probably left it open for me. Who was I to walk away from an open invitation? Certainly not Cole Masterson! Leave the door open on a rumored haunted property, and I'd walk right through it every time.

I wandered further into the exhibit room. The hairs on the back of my neck suddenly prickled as the atmosphere seemed to crackle behind me, and I spun around, expecting to find someone watching me. Instead, there was empty space. I was utterly alone, but I sure as hell didn't feel alone. I found it confusing because the sensation was so intense.

I rubbed the back of my neck, inspecting the room for the source of my discomfort. It lacked personality, but why should it have any to begin with? This part of the ship had been isolation for the sick and for those who'd stowed away to be kept from the main population. The luxury of the decks above had no place here for the less fortunate passengers. Once the Queen Mary had been commissioned into war, it was the thousands of soldiers being transported who may have suffered the most.

Shrugging off the odd sensation of being watched, I went back to investigating and snapped pictures of the bunks, noting that, even with a mattress, they had to feel like a board. I certainly wouldn't trade the amenity of my Sleep Number bed for one of these, for any extended period of time, for anything. I took several more pictures, then covered the lens and turned off the camera.

"Other than my nerves, all is quiet in the Isolation Ward. Gonna call it a night." I turned away from the beds, then shuffled toward the sinks.

A low groan filled the air, stopping me in my tracks. But glancing back, there was no one. Had I just imagined it? Were my nerves playing me up?

"Who's there?" I double checked the recorder, finding the new batteries kept it barely running. Shoot, why I hadn't thought to bring an extra set of batteries? Normally, I would've done that, but tonight was far from normal. "Listen, whoever you are, I'm going to bed now. If you want to talk to me, you'll have to find me tomorrow."

Quickly stepping out of the ward, wanting nothing more than to get my head on straight, I inched past the attendant's room and hustled toward the stairs that would take me above deck.

"Dr. Masterson!" Clicking heels hurrying along the floor echoed softly behind me.

The soft feminine English-accented voice made me freeze as every hair on my body suddenly stood at attention. Oh, my God, I hadn't imagined her. I spun around, eager for a glimpse of her, hearing the urgency in her voice, and groaned when I found no one there. Damn, if she was so eager to reach out to me, why wouldn't she appear?

"Dr. Masterson, please!"

The disembodied voice made my heart ache and my fingers tremble as I, once again, checked the power of the nearly drained recorder, hoping it caught her voice.

Swallowing the lump in my throat, I said, "Yes?"

·♥·♥·♥·♥·♥·

"Dr. Masterson, please!" Hanna pleaded once more, relieved when he turned in her direction.

At least they'd established communication of a sort, but he still didn't see her. She could tell by the way his eyes darted back and forth, searching in the dim light of the room for her. His simple response, edged with questions, made her heart flutter with heat. His voice, it was the same familiar sexy tone, thick and rich like honey, even though his body looked different. Fascinated, she looked him over carefully, his new lighter skin than the ebony she remembered it being when he'd left the ship to go on leave. His eyes remained the same, though, a deep brown that lit the room and sent shivers through her soul.

His movements through the ward were also reminiscent of Bill's easy lumber. *How could it be that Bill and this stranger are one?* The man's slow, easy approach as he took every nuance into consideration was identical to Bill's caring manner.

I don't understand why he didn't say hello to the soldier who smiled up at him and said, "Evening, Doc." Surely, he saw, if not heard, the poor man. He looked right through him as if he wasn't there.

It was painful that he was unaware of the greetings of the wounded soldiers all around her. Soldiers he couldn't see.

She came up behind him and reached for him, longing to feel the warmth of him on her fingertips again, and gasped when a barrier stopped her short. But, why? She wanted to cry to the fates. *Because you're on different planes.* Then, while she stood blinking back tears, Bill backed away, grumbling as he toyed with some black box-like thing. *Pay attention to me*, she wanted to wail.

Glaring at the small black box in his hand, her eyes widened when he brought the device closer to his mouth and spoke.

"Hello, my name is Cole. I won't hurt you."

At last, a way to make him hear her. She could have danced a jig if she wasn't so carried away by his honey tone. His words, dripping sweet and sticky, fueled her memories of the way Bill would talk to her, all slow and saccharine, carrying a hint of a night filled with passion. It made her want to kiss him...if only she could. And what about him calling himself Cole?

Then it all came to her—Cole was the vessel, and Bill was inside him. That had to be it, much as she rejected spiritualism in her day.

"Cole?" She circled her fiancé, appraising him from head to toe. "Bill is in there. I know it!" Other than his eyes, nothing about this man on the outside indicated Bill Masterson. Where Bill was tall and lanky, this Cole was broad-shouldered and muscular. His arms hard and ready for heavy-lifting, while Bill's were made to take care of people. But all that didn't matter. Bill's spirit survived inside Cole. She'd sensed it deep inside the man from the start.

There was only one way to test her theory, but was she brave enough? Goodness, yes! He was worth risking her heart and her virtue. Somehow, she'd have to get him into bed. Once they made love, he'd remember her. She didn't know how she knew, but she did. Making him remember the summer they'd spent healing the sick and wounded was the only way to pass them both on to eternity together.

He frowned and spoke into the device again.

"Look, I'm not going to hang out here, waiting for you to make yourself known any longer. If you want to play games, it'll have to wait until another night."

He turned away, and she couldn't resist touching his arm lightly, getting only a tingle as she came up against the barrier of his skin. It only made her ache all the more to touch his warm, mahogany skin, like a drunk looking for her whiskey bottle.

"Did you change your mind?" He scowled, unseeing, down at her hand trying to touch him.

He might not see her, but he could sense her. That was a good sign. She couldn't help noting the amused light in his eyes was gone, leaving annoyance in its wake instead. The irritated expression took her breath away, leaving her worried she'd been wrong about Bill. Then his face softened with a smile, and she knew in that instant she was right.

Although she knew next to nothing about Cole, the man carrying Bill's spirit, she sensed he was a good man, a kindred spirit, otherwise Bill wouldn't have chosen him. Somewhere in that handsome, all-male body, Bill lay in wait to return to her. She just had to make him touch her, and the barrier would be broken.

I brushed away the tingling chill on my arm, knowing something otherworldly had touched me. A cobweb wouldn't be strong enough for me to feel that kind of intense sensation. This was more like fingers glazing over my skin—soft and tentative.

I'd had this happen on investigations before, but not with the palpable intensity of this one. The soft, chilly touch was oddly, heartbreakingly familiar, like that of a former lover, yet I didn't know why. As far as I knew, all my exes were alive and well, and none had ever been on the Queen Mary.

"Hello?" Backing up a few steps, I found myself just inside the male Isolation Ward. "Is there something you need from me? If so, show yourself."

"Doc?"

The male British voice made my hair stand on end as I spun toward the last bunk I'd paused by. It was as empty now as it had been moments ago, not even so much as a spider lurking in the corners. No doubt about it, the voice, male and English, had definitely come from that bunk. I only hoped my equipment had picked it up along with the woman's.

"Hey, Doc, where's that pretty nurse of yours?"

This one was deeply southern, not in quite as much pain, from a bunk against the wall.

"Nurse?" That would've accounted for the female voice that had moved me to tears for some reason. I checked the recorder, noting the battery was almost drained of its power.

"Did I get any mail today, Doc?"

Male voices, seeped in pain, filtered through my mind. Pictures of men lying with bandages around various limbs flooded my memory banks, and I couldn't blink them away. All of them were looking to me for help, answers, and God knew what else they thought I could provide. I needed to close my mind, lock the visions out. Only then would I dare look around once more.

I'm not sure what was going on, except I needed to get a grip.

"I hope you don't mind if I take some pictures." Taking a deep breath, I put the camera on burst mode, then held down the button, taking several photos continuously. Whatever was out there should show up on one of these pictures. At least, I hoped so.

"Dr. Masterson?"

The soft female voice sent a warm current through me. I turned toward it, clicking more photos as I did so. Her voice was so sweet, soothing, and gentle—and at the same time, arousing. My body hardened, and something told me it wasn't the first time with her around. A current of heat soared through me as I gazed at the watery image of a captivating dark-haired woman in a crisp white nurse's uniform. Her gaze, one of familiarity, pricked at my senses.

"Yes, Bill, I'm here. Thank goodness you can finally see me."

The light touch of her fingertips on my shoulder seared my skin as they pushed past a tingling barrier and caressed me. The tender sensual heat they left in their wake was almost unbearable. I found myself gazing into the eyes of the woman in my great-grandfather's locket. The one housed snuggly in my pants pocket. And for a moment, it wasn't me staring at her, but another man.

Good Lord, I was losing it.

"No, it can't be." I stepped back, breaking the contact so I could think.

It was like I was going crazy, seeing another man's sights, feeling another man's emotions. My great-grandfather William's, to be precise. It was the logical conclusion, but I was in no shape to deal with it tonight.

"I've been waiting for you to return, Bill. We all have."

"No, no, no. I'm overtired. Need to sleep." I continued retreating from the ward, then down the hall, until the back of my leg banged against the bottom step leading to the upper deck.

"Bill, please...wait!"

The desperation in her gentle voice sizzled my soul, beckoning me to go to her. No. I couldn't deal with this. Not tonight.

Mustering my will, I turned and then leapt up the stairs two at a time. I didn't look back even after I'd reached the elevator to M Deck.

Three

Pressing the button on the elevator, I stumbled onto it as the doors slid open, running away from the past. A sense of urgency told me to hurry, to get off the deck as soon as possible or it will be too late.

My stomach churned out a warning: *I'm about to lose my cookies or kiss the floor if I don't make it back to my room.*

Frantically, I pushed the button several times, closing my eyes to the sensation taking hold of my clammy body. Sweat had gathered at my temples and on my upper lip. I needed air—cold, crisp air—to cleanse the nausea seeping from my stomach.

The doors opened, and I stepped out, sucking in deep breaths with each footfall. Turning left onto the deck, I wobbled around the bow like a drunken teenager. The churning in my stomach was finally settling to a light wave. The urge to get as high as possible still possessed me.

Leaning over the railing, starboard side, I stared at the rippling reflection from the lights of Long Beach on the dark, glossy water. The nearly uncontrollable urge to go out to sea, far from civilization as humanly allowed, flooded through me.

"What the hell is going on?" I mumbled as I moved unsteadily along toward the bow until I set foot upon a staircase leading to the top deck. "I've got to get more air and clear my head."

Pulling myself up the stairs, my feet felt like lead weights. Sucking in a deep breath, I finally obtained a bit of relief in the pit of my belly. The crisp summer night air filled my lungs, calming quaking nerves. Slow, long breaths cleansed me, inside and out.

Damn, what had happened down there? One minute, I was completely alone, the next, men were calling out to me. Soldiers wrapped in bandages. And that woman—no way she could have been...

Taking out the worn gold locket, I rubbed the cool smoothness between my fingers. As I wandered along the deck, I continuously caressed the keepsake, searching for a rational reason for my ghostly encounter. Was it possible they were residual hauntings in the sick bay, particularly in the Isolation Ward? Were the spirits using my great-grandfather's name when calling out to me? This had never happened on a case before, but it had seemed to ground me to the place and time. Was it totally possible here on the haunted Queen Mary? Except, I didn't look like William Masterson, at all. He'd been a handsome ebony-skinned doctor of military bearing. I was a mixed heritage nomad who hunted ghosts for a living. Totally different beings...but not since I came aboard, I had to admit to myself.

What the heck are you doing to me, great-granddad?

It could be my subconscious playing tricks on me, as well, but somehow, I knew better. My mind had been flooded with William's thoughts and memories, I realized in the clarity of the open deck. Maybe I'd brought it on myself. To say I'd been obsessed with finding out more about great-grandfather was an understatement.

True, he was of mixed blood. So am I. And yes, I've been told I have my great-grandfather's eyes. But I'd never felt him as strongly like now. As my grandmother had grown older, she'd begun to tell us stories about her father and how much of him she saw in my warm dark eyes every day, that one day, I would have a great love in my life, just like my great-grandfather. A love that an act of time and circumstance may take away from me. I'd eventually settle for the love of another woman, only to mourn the previous one every day like her father had.

I never understood why Grandmother felt this way toward me, but she had since I was old enough to know about girls. I always thought it was the ramblings of an old woman retelling fabricated stories of her father.

But then there was the journal, the very one I'd packed in the suitcase when I'd taken this case. The one we'd found tucked away at the bottom of the worn chest under William's uniform and WWII medals...long forgotten.

·❤·❤·❤·❤·❤·

Hanna stuck like glue to Bill, shuffling behind him, afraid that he'd topple over and out into the ocean. She'd lost him once, and sure as hell was not about to let it happen again. She hung on to him as he wobbled around the deck, resting here and there, until they reached the stairs to what had been his quarters.

He doesn't fully realize that he's Bill, but he will before the dawn breaks. I'll make him remember the men, his service, the months at sea...and me.

Walking ahead of her, Cole stumbled toward the staircase, grasping the railings as he tripped over the bottom step. His tread was slow and wobbly on the steady climb up to his cabin. His body trembled slightly under her hand, and she hurt for him. This had to be quite a shock.

His sleek, bald head was gleaming with moisture. She'd never found bald men attractive before, but this man was different. She couldn't help finding him pleasant to gaze upon.

No matter, it was Bill who she loved. She only feared Cole would pass out and collapse, hit his head on the steps, and perish before she could get him to the bridge and Bill's quarters. Although his demise may solve her situation nicely, she couldn't risk losing Bill forever if his spirit was released from its vessel too soon. No, better to help this man understand that, inside him, beats the heart and soul of her beloved.

This Cole must be a relative, though. I can feel the family connection in my heart. He's a part of Bill somehow, which is why he chose Cole to carry his spirit back to me. Why else would he have my locket? The one I had the captain give Bill when I knew I wouldn't be returning to him.

All I have to do is get him up one more deck, then things will fall into place. His memory will come back. Even if Bill didn't remember the men he treated in the Isolation Ward, or the months at sea...he'll remember me and how much I love him.

· ♥ · ♥ · ♥ · ♥ · ♥ ·

I stumbled up the final step, almost landing face-first on the deck. What the hell was wrong with me? Fortunately, I caught myself in time. Running a hand over my head, I was unsure of why I ended up on the Sport Deck, standing outside the bridge and officer's quarters. I only knew it felt right. There was an air of freedom this high above the ocean I found an odd kindred for, and it called to me.

"Well, since I'm here, might as well take advantage of it and check things out."

I checked the batteries in my EVP recorder, noting they were a smidgen close to being totally dead. I could only hope my camera was in better shape.

Taking a step forward, the ship listed slightly under my feet, which was weird seeing as it was moored.

"Tremor?" I muttered, grabbing the railing as another shift caught me off balance again. Earthquake, maybe. I glanced over the side, expecting to see a ripple in the glass-smooth surface.

"Hmm, wonder what that was all about." I shrugged my shoulders, then walked onto the docking wing on starboard. The lights of Long Beach were like beacons in the night, letting sailors know they're there, waiting for all who make the city their next port of call.

I snapped a few pictures, hoping to capture the subtle beauty of those lights. I took one last glance before heading onto the bridge—where I'd always fantasized about being the captain of a ship. Boyhood dreams aside, looking out the massive windows over the bow was impressive, even at night.

As I rounded the hallway into the officers' quarters, the ship listed under my feet again. Why weren't there alarms going off if there's an earthquake? Surely, if I noticed it, everyone else aboard had.

I ran my hands over my head, not sure what was happening anymore. In a matter of hours, I was totally lost between reality and...

Maybe it's just my head coming out of its funk from seeing Hanna—or what my mind believed to have been Hanna Amery—in the Isolation Ward.

I wandered through halls of glass displays, feeling like a peeping tom looking through a one-way mirror. I got the odd sensation as I peered through the glass that if there were people in these cabin displays, they'd be totally unaware of me standing, watching their every move.

I approached the Capitan's Quarters display and paused. There was the sound of music. Not the musical. This piece was from the thirties or forties, I'm not sure which, but I could've sworn it was Al Jolson's voice as the song faded.

"Get it together. You've been thinking too much about William and not enough about the job you were hired to do."

With a good mental shake, I stepped away from the window.

The ship shifted again and tilted me off balance for a second. My body was a bit fuzzy, but not like I was going to pass out or anything. More ore like my blood pressure had suddenly dropped, then rose back to normal.

Moving in my own mental fog, it seemed as if parts of me were fading away. Then, from far away, I heard the music become clearer.

"You must remember this..."

And then, Hanna appeared, and I ran to her, knowing I wasn't Cole anymore. I was Bill. I sweep her into my arms, and my heart has found its home once again.

Four

"William," Hanna cried as he drew her into his arms.

Her now tingling warm body pressed against his powerful one, his heart beat against hers, welcoming his love. Almost fearfully, she looked into his eyes, expecting rejection, but Bill's warm, merry gaze looked back at her. She'd know the force of that personality in any form. Tears slipped down her cheeks as she went up on tiptoes to kiss him. His mouth slanted hotly over hers, his body tightening against her, growing hard with need. They'd never taken that last step, leaving it for their wedding night, but now the time seemed right as the last of their barriers melted.

He broke the kiss to hold her tighter.

"I've missed you so much," she whispered, her words tumbling urgently. It had been so long since they'd touched, kissed. She needed more. She needed him. A fire burned in her belly only he could extinguish.

His lips, their movement, seductive and teasing, sent her head into a tailspin, quivering from want and mounting need. If he didn't make love to her soon, she'd be nothing more than an evaporating puddle on the floor.

"Hanna, my sweet Hanna." Bill's kisses covered her face, kissing the tears away. "I'm so sorry I'm late getting back to you, but please believe me, I've never stopped loving you." His eyes twinkled with recognition, and her heart soared with happiness.

Cradling his stubbled face in her hands, she smiled up at him, loving the feel of his whiskers against her palms, so alive again, so real. "I know—I felt you in my heart day and night, and I refused to leave until you got here."

"Sweetheart, I don't know what I did to deserve you." He kissed her again, crushing her against him like a life preserver. He was never going to let go, she could sense it, even if there might be more trials to go through. He'd found a way to come back to her—they'd find a way to insure forever.

Bill clung to Hanna, the luckiest SOB on earth. That his angel had waited for him, still loved him, touched him deeply. He had no inclination to ever let her go.

"Hanna," her name slipped off his tongue like honey on a warm summer day. He tasted her lips' sweetness with his tongue. "Hanna, my sweet, sweet Hanna." The sound of her name filled him with a desire he'd never encountered before. A fire burned in his body, fueling the hunger growing deep in his groin.

He felt alive for the first time ever. Like a baby coming into the world, discovering the light and warmth of its mother's loving embrace. He was home, and wanted nothing more than to bury himself deep into her.

Her brown eyes twinkling through thick lashes, a sexual craving lurking on their surface. *How can this woman want me as much as I want her? Could a man get lucky twice in a lifetime?*

The smooth, soft curves of her bobbed hair were like dark waves upon the ocean in a night's light breeze. The urge to run his fingers through them overwhelmed him. Slipping his fingertips through their silky strands, he captured her lips with his again.

Her mouth moved with the sweet surrender of an innocent girl handing her heart over in trust. In that moment, he made a silent vow to never hurt this woman, for to lose her, he'd lose his soul, as well.

"I wandered around and finally found..." Their bodies swayed to the soft, sultry voice of Vera Lynn. Dancing around the room, the heat built between them—an unbearable sensual thread burning into his heart.

Placing his hand on her lower back, he pulled her closer, kissing the small spot between her neck and shoulder. Her pulse throbbed against his lips, encouraging him to go on. Unspoken words passed between them as they clung to each other, exploring one another with the intensity of newlyweds.

Sweeping her into his arms, he carried her across the floor to his sleeping quarters. Her head rested lightly on his shoulder, her lavender perfume covering him with seduction. It brought back so many sweet memories, it made his heart weep with happiness.

Laying her gently on the bed, he slowly unbuttoned her dress, exposing her breasts. The strawberry-pink nipples were hard, tenting the white cotton covering them. She was perfect, seductive in her innocence.

He sucked in a breath as her fingers worked the buttons on his pants, one-by-one, until his manhood was freed of the restriction and throbbing against her, aching to possess her. Her legs opened, promising paradise, and the glimmer of lust clouds made her brown eyes darken until they appeared black, oozing with passion.

Drawn to her heat, he nestled between the folds of her thighs. Capturing a tented nipple between his teeth, he smiled at her moan of pleasure. She touched his throbbing manhood, stroking it to fullness as she arched, trying to complete the act. The excitement of knowing she wanted him only fueled him to grow harder with the manipulations of her hot little hand.

"Bill, please make love to me." Her whispered plea brushed against his ear, urging him to take control. "I…I can't wait a moment longer. I've already waited far too long for you."

He pushed her dress off her body, his hungry gaze eating her up. That she was nude but for the garter and stockings covering her shapely legs came as a bit of a surprise—a welcomed one. He grinned down at her as she hungrily ground her hips toward his, licking her lips as she watched him slip down his pants. This was worth waiting for, for both of them. Aching with need, he wanted nothing more than to feel his full length in her.

·❤·❤·❤·❤·❤·

Trembling under him, Hanna gazed up at Bill in a fevered haze. They'd waited so long, and she couldn't wait a minute longer. "Please," she murmured, arching.

"Hanna, I will," he whispered.

She gasped as he pushed through the maiden barrier of her womanhood. She tensed, letting the sharp prick subside, becoming unbearably full.

He whispered sweet sounds into her ear. "Easy, buttercup," her whispered pet name only he knew. He might look like Cole, but it was Bill making love to her. Motionless, except for the drumming of his heart against her breast, he said, "I'm sorry for the pain, buttercup." He shifted a little.

She gasped with ecstasy as it made him brush against the throbbing nubbin of her clitoris. *Oh, my!* Obviously mistaking her gasp for pain, he started to extract himself from her folds, and she cried out in protest, wrapping her legs around him. She was far from ready to let him escape when they'd just begun. She wanted that tingle of pleasure again and maybe more.

But even as she thought it, he was fading back to the spirit world. She sensed the shift.

"Bill, please don't go," she begged, moving her hips in a rhythm of love that made him gasp and stay with her. She had to keep him with her, complete this bond. *If I continue to move, to keep a hold of him, would he fall into rhythm with me? I can only hope and pray he will.*

Thrilled her tactic had worked, she could only moan as he moved deep inside her, driving her to the edge of bliss. He was moving with her, not fading away.

Oh, God...the sensation is...Bill...

She fell away from her conscious thought, concentrating on the movement of him inside her. Rocking up to meet his thrusts, she could only whimper, clinging to him as her body tightened around him, her muscles rippling like a spring wound too tight. She knew in a matter of moments that spring would pop, and this moment in time would be over. She wanted to cry with regret. She refused to lose him again, but knew she might, and this time forever. She didn't care. If she could only have this moment in time with him, she'd take it.

As if reading her desperate thoughts, his thrust deepened, his rhythm picking up. "You're mine," he groaned, his fingers pinching her love-swollen nipples, making them tingle, and she gasped as a gush of ecstasy filled her body. She tingled everywhere possible at the same time. Her head spun like a top as he brought her to peak after peak of bliss and beyond. Her last conscious thought was love as he came deep inside her and they convulsed together.

When he collapsed in a sweaty heap on top of her, she gloried in the sensation, cradling him against her. This was Heaven. Breathing deeply, the spicy fragrance of their love filled the air, along with the tandem beating of their hearts. *Tonight may be all we have in time and space, and we have to make the most of it.*

A change went through him as he stirred on top of her. He raised his head and gazed down at her in confusion. Looking into his eyes, she could tell Bill's consciousness had slipped away and Cole's took over.

Wanting to cry, she blinked back tears, wondering what Cole would make of the situation. How the heck could she explain this?

Lord, she did not want to talk about it. He would not believe the truth. Luckily, she didn't have to because, moving in a kind of trance, he simply rolled off her, turning his back.

Curling up in a ball of pain, she watched him walk away as if nothing had happened, and she wondered what to do next. There had to be a way to get Bill back permanently.

Five

Jolted abruptly in bed by the alarm I'd set the night before, my head ached like I had a hangover. As I flopped back down, I rolled over, reaching for the pack of cigarettes I no longer carried with me. For whatever reason, I was craving one of the cancer sticks like a john after a nightlong session with a hooker.

Speaking of hookers... Some flicker of a memory was on the edges of my mind. Soft skin, hot kisses... As I tried to focus on it, the sensation vanished.

Well, hell!

"This is totally nuts." I stretched under the blanket, not wanting to get out of bed, fully satisfied to stay here in my safe little cocoon. I mentally ran through the events of the night before, coming up with no reason why I should want a cigarette or why I could smell lavender. I hadn't been with a woman last night—at least, not that I remember. And believe me, I would remember if I'd been with one. There's nothing like the feel of a woman...

Hell, I needed to clear my head with a cup of strong coffee and a dose of fresh air, so I'd better roll my sorry ass out of bed, shower, and get dressed. I had several digital photos to look over, EVPs to listen to, so I might as well do it outside before the other guests started milling about.

I grabbed the laptop, digital camera, earbuds, and recorder, then made my way to the Promenade Café for breakfast and hot coffee. For some reason, in addition to wanting that damn cigarette, I'm famished. One would think I hadn't eaten in the last twenty-four hours, or had a marathon session of sex, which was totally wrong on both counts.

Thankfully, I was the first customer of the day, so I quickly got my breakfast sandwich and two coffees—black with 2 sugars—to go. I wanted to sit outside on the deck and suck in some fresh air to clear my head a bit. Not that it was doing me any good because I couldn't remember a damn thing once I'd left the Isolation Ward last night and started feeling sick. Maybe it was jet lag. Sounded reasonable to me. I let it go with that explanation.

With my laptop and camera bags slung over a shoulder, and my breakfast and coffees in both hands, I headed out onto the Promenade Deck to find a deck chair far from prying eyes. The morning fog was thick, and there was a slight chill in the air. Good thing I'd gotten two hot coffees because in short sleeves and shorts I was getting chilled. After all, who would expect fog on a July summer morning in Long Beach, California? Obviously not me...or the woman sitting alone starboard near the Isolation Ward.

The gentle waves of her dark hair hung lightly at her shoulders in the morning dampness. Before I could take another step down, I found myself mesmerized by those luscious waves and her even more luscious curves. Who was she? I wanted nothing more in that crazy moment than to drop everything and walk over to run my fingers through her hair. There was a stirring of familiarity itching near the surface of my memory banks that made me ache with longing. The wind blew out of the southeast, carrying the light scent of lavender with it.

Maybe I had been with this woman last night, or at least, in close proximity to pick up her scent. That might account for my hangover and fuzzy memory. Maybe I had gotten drunk and just couldn't recall. This was so unlike me. I wished I knew why there was a nagging part of me that said we'd met before. All I could make out was the back of her head, and my heart pounded like a stud ready to mate.

"Well, ole man, there's only one way to find out. After all, you've got two coffees in your hand."

I decided it was time to squelch that nag and get my head back on straight by facing the thoughts head on. As my grandmother would say, no better time than the present, so I headed down the stairs and made my way over to the woman.

·♥·♥·♥·♥·♥·

Vanessa Amery hated that feeling when someone was staring at her. It gave her the creeps every time. The hairs on the back of her neck stood on end, telling her she was being watched, and a shiver fluttered through her already chilled body. It was bad enough the sea air was damp and cool out here this morning, but now there was an added disturbing atmosphere. She wished the nosy person would just go away.

Maybe if she didn't turn around and acknowledge them, they'd give up and go back to where they came from. She didn't care where that may have been—the café, their stateroom—as long as they mind their own business. What were the odds—one out of ten? If she was lucky that was, but wasn't sure how many of her lucky stars were still shining.

Ever since she'd signed up for this assignment, it had been weird. Dreams of great-aunt Hanna, followed by a sense of grayness plaguing her, like being caught between light and darkness, assaulting her sleep. Not to mention, the sadness of the dreams. Never could figure out why that's all she could remember—no faces, just feelings. Happiness, despair, fear...all there in glimpses, but enough for her to feel their presence. If only she could remember more than those little aspects for longer than thirty seconds after waking up, she might know how to fix the problem.

If this assignment hadn't been on the Queen Mary, she never would've taken it. Never in a lifetime would she film a ghost hunting documentary—no way. Just a bunch of silliness in her opinion. At least, that used to be the case before Hanna came to her. Now, this job was a way for her to possibly find out more about her great-aunt and her part during World War II. Her family knew so little, other than the few letters passed down to Grammy, and those were sketchy at best.

Grammy believed her only aunt had gone to a watery grave not knowing what love was. Vanessa got a totally different impression from the recurring dreams—a warm ethnic doctor with a gentle laugh and a loving touch. So far, that was all Hanna had inadvertently shown her. But those glimpses told her she knew more than she was letting on, and something had held her back in sharing those feelings with her family. She couldn't put her finger on it, but something about the dreams felt so real to her. As if...

A shadow crossed over her, blocking out the sun breaking through the fog in the west. A chill sent shivers through her body, and she tried to shake it off, but couldn't. There was a sense of urgency for her to turn around, coming from the person lingering behind her.

Then it happened, a tenor voice saying, "Good morning," and it spread over her like butter melting on warm toast.

·❤·❤·❤·❤·❤·

I'm close enough to smell her shampoo, strawberry I think, and catch the sharp inhale of her breath. The young woman turned to look at me, and I melted into the depths of her caramel, almond-shaped eyes.

Wow! There was a brightness lingering behind the thoughts I'd interrupted.

"I'm sorry to disturb you." I set the paper cup holder on the table, then offered one to her. "You look like you could use a cup of hot coffee, and I just happen to have an extra. Hope you like it black with two sugars."

"I, um, well..." She looked at me as if I was a two-headed snake waiting to gulp her down for breakfast, and I guess several years ago, I may have been one. She gathered her bag and readied to push herself from the chair. "I really should be going. There are people expecting me, and I've arrived a few hours early. Anyway, thank you for the offer, but no."

She blew me off, but I'm not about to let her. I've got to know who she was. This driving force pierced my heart, urging me into a boldness I gave up years ago. Now that I'm this close, I have to get a better look at her face, but the damn fog decided to lift, and I squinted just to catch what I could.

I offered my hand, hoping she'd wrap dainty fingers around it. "Hey, I'm pretty rude. My name is Cole, Cole Masterson." The sun dipped behind a cloud and out of my eyes for a moment.

The surprised look on her face took nothing away from the softness at the corners of her mouth. There was a sweetness fluttering gently along her jawline and around the curve of her chin, framing her simple yet amazingly attractive face.

"Cole Masterson of G.H.O.S.T.?" Her laugh was like a songbird, light and feathery. "Well, seems the joke's on me this morning. Please forgive *my* rudeness."

She knows me? I must've looked as perplexed as I felt because she giggled again. Her smile lit up her face and eyes, and I melted before her.

"So, you've heard of me? I hope nothing I'm bound to live up to." My hand lay lightly on the pocket with great-grandfather's keepsake in it. The oval shape seemed like it had come alive, vibrating slightly on my hip.

"Well, sort of." She took a sip of the coffee, her nose wrinkling slightly in the steam. "I'm your new film production manager from American Ghost Hunters."

I breathed in, slightly calming my quacking nerves. At least she's not a beauty I bedded then totally disregarded. Even so, the slight tilt of her head and the way her turned up nose crinkled reminded me of someone. I must've seen her picture in one of the trade magazines. Why else would I feel like I've met her before?

"Ah, well then. I hope you're ready to get to work. What did you say your name was?"

"Vanessa. Vanessa Amery."

Six

"Amery?" The locket in my pocket called out to me, and I leaned further back in the deck chair to ease the tension growing. It was a common name, and could no way be connected to Hanna Amery. And William's journal indicated Hanna was English. "English, right?"

"Actually, the origin is Germany, although there's more English in our blood than our surname indicates." She took another sip of her coffee, the glint in her eye sending shivers of recognition through me. I've seen it before, felt its impact, but when and where?

"Listen, I have to be honest. I don't believe in all this talk about spirits walking the halls or reliving their last moments in places after they've died." She was staring past the latest Carnival cruise ship docked close by, the tone of disbelief heavy in her proclamation. "I'm here because it's my job and happened to be available at a time when I wasn't out on another assignment. So, I took it."

She turned and looked at me as a cloud covered the sun completely. Finally, I had a good look at her face, and I couldn't believe I was gazing into the face of Hanna Amery. But that was totally impossible, as Hanna Amery had never made it to dry land again. She'd never made it home to her family or to the man whom she'd loved so dearly—or so it appeared from William's journal and the locket.

"I've never been here before. I thought it would be a great place to stay with all its history and whatnot. Besides, Long Beach is great any time of year in my book." Her smile was demure, yet lit up her face.

My heart soared as the twinkle returned in her eyes. She was a beauty that any man could easily fall in love with. Unfortunately, I wasn't any man.

"Well, Ms. Amery, while we're being perfectly honest, why did you take this job really? It's pretty evident you don't believe in our cause or what we do, so why put yourself into the situation to begin with?" She had something to hide, and I had to find out what it was before we started tonight, or the entire project would be jeopardized. Was there any connection between her, Hanna, and William?

Why in the hell wouldn't my mind just let it go? Why was I so insistent on finding out about Hanna Amery, a woman none of my family even knew existed, plus great-grandfather William?

"Think about it, Mr. Masterson. You've got a couple of bags there I'm sure you had some intention of doing something with that are, no doubt, some kind of "evidence" or some such thing from an investigation. You haven't even touched them yet, so whatever is in there can't be all that important." The light in her eyes died, replaced with a darkness that hallowed her otherwise beautiful porcelain skin. I wanted to take her in my arms and chase away the clouds of despair she tried to hide, marring her ivory beauty. "At any rate, you go around in places like this, or people's homes, invading the privacy of those around you, and all for trying to catch the uncatchable because it doesn't exist. *That* is totally nuts, but that's just my opinion."

Her words were carried away with the wind that had just kicked up, almost in protest of her opinion. The chill in the air returned, and the hairs on the back of my neck were prickly.

· ❤ · ❤ · ❤ · ❤ · ❤ ·

Hanna stood in the shadows, at her wits end. Young people can be so stubborn. She had to admit, she'd been the same way once. It seemed her great-niece was just like her. She doesn't know how to draw Bill out from Cole's body—short of seducing him again. Certainly, she couldn't do that here on the deck. What would the young lady think? If this girl was her great-niece, and from the looks of her, she was, she'd grab the opportunity and make him hers. For some reason, she didn't think that would happen, and wondered why exactly.

"Bill, if you can hear me, please come back to me now. There's no time to waste any longer after last night. You found a way back and it worked."

Walking around Cole, she sent her message into his soul where Bill resided. He was so close to finding his way out without her help, and he has to take that final step without any aid from anyone on the outside.

"Bill, these children need our help, or they'll never surrender to love. These are our great-grandchildren. How can you stand by and watch them—"

"Hanna, why do you think I'm staying where I am? Cole needs all the help he can get with that grand-niece of yours!"

Bill's honey voice reached her, sending her heart into a triple flip. He was here, but not in the flesh, and she couldn't wait to hold him again.

"William John Masterson!"

His rich, timbered laugh penetrated her, warming her soul with lust and desire.

"It's good to hear your voice again. I missed you."

"Now, Hanna, don't go blubbering. There's work to be done here. It won't be long, my love. We've waited this long, what's a bit longer?"

He retreated back into Cole's mind and spirit. In that moment, she looked closer at Vanessa, and realized why he'd stayed with Cole all these years.

Somehow, Bill knew one day these two would find each other aboard the Queen Mary—just like they had. Only now, skin color won't matter.

· ♥ · ♥ · ♥ · ♥ · ♥ ·

Talk to her, man, before you lose this chance forever, like in the past. Yeah, I know. According to the journal, it was under different circumstances—I'm of mixed blood, she's white—but she died before I could get back to her. Don't let it happen to you, too, Cole.

"I'm not much on formality, so I hope you don't mind if I address you by your first name." I stood to leave because it was pretty evident Vanessa Amery's was not into this at all. By "this," I meant getting to know the man she'll be working very closely with over the next forty-eight hours. "As you say, I've got bags of work to get done, and I've wasted far too much time as it is."

I reached down and gathered my equipment, bound and determined to leave her and her lonely thoughts on the deck. A soft *ka-chunk* reached my ears, and my hand automatically went to the pocket housing William's locket. My heart flew into a panic. It wasn't there. I think I actually stopped breathing.

"Did you drop something in your haste?"

My gaze followed Vanessa's lightly painted nail pointing to a spot on the deck floor. The sunlight caught the gold metal under the chair I'd just vacated. Air filled my lungs with relief, and I bent down to pick up the keepsake.

"Thanks, it would have been a shame to lose this." I rubbed it lightly between my fingers, reveling in its warmth. "A family keepsake that once belonged to my great-grandfather, William."

For whatever reason, I placed the locket in her open palm. The current of electricity at the contact startled us both as we jumped from the jolt. She closed her fingers around it, breathing deeply. Her face relaxed, and she smiled so brightly, I could've sworn she was a different person. All the loneliness that had lined her face moments ago were whisked away.

"Mind if I look inside?" she asked.

I had no inclination to tell her no. I mean, why should I? The pictures in there meant nothing to anyone but me. She'd just see two old photos of people she didn't know, make a comment about them, and then hand the locket back to me. End of story. No worries to explain why a man of color and a white woman were together in a locket this old.

"No, go ahead." I watched her gently snap it open, and her gaze went from William's photo to me.

"You look like this man. Is he a relative?" Her smile was gentle within the curve of her lips. I'd love nothing more than to feel those pink lips against mine.

Instead, I shook the thought from my head and laughed. "It's odd a complete stranger would catch our resemblance. Yes, he's my great-grandfather, William, and was aboard the Gray Ghost during World War II."

"I had a relative aboard her for a short time, as well. Odds are they never knew each other, though." I wondered if she'd recognize the picture as that long lost relative. Her gaze traveled over to the picture of Hanna Amery, and her body went rigid. She sucked in a breath before turning an angry gaze toward me.

"This is my great-aunt Hanna! Why the hell is it in your locket, and what are you doing with it?"

Seven

As much as I half expected to hear Vanessa's declaration, it still hit me like a load of bricks. How do I tell this woman that her great-aunt and my great-grandfather appeared to be having a love affair?

"Ah, from what I know, she gave it to my great-grandfather, William." The way her eyes had darkened, I could tell she was having second thoughts on whether or not to believe me. I could hardly blame her. If roles were reversed, I might've had the same reaction. Although inter-racial relationships were commonplace in my family, I suspected they weren't in hers at all. Even in today's world, some people still had issues with it.

"What do you mean *she gave* it to him? My great-aunt died from the flu on a return voyage to the States. Her few belongings were sent home once the ship docked in New York. How could she possibly have known your great-grandfather out of thousands of soldiers on the Gray Ghost?"

She placed the open locket between us on the table, Hanna and William's profiles facing each other. It was plain as day to me what these two war heroes felt for each other. I had a feeling Vanessa had drawn a line in the sand, and it was due to our family connection.

"All I can tell you is, based on my great-grandfather's journal, he had a great love for Hanna." Maybe she would leave it at that, because I'd hate to tell her that her great-aunt's last thoughts weren't of her family back home. They were of William. I'd be crushed, broken-hearted, and mad as hell if someone had told me the same news. "I know it's a lot to swallow coming from a stranger, but I think we have something in common here."

She bounced against the back of the chair, her arms crossed over a pair of full breasts like a wall firmly in place. If only she knew how beautiful she was, looking like a mad wet hen. I'd like to tell her sometime, but I think I'd better wait for a better opportunity to present itself. Of course, presuming there's a chance of it ever happening and, after this, I sincerely doubted it.

"So you say. I can't, for the life of me, wonder what, other than you knew I was going to be here, did some research on me, then found an old picture of my Aunt Hanna to paste into this tarnished locket!" She smirked like she had all the answers when, truth be told, she had about as many as me. I take that back, she had less than I did. Damn it, I was going to have to share, and that was the last thing I'd wanted to admit—using an investigation for my own personal agenda.

"I really hadn't wanted to do this." I looked past the deck railing out to the ocean, searching for the strength to admit my unprofessionalism with this assignment. "I took this case at first thinking what a great place for rich history, then I found out my great-grandfather had been stationed aboard the Gray Ghost during World War II. We found the locket and his journal in an old chest, buried under his uniform, after my grandmother passed away.

"I'd grown up hearing stories of how he never loved his wife with that all-consuming love you hear about. That his heart had always belonged to another woman during the war, and he never got over that loss. In fact, we thought they were just stories from an old lady with a vivid imagination. Until after Granny's passing when we found the journal and locket wrapped in a protective cloth."

There it was, out in the open, like a toe poking out from a hole in a sock. It was a cold secret that poked its head out, testing for warmth.

"I have the feeling your reasons for really taking this assignment are similar to mine."

She inhaled deeply, unfolding her arms and opening herself up for the defense. Before she could utter a single word, my hand went up, stopping her from uttering any protest.

"There's more, so let me finish before you say anything."

She nodded, relaxing a bit, waiting for me to tell her the rest of my story. A story that consisted of my seeing Hanna in the Isolation Ward, of hearing soldiers refer to me as "Doc," me getting ill, and then the blackout, followed by the scent of lavender in my cabin. Of course, she'd look at me like I'm nuts. After all, it's a story only a believer of the spirit world would consider.

Now that I'd finished with my crazy family history, she didn't say a word, just got up and started to leave. I was so oddly struck by it that I watched her walk away, feeling as if I was going to lose that once in a lifetime chance for a great love. Why in the world I thought that, and not how she found me totally nuts, was another unexplainable crazy notion. Maybe she did and that's why she was putting distance between us. Not that I blamed her.

She reached the steps to the Isolation Ward and paused for a moment. Wrapping her fingers around the railing, she cocked her head slightly as though listening to something. Taking a step back, the heel of her sandal caught on the deck floor, and she stumbled, turning back around.

I jumped to my feet and reached out for her, knowing I was too far away.

She regained her composure and took a deep breath. "Okay, if what you say is true, could there be proof of it on your equipment?"

I reached for one of my bags, pulling out my laptop and camera equipment. "Absolutely!"

· ❤ · ❤ · ❤ · ❤ · ❤ ·

"Hanna, my dear, you've struck gold!"

Cole hooked up his camera to the thin, silver box on the table. Hanna wandered over, watching in amazement as a picture of the Isolation Ward came into view. What a marvelous world this had become in her absence.

"I'm going to hook up the recorder and play it simultaneously with the film to see if I picked up anything worth perusing." Cole plugged a cord into the flat box, and for a moment, all Hanna heard was static and the sounds of the ship at night. No voices from the soldiers, nothing that would suggest he wasn't alone that night. And by God, he wasn't. The men in the ward needed to hear his soothing voice telling them home was on the horizon. For some, it was.

His taped voice gave information about the ship and where he was located. Then, there it was, Hanna's voice calling out to Bill. Cole had turned his camera, and she came into view on the screen—a ghostly person in a nurse's uniform. She hadn't even realized she still wore it!

"Oh my, Cole!" Vanessa's mouth hung open in surprise, the look on her face surely matching the one of disbelief on mine as well.

I've never captured anything like this before. The apparition was so clear, we can make out her face and the gentle wave in her pinned hair. The woman who we'd heard moments ago call out to my great-grandfather was Hanna Amery!

I plopped into the seat, the faded image of Hanna frozen on the screen. "Well, here's the evidence we've both been denying. Ghosts really do exist. The proof is in the pudding, and there it is. Now, I was in the sick room. Let's see if there's anything else."

I pressed the Play button, and the photo slideshow moved from one shot to another. The recorder echoed my voice as I explained where I was and what I was doing.

"Hey, Doc." The two words were a mere whisper at best under the surface of noise.

"Did you hear that?" I glanced over at Vanessa's bewildered face. "Vanessa, did you hear that?"

"I...I...I don't know. Maybe."

I rewound and played it back until those two faint words emerged from the white noise of the ship at night. "Well, I'll be damned!"

Vanessa pushed away from the table and headed toward the Isolation Ward. I didn't have to ask why because I suspected she wanted to see things for herself. I followed her down to the ward, hoping to hear the voices again, but doubting we would.

Eight

"Hanna, don't dawdle!" Bill's smooth voice floated to Hanna as Cole and Vanessa jogged down the steps into the Isolation Ward.

His voice breathed new life into her spirit. *I know I'm not here as Cole and Vanessa are, but I'll stay here as I am until I have Bill in my arms again. There's no time to lose. I must find out if my love has truly returned to me or not.*

She jogged across the deck, down the steps, turning the corner as they stood outside the entrance to the ward.

Cole turned and looked *at* her, not *through* her, a slight grin on his face. He winked, took Vanessa's hand, then stepped into the room filled with sick and injured men.

"Cole, will you..." Vanessa protested as she floundered into the room after him.

Hanna hurried down the hall to see if she'd imagined Bill's gaze upon her or not. She followed as close as possible.

Yes, it was true. The heart and mind did strange things, even to a spirit.

"Shh, can you hear that?" He cocked his head toward a soldier lying in a bunk. "Can you hear their moans, Vanessa?"

"Whose moans, Cole? I only hear the sounds of the ship." She stared at him like he'd lost his marbles.

Bill came out of hiding, and Hanna had a feeling her great-niece sensed it because she pulled back from him. She had to do something to prove to her they were all here—the soldiers, Bill, and herself—even Cole was here in body.

"Bill, are you here? Can you step from Cole again?"

Hanna stepped between Cole and Vanessa, gazing into his eyes in search of her beloved Bill. That twinkle she fell in love with was just below the surface.

"Thank goodness, you're here. We've got to do something, Bill, or all will be lost."

Cole stumbled forward into Vanessa as he turned to leave the Isolation Ward. His arms wrapped around her, then his lips ravished hers.

Hanna watched, afraid she'd lost Bill to another, when a cough sounded from inside the ward. One of the soldiers needed attention, and she did as she was trained, to help the sick and wounded.

Walking into the ward, she found Bill examining the man. As hard as it was, she controlled the urge to run to him. Instead, she stared in disbelief.

"Come now, Hanna, these men need attention, and so do I." Bill looked at her, his smile brightening the darkness trying to dissolve her spirit.

Running into his open arms, she barely heard the cheers of their patients. "You certainly took long enough," she whispered against his lips, reveling in the long-awaited kiss.

"Sorry, my love, I had to wait for him." Bill nodded toward Cole and Vanessa, locked in each other's arms.

Hanna knew, in that instant, they would fall in love, just as she and Bill faded back into theirs.

Heat Rating: 1

April at Christmas

When April drove to the Franklin's
to decorate a house for a Christmas fundraiser,
she never imagined she'd meet a
disagreeable man and fall head over heels in love.

Sharon Addy

APRIL AT CHRISTMAS

Sharon Hart Addy

April slowed the company van to a crawl. Scanning snow-covered lawns and frost-glittered pines, she searched for a driveway. A swirl of tiny snowflakes created a fog-like haze. Windshield wipers swiping back and forth at top speed didn't help. The weather was providing the perfect setting for the Charity Open House, but the amount of falling snow made it hard to find the historic house they were hired to decorate.

"What was the address?"

Cassie consulted the papers on her lap then looked at the high, red brick wall along the street. "You don't need the address. We're here."

"Where?"

"Right there. Can you pull into the drive?"

"I'll try." April eased the van into a turn and started around the wide semicircle of asphalt that defined the massive front lawn. The drive led to a triple garage before it swooped past the front door. At least the angle of the driveway and the placement of the large Tudor house and garage suggested that layout, but a white pickup seemed to spring out of the snow and block the way.

She hit the brakes. The van slid, then lurched to a stop, inches from the front of the truck.

"Hey!" A loud male voice shouted. "Watch what you're doing!" A man appeared out of the falling snow, red-cheeked, with white flakes dotting his dark hair.

Cassie didn't have to open her window to hear him, but she opened it anyway.

He bent toward the van, his face inches from hers, his brown eyes slits, his forehead crumpled with fury. "Where did you learn to drive? California? Don't you know better than to slam the brakes on snow? You could have wiped out the front of my truck!"

April's temper rose. "Me? Where did you learn to drive? Even an idiot would know better than to block the whole driveway! There's room for two cars to pass, but you had to take up the whole thing!" The guy opened his mouth. Before he could say whatever prompted the angry look on his face, someone shouted something. He turned his head and stomped away.

April stared at his retreating form. The man was definitely short on brain power. How dare he insult her driving? California, indeed. She'd been driving on ice and snow since she was a teenager. She'd even taken her driving test when it was snowing.

Cassie broke the silence. "Well, that was exciting. A great way to start the day."

April clenched and unclenched her teeth. Finally, she let out the angry breath she'd been holding and loosened her grip on the steering wheel. She sat a moment longer, letting the fury drain away. It was another minute before she could manage a civil answer.

"We might as well park here. We can't get any closer to the house." Even she could hear the annoyance in her voice. "I hope you're in the mood to haul things."

Cassie shrugged. "Anything to get the job done." She unbuckled her seatbelt. "Let's get started. My kids expect me to be home on time tonight."

Carrying wreaths and boxes of garland across the slippery asphalt proved to be a challenge. April wished they'd brought a dolly so they could stack their supplies and wheel them to the house. They'd already carried the first load in when they returned to the van and found a dolly waiting for them.

A silver-haired fellow in jeans and a heavy sweatshirt stood beside it. He smiled. "Elaine, the housekeeper, saw you carrying things in and suggested you could use this. Leave it in the garage when you're finished."

Cassie loaded boxes while April said *thank you.* They wheeled the next two loads to the house, stacking their supplies in the main hallway. Finished with the dolly, April returned it to the garage.

The red-faced owner of the truck glared at her. "What's the big idea? First you almost hit my truck, then you use my equipment?" He jerked the dolly out of her hands. "Use your own stuff."

April watched him clomp off, her mouth open in astonishment. He didn't even give her a chance to explain or apologize. And, she would have apologized for using his dolly—although she wasn't sure it would be a polite apology. If she'd known it was his, she definitely wouldn't have touched it.

The elderly fellow stepped out of a shadow. "I'm sorry about that. I didn't think the guys needed it."

She nodded and took a deep breath to cool her temper. "Well, thanks. It was a big help. I'm sorry you got into trouble over it."

He shook his head. "There was no trouble. At least, not for me."

"I'm glad." She glanced at the snow-covered lawn where the guy stood talking to another fellow. "He sure has a short temper."

"He's usually pretty cool and collected. That's one of the reasons I hired him." The man held out his hand. "I'm Mr. Franklin. This is my house."

She shook his hand. "April McGuire, designer for Green and Growing Greenhouse. I'm pleased to meet you."

"McGuire. That explains the red hair."

She laughed. "Yes, it does."

"Well, April McGuire, the Charity Open House is in a few days, so you're working against a deadline. If you need anything, mention it to Elaine. She's the housekeeper. She'll help you out."

For April, the rest of the day went rather smoothly. Elaine supplied a stepladder, and April and Cassie hung wreaths over fireplaces in the living room, the den, and three bedrooms upstairs. They wrapped red velvet ribbon around evergreen garland and draped the colorful swags along the mantels. Red candles in silver candleholders completed the look and the house took on the brisk, clean scent of pine.

At five, April stepped outside to an awful mess.

A stack of plywood leaned against the garage, and odds and ends of lumber littered the sawdust coated driveway. Lights glaring from the front of the garage cut the early evening darkness and helped her pick her way through the maze.

Cassie, following April, mumbled something. The whine of an electric saw cut the air.

April stopped and looked toward the sound. Two men, one of them the dark-haired truck owner, wearing protective glasses and earmuffs, concentrated on a two by four as the saw ran through it. The other guy, the one with sandy hair, held the wood steady.

April put her hands over her ears and headed for the van.

Cassie tapped her shoulder and pointed. The skeleton of a shed sat on the massive front lawn. Four six-foot pieces of lumber defined the corners with the start of a slanted roof over them.

Cassie shouted, "Looks like they're building a manger."

April caught some of what Cassie said, but she wasn't sure. The saw stopped just as April hollered, "A manger?"

A familiar male voice rose from the garage. "It's definitely not a coat check. Of course, it's a manger."

April turned to face the guy. "I didn't mean to insult your work. The saw was going. I was just making sure I heard right."

"Sure, missy, and that's not snow on the ground."

She stared at him. What did he mean by that? She certainly didn't intend to insult him, but apparently, she had. Or, somebody else had and he was taking it out on her. That wasn't fair, or nice.

"Is there anything else?"

His tone set her nerves on edge. "As a matter of fact, there is. Tomorrow, I'll be eternally grateful if you don't block the entire driveway with your monster truck."

"Now, look here, missy.

"April," she growled through clenched teeth. She might be tiny, but she wasn't a child.

"April," he repeated. "It's December, not April. And don't change the subject."

"I'm not talking about the time of year. My name is April, and I prefer that to missy."

He seemed stunned, then puzzled. "Why would anyone name—"

"April was my mother's favorite month." She considered elaborating, but gave him the short version. "Flowers come up then."

"Oh." His eyebrows dipped and a faint color suggesting embarrassment appeared on his cheeks. "I never knew it was a name. I guess I owe you an apology."

"You owe my mother one, but it's a good thing she's not here to hear it." She clenched her teeth and marched away.

Cassie caught up with her. "He apologizes nicely."

April nodded in agreement, her cheeks burning. Why did she get so huffy and make a fool of herself? A lot of people commented on her name. She almost never exploded at them. She reached the van, opened the door, and looked back. The dark-haired guy hefted the sheet of plywood, carried it across the driveway to the structure on the lawn, set it in place, and used a nail gun to hold it there. She watched him walk back to the garage, check a few things, and talk to the man he was working with.

Cassie climbed into the van. "Tomorrow, let's try to leave on time. The kids' holiday concert starts at six, but they have to be there at five. You're welcome to join us."

"I'll think about it." April got behind the wheel. "We should get out of here early tomorrow. We only have to place the table pieces, do the banister, and the windowsill on the landing. The trees will be delivered in the afternoon. If we can, it would be good to get a head start on them."

The next morning, bright sunlight glared off crusty snow as April maneuvered the company van onto the curved driveway. She moved slowly, ready to stop if a certain white truck blocked the way again, but the drive was empty.

She parked in front of the garage.

Cassie jumped out, opened the back doors, and stood looking at the boxes stacked there. When April joined her, Cassie moaned, "We forgot a dolly."

"There's not that much." April piled two boxes, one on top of the other. "We'll just have to carry them." She led the way to the side door. She slowed enough to look at the closed garage. Obviously, the guys working on the manger weren't there yet. She hid her smile. She was glad. She'd had enough run-ins with that good-looking dark-haired brute. She wondered if he'd quit or if he was just late.

What difference did it make, and why did she care?

She juggled the boxes in her arms and kept walking.

Before she reached the house, Elaine opened the kitchen door. She took the top box from April's stack. "Where do you want these?"

"The front hall." She crossed the kitchen and set her box on the stairs to the second floor.

"Do you have more? Should I get a dolly?"

April laughed. "Not if it belongs to that short-tempered guy building the manger."

"Do you mean Garth?"

"Does he have black hair, a loud voice, and a white truck?

"That sounds like him, but I've never known him to be short-tempered."

"Well, he was yesterday."

"I'm sorry to hear that. He's usually pretty easygoing."

"So I keep hearing." April shook her head. "He can be anything he wants as long as I can avoid him."

Cassie caught up to them and set her boxes on the steps. "Are you talking about Garth? I just met him and Nate. He's in a better mood today. Actually friendly."

"Hmm," April mused. "A real life Dr. Jekyll and Mr. Hyde?"

Elaine shook her head. "Don't be so quick to judge."

"It doesn't matter." April opened a box. "We have today and tomorrow to finish decorating this house. That's not a lot of time."

Elaine collected their jackets, promising to hang them up. "There'll be coffee and fresh donuts about ten."

April and Cassie thanked her and turned their attention to evergreen garland wrapped in twinkle lights and a box of large red velvet bows.

Starting at the top of the stairs on the second floor, April tied the end of the garland to the banister with one of the bows, let the garland swoop in a gentle curve past three spokes and held it while Cassie fixed it in place with another bow. The smell of fresh donuts reached them as they finished the bow on the newel post at the bottom of the stairs. April plugged in the twinkle lights, and they stood back to admire their work. The bright red ribbon, the dots of light, the varied green of the garland, and the banister's gleaming walnut complimented each other.

Mr. Franklin came out of the den and stood with them. "It looks great. Very Christmassy." He turned toward the kitchen. "Do you smell those donuts? Come on, let's get some. I'm sure there's coffee, and it sounds like the guys just came in."

He led the way to the kitchen with Cassie right behind him.

April lagged. One of the male voices emulating from the kitchen sounded way too familiar. She edged her way into the room. The two fellows building the manger sat at the table, drinking coffee. When she hesitated, Mr. Franklin pulled out a chair for her. She eased into it, smiling as Elaine filled the cup beside her plate. Cassie, seated next to her, passed the platter of warm, sugar-coated donuts. April took one and handed the platter across the table.

The dark-haired grump took the platter with a wide smile. "Elaine, you're a peach. Apple cider donuts. My favorite!"

"There are plenty of them. Eat up!" Elaine rounded the table with the coffee pot, giving refills.

Mr. Franklin settled at the head of the table. "Garth, how's the manger coming along?"

"We came up with a solution to the problem, but there are a few details we need to discuss. Lighting is one of them."

April held her coffee mug and studied him. Garth, she reminded herself. Mr. Franklin had called him Garth. Now that he wasn't scowling, he was good-looking in a rugged, square-jawed way, and his voice, now that he wasn't shouting, was a pleasant bass. She wondered, briefly, what yesterday's problem had been. Today, he seemed like the easygoing person she'd been told he was.

"Refill?" Elaine stood beside her with the coffee pot.

April held out her mug. Her concentration broken, she heard Mr. Franklin say, "And, of course, you'll help these young ladies with the trees."

Garth turned to April and Cassie. "When are they coming?"

Cassie answered. "This afternoon."

Garth gulped his coffee and pushed back his chair. "Come on, Nate. We better get busy." He grabbed another donut and was out the door, Nate right behind him.

April and Cassie got back to work, doing the other banister on the grand staircase, then carrying premade table decorations from the van and placing them around the house. When the trees arrived, they held doors while Garth and Nate carried a six-foot long-needled pine into the den, then set up an eight-foot balsam in the living room, filling the space with the fresh, crisp scent of the great outdoors

April opened a box of the old-fashioned tree lights and asked Cassie, "Are you going up the ladder, or am I?"

Cassie moved their aluminum ladder next to the tree. "Before I answer, tell me, did you have lunch? You know how dizzy you get if you don't eat."

She smirked. "I ate. You saw me."

Garth interrupted. "I'll go up for both trees and we'll use my ladder." He walked out.

April and Cassie exchanged a glance as Nate folded their ladder and set it to the side. "Garth's stepladder is taller."

April shrugged and let it go.

Garth arrived with his ladder. He looked from Cassie to April. "Do you ladies have a plan?"

"Usually," April explained, "one of us stands on the ladder and the other one walks around the tree feeding her the lights while she places them on the top of the tree. When she can't reach around the tree anymore, we walk around the tree together."

Garth climbed the ladder. "Bring on the lights."

Nate hit the button on his portable radio and Christmas music filled the room.

"This goes up first." April handed Garth a large star.

As he took it, his fingers wrapped around hers, and a shiver-like tingle shot through her body. She glanced up at him, her heart thudding. His brown eyes swept across her face as if he was trying to memorize it. The world seemed to stand still.

Something bumped April's arm, breaking the spell. She turned to find Cassie holding out the end of the light string. April stepped aside to let Cassie pass it up to Garth, her face hot. She cradled the fingers he'd touched. What just happened?

She moved to the back of the tree. Cassie and Nate stationed themselves on either side of her. They passed the strings of lights as Garth set them in place around the top of the tree. As they worked the lower branches, they each positioned the lights. When they reached the bottom, April flipped a switch, and pools of red, green, blue, and yellow light spotted the branches.

She shared a happy smile with her co-workers, but her gaze lingered on Garth. He returned her smile with a happy glint in his eyes.

Cassie opened another box, handing out silver and gold ornaments. Their shiny surfaces reflected the lights, creating an overall glow.

With that tree finished, they moved to the one in the den. Once those lights were in place, they decorated the tree with the family's treasured ornaments.

April stepped back to admire their work. From the antique angel on the top to the personalized messages on the lowest ornaments, the tree sparkled and spoke of family. She gave a satisfied sigh and swung around to thank her helpers.

"We're finished!" She glanced at Nate and Garth. "Thank you for your help. We're done early because of you."

Nate shifted from foot to foot. "Glad to help, but we've got lights to hang outside."

Elaine appeared in the doorway with a tray.

Mr. Franklin stood behind her. "Nobody leaves until we toast the trees with a cup of cider."

April reached for a cup just as Garth did. Their fingers touched, and a tingle went through her again. She looked up and found him staring at her. Her heartbeat quickened as he examined her with a puzzled expression.

She took the cup and lifted it, all too aware he stood beside her, close enough she could feel his warmth.

Mr. Franklin raised his cup. "Merry Christmas!"

April lifted hers. She touched Cassie's cup, and Nate's, Mr. Franklin's, and Elaine's. Turning, she grazed Garth's shoulder as her cup touched his. She didn't have the courage to look at him. The toast over, she stepped closer to Cassie—closer to safety, away from Garth's magnetic field. Under the guise of putting her empty cup on the tray Elaine offered, she peeked at him.

He stared into his cup as if it held a potion he'd never had before. In one swift movement, he emptied the cup, put it on Elaine's tray, and started for the door. His voice seemed deeper as he said, "Come on, Nate, we need to get back to work."

Cassie called after them. "Can we help?"

Garth's back stiffened. He didn't turn around to respond. "No. We got this."

Nate clunked his cup onto Elaine's tray and hurried after Garth.

Cassie grabbed a bit of tissue paper off the floor. 'I guess we're the cleanup crew."

An hour later, a sliver of moon hung in the sky as April stepped outside and paused to enjoy the fresh air.

Cassie stopped, too. "We got a lot done today. What's left?"

"Lighted garland outside around the front entry, a wreath on the door, and mistletoe somewhere. About a half a day's work."

"Good. If we leave early, I can get some shopping done."

Nate came out of the garage. "You get to leave? Man, you're lucky. We'll probably be here till midnight."

"Really? The manger is finished. What else do you need to do?"

"The figures. When Garth signed on for the job, we were just supposed to do the manger, but the actors backed out, and now we have to do the figures, too. We're also putting up the outside lights and decorating the brick wall along the street."

April sent a silent question to Cassie. After Cassie nodded, April said, "You helped us, so we'll help you. What can we do?"

Nate lifted a shoulder. "I don't know. Maybe string the garland on the wall by the street?"

"We'll do it first thing tomorrow," April promised. "Just tell us where the garland is."

·❤·❤·❤·❤·❤·

Hanging evergreen garland on the brick wall along the street turned out to be an easy task. In the past, someone had added permanent hooks to the masonry, so April and Cassie simply had to move their ladder down the sidewalk, measure the appropriate amount of garland, and catch the next hook. They were finished and heading to the house when Garth's white truck pulled into the driveway and parked near them.

He rolled down his window and leaned out. "That looks great, but you weren't supposed to do it."

April walked toward the truck, trying to ignore the sprig of joy that made her want to skip like a child. "We're just returning the favor. You helped us, we helped you." She gave a quick wave. "See you later."

He waved back and she watched him get out to drop the truck's tailgate. How could she control this feeling that took over whenever she saw him? How could she go back to just thinking about him as that dark-haired guy? But there was something about the confident way he moved, and the easy smile lurking at the corners of his mouth, ready to broaden into a grin. A grin that suggested a great sense of humor. His sense of self was the most irresistible thing about him. He knew who he was and was happy with it. She watched him climb back into his truck with an easy grace and wanted to sigh as he drove away.

Draping lighted garland around the windows and doors proved to be as easy as decorating the wall along the sidewalk. A massive wreath on the front door was the final touch.

"All that's left now," Cassie reminded April, "is the mistletoe. Do you know where Mr. Franklin wants it?"

"We can check with Elaine. She'll know."

Elaine did know. "He usually hangs it in the arch leading to the living room. You'll see the little hole from the thumb tack. I'll have coffee and sweet rolls for you when you're done."

The mistletoe hung, April climbed down the ladder. She folded it and carried it to the garage, glad to be finished for the day. The saw was zinging as she stepped inside, but the noise quickly stopped.

Garth removed his safety glasses and what looked like headphones. "You should have let me know you needed to put something up."

"It wasn't much of anything, and it's done."

Turning so her back was to him, she leaned the ladder against the wall. Her cheeks grew warm at the thought of him helping her hang the mistletoe.

She'd be up on the ladder, and he'd be right behind her, his arms kind of around her as he held the ladder steady.

She blinked the image away. Why couldn't she control the crazy ideas that snuck in whenever he was around? She put her hands on her cheeks to cool them.

She could all but feel him watching her as she moved toward the door.

"Don't go. Nate's gone, and I could use a hand cutting this stake."

She turned to face him, hoping her expression wouldn't betray her runaway thoughts. "What do you need me to do?"

"Hold the end of this one-by-four against the top of the sawhorse while I cut it. I didn't bring enough claps from the shop."

"You have a shop?"

"Workshop. Robert Fariday & Son. I'm the son. Dad rents me out for big jobs."

She chuckled at his being 'rented out.' "What does Fariday & Sons do?"

"Carpentry. All kinds. Sheds and," he grinned, "actual mangers. Chicken coops. We've redone porches and replaced doors. Installed paneling. We do anything involving wood. Everything from rough work to fine refinishing. We even repair furniture."

"It must be interesting work."

"It is."

He held out a small package with foam earplugs. She shook her head. He took her hand and put the package in it.

She stared at the earplugs, her hand still warm from his touch, aware he was very close. His voice, so near, so soft, cut through her haze.

"If you're going to help me, you need to put them in."

She nodded and fumbled to rip the plastic.

He took it from her and opened it. "Look at me."

She tipped her head and found his face inches from hers. She couldn't breathe. Her heart pounded.

He leaned closer. "I'm not very good at this."

He pushed her hair behind her ear, and his other hand caressed her cheek. He blinked and quickly stepped away from her. He shifted closer again and blinked several more times.

"It's better if you put them in yourself." He held them out to her.

She nodded and opened her hand to take the earplugs. He dropped them onto her palm. She looked at the earplugs, but didn't see them at all. Seconds passed. Her breath came and went. Her heart slowed.

Something moved nearby. She looked up and saw him holding a long thin piece of wood.

"Ready?"

"Not quite." She rammed the foam plugs into her ears.

He slipped on his goggles and protective earmuffs, flipped the switch to start the jigsaw, and swung the one-by-four along the top of the sawhorse. She pressed down on the wood, and he started the saw. The whine's pitch changed as it bit into the lumber. A tense few minutes and three cuts later, the long piece was reduced to four short ones.

Garth shut the saw off, set it aside, and slid off his earmuffs. She pulled out her earplugs.

"Thanks. You make a good handyman's helper."

"Thanks, I guess. I should get back inside."

"Just so you know, that's not the safest way to work with a saw. The board should have been held in place with clamps."

She grinned. "I guessed that, but it's too late now."

He grinned in return, his gaze finding hers. "It certainly is."

She floated into the kitchen, smiling.

Cassie got up from the table and carried her coffee mug to the sink. "I did the final walk-through. Everything is ready for tomorrow." She pulled on her jacket. "It's after five. I have to get home. The kids' program starts at six."

Elaine gave April her jacket and walked them to the door. "It's been a pleasure having you here. You'll come to the Open House, won't you?"

"I can't make the Open House," Cassie said. "But I'll see you afterward for cleanup.

"I'll come," April promised. "It's always fun to see how people react to the decorations."

.❤.❤.❤.❤.❤.

The next morning, April laughed when she drove past the Franklin house and recognized the sticks jammed into artfully contrived mounds of snow and holding the signs for the Charity Open House. She navigated the narrow street, the lanes tighter than usual because of the cars parked on both sides, and found a parking spot two blocks away.

Walking back toward the house, she met smiling people who'd been on the tour. Bits of conversation she caught told her everyone seemed delighted with the way the house was decorated. She stepped into the line leading to the front door, glad she'd worn a long coat and remembered her hat. She jammed her hands in her pockets and prepared to endure the next few minutes in the cold. At least it wasn't snowing.

Soft music filled the air as the line moved forward. The folks ahead of her murmured and pointed to the manger scene on the lawn. The hands of the wooden silhouettes of Mary and Joseph that Garth and Nate had created were raised as if in awe. They'd been painted a flat black, making them resemble shadows. A rough-hewn manger sat between them, but instead of the usual figure of a baby, a brilliant light beamed up from the straw. The light drew everyone's attention and praise. April did her best to catch everything said, hoping she'd have a chance to share the comments with Garth.

Garth. She shook her head. He always seemed to be in her thoughts. What was wrong with her?

The line moved, and within minutes, she was in the house, enjoying the scent of evergreens mixed with the aroma of hot chocolate. Trailing the people in front of her, she absorbed everything they said about the decorations. The tiny lights blinking in the garland drew the most attention. Everyone seemed to like them, and the wide red velvet ribbons and bows. The tabletop centerpieces of Christmas tree ornaments with red and green plaid ribbon drew compliments. By the time her tour reached the kitchen, and the hot chocolate, she was pleased with what she and

Cassie had done. She slipped out the kitchen door and headed for her car, filled with the satisfaction of a job well done.

Shopping took all afternoon. She found gifts for her mom and dad, her brother and her sister-in-law. Finding something for Cassie wasn't as easy. She finally settled on a hat and scarf set, and was debating between the red or the navy blue when a familiar voice spoke beside her.

"Blue, definitely the blue."

She looked up and found Garth next to her. Her pulse quickened, and for a second, she couldn't think.

She managed to say, "It's for Cassie."

"Definitely the red. For you, it would be the blue, but for Cassie, the red."

She laughed at him. "You're certainly sure of yourself."

He grinned. "I'm used to shopping with my sister. If I didn't tell her what to do, we'd never finish."

April shook her head, laughing. "How old is your sister?"

His expression grew sly. "That would be telling, and she wouldn't be happy with me."

"Is she with you today?"

"She just left, and I'm ready for a break. How about you? A cup of coffee and a chance to sit for a while?"

"That sounds good."

She claimed a table for two, the only empty one in the coffee shop, while he stood in line to order. She couldn't keep herself from watching him as he chatted with the folks around him. He was, she saw now, easygoing, which made her wonder why he'd been so irate that first day at Mr. Franklin's.

She asked him after he put their coffees down and settled across from her.

"Nothing much." He hid his expression by stirring his coffee.

She found that hard to believe. "It had to be something important."

"It was. An argument, actually. It really riled me up." He shifted in his chair and avoided looking at her.

"I'm sorry I brought it up. It's really none of my business."

He shrugged and gave her a half smile. "An old girlfriend. She knows how to rattle my cage."

"Oh." She concentrated on her coffee while the word 'girlfriend' echoed inside her head.

She should've known he'd have a girlfriend. Maybe two. She bit her lip as sadness filled her. A girlfriend. Of course, there'd be a girlfriend. He'd called her an *old girlfriend.* Did that mean she was someone in his past or that she'd been his girlfriend for a long time? She'd been so silly, daydreaming about him like a teenager. Thinking he might be interested in her. She sipped her coffee, then stared into her cup.

"It's all settled now." His voice carried a light note, a happy sound.

She felt worse, and felt bad about feeling worse. If he was happy, she should be happy for him. She took another gulp of coffee, wishing she could swallow the rest of it and leave, or better yet, just vanish into thin air.

Cassie popped up out of nowhere. "Hey! I'm dying to sit down. Can I join you?"

Garth jumped up. "Sure. Take my chair. I'll get another one."

Cassie plopped across from April. "What's wrong? You look miserable."

April glanced at Garth, chatting with folks a few tables away. "I don't want to talk about it."

"So, it's Garth. What did he do?"

"Nothing."

"I don't believe it. He did something. The two of you didn't argue, did you?"

"No. Nothing like that." She blinked away the moisture gathering in her eyes. "He has a girlfriend."

Cassie shook her head. "Of course, he has a girlfriend. He's not a monk, but that doesn't mean he's not aware of other women. Lovely women."

She glanced at Cassie, annoyed. "If he has a girlfriend, he shouldn't be looking at all."

Cassie laughed. "Oh, you have it bad, my friend."

April got up. "I'm not going to stay here and listen to you make fun of me."

"What will I tell Garth?"

"Just tell him I had to leave." She pulled on her jacket, picked up her things, and fled.

Driving home, she turned up the radio, hoping music would lift her mood. Cheery Christmas songs only made her feel more awful. She shut the radio off and drove home in silence. She paced her apartment until, exhausted, she curled up on her couch.

Over and over, she told herself she was being foolish. She'd only known him a few days. How did he become the center of all her hopes and dreams? What was it about him that drew her to him? He was good-looking, but he wasn't classically handsome. He was easygoing, but he also had a hot temper. He definitely wasn't perfect, but she couldn't help wishing she could rest her head on his shoulder while he held her in his arms.

After an almost sleepless night, April picked Cassie up with the company van. As they headed to Mr. Franklin's house, April explained what they had to do today. "Mr. Franklin decided to keep the trees and garland for the rest of the season. We just need to pick up the table decorations."

"That's good. The kids and I are baking this afternoon. Pecan fingers, spritz, and date pinwheels. It's going to be messy."

"Sounds fun."

"You can join us if you'd like."

"Thanks, but no. That's family stuff." And she wasn't family.

"So, will you come to bake cookies?"

April shook her head and said the first thing that popped into it. "I have to finish shopping."

"You don't need to sound so sad about it. It's Christmas. Cheer up!" Cassie reached over and turned on the radio. "Maybe music will help."

April switched it off again. "Music does not help." She swung the van into Mr. Franklin's driveway and stopped at the front door. "Let's get this over with."

Cassie frowned, but climbed out.

Elaine let them in and offered coffee, eager to share stories of the open house. Cassie stayed to chat, but April bustled off, saying she needed to get the returns back to the store. She gathered the table decorations and extra candles, ignoring the trees and the memories they triggered.

She was on her way out when Mr. Franklin asked, "What's your hurry?"

She stopped, calmed by his quiet presence. "Nothing, I guess. Just want to finish up."

"Well, you and Cassie did a marvelous job. The house was beautiful. Everyone said so."

"Thank you. I'm glad you were pleased."

"I'm having a little Christmas party next weekend. I hope you and Cassie can come. Feel free to bring a friend." He handed her a printed invitation.

"Two o'clock next Sunday. I'll be delighted."

"Good. I'll look forward to seeing you."

The week passed quickly enough. April refused to look at any of the manger scenes Cassie pointed out on the way to and from their decorating jobs. She definitely didn't want to think about Garth, but he invaded her thoughts constantly. She almost wished she'd never met him, but if she'd never met him, she wouldn't have those wonderful daydreams about him—walking through the snowy landscape with him, talking, laughing, stopping for hot chocolate. Her daydreams were better than a Hallmark movie. When she realized he'd be at Mr. Franklin's party, her imagination had him catching her under the mistletoe and...

The thought of his arms around her and his lips close enough to kiss nearly made her swoon.

And then she remembered. *Girlfriend.*

She forced herself to think about what kind of partner he'd have. Someone beautiful, with long brown hair, not the curly red stuff on her head. Someone athletic, who'd love skiing and lounging around the lodge's crackling fire with a glass of wine. Someone sophisticated and alluring. Someone depressingly not like her.

Cassie kept teasing her about her mood swings. In her defense, April grew silent. As the week moved on, she wavered between looking forward to Mr. Franklin's party and deciding not to go.

Sunday morning, she looked through her closet. If she went, what should she wear? Her little black dress wasn't anything smashing, but she could dress it up with jewelry. She laid it out on the bed. The color made her think of funerals. She hung it up again. She pulled out her emerald green sheath. A green dress with her red hair? She'd look like a walking Christmas ornament, but she liked the dress, and wearing it would put her in a party mood. A soft knit, it was comfortable, and the draping neckline would show off her one nice glittery necklace.

She found the dangling earrings that matched the necklace and held them next to her face. She turned her head, and the pendants sparkled. She grinned at her reflection. She'd wear the green dress and live a little. If Garth brought his stunning girlfriend, she'd at least look festive.

Cassie picked her up, and they drove to Mr. Franklin's, listening to Christmas music. April wanted to shut the radio off, but it wasn't her car and Cassie seemed to be listening. April stared out the window instead at the houses bright with multicolored Christmas lights, trying to ignore the songs about hope and love and jolly times.

They left the car on the street and walked in. Elaine met them at the door, took their coats, and directed them to the living room. Mr. Franklin left the group he was with to greet them.

"I'm glad you were able to make it. I think you might know some of the people here."

April looked around the room, and recognized most of the guests were people she'd worked with as they organized functions for various organizations. The couple in charge of the Charity Open House waved at her from across the room.

Later, April thought, she'd visit with them. For now, she took an offered glass of wine and smiled as Mr. Franklin introduced his daughter, Rebecca, and son-in-law, Mark. He left to greet more guests, and April stood with the little group as Cassie and Rebecca chatted.

A minute later, Mr. Franklin was back, Garth beside him. "I think you all know each other."

April glanced at him, then quickly away, afraid her face would show the wild surges of joy and despondency that made it hard for her to breathe. He stepped beside her, she couldn't breathe at all. Her ears buzzed.

She barely heard Mark say, "Garth, it's good to see you again."

A weird, tight feeling crawled up the back of her neck. The strange feeling continued. She felt woozy. She reached for something to hold on to and—

Groggy, she woke to Elaine leaning over her, her image fuzzy.

"There you are. You gave us quite a scare."

April looked around the room, confused. Where were all the people? There'd been a crowd, laughing, talking, drinking wine.

Elaine smiled. "You're on the couch in the den. I have to leave now, but Cassie and Garth are here if you need something."

Elaine left, and Cassie appeared. "You fainted! I never saw anyone crumple like that. One minute you were standing next to me, and the next minute Garth was catching you. You caused quite a stir."

April turned her face toward the back of the couch, her face on fire and stomach pitching. She fainted? Like some simpering Victorian lady. How embarrassing. She wished she could disappear.

"Garth is getting you coffee and cookies. Elaine thought caffeine and sugar might help."

April tried to sit up. "No, don't let Garth—"

Cassie put a restraining hand on her shoulder. "Don't get up. You're as white as a ghost and your eyes still don't look right."

April gave up and relaxed against the cushions. She closed her eyes, hoping the darkness would return and she wouldn't have to live through this nightmare. She'd actually fainted. At Mr. Franklin's party. In front of all those people. And Garth had caught her. She'd daydreamed about being in his arms, and when she really was, she'd been out cold and couldn't enjoy it. She turned her face to the back of the couch again, afraid she might cry.

Cassie patted her arm. "That's right. Just rest. In a little while, you'll be right as rain. Garth's here, so I'll go back to the party to help Elaine. See you later."

April kept her eyes shut, but felt Cassie rise with a shift of the cushions.

"April?" Garth whispered. "Are you okay?"

She nodded.

"Can you look at me?"

She shook her head.

"Why not?"

"I'm too embarrassed."

"You fainted. That's nothing to be embarrassed about."

"I never faint."

"Well, you did today. I brought you coffee. Are you ready to sit up and drink it?"

She sighed. She'd have to face him eventually. She sat up, watching him as he watched her.

"You still okay?"

"Yes," she lied. She'd never be okay again. She shook her head to get rid of the thought. She didn't know him long enough to feel so strongly.

He handed her a mug and set a plate of cookies on the coffee table. "Here. Be careful. It's hot."

She took it, her fingers brushing his as she took the mug. She longed to put her hand in his, or better yet, put her head on his shoulder and rest there. She sipped the hot brew and leaned forward to set the mug on the coffee table.

He sat next to her and, when she straightened, his arm was behind her. She rested against it and didn't object when he pulled her close.

"Are you feeling better?"

She nodded, glad he couldn't see her contented smile. Yes, she was definitely feeling better.

"You gave us quite a scare."

"That's what Cassie said." His breath caressed her cheek. If she turned just a bit, her face would be close to his.

She turned.

Her lips found his. They were soft, so soft. Softer than she'd imagined, and his arms were solid as they wrapped around her. His lips left hers, and he cradled her head against his shoulder. She closed her eyes and cuddled against him, dizzy again, but for an entirely different reason. She'd never felt this alive before. Every part of her, every cell in her body, was more awake than they'd ever been. She could stay like this forever.

Someone cleared their throat.

Garth jerked and let her go.

She sat up, back straight, alarmed.

Cassie chuckled. "You two can get back to whatever that was in a minute. April, I came to tell you I'm leaving. I promised the kids I'd take them sledding."

"Oh," April looked around. "As soon as I find my purse, I'll be ready."

"You don't need to rush off. I'm sure someone will give you a ride." Cassie's smile seemed ready to bloom into laughter.

April frowned at her. She didn't want to make Garth feel he had to give her a ride. She'd go with Cassie. She stood up quickly. That strange warmth at the back of her head reappeared and darkness started to close in on her. She swayed and shook her head to fend off the feeling. Dang it, she'd forgotten to eat today.

Garth shot up beside her, holding her steady. "You need to sit down again."

Unable to do anything else, she plopped on the couch and sagged. She closed her eyes, Garth right next to her.

"I'll take her home."

Cassie laughed. "I'm sure she won't mind."

April opened her eyes and pulled herself upright. She wasn't going to let Cassie taunt her like that. "I'm okay," she insisted, even though she knew that wasn't true. "I just need a minute or two."

"You need more than a moment. If you really don't want Garth to drive you home, give me a call, and I'll come back for you." Cassie waved and left.

April drank her coffee. Her stomach rumbled, and she reached for a cookie. "I guess I skipped eating today."

"You need more than cookies. I'll fill a plate from the buffet." He rose.

She caught his hand. "Don't go." Her fingers tightened around his. She'd dreamed long enough. It was time to follow her heart, but... "You have a girlfriend."

Confusion wrinkled his brow. "I don't have a girlfriend, just an ex-girlfriend."

"An *ex*-girlfriend?"

He seemed to connect the dots on the miscommunication. "That's all, until now."

"There's no mistletoe, but it doesn't matter." She stood up, slipped her arms around him, and kissed him. A long, sweet, lingering kiss.

He pulled her closer. "We don't need mistletoe."

She tilted her head to accept his kiss. A soft warmth eased through her, something like fainting, but oh, so much better.

Dance With Me

Marianne is getting married and needs to learn how to dance,
so she enlists the help of Robert, an accomplished instructor.
But when she begins to have feelings for him,
she questions whether her fiancé is the right match for her,
and if she should be getting married in the first place.

Veronica Leigh

DANCE WITH ME

Veronica Leigh

Marianne timidly entered the airy room of the dance studio, wiping her damp palms on her A-line skirt. The whitewashed walls smelled newly painted and the hardwood floors gleamed beneath the bold chandeliers hanging above. *Monroe's Dance Studio* on the front of the building beckoned her inside.

"What am I doing here?" she mumbled, a throb of tension mounting in her shoulders.

Her past experiences with dance had been horrendous. Her father once tried show her a simple step. *"Stand on my feet,"* he had urged. She was five-years-old and took that to mean she was supposed to stomp on the bridges of his feet. And so, ended his sole attempt to educate her. By her teen years, she was an ugly duckling. On prom night, she was parked on the living room sofa, stuffing her face with chocolate ice cream, watching "Pretty in Pink."

And now, at thirty-two, she was engaged. Her fiancé, Elliot, was a fantastic dancer and there had been dozens of failed attempts to teach her, all of which ended with him shouting and her in tears.

Six weeks, she reminded herself.

Six weeks to learn to dance. That way, she wouldn't be a disaster at the wedding. However, if her talented fiancé couldn't help, there was no reason for her to think a dance instructor could.

Marianne detected movement out of the corner of her eye. Turning around, she exhaled a lungful of breath she'd been holding.

"Hello?" A man dressed in jeans and a polo gave her a shy wave. He was a few inches taller than her and his compact wiriness gave him an energetic appearance. "May I help you, miss?"

"I hope so." She gulped and stepped forward. She had to be brave, otherwise she'd make a fool of herself at the wedding and ruin the Big Day. "Are you Mr. Monroe?"

"Monroe, yeah." The man nodded, the corner of his mouth twitching. "Mr. Monroe was my father, though. I prefer Robert." The more he spoke, his low, husky voice sent delicious shivers through her. "And you are?"

She shook the hand he offered and was a little overwhelmed by his firm, but warm grip. "Marianne Reynolds. I need to learn how to danc e...in six weeks." She extracted her hand, wondering why she enjoyed his touch so much.

"Six weeks!" Robert repeated, and let out a shrill whistle.

Blood rushed to her cheeks. In all likelihood, six weeks wasn't sufficient enough time to master the art of dancing, but she had no other choice.

"That's when I'm getting married. I'd like to be able to dance at my wedding." She clenched her fists, longing to grab hold of something, but nothing was in reach. Other than Robert's hand. "My fiancé is a wonderful dancer and I...suck."

That she sucked was an understatement of the century. She was a menace on the dance floor, a danger to herself and to anyone within an arm's length. An accident looking for a place to happen, she had broken a number of Elliot's toes, tripped herself, and per Elliot when the *"music moved her, it moved her ugly."*

And she didn't want to be ugly, especially on her wedding day.

Robert's soft gaze swept over her, and she felt a fluttering in the low pit of her stomach like butterflies. His eyes were ambers, deep and warm.

"I'm sure you don't suck." He gave a lighthearted chuckle. Cupping her elbow, he led her inside and coaxed her to the center of the room. "Let's try something very simple. The waltz has three steps, and we'll start slow."

Out of habit, she tensed as his arm curled around her waist and drew her closer. There was nothing inappropriate about the way he cradled her, but he was close enough for his spicy breath to tickle her chin. Close enough for him to look in her eyes and search out what was in her soul. Meeting his gaze, she was sharing an intimacy with him she had never shared with Elliot. It was unsettling.

Robert counted off, "One-two-three, one-two-three, one-two-three..." With each movement and every turn, it was followed by a grunt or an "ouch" when she stepped on his toes.

When he let out a sharp yelp, she disengaged herself and shrank back, clasping her hand over her mouth. "I'm sorry. See, I told you I sucked!" It was no use. There was no overcoming her two left feet. "This is a mistake." Tears blurred her vision and were soon spilling down her cheeks.

"What?" He rummaged through his pocket and pulled out a handkerchief. Giving it to her, he claimed her hand and led her towards an empty table in the corner. "No, here, come sit down."

She slumped into one of the chairs and dabbed the cotton handkerchief–which was still heated from his thigh–to the corners of her eyes. She didn't know why, but she was crying more and more these days. She would have breakdowns where she would end up in the fetal position, usually in her bedroom closet, gasping for breath. Anxiety attacks had cropped up off and on in her life, but this was different.

Robert sat beside her and placed his hand on her wrist. The pads of his palms were much gentler than Elliot's. She found herself wondering what it would feel like if he massaged her pulse point...or someplace else.

"You're putting too much pressure on yourself." He tilted his head and sighed. "Dancing is meant to be fun. Therapeutic."

She made a face of disbelief. Dancing was anything but fun, let alone therapeutic. If she didn't *have* to learn, she wouldn't. She would avoid it altogether.

But her relationship with Elliot was on the line. Couples had to make sacrifices for one another. This was important to him, therefore, it was important to her, too.

"I have to get this right. I don't want to embarrass my fiancé." She made an unattractively loud sniff.

Robert looked confused, but waved her worries off. "Your fiancé loves you. How could he be embarrassed by you?" He gave her wrist a final, comforting pat. "Listen, we have six weeks. We'll make a dancer of you yet. I promise."

She nodded and, despite her reservations, found herself taking Robert Monroe at his word.

Robert rubbed his side, the spot still sore from where Marianne had jabbed him in the gut with her boney elbow. He'd have a bruise there tomorrow, no doubt, as well as a broken toe or two.

She wasn't kidding when she said she was a bad dancer. Well, she wasn't so much bad as clumsy, and not so much clumsy as terrified. He was no expert, but something set her on edge, and that nervousness transferred to her dancing, and probably other parts of her life. Still, he never would've guessed someone so small could cause such pain.

He released the trembling woman and dragging his hand through his sweat damp hair. "Let's, uh...let's take a break."

She seemed to be on the verge of tears again. Clasping her hands in front of her, she whimpered, "I'm sorry."

"Really, its fine." He hoped she wouldn't fret over it. Bruises healed, it was as simple as that. "We all have to start somewhere. It can be frustrating."

"I think I'm getting worse, though." She hugged herself, looking smaller than before. If that were even possible.

When Marianne Reynolds had traipsed through the doors of the dance studio, he'd nearly fallen over. She was so...beautiful. Auburn curls cascading down her shoulders, piercing blue eyes, pert nose, plump pink lips. She reminded him of one of those Old Hollywood actresses. Not only did she possess outer beauty, she had inner beauty, as well. Smart, sweet, kind, funny...

His heart had literally skipped a beat when she'd said she needed to learn to dance. And then it had broken a second later when she'd mentioned her upcoming nuptials.

I never stood a chance.

He'd gone directly home after their first lesson to lick his wounds. Naturally, someone as lovely and sweet as Marianne had a fiancé. Made sense.

By the second lesson, she looked as though she wanted to flee. In fact, she always had that look. Like she was frantically searching for the nearest exit. What she was trying to escape, he couldn't say. Everyone had their demons. His arms ached to hold her, to offer her some comfort and assure her that all would be well, but he got the distinct impression she did not like to be touched. She tended to flinch when he held her hand or placed his arm around her. Perhaps she didn't want to get too close to him when she had a fiancé at home waiting for her.

Still, something seemed off.

Robert retrieved their water bottles from the table, handed Marianne's to her, and then unscrewed the lid on his. He took a swig and swallowed.

"Well, in my opinion, you're getting yourself worked up, and that's what's causing you trouble. Is something bothering you?"

She averted her gaze and shook her head. "Just that my wedding is in six weeks, and I need to be the perfect dancer." She limped over to one of the chairs and flopped in it. "But I'm not."

Placing her bottle on the floor, she kicked her heels off and wiggled her toes. She bent over, stroked her ankle, and gave a little groan.

Robert frowned. He'd tried to warn her that, for beginners, dancing was hard on the feet. Better to start off in comfortable footwear, but she seemed determined to take the hard road. She insisted on wearing heels because that was what she would wear at her wedding. Whatever it was that was driving her to succeed, it was a cruel task master. One that needed to be expelled from her life.

He set his water bottle back down, scooted a chair opposite of her, and took a seat. He patted his thigh. "Here, let me see."

Her brows furrowed. At first, he assumed she didn't want him to touch her, but realized she had no concept of what he was offering to do.

"Your feet." He gestured.

"Oh, you don't have to do that!" Her cheekbones reddened furiously.

"I know I don't have to, but I want to."

It took some coaxing, but he lifted one of her delicate feet into his lap. He pressed his thumbs along her instep and kneaded the muscles, guided by her tender, little moans.

"Why don't you tell me about your wedding?"

He waited for her to start babbling about wedding plans, and caterers, her dress, the fiancé—whatever. However, her monotone responses to his inquiries left a bad taste in his mouth. Not at all the way a blushing bride should be. She might as well have been planning her own funeral.

Her lower lip quivered as she watched him massage her feet. Why a simple foot rub would upset her so was beyond his imagination. But it seemed to affect her.

"How did you become a dance instructor?" Her tone was strained, again from unshed tears.

He chuckled. Reserved as he was, no one ever pegged him for a dancer. But as a boy, his grandmother had taken him in hand, and the rest was history. Granny had been a professional dancer, and had later opened her own studio, which he'd inherited. Dancing, feeling the blood rage through his veins, moving to the music? It unlocked something inside of him.

"It's a long story," he admitted shyly, and motioned for her to switch feet.

She slid her foot off his lap and replaced it with the other. "I love long stories."

She offered the first genuine smile she'd bestowed on him all evening. He'd never seen anything prettier.

"All right." He continued to caress her foot, and though his tale had some sad parts in it, he didn't mind sharing with her. Anything to amuse her. Best of all, her limb was less ridged beneath his fingers, indicating she was calming down and beginning to trust him. "My parents died when

I was young, and my grandmother raised me. She owned a dance studio, and to help me heal from my parents' deaths, she taught me to dance."

She sighed, and the light slowly returned to her eyes as he told her the rest of his story.

"Marianne, you're doing beautifully." Robert spun her around and then dipped her low.

"Don't let go!" She giggled, letting her head fall back, her arms encircling him. Her fingertips scraped, detecting the warmth of his muscles beneath his cotton shirt.

He hung onto her. "I won't. I promise."

She allowed herself to be swept upwards and threw her arms around him for a proper hug. "I can't believe it! We made it through an entire lesson, and I haven't hurt you once!" She shook her head as she parted form.

"You're a natural."

Gone was her irrational fear of dancing and of making a fool of herself. She didn't know whether she had any talent or not, but she felt good and she was having fun. Three weeks of lessons, every night, were working a miracle.

Despite all of her gaffs and the physical pain she caused Robert, he never once lost his temper. Never yelled or swore. No matter how many times she made a mistake or cried, he was always kind and patient. Always ready to offer her a listening ear or a handkerchief. No longer did she tremble or cry when he was close by. Robert was so unlike Elliot. Elliot had left bruises on her from holding her too tight, bruises that took weeks to heal. His manner of dance was sharp, angry, severe even. She once heard how someone danced was an example of how they would be in bed. She and Elliot opted to wait until their wedding night before having sex, but she often wondered how her future husband would treat her. Would he be too rough as he was on the dance floor, and leave further marks on her?

Robert wouldn't. Sweet, gentle, tenderhearted Robert… She had been enamored with him since he'd shared his story. After each lesson, he rubbed her feet to help her feel better, to relieve the tension. His nimble fingers always worked a miracle on her. Elliot would never do anything so humble, so thoughtful.

Robert would be the perfect partner–on the dance floor, in bed, and in life.

She gave a slight shake of her head and hoped he didn't notice. *Don't go there.* She was engaged and the lessons were for her wedding, for crying out loud! The last thing she needed to do was fantasize about Robert Monroe.

Why couldn't I have met Robert before Elliot? She grabbed her towel and patted her sticky brow. *Stop it. You're just having cold feet!* This was common for brides. She was just stressed out.

"My grandmother once told me everyone has One Thing. One Thing that gets you up in the morning and helps you put one foot in front of the other," Robert said without batting an eyelash. "It's the One Thing that can breathe life into us. For me, it's dancing."

She gaped at him, amazed by the onslaught of words that had tumbled from his lips. The quiet gentleman had more passion than he let on. His little speech stirred something within her, perhaps her own passion that had been lying dormant for years. Passion that had been buried beneath mounds of pain and sadness. Pain and sadness that could be exorcised.

His thin lips curved into a crooked smile. She wanted to try it on for size, to sample and savor. *Our mouths would fit together perfectly.* She measured the possibilities in her head. Again, she knew it was wrong to think of him like that, to desire him when she was engaged.

"That was beautiful, Robert." She pressed her hand to her chest and counted the erratic beats of her heart. "The One Thing?"

"You'll find your One Thing, too, I promise."

The door creaked, but she didn't pay much attention to it, shrugging it off as another one of Robert's students.

"Marianne, have you been dancing?"

She jerked at Elliot's strong baritone.

The blood drained from her face. Neither she nor Robert had done anything wrong, yet she felt as though she'd committed an unpardonable sin. Since they'd gotten engaged, she was never in the company of other men.

She slowly faced her fiancé and hugged herself. "Elliot, hi. Robert has been kind enough to teach me." She didn't dare look at Robert, not now.

Elliot crossed his arms and puffed his broad chest. He was a handsome man—tall, black wavy hair, dusky complexion, muscular. And he knew it. He could have his pick of the ladies, but for whatever reason, he had chosen her. Strange, awkward, clumsy Marianne!

"You must have the magical touch," Elliot drawled, his steely glare challenging Robert. "Nothing I tried to teach her stuck, then she nearly broke my foot during our last lesson."

She dropped her gaze to the floor, wishing this conversation would come to an end. She had never intended for Robert and Elliot to meet. Robert was too sweet to be subjected to Elliot's abrasive personality. And Elliot would only accuse her of cheating on him with Robert. It had happened before, which was the reason she no longer had guy friends.

Robert stood at her side and didn't waver, not for a second. "Marianne is a wonderful dancer. A wonderful woman, in fact." There was a hard edge to his words, one she didn't know he was capable of. "You don't know how lucky you are."

She ventured a glance at Robert as he sent her an encouraging smile.

"Yeah, well, are you about ready?" Elliot checked his watch, tapping the face of it. "We have reservations."

She nodded. "Let me get my things."

After working all day and dancing for an hour, she was really in no mood to go out to dinner. Her feet ached, her muscles were taut, her body throbbed, and she was perspiring all over from the exertion. The only thing she wanted was a hot bath and a bed.

But it would be useless to argue with Elliot.

She went to retrieve her purse and water bottle from the table, Robert's light footsteps behind her.

Robert snatched up his own jacket draped over the chair and handed it to her, his expression clouded with concern. "I'll see you tomorrow. Same time?"

"Yes, I'll be here." She longed to hug him for his thoughtfulness. She had forgotten to bring her coat.

She slipped his jacket on and sniffed the collar, enjoying the hint of cologne which always seemed to cling to his skin.

Elliot could rant and rave about it, but she would not give up her dance lessons. Not only did she enjoy spending time with Robert, she had learned so much, and her confidence was returning. It had been ages since she felt good about herself.

She trailed her fiancé out to the parking lot and tugged the jacket closed. The night air on her sweat-dampened skin should have chilled her, but Robert's tan jacket protected her. It was like he was wrapping her in a hug. *Perhaps I can forget my coat again tomorrow night, just to have an excuse to hang onto his.* She chewed on her lower lip in contemplation.

"I don't know if I like you dancing with him." Elliot sauntered to the car. "The way he looks at you." He stuck his hand in the pocket of his pants and withdrew his keys.

"What?" She stopped abruptly. A small spark of anger ignited within her. That he accused her of being less than faithful was nothing new. That he implied that Robert Monroe was lecherous upset her. "Robert is a gentleman. He is giving me dance lessons so that I won't ruin our wedding," she shot back.

"C'mon." He snorted. He pressed the button on the remote and the doors unlocked. "A few lessons will hardly make you an expert. It took me years to get where I am today. Knowing you, you'll only end up looking like a fool."

"I'm trying!" She protested, then let the sentence hang. There was no use in defending herself. Once Elliot's mind was made up, it was made up. Her shoulders slumped, and it was only then she realized how tired she was. Not from work or dancing, but from being in a relationship where she was constantly criticized. Being engaged to Elliot was sapping her strength. "I'll never be good enough, will I? Not for you."

Her chest grew heavy. Tears stung her eyes. It had been days since she had cried. Dancing was healing her soul, just as Robert predicted it would. Of course, spending time with a man who was kind, considerate, and sweet made a difference, too. She had found her One Thing!

She blotted her tears on the sleeve of Robert's jacket. *I can't do it! I can't give up Robert or dancing!*

"Knock it off." He huffed, rolling his eyes. "I won't listen to a hysterical woman."

She didn't have to listen to his insults, either. She spun around and stalked off in the opposite direction. Luckily for her, her hometown was small, and her apartment was only five blocks away. Disregarding Elliot's shouts for her to return, she continued on her own.

She needed time to think. Besides, a bath and bed never sounded better.

Robert favored his right foot as he disengaged from Marianne. Gritting his teeth, he swallowed a grumble. He wasn't upset she'd stomped on his toes again. He was upset she had resumed her skittish behavior. She'd been freeing herself from fear. While she would never be a professional dancer, she could hold her own on the floor. And when she was happy, she moved gracefully, like a swan.

Then her fiancé had showed up at the end of their last lesson. Now she was back to trembling whenever Robert touched her. He wasn't an expert, but it was obvious she was in an abusive relationship. Maybe not physically abusive, but she was heading down that road. All of the signs were there, but she didn't see it. Or didn't want to.

Her two front teeth sank into her lower lip and her arms wrapped around her middle.

"Marianne, are you all right?" He steadied his voice to not let on he was angry.

How anyone could be cruel to Marianne—who had to be one of the sweetest women alive—was beyond him. He was easygoing by nature, but he wanted to beat the hell out of Elliot. The guy had this priceless treasure, and he took it for granted.

"Have you ever been in love?" She shook her head, her pretty mouth twisting into a pout. "Sorry, I'm just not the best student today."

He shrugged it off. She was more important than some dance lesson. "Dance is more than movement. You're allowing your soul to be on display. And if your soul is troubled…" He hesitated. The last thing he wanted to do was scare her off. "I've been in love before."

"It didn't work out?" She blinked in surprise.

He gulped. His wife's death was not something he liked delving into. Not until he really got to know someone. Sometimes, he could barely get the words out.

But this wasn't about him. This was about Marianne, and the focus needed to remain on her.

"No. My wife…she died in a car accident." He left it at that, warding off the memories of his wife's car wrapped around a tree. "I've been alone ever since." He cheered inwardly while he observed her slowly unwind. Her body language implied she was relaxing. "How did you and Elliot get involved?"

She sighed and ducked her head as though she had something to be ashamed of. "Blind date." Her tone was devoid of all emotion. She had no love for Elliot. Those lovely blue eyes that glittered when she danced and talked of her hobbies, her work as a schoolteacher, looked fraught with sadness. "We continued to date. Six months later, he proposed."

He shook his head. *It's now or never.* He had to say something, or else she might make the biggest mistake of her life. "Why are you with him, Marianne?" He held up a finger apologetically for broaching a subject that would cause her pain, but if it spared her from further suffering, then it was worth it. "I'm sorry, but it doesn't make any sense. You deserve to love and be loved. You should be cherished."

When she didn't respond right away, he slightly probed by murmuring her name.

"I'm in my thirties." She closed her eyes, and a lone tear trickled down her cheek. "My friends all have someone to love. They're marrying and having children. I want to be a mother. I want a baby." Her voice cracked on the last word, and her hands cupped her abdomen. "Every year that passes, it's less likely it will happen for me."

He rubbed his jaw. Now that made sense. Marianne was so passionate and loving. Of course, she wanted a husband and to have children. But shackling herself to Elliot out of sheer loneliness was dangerous.

Elliot shouldn't be her husband, and he shouldn't be a father.

Why couldn't I have met Marianne earlier? There was a time in his life when he'd wanted a family. He had his dance studio, but a wife and children? That had been the ultimate dream. His wife's death killed that dream, and he had been in turmoil for a long while. Now he was on the wrong side of forty. It was too late for him.

But it was not too late for Marianne. She deserved the best.

He grasped her hands and cradled them inside of his. "Elliot has abusive tendencies. I know that's not what you want to hear, but it's the truth. You shouldn't marry him. He would make a horrible husband and a terrible father." He lifted her knuckles to his lips and kissed them reverently, savoring the soft feel of her. "You could have any man."

He waited for her to lash out at him for overstepping his bounds, for prying into her private life.

But she gaped at him, her eyes watering. "Could I have you, Robert?" she whispered.

Rising up on tiptoe, she brushed her mouth against his. It was simple and sweet, and better than he could've ever imagined. *Am I dreaming? Is this real?* His heart raced, unable to fathom she was kissing him.

He made a strange sound at the back of his throat, a noise of disappointment when she pulled away.

She touched her fingertips to her lips. "I'm sorry. I have to go."

She sprinted out of the room, leaving him alone with his thoughts.

I screwed up! He exhaled and squeezed his eyes shut. He slammed the heel of his hand against his brow.

Marianne had had feelings for him all along, and he'd missed it. He had ruined everything, and now she was going to return to her fiancé!

Marianne lingered outside her fiancé's office, attempting to rally whatever courage she had left inside of her. Elliot had only invited her to office parties and social functions. She'd visited one time at lunch as a surprise, and was lectured for showing up unwanted. He'd be more than annoyed for her to drop by now, especially considering what she was planning to tell him.

She'd been so stunned by what Robert had said, and though she wanted to deny it, she couldn't. *How could I have missed it?* She'd asked herself over and over again. Elliot was verbally and emotionally abusive. He'd even left bruises from gripping her too tight. He was controlling and harsh and impatient. She had overlooked it all in her desperation to have a family of her own. Countless times, she blamed herself, believing her own behavior caused him to lash out and be rough. *If I had been smarter, quicker, better, prettier...* It was a cycle she fell into. Robert's kindness, his gentlemanly behavior, his patience–it showed her Elliot's abusiveness wasn't her fault.

Then Robert had claimed she could have any man, and kissed the back of her hands. Touched, she'd asked if she could have him, and she'd impetuously kissed him. Then bolted like a frightened little rabbit. Whether she and Robert had a chance, she didn't know, but she couldn't continue on with this sham of an engagement. It had taken her two weeks to think things over and prepare herself, but now she was ready.

She rapped her knuckles on the door and entered when her fiancé beckoned her inside.

His head snapped up, and he scowled when he realized it was her. "Marianne? What are you doing here?" He pinched the bridge of his nose. "I don't have time for this. I have to—"

"Elliot, stop." She shut her eyes briefly and drew in a sharp breath. "You never let me speak, you never listen to what I have to say!"

When she opened her eyes, she wasn't surprised to find him red-faced and his jaw clenched. He didn't like to be interrupted, not by her. But this was long overdue.

She balled her fists, her nails biting into the palms. "A wedding is something the bride plans, but you have made all of the decisions. You even chose what dress I would wear. I hate the princess style." Somewhere along the way, she'd lost herself, her voice, and she had lost her way...but no more. "I was so grateful not to be alone anymore that I went along with whatever you wanted."

"What are you saying?"

"We never once said we loved each other or talked about feelings." She blinked back tears. In her short acquaintance with Robert, they'd shared more than in her year-long relationship with Elliot.

He made a fist and slammed it on the desk, hard enough to rattle the coffee cup inches away. "Damn it, Marianne! I can't believe you're doing this. Stupid, ungrateful bitch!" The venomous words spewed out of him like black bile.

She cringed. He'd never called her such things before, but there was no doubt in her mind he would have when they were married. Who knows when the violence would begin?

She really did deserve better.

She twisted the ostentatious diamond off of her finger and placed it on the desk. "It's over," she declared coolly.

"Marianne, please!" The anger had drained and, for once, he seemed desperate. His eyes were wide and bloodshot. "Don't do this. I know I've been impatient lately, and that hasn't been fair to you. I'm really sorry. I'll do better, I promise." He gestured towards the ring. "C'mon, we love each other."

She wasn't fooled by his sudden change of tactics. It was all an act. Elliot would never change, not for her. Even if he was willing to try, she had endured too much pain to fully trust him.

"It's over, Elliot."

He spewed out a string of profanity, and it reassured her she was making the right choice.

"This is a mistake!" He shot to his feet and braced his hands against the desk. "You think it will be easy starting over at your age? No one will ever want you."

"Maybe not." She shrugged. There were worse things in the world than being alone. She would find happiness somewhere or make her own. "But that doesn't mean I deserve a lifetime of abuse. I deserve better." She first pointed to her chest and then directed her finger at him, shaking it. "And you need some serious help. Goodbye, Elliot."

She swept out of his office and down the hall, disregarding his shouts for her to return.

It had been ages since she felt free.

Robert sank to the floor, resting his back against the wall, and crossed his legs at the ankle. A chair would be more comfortable, but he felt low and figured sitting on the floor would better suit his mood.

He'd canceled this evening's class and opted to give the studio a good cleaning. Smelling of solution, the room was bright and prepared for another week's worth of classes.

It had been two weeks since he'd last seen Marianne. Not that he was surprised. Telling his student she was in an abusive relationship and needed to get out, then kissing said student, was bound to make things awkward. He'd stopped himself a dozen or more times from seeking her out. She already had one crazy man in her life. She didn't need another stalking her.

She may have expressed some desire for him, but she was engaged. And lonely.

He let his head fall back and shut his eyes. He'd give anything to be with Marianne.

Can I have you, Robert? Those words played over and over again in his mind.

Yes! Every fiber of his being cried out.

The door hinges squeaked. His eyes slid open, and when his gaze focused, he gasped.

Marianne was walking towards him wearing a gauzy pink dress. The way she moved, she was like a soft, pink cloud. Her long, shapely legs went on for miles. Her hair was drawn up in a messy bun, a few curls escaping from a clasp.

He scrambled to his feet. "Marianne? What are you doing here?"

"It's time for my lesson." She stopped no more than a foot from him. Her coloring looked so much better and her eyes were sparkling.

He dropped his gaze to her lips. He was thirsting for her kiss. One kiss was all they'd shared, but he yearned for much more.

"You were right. Elliot and I didn't make sense." She offered a demure smile. "I called it off."

"Really?" He couldn't believe what he was hearing. It seemed too good to be true.

"Really and truly."

"Thank God," he mustered.

In one short stride, he gathered her into his arms and slanted his mouth over hers. He drew her lower lip into his mouth and sucked on it, savoring her flavor. She tasted heavenly, like the sweetest candy. He moaned as her fingertips threaded his hair and scraped the base of his neck. His own hands were splayed against the small of her back, pressing her closer to him.

Breathlessly, she drew back slightly, whispering, "So, can I have you, Robert?"

"Yes." He nodded, his heart soaring. He was tempted to pinch himself, fearing this was a dream. But no dream could be this perfect. He cupped her cheek and stroked the curve with his thumb. "I'm all yours."

She nuzzled her lips against his, and he nearly lost control when *she* nibbled *his* bottom lip.

He angled his head, placing a kiss on the patch of skin near her ear. "Dance with me?" he whispered.

"Absolutely." She laid her head on his shoulder.

His arms loosely encircled her waist and, together, they slow-danced to a tune she was humming.

First, they were partners in dance, and from now on, they would be partners in life.

The Evolution of Richard Hale

Time-traveling, dimension-hopping, parallel-universe visiting Arthur and Ellen Hale are back from their first year gallivanting around the multiverse, but return with a mission. Their son, Richard, is successful, financially secure, and admired. But he's missing out on the one thing his full-steam-ahead career cannot offer: romance. So his parents deliver a message--a chance for love their son desperately needs.

Victor Kreuiter

THE EVOLUTION OF RICHARD HALE

Victor Kreuiter

Friday evening, early

"Let me see if I've got this straight."

Richard Hale, thirty-seven, was Senior Vice President at Gaither Partners, dressed in a seven hundred dollar suit, sporting a sixty-dollar tie, and two hundred dollar wingtips. He leaned across the table and took stock of his father, who wore cargo pants, an Eastern Illinois University sweatshirt, and sandals with socks. Typical Dad. Glasses clinked around them. Waiters moved silently. They were on the patio of an upscale restaurant.

Richard dropped his chin and looked over his glasses. "You've traveled through parallel universes and navigated other dimensions. That's what you're saying? You and Mom? And you've returned to this dimension, *our* dimension, to..." He stopped and cocked his head. This was nuts.

His father ignored the sarcasm. "You're close."

"Am I close?" Richard asked.

Dad smiled.

"Okay, what am I missing?"

Dad leaned forward and whispered, "Did I mention time travel?"

An hour later, dinner done, the drive to Richard's apartment was quiet. He was puzzled with his prodigal father's return, worried about his dad's fanciful travel tales, and curious about where his parents had been for the past year. They'd just disappeared. They'd done it before, but not to this extent.

And, by the way, where *was* Mom?

"You look good." Dad leaned his seat back, head on the headrest, seemingly impressed with Richard's luxury car. "This a Mercedes?"

Richard looked over at him, nervous. Gadabout father showing up, telling tales of excursions in other dimensions, alternate realities, and parallel universes. Time travel? Really?

"I bet this thing costs a pretty penny, huh?"

Richard laughed, embarrassed. "It's leased."

Dad nodded. "We use a lot of public transportation, and what's funny is, you skip over a dimension or two, and you'd think transportation would be similar, right? And in some ways, it is, but..."

Richard's heart sank. His dad looked like a hippie gone to seed. Was he using drugs?

"Like, there's stuff I just can't wrap my head around. We were in one of those weird dimensions—six or seven, I'm not really sure—and one minute you're thinking about going somewhere, and the next minute, it's like your thoughts are, I don't know, marinating, but you find yourself *there,* and you don't remember *going*—"

"Dad?"

His father stopped, turned, and sighed. "I know. I get it. I'm not explaining it clearly."

"Dad, come on."

If child is father to the man, what kind of childhood had Dad had? That's what Richard wanted to know.

"Are you okay?" he asked, fingers tightening on the wheel. "I mean, *are you okay*? You're talking about crazy stuff like it's normal."

His father went silent.

"It's been a year," he reminded his father. "Where have you been? You couldn't write? Call? Let me know you're okay?" He tapped the brakes. Traffic was getting heavy.

"You cross over a couple dimensions, and time gets dicey. I'm not making excuses, I'm just saying a day, a week, a month, a year? You get involved with one thing, and then another thing pops up, and..." Dad stopped, took a breath, pursed his lips, and seemingly organized his thoughts. "To be honest, it's just like here. Things come up, you get busy, lose track of time, and..."

Richard was struggling to hold back...what? Anger? Dismay? Emotions were not his strong suit. His breathing was shallow. His neck and shoulders were tight. He forced himself to take a few deep breaths, trying to ignore his father's words, and repeatedly blinking.

Why was traffic so slow? He concentrated on the car in front of him, relaxed his grip on the steering wheel, formed an "o" with his lips, inhaled, exhaled.

His father had stopped talking.

He glanced at him, and looked back to the road. "Where's all your stuff, Dad?"

Dad leaned over, pulled something from a pocket in his cargo pants, and held it up. A gray slab, the size and shape of a cell phone. He held it out in front of himself, let it go, and it remained there, floating. He pointed at it, flicked his finger up, and the slab expanded in size. He continually flicked his finger, and the object grew proportionately. He rolled his hand in a circular motion. The thing rolled over. Then he clapped his hands, and it shrunk back to its original size. He then shoved it back into a pocket.

Richard blinked, forced his eyes straight ahead, and shifted in his seat. Rapid breathing. Something raw roiling in his throat. What the hell?

"That thing holds our stuff," Dad said. "Crazy, right? Somebody invented that!" He laughed. "It holds everything, and I mean *everything*. Personal papers, financial records, health care stuff, a couple currencies. And, this'll kill you." He stopped, looking at Richard, who was eyes-forward, a death-grip on the steering wheel. "Our clothes are in there. Really! Well, not your mother's, but mine. All my clothes!" He beamed. "I can't remember where I got it. Some parallel place, maybe?"

Richard said nothing. What could he say? He was starting to think *he'd* lost his mind.

"Think about it. Most of the universe is empty space, right? That's science! I mean, you, me, this car, everything—ninety-nine percent empty space. I'm not saying I understand it, but I think that's right, isn't it? I think it is. This thing, it *evaporates* stuff. *Condenses stuff.* Something like that. Takes out all the extra space between atoms or something. Hell, don't ask me what it does, I have no idea. But it works! And I got it cheap!"

Traffic started moving, got up to speed, and Richard swallowed hard. He pushed back against his seat, and didn't want to think about what he'd just seen. A trick? A magic prop?

He asked his father what he'd been wanting to ask since he'd first showed up. "Where's Mom?"

"Well..." Dad shrugged. "Don't panic, but I'm wondering that myself."

Richard put on a blinker, pulled to the shoulder, and let three lanes of traffic whiz by as he leaned over to look his father in the eyes. "You don't know where my mother is?"

His father looked sheepish.

"You lost her?" In a flash, Richard envisioned himself telling this story on *Dateline.*

Dad licked his lips, leaned closer, and lowered his voice. "Look, we weren't always sure where we were, or *when* we were. It's not like the movies, you know. You can't dial up what day you want, what year. What dimension or what alternate reality. You just go! Go with the flow. But we got spooked, okay? Felt like we were being followed. Stalked maybe, so we split up a about a week ago, and decided we'd meet back here. At your place."

Richard took a moment, pulled a breath, counted to ten. Where in God's name was all this traffic coming from? *Jesus Christ, people, get home!* He calmed himself.

His father stayed silent. Was this—his father sitting in his front seat—going to be some sort of problem? Had his father done something to his mother? Was his father psychotic? Worse?

"I'm an optimist," Dad said. "I have confidence in your mother. I do. Sometimes, you gotta have faith."

Friday evening & Friday night

His apartment was in a development boasting a professional-level golf course, a tennis club, a spa, two Olympic-size pools, and a one-star Michelin restaurant. His apartment was twenty-one hundred square feet. He paid extra for maid and laundry service. It felt like the size of a shoebox at the moment.

"Nice place," his father said.

Richard stopped at his kitchen counter, dropped his wallet and keys, loosened his tie, took off his jacket, walked into his bedroom, and hung it in a walk-in, then walked back to the kitchen.

His father was in the entry, scoping everything out. Richard wondered whose fault it was they seemed separated by, what? There'd been a gulf between them for how long? A gulf between him and his mother? Yeah, that, too. He loved them. Who doesn't love their parents? So, why the jumbled feelings? He knew, deep down, his feelings about his parents were not kosher. He'd held them at bay for some reason, and he carried around remorse and a vague sense of inadequacy. Now, his father had returned, mother missing, and feelings surfaced. He didn't want to think it was all on him. It wasn't, was it?

His father, hands in pockets, rocking slightly, studied the apartment. There wasn't a single item hanging on any of the walls. No photos, paintings, photographs. No knickknacks scattered around. No books. Who lived without books? The apartment looked unlived in. The kitchen looked unused. An enormous television looked lonely. Maybe he should fix that?

Dad sauntered toward him, and Richard's nerves jingled. His father, smiling, kept coming, and it was as if Richard was bolted to the floor. His father wrapped his arms around his neck, hugged him without saying a word, and Richard eventually put a hand on his father's arm. What was he feeling? He'd felt it before and failed to identify it.

His father stepped back, found a stool at the kitchen counter, and sat. "We're about as unlikely a family as there could be, wouldn't you say?"

There was tightness in Richard's chest, through his shoulders. At his core, when he was aggressively pitching a client, when he was laying out a strategy to his team, when he was selling himself to his boss, he was insecure. He hated his insecurity. He and insecurity fought. Regularly. Richard won most of the time, but winning came with a price.

"I love you," Dad said, "and I'm not sure I let you know that enough. When you were growing up, did I say it enough?"

Embarrassment. Discomfort.

Richard did not respond.

"Listen," his father continued. "Most of my life, I've felt like a fish out of water. Your mother, the same." Dad glanced at him, and Richard probably looked as confused as he felt. "About what we've been up to, let me show you something. Save us some time."

He walked to the mouth of the hallway, turned to him, and said, "Watch this." He took two steps into the hallway, turned, and gave Richard a thumb's up, took one more step, and disappeared.

Richard's jaw dropped. The hair on his head stood up. Gooseflesh covered his arms.

Almost immediately, a loud knock came at the door, and Richard shook his head, dazed. He ran to the door and opened it.

It was his father, wearing a sheepish grin.

"I know," he said, "it's weird. There're these portals everywhere, and…"

Richard, unsteady, took a few short breaths, shuddered, then everything went black.

Saturday morning, early

He woke slowly. A toilet flushed in the background, then footsteps tapped. He rolled to one side, blinked, and realized he'd spent the night on top of the covers, in the sweatpants from the previous evening, and socks on his feet. He had a headache, was foggy, and slowly blinked himself awake.

It was Saturday, right?

His father had returned. The shock of seeing him, the uncertainty, why was it always like that? He wondered about their relationship, their bond, and the thinking felt remote and unfocused. He wanted to be alert, but alert to what? The room had whirled the last time he'd tried to sit up, so he carefully rose on his elbows, breathing slowly.

"Hey, buddy, you awake?"

He twisted his head toward his father in the doorway. The room spun, settled, spun more. His stomach rolled over.

"I'm okay," he said, and his eyelids fluttered as he lowered himself back down.

"Let me give you a hand." Dad walked to the bed, put his hands on Richard's head, and slowly traced his hairline, rubbing gently. "Keep your eyes open, if possible, but don't speak."

He worked his hands to the jawline, applying pressure, worked down the neck, pushed hard on the collar bone. He went to the ankles, carefully rotated each. "Look straight up, not at me." He straightened each foot, pushed it toward the knee, then went to the knee, pinching the fibula, crimping. He stepped back. "Close your eyes. We're almost there." He went to the indent at the back of the head, top of the neck, and massaged.

His father's fingers landed on Richard's eyelids, moved to his nose, then clamped around his throat. Panic clutched his airway and his eyes flew open. Pressure increased until breathing grew difficult. Pressure on the neck. Then, his father clamped his nostrils shut, and he kicked his feet, flapping.

"Open your eyes."

He hadn't realized he'd closed them again.

His lids lifted, and he immediately realized he was floating inches above his bed.

His father leaned down, their eyes locking. "Take a deep breath and hold it until you can't hold it anymore."

He obeyed. Why, he didn't know.

His father stepped back and smiled. "You feel better, right?"

And at that moment, he didn't feel better. He felt best. The best he'd been in he didn't know how long. Serenity washed over him, and it was so *physical*. Was that a thing? Physical joy? He was rejuvenated. Relieved. Such relief—mind and body.

Then, a touch of panic strangled him. Drugs? Had his father administered drugs?

"I have a surprise for you," his father said. "Come on."

Dad turned and walked into the living room.

Richard descended onto the bed, no longer hovering. Had he willed that?

He rolled out of bed and followed his father

"This has been stressful for you," his father said. "I can tell. Me showing up, saying what I've been saying. So, I'm going to try to explain something that isn't easy to explain. I know you haven't experienced what I've experienced, so this is the best I can do right now."

Richard shrugged, nodded. What the heck, why not?

"You've heard the phrase *things aren't always what they seem*, right?"

Richard nodded. Why did he feel so good?

"Well, there's—"

Richard held up a hand. "Am I intoxicated?"

Dad puffed his cheeks and blew out air. "What?"

"I wake up in bed feeling weird, and then you do that stuff in there, whatever that was, it was *really* weird, and..."

"Oh, that. I just removed your stress. Most of it. You can carry stress around so long, it becomes your normal. Everybody does. I know I did, but then I—"

"I'm not intoxicated?"

"Richard, why would you ask that? What are you worried about?" His father frowned. "Come on, let me get to the point. I've got a surprise."

He leaned toward his father. "Dad, it's been nothing but surprises since you showed up." Cordially spoken, despite his irritation.

It was his father's turn to shrug. "Okay, so things are not what they seem." He inhaled, exhaled. "Pay attention, please. Things are not what they seem, that's true. But Richard, just as often as not, things *are* just what they seem. See, it's complicated. The mystery of life and all that. It takes experience to make an accurate assessment, okay? Like, is something what it seems to be or is something *not* what it seems?"

Richard was listening without judgment. Not necessarily getting it all, but paying attention. He was intrigued. Where had that come from?

He held up a hand again. "So, this surprise. Is it what it seems or is it not what it seems?"

A smile bloomed on his father's face.

"A stupid question?"

Dad beamed. "No! No! That's the question! Good for you, son! You got it!" He walked to the spot in the hallway where he'd disappeared the previous evening, whispered something to himself, then swept out an arm. "Voila!"

One moment, nothing was there, the next, there his mother stood.

Richard was dumbstruck. He shivered. Goosebumps formed. He took a few steps, looked at his father, looked at his mother, and couldn't believe his eyes.

She was posing, arm slung over her head. She twirled, giggling. "Richard, watch this!" She hopped backward and disappeared. A second later, she reappeared, laughing. She looked at him, grinning ear to ear. "We're not sure where we've been, but it has been *one wild adventure*!" She hopped back again and disappeared.

Seconds ticked by.

Richard raised a hand, attempting to speak. He turned to look at the door to his apartment. Would she come in there?

She landed back in the hallway, laughing even harder, hand over her mouth, shaking her head. "Richard, sweetheart, the world is so..." She put a finger to her lips. "It's crazy! The world is so much bigger than I ever imagined!"

One more hesitant step forward, and Richard attempted to speak again, but he got light-headed. "Mom?"

He attempted a smile, could only produce a grimace, then took a nosedive.

Still Saturday

Late afternoon, Richard woke, mouth dry, and skin clammy. He stayed perfectly still, slowly breathing, running through the events of the last twenty-four hours. His mother and father, their stories, that crazy disappearing act. What the hell? He could feel his discomfort rising. That always happened. Where did that come from? Did he turn every emotion into a negative? Did he do that? He revisited his father's tales, his mother's actions. When he pictured his mother hopping backwards, disappearing and reappearing, all laughter and excitement, he sighed.

"You're awake." Her voice came from across the room.

He craned his neck and found her sitting in an armchair in the corner of his room.

"This has been a real hoop-de-do for you, huh?"

Hoop-de-do? He'd never heard her use that term before.

"Your father has gone to the house to check things out. We've haven't been there in a year. He's hoping the key still works." She chuckled. "We're looking forward to some downtime. Enough with the bouncing around."

Richard didn't move or speak, letting her run the show. He needed answers.

"We made some friends traveling, and invited them to visit us. They live here. *Here*, this reality, this universe, or whatever. I'm never sure how to say it. Helmkamp, that's their name. Older than us. Very nice." She paused. "I couldn't tell you if we met them in another dimension or an alternate parallel elsewhere. I can't tell the difference."

He stopped himself from rolling his eyes.

"Anyhow, before I go, I want to tell you something. You feel up for that?"

Here it comes. Then he ridiculed himself. *Jesus, can't he just listen for once in his life?* What would it hurt to just take a moment and listen to his mother?

"Sure," he said. "But, Mom..." All of a sudden, he choked up, emotional. Head to toe. Throat tight, eyes burning. He held back tears, wondering what was going on.

"I know." She stood and dragged her chair over.

He rose onto his elbows.

She got the chair next to him, walked around the bed, and grabbed a pillow. "Lean up."

He did, and she stuffed the pillow behind him.

"Stay there." She left the bedroom, and he heard her walking around before she returned with pillows from the couch. She arranged them behind him. "That better?"

"Yeah," he said.

"You hungry?"

He shook his head.

"I'm not, either."

She sat, took a breath, looked around the room, and started. "I'm not going to try to convince you of anything. Just hear me out, okay? This might take a while. You can say whatever you want when I'm done."

He nodded. "Sure."

"Okay, here goes."

Mom's story

"Our traveling," she said, "is not what it sounds like." A slight hesitation. "And then again, it's just what it sounds like."

He all but rolled his eyes.

"Did your father use that line on you?" she asked.

"Something close," he admitted.

"Okay, bear with me." She paused, nodded. "So, your father and I and our traveling—dimension hopping, that's your father's term—time travel and the alternate universes and realities.... I don't know which is which, never did, and neither does your father, but he won't admit it." Her expression was that of the self-assured mother he'd seen his whole life. "Your father is a true believer. He's always talked about this *traveling* for years. I figured it was comic book stuff, all the stories he was reading. Him and his UFOs. Aliens. I always let him ramble. What could it hurt? So, when we actually succeeded, when I could look around and say, you know, this isn't Kansas anymore, I was completely dumbstruck. It was astonishing. Your dad can be a bit out there, you know that. I like that about him."

She sighed and stretched. "So, anyhow, when we left, we started off for somewhere with nowhere in mind. We went up the Great River Road, zig-zagging up the Mississippi River valley, crossing back and forth between Illinois and Iowa whenever there was a bridge to cross. It was your father's idea. At some point, we were in a state park above Dubuque, and Arthur gets all excited. We're parked at a look-out point, looking down on the Mississippi, and he gets super excited. Frantic. We're hiking on a trail, going down toward the river, and I'm being careful because it's steep in places, and we step into a fog. It was a visual mist, all blurry, and he stops to say, 'Okay, take a look,' like I haven't been looking. He steps away from me and vanishes. Then he's back, right away. I get all giddy. Dizzy, too. I think he had to grab me to keep me on my feet."

She leaned forward and slapped at his arm. "I almost tinkled in my pants." She made a face. "I got spooked, then for some reason, I started laughing. Outrageously. And then he starts laughing and we're hugging and we're laughing so hard we're crying."

She stopped, they went quiet, and when Richard looked at his mother, there were stars in her eyes. Real stars. In her eyes. How could that be? Goosebumps rose on his arms. He raised a hand, leaned toward her, and she shook her head.

"Richard, I'm still processing what I saw. What *we* saw." She put a hand on her chest and drew a breath. "We were on the trail, but not *there*, that's how I saw it. Wherever we were, whatever we stepped into, I had no idea, and neither did your father. Everything was changed, and yet nothing had changed, and I'm sorry, but that's how it was. Everything was similar, but not the same. The river looked further away. The trees were either bigger and taller or smaller and skinnier. Different in some way, and the trail was more narrow, the woods were more dense, and the *light* was different. *Really different.* We noticed that immediately, and your father kept saying 'It's refracted. The light is refracted.' I just wanted him to be quiet so I could take it all in. By the way, your father was right. The light was refracted."

She waved her hand dismissively. "Anyhow, that first day in Iowa, we just took it all in, and we've talked about that experience ever since. Your dad calls it our maiden voyage. Your father's words, not mine."

Richard had been listening closely. What she'd spouted was nuts, so why was he wanting to hear more?

"That's what we've done for the last year. Chase that experience."

He shifted, pulled himself up in the bed, and adjusted the pillows.

"You want to know what worried me the most?"

He nodded.

"The car." She laughed. "I don't know how long we were in that spot. It was unnerving, really. Your dad was so calm. He was excited, joyous, but was basically calm. He didn't seem at all worried. He seemed gratified. We wondered whether we were in a different reality, a parallel universe, or some other dimension. Then, all of a sudden, it hit me—how do we get back? You know, *what if we can't get back?* I asked him where the car was. He looked at me, so composed, and he said, 'In the parking lot, where we left it.'

She leaned back in the chair, dropped her arms, and took a breath. "Your dad took my hand and pulled me. We started walking up the trail, the one we'd come down, and when we got back to the outlook, there was the car. On the way back, I kept looking for *something*, some doorway or gate or something that marked where we left *that* place," she waved a hand around, "and got back to *this* place."

Richard sighed. He let his head go back slowly and closed his eyes. He kept them closed. "Mom, are you—"

"Go ahead. Ask away. It's okay."

"Are you and dad taking drugs?"

She dropped her chin. "Drugs?"

He stared at her.

"Wait a minute." She sighed, pushed her hair around. "You saw me arrive, right? You saw me step into and out of your apartment, didn't you? Through a portal. That's what it's called, a portal. Richard, that wasn't magic. To be honest, it wasn't much of anything. It's easy if you know what you're doing. What you witnessed was *real*. I promise. And nobody is on *drugs*. Are you looking for an excuse not to believe your own eyes?"

No comment, he thought.

Mother went quiet.

"Drugs?" she finally said. "If you have to know, I smoked marijuana as a young woman, years ago. Big deal! What I want to talk about is what your father and I saw. Lived through. Learned from. Is that okay?"

She didn't wait for an answer.

"Okay, so quickly, about time travel. We went into the future and into the past. For sure, we did, but we had no control. Regardless of what your father says, we had no control. None. It was like being blown around. We didn't stay long, if that means anything." She paused, putting a fingertip to her mouth. "I was never comfortable with time travel. I never knew how to manage it. Your father, though..."

Richard coughed. He held up a hand, asking permission to speak. "That thing dad has, that little box thing that gets bigger and smaller? It holds all his stuff."

"He has that with him?" She frowned and straightened. "He shouldn't have that. I wasn't with him when he got it. We got separated at times. I told him to get rid of it."

He puffed cheeks and exhaled.

"Listen," she said, "there's more I want to tell you. We never really planned the time travel. I don't think it can be controlled. We just stumbled around in it. Your dad kept saying it was what we were going to do, but it wasn't like it was planned, or like it was scientific, not the way we were doing it. I think your father mentioned he thought we were being followed. He got a bit wound up. You know him. And, well, there was someone, not following us, but someone who wanted to talk to us. Talk to *me*, it turned out. I had a nice conversation with this person, and it was special."

She sat back, tongue working over her teeth. She eventually stood, walked out of the room, and he heard her dialing the phone, mumbles followed, and she hung up.

His mother walked back into the room. "Your dad's gonna come get me."

Already? She ranted a mile a minute, then wanted to leave? "What's the rush?"

Mother sat, ignoring the question. "Before I go, let me tell you something I learned that I think is so..." Fingertip to her mouth again, her eyes cast down. "We met a very nice man, a fellow traveler, and we spent some time with him, just relaxing. He was Latino, but I think he was, you know, not from *here*. He knew we were travelers and said he'd done some traveling. One evening, we had this lovely conversation with him, and it turned to emotions, human emotions."

She glared at him. He must've rolled his eyes again.

He sighed. "I'm listening."

She looked at her watch. "Here's the bottom line. Jorge was his name, and he said emotions are evolutionary. Emotions *evolved*, like in *evolution*. Emotions came into being and evolved because they were required for survival. They were critical for the human species. *Are* critical for humans. Without emotions, human civilization would not have occurred, would never have advanced. It's scientifically studied. And love is evolutionary. It's a real thing. Chemical, physical, and biological, developed by humans, required for humans."

She stood, clasping her hands, then abruptly sat again. "Someone's coming to see you. Here."

He looked at her. *Come on.* Drama? More drama, *now*?

"Who?" he asked.

"I'm heading out," she said and stood. "Arthur's going to pick me up. I'll wait in the parking lot."

"Wait," he said. He sat up. "What's going on?" Christ! A rush of frustration slammed in his head, more shallow breathing, more anxiety. "Mom! What do you mean? Who's coming?"

She put a hand on the headboard, leaned over, and kissed him on top of his head. "Richard, mothers want things for their sons. That's the way it is. That's the way *I* am. You'll make up your own mind. Just be calm, if that's possible. Keep an open mind about her."

Her, who?

She laughed, put a hand over her mouth, and her eyes went misty.

"Mom, come on! What?"

"I love you." She turned and left.

His feet hit the floor, but his apartment door opened and closed.

He ran and caught up to her, standing inside the doorway.

"You're doing well at your job?"

Talk about a topic change. His head spun.

He nodded. Why had that come up?

"Let me ask," she said. "How much effort do you put in? How much thought? Think about how you've committed yourself to your job. Then, think about what commitment can achieve."

Before he could respond, she turned, headed for the elevators, and never looked back.

Emotions are evolutionary

As a boy, Richard was drawn to math and the sciences, anywhere there was only one right answer. No hemming or hawing, no nit-picking. He wanted a yes or a no. Insight? Did he need insight? Insight into what? He wanted a yes or no answer.

Watching his mother step into the elevator, he remembered an afternoon years ago, him in high school, his mother blithely describing her beliefs, her perspective on life, living in the world, religion and spirituality, and the guideposts they provided. How she wanted to be treated, how she wanted to be respected, how she wanted to respect others and their beliefs. For her, the conversation with him had been pure heaven.

Teenage Richard had poo-pooed it.

Why was he remembering that conversation now? The way he'd spoken to his mother that day? How many times had he looked at her and said, "Mom, that can't be. That just can't be. What you're saying, it's wishful thinking." The disappointment on her face. Why remember that now?

A cough came from the other room, followed by a sneeze.

He walked into his living room, and stood still. In the hallway, to his left, the hallway where his father had disappeared and his mother had appeared, came a movement. A foot showed up, then a leg. Nothing else. Foot and leg withdrew.

His breathing picked up. He rolled his neck to stretch it and bit his lip.

A woman stepped into his hallway, stopped, spotted him, smiled, and stood perfectly still.

Did he recognize her?

The optic nerve connects the eyeball directly to the brain. It is composed of over a million nerve fibers and is more closely related to brain tissue than nerve tissue. That meant information collected by the eyeball is delivered to the brain really, really, really fast.

Yeah, he knew her. Standing in his hallway was Katherine Winter. His ex-fiancé, his former love. Love of his life, actually. The one who got away. He hadn't seen her in ages, had thought she'd gone...missing? They'd left things bitter and sad when they'd parted.

This was who Mother said was coming?

His first thought: Katherine was still really beautiful.

He tried to think beyond that, got a bit woozy, stepped sideways, and put his right hand on the wall for balance. He was breathing through his nose, lips clamped tight.

"Are you all right?"

Her voice was melodious. He'd never told her that and should have. He staggered.

She walked to him, her hand out.

He straightened on shaky legs. "I'm ..." He looked down and swallowed.

Her hands were clasped in front of her. She wore a summer dress, dangly earrings, a bracelet, with a pendant around her neck.

"I'm barging in," she said, yet she remained motionless.

A chill rolled across his shoulders.

Saturday, noon

"I was nervous," she said. "Ronke kinda settled my nerves."

Kate Winter was sitting on Richard's couch. He'd watched her materialize in his hallway.

She was sitting on the floor beside him, dabbing at his forehead with a damp cloth. She'd helped him walk into the living room, got him on the couch, and gave him a drink of water. All that was done quietly, no fuss. She was efficient. She'd always been like that. She was the kind of woman who could take charge effortlessly, who knew what had to be done and would do it, the whole time acting as if it were a pleasure.

She was talking about being a nurse, the people she worked with, how healing was both physiological and spiritual, and how modern medicine was only half the game because there was the incarnate and the disincarnate.

He was thinking, *Am I in some other dimension?*

"Ronke, you met her once, remember?"

He didn't remember, and embarrassment heated his cheeks.

She spouted a whole story about seeing someone in an ICU room who no one else could see, how it wound up being a God of some kind named Oshun, and then she'd somehow gone to another dimension.

"So, that's how I wound up somewhere I wasn't going, and I know it wasn't here—like *here,* here—but it wasn't frightening. Somehow, I got there and back, and I think I wound up there because I was *supposed* to be there. I was supposed to meet Oshun, and we talked—she lectured me, actually—and she told me to go get my love."

He was confused as hell. He didn't want to be, didn't know why he was, and yes, he'd heard what she'd said, but he was spending more time wondering about why he felt so confused. Was he always separating himself? Moving away? Kate was right here, on the couch, but he felt distant and didn't want to be.

"I didn't think of you right away," she said.

He wondered why she'd said that, and it probably showed. He cocked his head.

"But the next time I visited that place, I thought of you. Standing in some kind of playground that wasn't there, I started thinking about you, and haven't stopped thinking about you since."

She paused, looked at him, and seemed to be debating something.

"Then, one day, I saw your parents. I hadn't stopped thinking about you. I *knew* a mistake had been made." She sniffed, tilted her head, dropped her gaze. "You'd made the mistake." Eyes up, her face was blank. "Or maybe the mistake just happened." She inhaled, sighed. "I don't know what I thought when we broke up, but after that moment at the playground that wasn't there, I knew a mistake had been made. I'm here to tell you that."

He listened, still confused.

"I saw your parents and I always thought your mother was such a lovely person, so I knew it was for a reason. I sought her out and we talked." She paused. "Your mother is very thoughtful."

The sound of her voice was jarring after all this time. Her on his couch, in his apartment, the whole thing was jarring. He'd been listening carefully, and was working on what to say–it had to be good–but he was drawing a blank, and the blank was making him wonder why he was drawing a blank, and why it was so difficult for him to just say what he was feeling.

If he could *just* understand what he was feeling...

She leaned over and tapped his leg. When he raised his eyes, they just looked at each other for a moment before she spoke. He knew she'd say exactly the right thing, and it would be so simple, he wondered how she could do that while he couldn't.

"That's what happened, what I've been thinking about, and here I am."

Monday night and Tuesday morning

For the first time in his life, the evening after a winning presentation at work, Richard was lonely. He couldn't help thinking about Katherine. He ate dinner alone in the complex restaurant, returned to his apartment, and stared out the windows. He turned on the TV and turned it off again, logged onto his work account, answered a few emails, wrote a few, and logged off. He stared at the golf course some more, then walked down the hallway and stared at the spot where his father had appeared, his mother had appeared, and Kate Winter had materialized.

It wasn't that he didn't believe what he'd seen. He did. He just had no way to understand any of it. Not understanding was a problem. Thinking about not understanding was going to consume him.

He went to bed thinking about Katherine, dreamt about Katherine, and when he woke up, he was thinking about her still. He stayed in bed thinking about her, got out of bed thinking about her, walked to the hallway in his apartment, and stared at the spot. He went into the kitchen, got a drink of water, walked back into his bedroom, and slipped on sweatpants. He retraced his steps, and stopped near the spot that he was thinking about when he was thinking about Katherine.

He sighed, put his glass of water down on the carpet, cleared his mind, shook his arms and shoulders, inhaled, and took a step forward.

It was immediate, and he just wanted to accept it. Couldn't he just accept something for once? Somebody had said something like that, right?

It was almost his hallway. Everything looked familiar, but felt different. Then he wondered if everything looked different, but felt familiar. He was woozy. His neck and shoulders tightened, his breathing was shallow, and he wondered if he was doing that to himself or if it was the result of...what?

He took a moment, steadied his breathing, relaxed as best he could and, thinking he might need to think a bit more about this idea, he retraced his steps, hoping to pass back through whatever he'd passed through moments before.

It worked. It was easy. Effortless.

But now there was a man in his apartment, older, looking confused.

"You're in my apartment." Richard turned and looked toward the portal. It was not visible. Had it ever been?

"What apartment?" the man replied. He looked to his left and right, and shrugged. "I'm sorry. I'm looking for Kate."

Richard's stomach turned.

"Kate Winter," the man said again. He was a bit older than Richard, a bit heavier. "I lost her here the other day, saw her walking in this park. I was following her. We've met and talked, and I don't know." His hands fluttered at his sides. "I was taken with her. It was instant, and nothing like that has ever happened to me before." He stopped and swallowed. "I'm afraid I'll never see her again, and I didn't have the nerve to say things to her and…" He took a breath, held it, exhaled, and straightened. "Love at first sight. It exists, doesn't it?"

Richard dropped his gaze, brain clicking away. Focus. Focus *now*.

This was not good. Whatever was happening, it was not good. His tongue slid over his teeth, his fingers rubbed his chin. "You're not seeing the hallway? You can't see you're in a hallway? Mine?"

The man shook his head, looking around. "This is Prospect Park, isn't it?"

Richard nodded. He faked a laugh. "Yes, sure, it is. I don't know this Kate, but if you're lost, just turn around and head back toward Goodfellow." He pointed, hoping he was pointing in the right direction. "Follow the walkway, and at Goodfellow, go left." He was nodding vigorously, agreeing with himself. "Remember that. Go left. That'll get you out of the park."

His visitor appeared not to hear him.

Richard approached him, put a hand on his shoulder, turned him slowly, pointed, nudged him and said, "See the playground? Is there a playground straight ahead?"

The man blinked. "Off to the right," he said. "It's off to the right."

Off went his visitor.

Richard turned and walked into his living room, past the kitchen, into his bedroom, grabbed the phone, and dialed as he walked back into the living room. He looked at his hallway. Empty.

His mother answered.

"I'm on my way over. You're not going anywhere, are you? We need to talk."

His parents lived in a brick ranch in an older neighborhood near the northwest corner of town. His mother met him at the door, got him inside, into an armchair, then sat beside Dad on the couch.

"What's going on?" she asked.

His father sat straight, hands folded in his lap. He looked exactly like a fourth-grade teacher.

Richard dropped his chin, his gaze, took a breath, and was about to speak when his father leaned forward.

"You've had a visitor?"

Looking up, Richard sighed. "Two visitors."

Shock spread on their faces as he explained a man appearing in his hallway, unable to actually *see* the hallway, searching for Kate Winter, and he was evidently in love with her. Richard rocked slightly the whole time he was speaking, one hand massaging his chin, the other resting on his calf. His breathing was audible in the quiet room.

He explained his attempt to mislead the man, then asked, "What do I do?"

His father raised his brows. "Richard, can't you figure it out?"

How could he?

His mother twisted her lips. "Richard, Kate Winter is in love with you." She let that hang for a moment. "She is in love with you the way a woman who has brains and is confident about herself and knows what she wants. It's that kind of love." Another pause. "You better listen to what I'm going to say next. If Kate Winter doesn't get what she wants, she'll move on, and I don't mean running through some dimension. She's here to see if you're interested in her. Got it? A second chance. You don't see that?"

There was a minute of quiet. No, more like two or three. Those minutes went by slowly.

His father stood, adjusted the waistband of his pants, and then tugged slightly at Richard's ear until they were standing face-to-face. Dad put his arms around him and patted his back. "Okay, tell me, how is it you are so good at your job? What do you know about research, finding these businesses, helping these businesses build their business? How do you *do* what you do?"

Richard's mind snapped to attention immediately. He took a second, was about to answer, started, and then realized the rationale behind his father's question. At that moment, he felt more connected to his father than he ever had before. He wrapped his arms around him.

"Dad, thank you."

Tuesday through Friday

On Tuesday, Wednesday, Thursday, and Friday, the days leading up to his date with Katherine, Richard performed his work with his usual efficiency. If his coworkers noticed anything different, it was never mentioned. Team members were introduced to a new client, assigned duties, and sent on their way. Older clients continued to be serviced. The days went by, business was handled, emails sent and received, phone conversations and Zoom conferences held, all bumps in the road navigated.

Did he think about Kate Winter?

When he was trying to focus on business, during lunch, drivetime, dinner, evenings, he thought about her, and wondered about the guy who'd come looking for her. Did he have a rival?

He reviewed his first round of courtship with her, his proposal, his fear of commitment (yes, that's what it was), his reluctance to actually share his thoughts. He remembered ending their engagement. It was difficult to think about. Shameful.

Would a woman forgive a man for that? He'd been self-absorbed, and that thought kept him awake at night. He wanted to call her every day, didn't, and finally broke down Thursday evening. He dialed, and their brief conversation was little more than a reminder they'd meet the next evening at the sports bar where they'd met the very first time they'd ever laid eyes on each other.

A second first date

"We met right here, at this table. You were here with coworkers. I knew one of them, Christine..."

He nodded. "Christine Wells. Still with the firm."

She smiled. "I came over to say hello to Christine. I'd been watching this guy with her, a handsome fellow. He seemed uncomfortable. Maybe not uncomfortable, that's too strong a word. Reserved. This guy was reserved and was hanging back, and he looked a bit out of place. Uncomfortable, like he was a tad unsure of himself. I wanted to meet him. That guy was you, and we talked a while, you and me. Christine, God bless her, she drifted off, and I flirted with you."

He smiled, remembering.

"You asked me out on a date. We went on that date, an easy one, right back here. Then we walked around the area for what seemed like hours. I kept hoping you'd kiss me and, if you remember, it was an early night. You kissed me when you walked me to my car in the parking garage across the street from this place. I wanted to ask you to marry me, but I didn't."

What emotions went through him at that moment? Her saying that. Why didn't he know what to say? That's what he was thinking, and he wanted to say something really good.

"I'm sorry," he said. Was that any good?

Kate sighed, pushed her hand across the small table in front of her until he reached out and put his hand on hers.

"I'm going to explain why I'm here," she said. "I want to you listen and not say a word until I'm finished. Is that okay?"

A stab in the heart. Fear ravished his chest. He looked at his hand on hers.

"Richard, I'm thirty-two years old. A woman's best, safest child-bearing years are late-twenties to early-thirties." She cocked her head as if asking, *are you listening?* "I've read everything there is to read about women wanting children, women not wanting children, women wanting careers first, and what happens to a woman's career when she starts a family. Want me to tell you about the chemistry of the female brain? I can do that, but it doesn't matter. Not to me. I want a husband, and I want a family, and so I came looking for you." She paused, frowned. "I want to know how you couldn't see me, see what I felt for you. See what we would be. What we could be."

His emotions were up and down, and up and down. Fear, confusion, anxiety. Hers seemed controlled.

"I remember our relationship this way," she said. "I remember coming up with ideas for us—things to do, places to go, movies to see. And you were wonderful, okay? You did those things. But I don't remember you taking charge. I don't remember enthusiasm, and I worried a lot. I felt like I was dragging you. Pulling you or pushing you."

There was her drink, not half gone, but his was mostly full. Some kind of appetizer was on the table in front of them.

She was going to leave. Again.

"I'm sorry." Panic rushed inside him. What to say? She came back for this? For him?

"Richard, this is clinical. What I'm going to say is clinical, okay? And in full disclosure, I've practiced this." She blinked, took a breath. "I'm running out of eggs. That's science. Women only have so many, you know. I want a family and a husband. I wanted you to be my husband from the start, right away, and I wanted—"

"I'll quit my job!" It came out loud. He looked around. A few heads had turned.

She drew back with a puzzled expression. "What? Why?"

He didn't know why. He didn't have an answer. But he'd said something. That was good, wasn't it?

"Richard, I need to finish what I have to say. Really. I want us together. That's what I want. I saw your mother, *somewhere*, wherever that is. I'm sorry if it makes you uncomfortable, it's weird, I know. And I opened up to her. Wherever we were, how in the world I wound up in there is beyond me. I told her I missed you. That you and I should have or could have..." She paused, inhaling, her eyes down. "I'm rambling. I want a relationship. With you. Courting. All that. All of it. So, here goes."

She stood up, leaned over until he raised his face to hers, and put her lips on his.

Soft, sweet, and brief.

"If you're interested—and please think long and hard about this—come after me," she said. "You need to think about it. I don't mean come after me tonight. Don't. I mean, think about it. Take some time. That's what I'm asking. If you think you're not ready or not interested, that's okay. I'll understand. I'll live. It's okay, I promise, but if you..."

She'd seemed to run out of words. "I don't know if it was love at first sight, or if that's even a thing." She straightened, and looked through her purse. "Am I leaving you with the bill?"

He swallowed, shaking his head. "No. Kate, no, I got this," and when he started to rise, she touched his face, turned, and walked out.

Late Friday

He'd never noticed his apartment was so big before. Did he need all the space?

Sitting on his couch, he weighed Kate's words, the excitement when she'd reentered his life, the exhilaration when he set eyes on her, the apprehension when she'd left.

Time. Ticked. By. Slowly.

At some point, just sitting there, it dawned on him he was using whatever energy he had to isolate and tamp down the same emotions he was trying to understand.

Was that realization a hint of progress?

He stood up, wandered down the hallway into the third bedroom, and went to the window with the view of the parking lot. Who did those cars belong to? Did he know any other tenants? Did he care?

In fact, right at that moment, he cared. He cared, and it occurred to him he *should* care. Shouldn't he be a real person? With friends? With neighbors?

That was progress, right?

Behind him, someone coughed and cleared their throat.

He shivered.

He walked to the bedroom door, stared down the hallway and, at the spot where everything had been happening lately stood a woman, dark-skinned, tiny, fashionably dressed.

He sighed, and everything about him went slack.

She stepped toward him and said, "Come on. Now, come on." She turned and disappeared.

He shook his head and followed.

He walked into that whatever space without hesitation. His stomach grumbled, his skin rose with goosebumps. His breathing became shallow and his chest tightened.

Hearing "come on over here," he stepped out of that something-or-other and found himself on a terrace. It was twilight and cool. There was a breeze, and the woman he'd seen in his apartment was sitting on a deck chair, pointing to the one beside her, motioning for him to sit.

He obliged, still trying to wrap his head around the current events.

"You know who I am?"

He shook his head.

"I'm a goddess," she said.

He shivered. "How sick *am* I?" He touched his forehead, grabbed his wrist like he knew how to find a pulse.

She watched him, pointed to the something-or-other he'd just stepped out of. "Lots of traffic through there lately, huh? Tough to wrap your head around that?"

He didn't respond because he didn't know how.

The goddess leaned back and crossed her legs. "I had no business going through there." She pointed at the portal. "I have a watchful eye, and I watch out for folks to protect them. I've been visiting family hereabouts and noticed the traffic. I got all curious and wanted to see what was going on. I see a mist like that, and I just want to feel it around me, you know? I know what that mist is all about, so I stepped through, saw you looking all forlorn, all lonely, and, well, I have responsibilities. I got a job to do."

He inhaled, puffed his cheeks, exhaled, drooping a bit. "Where are we, really?"

"Interesting question," she said. "It's the world. It's just the world."

He nodded, trying to understand.

"Does it matter where we are?" she asked after a few moments. "You're here, I'm here, we're here. Soon, you'll be there, and I'll be somewhere else. No point in worrying about here or there right now. Believe me. But looking at you, at the expression you're wearing, the look in your eyes, I pretty much know what your problem is."

That made one of them.

She hitched herself up in her chair. "Don't you want love?"

He dropped his chin, felt a chill, and went bleary-eyed. A tear popped, then another.

She watched.

Researchers claim emotional tears are influenced by biological, social, and psychological factors, and releasing emotional tears activates the parasympathetic nervous system, and that restores the body to a state of balance. There's evidence that emotional tears contain proteins and hormones that may have calming or pain-relieving effects. So, releasing tears, like he was doing, stimulated the production and release of positive endorphins.

His tears? Progress.

"It's not complicated," she said. "To be honest, I give the same advice the same way to everybody." She cocked her head. "Doesn't say much about me, I guess. You know where your love is. Don't act like you don't. If you want love, you need to go where your love is. Understand? It's not complicated."

She stood and placed a hand on his elbow, pointing him toward home. "You remember where you came in?"

He couldn't speak. Eyes damp, nose spicy, throat clogged, he nodded.

"Click your heels," she said, and laughed loud. "Why the struggle? You're fighting yourself, you know." Then she turned, walked across the terrace, and he saw, for the first time, a small river flowing by. It was whispering, and the water slowly rose out of the riverbed, turned into a spray, a thin mist, then eventually faded. She looked at him and shrugged. "The world's not always stable, but that's not necessarily bad. Not like it sounds, at least. Just look for balance, Richard. Love balances, that's what love does. Ying-yang, positive-negative, in-out, up-down."

She retraced her steps across the terrace and pointed toward the portal. "You want that thing closed up?" She waited for a response, but he didn't give one. "I'll see if I can't find somebody who knows how to close that thing, or move it somewhere else. I'll ask around. Looks to me like you've had enough."

Saturday

"I have some issues."

He blurted out the admission to Katherine on Saturday morning, unannounced, the minute she opened the door.

"I need to talk," he said.

And that's what he did.

Childhood? His idea was to start there.

"I was distant. Remote. I don't know why. I felt like I didn't fit in, and I wasn't trying very hard, or what's worse, I wasn't even interested. If that's true, what does that say about me? I mean, what's wrong with me?

"I remember my grandfather, my mom's dad, always piddling with something. I remember him always including me, always wanting to show me how to fix something around the house, and as I got older, I was embarrassed by him. I don't know why. There was no reason, really." He stopped abruptly, looked at Kate, her in sweats and a t-shirt. "I'm sorry. I barged in."

She looked at him and ran a hand through her hair.

"This isn't right," he said.

She dropped her leg, leaned forward, stood up. "Richard, can you give me a couple minutes?"

"Listen, Kate, how about lunch? How about I take off now and..." He jerked his head toward the door. "How about I come by..."

He was out of words. No plan. What was he doing?

She took the few steps to him, put a hand on his arm, and looked into his eyes. "Are you asking me to lunch?"

He nodded. "Yes."

"Okay, so how would a guy do that? What would he say?"

"Would you like to go to lunch? With me?"

"Thank you. Okay then, let's say one o'clock."

He nodded. Had she saved him? That's what he was thinking. She'd saved him. Maybe not yet. Maybe he wasn't saved yet. He kept nodding his head.

She kissed him on the lips, and he would wonder for the next several hours if he'd kissed her back. Christ! Didn't he know enough to kiss back?

"It's my treat," she said.

He started to shake his head, and she waved a finger in front of his face. "I pick the place. I pick up the tab, and you talk."

He nodded, relieved.

"Some guy stepped into my apartment," Richard said later at the restaurant, "looking for you."

Her eyebrows rose, but she shrugged. "I know. He found me. We talked. He's from somewhere else and...well, I explained things to him."

He sipped his water, eyes on her. "This is awkward," he said, looking away, hoping she'd pick up the conversation. When she didn't, he filled the silence. "This moving around business, dimensions, realities, parallel universes—is that what it is?" He waited, and when she didn't speak, it occurred to him she was playing a waiting game.

He took a breath. "It's unnerving. It's nutty, right? It's, uh ..." He paused, glancing around. They were seated outside amongst a few other tables. "Should I talk about my parents?"

"Your call," she said.

He dropped his gaze, trying to think. If planning was his strong suit, what was the plan?

"I'm not always happy," he said. "And I've never done much thinking on it. Or, I've tried to avoid thinking about it." He remembered saying those exact words before. He was certain he had. To a therapist. He'd gone to a therapist, and never told that to anyone.

"My parents are eccentric. That's a nice word for it, I suppose."

No response from Kate Winter.

"My childhood was interesting." He leaned toward her as if delivering a secret. "My folks were eccentric, yeah, but happy. I never heard them argue about anything. And thinking back, for all their crazy notions and dreamy philosophy, they were disciplined in their own way. I didn't see that, I guess. As I kid, I was...what? Unsatisfied? Dissatisfied?" He made a face. "Dissatisfied. That's how I remember me, and it's weird, because I had everything a kid needed. Parents and grandparents. I didn't socialize well, I know that. That bothered my parents, I think. At least, I remember thinking that. And then when I was a teenager, and you know, you turn into a teenager and everything you hear your parents say is stupid, and I was that way. I might have been that way before my teenage years. And now I think it was me that was the distant one. Difficult. That's the word. Difficult."

Her paying attention made him feel good. She'd always done that. Paid attention and made him feel good. What was that worth? He wanted to touch her, and then realized he wanted her to hold him. Was that weird?

He changed direction. "Tell me about this dimension business. Tell me what you've seen. Is it real or is it, I don't know, like, a psychosis?" He winced. If it was a psychosis, was he psychotic?

"Tell me about your job," she said instead of answering.

"Well," he said, "there's research, which I do with my team. I direct that. There's finance. I have people on my team who are good at that. There are communications, which we do as a team, and then it's media development, media contact, media placement. That's what we do." A pause. It had been abbreviated, but he'd been accurate. "We're good at it. I know it sounds dry, but it's not. It's a challenge. For me, at least. For me, it's like defining and redefining, rethinking, really. It's listening to people and hearing them and getting their perspective and seeing where they are and seeing where they want to go, what they want, then helping."

She'd been listening to him, and he'd been listening to himself, and he wondered how she'd pulled that out of him.

He reached over and took her hand, and they sat like that, looking at each other until the food arrived, and then they ate in silence. When the bill came, she paid, and after, they went out to the lot. They got in his car. She directed him to go north, out of town. They drove until they came upon one of those little unincorporated towns that dot the landscape in the Midwest, and she had him pull into a little park with a playground area.

They sat on a bench and stared at clouds floating by, and eventually, she looked at him.

"I like it here."

He took her hand and held it, afraid to look at her.

After the sun went behind the trees, he said, "Is this, like, *somewhere else*? You know?"

"No." She laughed, scooted closer so their legs were touching, then twisted a hip and leaned back on him. "This is just where we are. We're right here. Those other places? Interesting, I guess, but there was never much there for me."

Almost a year

Their second traditional courtship lasted almost a year. He was afraid every day he would mess up. As good as he was about not obsessing about unnecessary thought, he could not shake that fear.

His work life changed a little. He still arrived early, but rarely worked later than six. He gave up working Saturdays. Mostly. He did not make partner during the next promotion cycle, waited a few months before asking for a meeting with upper management, went in and said, "You know how much I appreciate the opportunities at this firm. You know my capabilities, my reputation, my work ethic. You know I want to advance, and I'd prefer to advance here, if at all possible. I do, however, have another offer. In fact, I have two offers, one very lucrative."

It was a bluff. He had no offers of any kind, nor did he even have an up-to-date resumé, but the bluff would work because, in all his years at Gaither, he'd never once bluffed.

He shook hands with his CEO and the CFO. "I'm out all next week. Christine Wells is in charge during my absence. He paused, nodding. "And, I'm going to ask my girlfriend to marry me this week."

Time will tell

On a Saturday morning, he and Katherine drove the Great River Road to the Quad Cities. There was a farmer's market to ramble around in, an art fair Kate wanted to see, and the annual Tugfest between Port Byron, Illinois, and Le Claire, Iowa.

Sunday, they slept late, stared at the river, went to a movie, out to dinner, and were asleep by ten.

Monday, they traveled from Davenport to Dubuque, lollygagging all the way, stopping at every historical marker, every fruit and vegetable stand, every scenic lay-by. The drive was seventy-plus miles, and it took three delightful hours. In Dubuque, they checked into a hotel, cleaned up, and drove to Eagle Point Park, where Richard's parents had their inaugural romp in the great wherever. His father had given him directions, his mother had quizzed him to make sure he was clear on them, and after parking his car at the correct trailhead, he led Katherine down the trail toward the portal he hoped was still there.

He would propose marriage and do so in some other place, some other dimension or universe or whatever. He just wanted it to be special, and he just wanted her to know he was capable of change, not the same man she'd been engaged to years ago.

That, and he wanted her to say yes.

He had absolutely no idea what he was looking for and couldn't find it.

Neither could she, although she kept telling him sometimes these gateways were easier felt than seen.

They were, though, on the correct path, and his mom's description had been quite accurate. The way was steep enough they kept hands elevated, near each other, in case a grab was needed to stop a slip-and-fall, and it was wide enough to accommodate them walking almost side-by-side. Erosion had created gullies that crossed the path on occasion, and there were spots where treated timbers were installed to put a stop to that. Those spots were a bit washed out, too.

"Are you okay?" he asked her after she'd paused. "What is it?"

She rubbed her neck and closed her eyes for a moment. Opening them, she turned in a complete circle, slowly scanning their location. There was a slight breeze. What was she observing?

"Kate, what is it?"

No reply.

"What is it?" he asked again, worried.

She pulled herself against him and set her chin on his shoulder. "Richard, we're married, and I am so happy we've been so happy. Don't you get it?"

Descent and Ascent

She stepped back, grabbed his hand, and smiled, then turned and started off down the path without him.

She'd looked a bit bleary when she'd spoken, and Richard, struggling to stay with her, watching his step, starting to feel the thud of the descent in his hips and his knees, followed.

They were married? Is that what she'd said? Interesting idea, but...

Down the trail they went, him falling behind, getting a bit rattled, then a bit vexed. His right side, that right hip was bothering him, and his knees and ankles were telling him to slow down.

"Katie!" he hollered, wondering what had happened to his voice. It was thin and wavering. "Katie, you be careful!" Damned knees. Damned ankles. Wasn't he in better shape than this? Was she in that much better shape than him, and since when did he call her Katie?

More twists and turns in the trail, more erosion to sidestep or step over, and eventually, the landscape started to flatten out. There appeared a country road to the left.

He was puffing pretty good, wishing his shoes were better suited to the activity. He'd lost sight of her. "Katie! Be careful!"

He went around a curve, and there she was, some small distance ahead, standing near the road, hands on hips. Across the road from her was a building falling in on itself.

She straightened when he got close, and seeing her, his jaw dropped.

Her hair had gone white. It was still as lovely as ever, but white? How could that be? On her neck, her cheeks, around her eyes, and across her forehead were.... Wrinkles.

He was staring. Should he be frightened?

He looked down at his hands, rubbing them together. They were wrinkled, too. They were resting on his belly. A belly? He had a bit of a belly? Since when? His hands. Wrinkly. The skin, like paper?

She approached him, still smiling, and took his hand. She stood tight against him, and he knew right then. He touched her hair, her neck, and was so relaxed. Suddenly, he was so grateful. He started shaking, just a bit.

How long had it been? How many years had they walked through, stepped over, just to get to where they were? Somewhere near the river, somewhere down the hill, across a path.

Their path.

He started to remember. Memories so vivid and, at the same time, surprising. How long ago had he proposed to her? Here? Yes, it had been here, in this place! How long had it been? And they'd come back... Is that what they'd done? Had they been lured into their past? Or was this their future?

"You should see yourself." She nuzzled his chin with the top of her head. "Still handsome."

He tried not to react, and didn't. He held her close, took a breath, raised his hand from her shoulder and studied it. The hand of an old man?

Is this what his parents had gone through?

His eyes were still closed when she patted his arm, and he kept them closed. She held onto him.

"How much time you think?"

She didn't reply.

He pictured them both, parking the car at the trailhead, heading over the path, and looking for some portal or whatever to get them somewhere or somewhen, wherever, whenever that might be. They stopped more than once, looked around, inspected the surroundings, expressed some frustration and disappointment. They'd enjoyed the day. Then the descent, them going down, and not going through anything he could remember, but the steps down had grown more difficult and his knees had started hurting, then the hip, and finally him catching up with Kate. She was as gorgeous a woman as he'd ever seen, and he wanted to walk right up to her and ask her to marry him.

How long ago had that been?

As new as it was to him, he wasn't sure if he was happier than he'd ever been in his life or on the cusp of being happy. It was a lot to take in.

He liked the idea of Katherine–in her sixties, was she?–going up and down hills, exploring, investigating, and scrutinizing, still looking at him with those kind eyes and one of the world's greatest smiles.

"How?" he asked. He waited for a response, and when none came, he finally opened his eyes and looked at her. All he could see was the top of her head. She'd buried herself against his chest again. He waited for an answer.

In her own time, she said, "Who cares? If this is real, hasn't being married been sensational?" She eased away from him, wry smile, slight nod, obviously pleased with herself.

He sniffed, went into his back pocket, and pulled out his wallet. The black leather was worn to gray. He flipped it open, skipped past the driver's license and the credit cards, and pulled out a clear plastic insert holding photographs.

"Look at that," he said.

Kate stepped closer. His hand started trembling. He handed her the photo and looked away, biting his lip.

That was her in the photo. Him, too. Three children, two girls and a boy. How long ago had the photo been taken? It was creased and fading.

"I'm not sure," she said, "but I don't think you've actually proposed to me yet." She shrugged. "I mean, how did we get here–kids grown and lives lived–and I can't remember your proposal, and I *really* want to."

He felt old, and the bonus was, he was pretty sure he wasn't permanently old. What a bonus. Get the outcome in advance and discover your life will be what you'd always wanted it to be. Does it get any better than that?

"You're still quite the looker," he said. "That's gotta make you feel good, right?"

"You know you haven't proposed to me yet. You did hear me say that, didn't you? Just now?"

He nodded. "I heard you," he said, looking back to the path they'd come down, and it was like any other path in any other park in any other state. Dirt, weeds, scrubs. "Maybe we ought to head back." He didn't want to be going up that path in the dark.

"There better be a ring up there," she said. "And a proposal. I'm not negotiating."

"Katie, come on. Look at your hand. You didn't think of that?"

She did, the left one, where there was the ring. "Okay, the ring's pretty."

She pointed. "But up there, I want the proposal. You love me a lot. So, I'm heading up for my proposal, and it better be a good one."

She led him to where they were only young lovers, where they were lovers traveling together, where they were wondering how to make a future together, and what that future might be like. At the top, she turned to him, and when he proposed, she acted like she was surprised.

Did she remember any of what she'd recalled at the bottom of the trail? Did he?

If she did, she didn't show it, nor did he. That's the beauty of it. They have to go through it to get to it. Sometimes, the going is confusing, and sometimes the getting to it is confounding, but the smart ones know.

Who wants to know what's coming?

The requisite epilogue

Richard made partner six months before their first daughter, Ellen, was born. He still liked going in early, but a couple times a week, he'd do breakfast with the baby. He liked to see her wake up and go wide-eyed, liked to hear her coo, and he liked to feed her what he referred to as "mush." She loved it, and he loved seeing her dribble all over her cheeks and chin, and giggle.

He always made it home by six. That was dinnertime. Always. And he gave up working Saturdays.

Mostly.

About
the
Authors

A career historian, Annie R McEwen has lived in six countries and under every roof from a canvas tent to a Georgian Era manor house. She is published by Harbor Lane Books (US), Bloodhound Books (UK), The Wild Rose Press, and Rowan Prose Publishing. When she's not in her 1920s bungalow in Florida, Annie lives, writes, and explores castles in Wales.
www.anniermcewen.com

Isaac Sher's books are known as out of this world magical escapism. He is a master at blending sci-fi, urban fantasy, and romance for a unique read. He is a two-time brain cancer survivor, and resides with his family near Chicago.
www.facebook.com/AuthorIsaacSher

Julie Castle has always had a love affair with the written word. As a child growing up in a small town, she loved visiting the local library, a converted gilded age mansion, and getting lost between the pages of a book. The drafty old mansion could be a spooky place, but she still loved it. She enjoyed poking into behind the scenes areas she wasn't supposed to venture into. She's still the same way, which is why she loves writing romance with an edge, paranormal, suspenseful, super sexy, or just laugh your pants off funny. She is an award-winner, and resides in Wisconsin with her family.
www.facebook.com/authorjuliecastle

Kathleen Lee is the author of sweet and sexy M/M romance novel-las. She is an Amazon Bestseller in Gay Romance. When not taking her caffeine by I.V. (well, not really) or plotting world destruction (this she does do) she can be found at home reading. She has since retired from writing (as of 2019).
www.facebook.com/AuthorKathleenLee

Alberta romance author Katie O'Connor can't live without her computer and e-reader, but she wants to use them in the woods while watching the deer frolic on her summer property, Sanctuary. She spends her summers with her husband hiding in the woods. Her passion, aside from romance and her grandbabies, is giving back to the writing community. She is a co-founder of Rowan Prose Publishing. If you need her, she'll be cozied up by the coffee pot eyeing the cookies. She's fueled by coffee and steak, and is fluent in sarcasm, cussing, dad jokes, and romantic jargon.
www.katieohwrites.com

Kelly Moran is an international bestselling author of enchanting ever-afters.

She is a RITA® Finalist, RONE Award-Winner, Catherine Award-Winner, Reader's Choice Finalist, Holt Medallion Finalist, Book Excellence Award Finalist, Amor Book Award-Winner, and landed on the "Must Read" & "10 Best Reads" lists in USA Today's Lifestyle section. Her books have foreign translation rights in Germany (where she is a Spiegel Bestseller), France, the Czech Republic, Romania, Russia, and the Netherlands. She also writes horror as Kelly Covic. In 2023, she founded Rowan Prose Publishing.

Her interests include: scary movies, all kinds of art, driving others insane, and sleeping when she can. She is a closet coffee junkie and chocoholic. Tell no one. She's originally from Wisconsin, but she resides in South Carolina with her significant other, her three sons, their wily dogs, a bearded dragon, and their sassy cats. She loves hearing from her readers.
www.AuthorKellyMoran.com

Mandy Eve-Barnett is a multi-genre author writing children's, YA, and adult books. Every story has a basis of love, nature, magic, and mystery. Her passion for writing emerged later in life and she is making up for lost time. With ten books published since 2011 and another five awaiting the editing process, she indulges her Muse in creative as well as freelance writing. Mandy regularly blogs at http://www.mandyevebarnett.com, where she encourages, and supports the networking of writers and readers alike. She is also prolific on social media. Mandy is currently the Secretary of her local writers group, the Writers Foundation of Strathcona County, she hosts the monthly Writers Circle meetings and creates weekly writing prompts for the website. She is past Secretary of the Alberta Authors Cooperative and past President of the Arts & Culture Council of Strathcona County Council.

Maribelle McCrea is a fourth-generation Atlanta native living just south of the city in a little town with 100 miles of golf cart paths. She loves all things Southern and wishes she could speak with that old, Georgia accent and say, "I do declare!" and feel faint about things.
www.maribellemccrea.com

Maxine Douglas
American Historical &
Contemporary Romance
Author

Maxine Douglas writes in several genres, including historical romance and romantic suspense. She is a current member of the Oklahoma Writers' Federation, Inc. and its affiliations, Central Region Oklahoma Writers, and Oklahoma Romance Writers Guild. A widow and Wisconsin native, Maxine now resides in Oklahoma.
www.maxinedouglasauthor.blogspot.com

Writing for adults is the newest wrinkle in Sharon Hart Addy's life as an author. She began her career writing obits for a local paper and went on to do feature articles. One of those features led to a picture book. After that success, she focused on writing for children. Along with more picture books, she wrote fiction and poetry which appeared in Highlights, Cricket, and other magazines for kids. Her husband's retirement brought a shift in her outlook, and she took up writing for adults: mystery and romance.

www.facebook.com/sharon.hart.addy

Veronica Leigh has been published in numerous anthologies, journals, and magazines. She aspires to be the Jane Austen of her generation and she makes her home in Indiana. www.facebook.com/veronicaleighauthor

The good news is, for Victor Kreuiter, that when he doesn't have a story to tell – and there are those days – there are others who do. If fiction were a country, he doesn't know that he'd emigrate, but he'd sure as hell visit often. He'll be seventy-five years old very soon, and writing – his or someone else's – keeps the celebratory alive, and if life ain't a celebration...

CHECK OUT THESE OTHER GREAT READS FROM ROWAN PROSE!

9 781961 967533